Praise for Iain Stewart's

Knights of the Air, Book 1: Rage!

"A remarkable historical novel... A sharp and effective blend of WWI aviation action and adventure, a hefty dose of emotion and human drama, plus a dash of romance, keep the pages flying. Finely written and vividly imagined, this is a complex, gritty novel delving into the brutalities of war. Stewart is an author to watch."

BookView Review, **Gold Award Winner**

"*Rage!*, the first book in Iain Stewart's *Knights of the Air* series, is about as realistic and loyal to history as they come... If *Rage!* is any indicator for the rest of the series, military history buffs better be making some room on their bookshelves now."

Independent Book Review

"Highly recommended... Splendid tale of aerial warfare in WWI... Book 1 of what promises to be a highly enjoyable series, and this reviewer, for one, is looking forward to the sequel."

Historical Fiction Company

IAIN STEWART

Knights of the Air

BOOK TWO

FIRE

atmosphere press

To my mother, for inculcating a love of good stories. To my father, for encouraging and funding my early flying. And to Cassia, for her understanding that sometimes my body was present but my mind was cavorting in the skies of the Western Front.

"Aye, aye! and I'll chase him round Good Hope, and round the Horn, and round the Norway Maelstrom, and round perdition's flames before I give him up."

—Captain Ahab in *Moby Dick*

~

"The essence of war is violence and moderation in war is imbecility."

—Lord Macauley, 1831

~

"It was like the lists of the Middle Ages, the only sphere in modern warfare where a man saw his adversary and faced him in mortal combat, the only sphere where there was still chivalry and honour. If you won, it was your own bravery and skill; if you lost, it was because you had met a better man."

—Cecil Lewis, RFC ace and author of *Sagittarius Rising*

1
Cock O' The Walk to Feather Duster

To each their own religion.

Let others go to church services on Sundays, seeking heavenly redemption on their knees. Lance Fitch flew to the heavens to extract revenge.

His SE5 clawed upwards through the thin air towards its maximum altitude of seventeen thousand feet, a beautiful frigid wasteland where only the hardiest ventured. Or those who nurtured bloody intent with the zeal of a Spanish Inquisitor.

The Huns had killed Lance's friend, Albert Ball, and revenge was his best form of grief control. Curious how revenge was the answer to so many questions. It filled the hole inside, got you out of bed burning with a purpose. Lance welcomed its cold rage; it was like a much-missed lover, familiar but still arousing.

Lance's fury wasn't exclusive to the Germans, neither was he damning God. They had both behaved as Lance expected. The Huns were supposed to try to kill you—although no RFC pilot had dreamed they would ever succeed with Ball, the British Empire's greatest ace. Meanwhile, God had done what

3

He always did. Nothing.

No, Lance was livid with himself. What a fool he'd been! He'd learned back in the trenches to never make friends. Watching them die left you an emotional wreck. Lance had thought himself tough, but the combination of shellshock, horror, and grief had taken Lance to the fringes of a breakdown.

The episodes came with a roar like storm waves breaking on the jagged reefs, a surf that tumbled his mind in white, threatening to rip it from its moorings. So far, the episodes had always receded like the tide. But each time it was a close-run thing, and what if the white storm sucked him under next time?

As a green infantry officer, he had seen a swathe of his mates cut down in stumbling charges across glutinous mud and sworn to harden his heart. Friends die on you. Feelings make you weak. Since joining the RFC, the horrific losses of the past year's Fokker Scourge and this year's Bloody April had only reinforced his vow.

But then he had let Albert Ball sneak under his barriers. Now the heartache dripped acid into his psyche, scouring away the defences that kept Lance on the margins of insanity, where you at least knew you were a lunatic.

Cross that fine line, lose that precious knowledge, and men in white coats strapped you into a straight-jacket and entombed you in a whitewashed mental asylum. Sometimes they called it shellshock, other times a breakdown. Same ending. The white hell of an asylum. He'd rather die. So, friends were a luxury Lance couldn't afford if he wanted to stay sane. So now Lance, like the good Catholic he wasn't, scourged himself mentally and physically at seventeen thousand feet above the battlefields of Flanders.

The icy slipstream battered past the open cockpit at hurricane speed, and at temperatures belonging to the North Pole.

4

His nose dribbled incessantly. Only the stinking whale oil slathered on his face prevented the snot from turning into ice on his upper lip. The fur-lined goggles bit into his eye sockets, but when he eased the strap just a fraction, the howling gale raged inside and made his eyes water furiously. He'd lost feeling in his toes despite his thigh-length sheepskin boots and double wool socks.

Breaths came in quick pants between pursed lips. Each ragged inhalation waged a bitter battle to suck oxygen from the arctic air, thin and as meagre of sustenance as Kikuyu gruel during a drought season back in East Africa. If you breathed too shallow, your head spun and your eyes clouded. If you breathed too deep, icy daggers stabbed the nasal passageways or lungs. Already his windpipe raged raw.

The RFC doctors called such conditions "extreme." Rod Andrews, the Australian commanding 100 Wing's Bristol Fighter squadron, called it "colder than a witch's tits." For Lance Fitch it was simply a killing perch, from where he could swoop on his prey while hidden in the sun's glare.

Killing perches are, by definition, uncomfortable. This one was excruciating. He gritted his teeth and hunkered lower in his cockpit. To stave off frostbite, he beat his gloved hands against his knees, slapped his numb cheeks, stamped his feet, and wiggled his toes inside his flying boots.

And waited for his prey.

"Patience is the cornerstone of a great hunter. Without it, other hunting skills, no matter how finely honed, can be useless." So spake Old Man Selous, Lance's godfather and the man Teddy Roosevelt called the "last of the great white hunters."

Before the war, Selous, Pa, and Lance had hunted rogue elephants who raided the local village shambas for maize and fruit, trampling or goring the tribesmen who tried to protect their food supply. When you hunted elephant, patience meant lying in wait, upwind and stationary, as the sun hammered you against the baking anvil of the parched earth. Sweat dribbled into the eyes, hot and salty, and a careless move scorched skin on rifle metal. Hunter patience meant lurking silent and motionless even as horseflies stabbed their red-hot needle into the tender skin under the ear.

Right now, Lance longed for that searing heat with a lover's yearning. But still he waited. And endured.

On such a cloudless day, sooner or later, a high-flying Hun reconnaissance aircraft would come prying. Rumours said a few Hun crews now enjoyed oxygen masks and electrically heated flying suits. These specialist reconnaissance planes carried Zeiss cameras with the most powerful lenses in the sky. They would snoop at towering altitudes, invulnerable to most fighters, the camera recording any build-up of artillery or men that would reveal the British Army's next attack. The naked eye could not pick out such details seventeen thousand feet below, but the camera's grainy black and white photographs would expose the Allies' attack plans with unerring accuracy. If the Germans knew where the assault would be, British blood would soak the Flanders' mud.

So, Lance closed his mind to his agony and lurked high in the azure sky. The minute hand on the dashboard clock seemed petrified in purgatory. The vast emptiness of the sky mocked his diligence. This high, and without clouds, there was no sensation of speed—the SE5 floated motionless. Below him, the earth rotated silently. Above him, the heavens stretched towards eternity. A barren, featureless hunting ground. An altitude headache throbbed, each pulse of his heartbeat a thudding pain in his skull.

He didn't care. Whatever the elements threw at him, it was a drop of spit against the unquenchable furnace of his revenge quest. Lance's vendetta didn't originate with Albert Ball's death. He had older and deeper scores to settle with the Huns.

Both of his brothers, for starters.

So be patient. Patience is a weapon. He checked the gauges: rpm steady, coolant temperature fine, plenty of fuel. His eyes quartered the sky methodically, using a soft focus. Eyes picked up movement better from peripheral vision, rather than staring.

When he first saw the dots, he thought he was hallucinating. He forced deeper breaths, each so cold his teeth ached. Then he squinted, willing his foggy mind and dry eyes to focus. He blinked. Two planes sliding towards him. He swore. It was hard enough to down one of these planes, but with an escort...

Lance turned, keeping the sun between the planes and himself, and waited until he could see more details. Then his frown cleared. The second aircraft was not an escort but a SPAD VII, a formidable French fighter plane. It looked like a puppy playing with its mother as the smaller SPAD gambolled around the sedate two-seater, only white streaks of tracer hinting at the deadly duel.

Until the SPAD exploded in a brilliant flash.

Lance grimaced. This prey had teeth. The disdainful ease with which the Hun dispatched the SPAD told of a skilled crew. The Hun's elegant fuselage and tall exhaust stack identified it as one of the new Rumplers—fast, manoeuvrable, and well-armed. Lance had seen these planes at twenty thousand feet before, a height even the SE5 could not attain. But this crew wasn't bothering to take the extra safety margin their performance ceiling gave them. They must prefer to fight than freeze, and Lance did not blame them. He couldn't even imagine the agonies at that altitude.

Lance took extra care. He let the enemy bore deeper across the lines. Then he swooped out of the sun.

The black crosses grew larger. Dappled green and purple camouflage glinted in the sun. Lance eased out of his dive and arced up from underneath the Rumpler until its grey belly loomed in his gunsight. He led the plane in his sights and thumbed both triggers. His guns hammered, spewing cartridges, hot gas, and the acrid tang of cordite. The SE5 shook. Tracer lines speared towards the enemy.

The Hun pilot chopped his throttle instantly. His Rumpler mushed as though he'd slammed on brakes, while Lance's SE5 hurtled onwards. *Jesus! We're going to collide!*

Lance wrenched back on the stick. Gravity punched his gut as the SE5's nose pointed to the heavens. The Rumpler filled his whole horizon. He kicked right rudder to skid past. And prayed.

The black Maltese cross on the white tail hypnotised Lance as it loomed towards him in slow motion. So close that the patchwork repair on the fabric showed stark as moss on a tombstone.

The Hun's tail slid a mere five yards past the SE5's propeller. Lance blew out a breath.

Until he saw the goggled gunner hunched over his machine gun, waiting for the SE5 to soar into his firing arc. *Oh shit!* The machine gun muzzle loomed as large as a railway tunnel. *Six hundred rounds a minute from twenty feet away— he can't miss.* Lance waited for the end, his jaw clamped tight. *For what we are about to receive...*

But the next sound was not the jackhammering of a machine gun but a dull boom. Flames sheeted backwards from the Hun's engine. The gunner flinched and his tracers smoked wide. Lance half-rolled the SE5 away, desperate to escape the next burst. Too late! Bullets stitched his plane's belly.

Lance kicked the right rudder and slammed the stick right and back to roll into an inverted dive, his horizon revolving crazily. Tracers flashed between his wings. He dived hard, then pulled up into a tight turn, head twisting to find the Hun.

Christ! The Rumpler was plunging towards him, wreathed in fire. Lance flung his SE5 into a hard bank away, and the

Hun slid past by fifty feet, a roaring mass of flames.

The pilot jumped, wreathed in fire. His arms and legs flailed as he fell through the weightless void. *Thud!* The petrol tank exploded and the plane crumpled, wings folding. Fragments rained downwards. But Lance could not tear his eyes from the pilot, a meteor growing fainter and fainter but still burning.

Lance vomited over his boots. Better there than over the side where the slipstream would fling it back in his face. Flamers always made him sick.

Lance's war had started with fire. Back in 1914 in Africa, German askaris had dowsed his friend Hamisi in petrol and set him alight. Then they cut Lance free and told him to help the man. Lance had scrabbled away in fear and horror, vomiting on his knees as Hamisi burned. He had done nothing for his friend in his hour of need.

Since the war started, Lance had accumulated regrets like barnacles, but none nagged at him more than his betrayal of Hamisi. Misjudgements? Plenty of those to keep each other company. Hurtful words that should never have left his lips, and healing words that should have? Roman legions were fewer in number. But only his abandonment of Hamisi defined Lance as a coward, at least in his own mind.

Since Hamisi died, not a week passed without a nightmare jolting Lance awake, gibbering and sweat-soaked, as Hamisi's flesh bubbled and melted to white bone, his lidless eyes shrieking inconceivable hell through dancing flames.

No surprise then that fear of fire now haunted Lance's every flight. All planes were combustible bombs, a pyromaniac's dream. Take one aircraft of dried wood and flammable fabric, add a petrol tank (partially empty and thus primed to explode with combustible petrol fumes), and place it between a red-hot engine and the pilot. Then mix in a sky populated with motivated murderers armed with machine guns and flaming tracer bullets.

Once the flames flickered on your plane, you had two choices. Jump into the void thousands of feet high or ride the meteor into a flaming hell. Lance knew his choice.

If no-one set you alight or riddled you full of holes, your reward was to repeat the nerve-harrowing two-hour ordeal four times a day, seven days a week. Lance had undergone this daily trial of fire in the skies since June 1916—a year by one measure, several lifetimes by another.

Lance spat the foul taste of puke and fear from his mouth. He checked his tail to ensure that no Hun had sneaked up on him while he wallowed in horror. All clear. Plenty of fuel and bullets left. He pointed the SE5's nose higher and climbed back to his killing perch at seventeen thousand feet. And waited with a predator's patience.

The ravenous cold set its savage claws into him again. Doctors said brain cells died from lack of oxygen if you stayed too long at this height. Too bad. Lance had debts to pay and if it cost a few brain cells, so be it. So long as the Huns paid in blood.

The German Colonial Army had invaded British East Africa in 1914 and ambushed Lance and his younger brother, Francis, before the brothers even knew that war had been declared. They had smashed Francis's knee so severely he was left crippled. When Lance and his other brother, Will, sailed for Europe to join the Western Front, Francis presented Lance with a copy of the Old Testament Bible. Inscribed on the inside cover was the exhortation "Hosea 8:7. They have sowed the wind: they shall reap the whirlwind."

"Promise," Francis said, his voice a whisper but bitter as bile. "I want the Germans to pay, to know there is justice in the world. When I grind my teeth in agony at every step, I want to know a German somewhere is paying the price."

Lance looked at his teenaged brother, crutch-dependent

and arthritis-ridden with pain lines etched on his old-young face, and nodded. "I promise."

Now Lance dedicated his latest kill to Francis. "Reap the whirlwind," he whispered.

He wasn't naive enough to think all Germans were bad. Far from it. Lance's ex-fiancée, Heidi Schumacher, was German. Her father, Herr Schumacher, had been Pa's closest friend. But the men in power in Germany today were brutal men from a harsh land—the militaristic and ruthless Junkers from the frozen wastes of East Prussia.

In Africa the German Schutztruppe had won a hard-earned reputation as the most brutal colonial army in the continent. When rebels in German East Africa killed fifteen Europeans, the Schutztruppe retaliation littered the plains with more than 75,000 native corpses. Namibia had been even worse. The German Army paper, *Der Kampf*, celebrated the "extermination of the Herero nation," and Kaiser Wilhelm hailed the perpetrators as heroes.

Lance had heard Herr Schumacher rage against all this before the war. But only when Lance was on the receiving end, did he understand Schumacher's assertion that such endemic cruelty pointed to a nation that had lost its moral compass.

Lance didn't fight for King and Country. He fought for revenge and to defeat the Hun. Only then could he return to his home, five miles from the border with German East Africa, and live without fear. Only then could he go back and find out what had happened to Heidi. Only then would he cease his quenchless feud.

He shook his head at the memories, then blocked out the self-indulgent thinking as his eyes scanned for another victim.

~

Ten minutes later he found another Rumpler over Bapaume. He stalked it, always hiding himself in the sun's glare. The crew never saw their nemesis. This time his tracers stabbed into the pilot's back. The plane jerked and fell away on one wing. It spun lazily for two minutes before crashing. Lance watched it all the way as he regained height.

That's more like it...Number Thirty. A good kill like this cast a welcome illusion of control. When Lance had been a lone wolf pilot, most days were like this. But when he accepted command of Ball's squadron, the world became complicated. People and their problems had a way of twisting you in knots. Flying solo against the Huns seemed simple in comparison, with a single rule—kill or be killed. That Lance could cope with. Leadership? Tougher, much tougher.

He'd had enough high-altitude punishment. He banked westwards and began to drain off height. Now came the price for the extended time at altitude. His eardrums pulsed with pain. He swallowed hard and banged his head to dry and clear them. Every little pop he wrung from them eased the pressure. His feet and fingers alternated between pulsing agony and stabbing needles as circulation returned. He beat his left hand against his thigh, then switched hands on the joystick and beat his right and wiggled his toes rapidly. Nothing did any good. He screamed curses into the slipstream and that felt better. Eventually the ears settled to a hum and the extremities to a dull throb. He blew his cheeks out in relief. Familiarity with the inevitable routine did not make it easier to endure.

As he approached the front lines, he spotted the white smoke of Archie bursts from the British anti-aircraft guns. He veered towards them. It turned out to be a two-seater DFW over Sanctuary Wood, doing an artillery shoot. Two Pfalz fighters rode escort above as the DFW traced leisurely figure-eight patterns over the target.

"Yes!" Lance exclaimed with glee as a cold anger spread its tendrils through him. He smiled and his cold-chapped lips cracked. He licked them and the taste of blood coated his tongue.

Back in 1915 when Lance was in the infantry, a similar plane had called down an artillery barrage on his regiment. The resulting bombardment decimated Lance's platoon and eviscerated his brother Will. Lance suffered a brief mental breakdown from the shellshock of that barrage. When he recovered, he joined the RFC. Since then, artillery spotter planes were his target of choice, his offerings to Will's ghost, a salve on Lance's guilt for not removing his platoon from a targeted crossroad.

Lance waited until the DFW's pattern took it furthest away from its escort, then dived underneath the two-seater. His stalk out of the sun was so stealthy that even the British anti-aircraft gunners did not see him coming. As he arced upwards for his usual attack in the blind spot, their 'Archie' shells exploded under the DFW, directly in front of Lance.

Shrapnel slashed at his plane's underside. The SE5 jolted as it snarled through the dirty white smoke. "Blind bastards!" Lance frantically waggled his wings at the British anti-aircraft gunners. Thank God they got the message and stopped.

Lance fired from forty feet, and the DFW fell apart. Engine and bodies hurtled earthwards while the fuselage and the wings floated down separately. He must have hit the bracing wires. Lance imagined the British troops below cheering as the bits plummeted to earth.

The two Pfalz fighters slashed towards him. He'd caught the bastards napping and they wanted revenge. Lance turned into the attack, then feinted left, suckering the second Pfalz. Lance sawed off both his right wings with a long burst. The one-sided aircraft flipped over and over. Then the left wings ripped away, and the fuselage plummeted earthwards like a coffin.

His comrade turned onto Lance's tail. Lance found himself in the classic duelling circle, the two of them seemingly alone in the sky. Across the circle, the slim Pfalz sported a pretty silver-blue paint job with the yellow nose and tail of *Jasta* 10. *One of Richthofen's pilots. He'll be good, then.* Lance settled into the duel, wary but confident in his own skills and the capabilities of his aircraft.

Soon he was sweating, only partly from his exertions as he threw his plane around the sky. Speed, not manoeuvrability, was the SE5's forte. Pfalz were not especially manoeuvrable either, and Lance had not suffered problems with them before. Yet this bugger flew with the agility of a witch on a broomstick, with lightning-fast chandelles and turns as tight as a Sopwith Camel's. Which should have been impossible for a Pfalz.

The yellow nose with its twin guns crept inexorably closer to the SE5's tail. Lance tried a quick reverse and right turn. A manoeuvre he could nail clean as a knife blade ten times out of ten. But on this occasion, harried by his opponent's skill, he skidded wide. *Oh bugger!* The skin between his shoulder blades prickled. *Stupid mistake, stupid time to make the mistake.* He stomped on right rudder and let the nose go. *The Hun won't expect that.* Tracers slashed inches past his head as the SE5 plunged.

Now Yellow Nose had the height advantage and rammed it home remorselessly, firing short bursts. Desperately Lance twisted and turned from the spiteful tracers, panting with the effort. His thigh muscles ached. Sweat rolled from his forehead. It seemed aeons since he'd been freezing.

The bastard was too good to give him an opening to run for home. Lance feinted a half-roll left and reefed hard into a right turn, trying to win enough of a lead to dive away without being riddled in the back. Yellow Nose turned inside him, and the tracers slid so close that Lance smelled the phosphorus.

The two planes swung into another pattern of hard circles, the Pfalz always holding higher than the SE5. Degree by degree, the guns on the yellow nose crept towards Lance. He flipped a quick look at the fuel gauge—getting low. Ammo must be low too. The strong easterly wind was pushing them deeper into Hunland. Place, wind, fuel, ammo, height, manoeuvrability—the Hun held all those cards.

If he straightened to run, the Hun would nail him with an easy non-deflection shot. If Lance stayed, he would run out of fuel or bullets soon. And the Hun was out-flying him. *Damned if I do, damned if I don't.* He was trapped.

The trench-scarred and shell-torn earth waited two thousand feet below. Another rotting carcass would make no difference.

A shadow ripped across his peripheral vision. Lance ducked. His plane kicked in turbulence. *What the heck!*

He twisted to look back at the Pfalz, but the German pilot seemed at puzzled as Lance, his head turning side to side as he too seemed to search for the cause.

Again, the air around Lance ruptured, and the SE5 bucked. This time, Lance glimpsed a giant howitzer shell, slowing near the apex of its arc. He blinked in disbelief. Then realised that as the duel lost height, he and the Pfalz had flown into the path of the artillery barrage that Lance's two-seater victim had been directing.

That was enough for Lance. He flung the SE5 away from the shells' path and fled for home, praying that the shells had distracted Yellow Nose enough to give Lance the few seconds he needed to escape. His shoulder blades cringed as he waited for the machine gun fire.

None came.

A quick look back showed the Hun turning for his home. Lance took a deep breath. His shoulders unhunched. Whoever that Hun was, he'd handed Lance a lesson.

Lance needed to improve his flying, that was for sure. His skid in the turn was a minor mistake, but this game allowed thin margins between victor and vanquished. If not for those howitzer shells...

But four kills on one patrol! Not even Albert Ball, God rest his soul, had achieved that. And despite Ball's recent death, he was still the RFC's leading ace with forty-four kills, twelve ahead of Lance. To be honest, Lance was reluctant to overtake his friend. He'd inherited Ball's mantle as 111 Squadron commander, and that was bad enough. Lance wanted to kill more Huns, but he didn't want to lessen Ball's laurels. And yet it was undeniable that four kills wetted the appetite rather than slaked the thirst. He basked in the glow as he headed home to Bailleul.

~

Home sweet home. Lance shut down the engine and eased himself wearily out of the plane. He loved the SE5 as a fighting tool, but it took a minor miracle to escape from the cockpit without burning himself on the exhaust stacks or smacking his head on the overhead Lewis gun.

His ground crew fussed around the plane. Digby, his chirpy Cockney fitter, waited until Lance removed his leather helmet before asking his habitual question. "Scorecard today, sir?"

Lance held up four fingers of one hand while ruffling his sweaty hair into some sort of order with the other.

"Bloody good show, sir! That'll teach them Huns!" Digby's ruddy face glowed with pride. His armourer, Murray, a mono-syllabic Ulsterman, handed Lance a damp rag to wipe off the foul-smelling whale grease that helped protect his exposed cheeks from frost bite. Murray's face seemed fixed in the grimace of a man suffering from gas.

"Are you alright, Murray?" Lance asked.

Murray looked even more pained but gave a thumbs-up.

Digby laughed. "Don't worry about Paddy, sir, that's his happy face. He just hates Huns, happy as a sandboy when you kill the bastards."

"You're a bloodthirsty crew," Lance said.

Digby cackled agreement and started circling bullet holes with chalk to mark the spots needing repair.

Lance's legs still wobbled. He walked around the plane to work off the trembling. Murray helped him strip off the layers of flying clothes, which reduced the other all-pervasive smell, the spoiled fish reek of castor oil thrown off by the engine. Now Lance just felt grimy. Sweat had pooled in his groin and boots, and his khaki shirt wore crescents of damp under the arms and down the back. His ears rang and throbbed. He rolled his neck, which clicked and grated after the hours of ceaseless turning to check his tail. Worst of all, his altitude headache pulsed against his skull.

"Ahoy there!"

Lance turned to face the 100 Wing's adjutant. Only Clayton talked like a caricature of an old salt. Too many admirals in the family, he always claimed. He limped towards Lance, one leg permanently shorter than the other thanks to an old bullet wound.

"I've had a complaint," Clayton said, "and I think you might be the culprit."

Lance scowled. He didn't want to chat, even with Clayton. His head was pounding and the adrenalin had leached out of him. He needed a shower and his bed.

"The Archie observers are complaining that the sky is raining Huns so fast they can't keep count. Then I see you landing and I dare say that two and two make four?"

Lance nodded.

"By Jove!" Clayton stroked his pencil-thin moustache in delight. "Four on one patrol! I believe this is the first time anyone has done that."

Lance shrugged. "Luck. A Rumpler almost drilled me, and a Pfalz ran rings round me. Thought my goose was cooked each time."

The adjutant's eyebrows rose at the frank confession. "A Pfalz run rings around the great Fitch? Surely you exaggerate!"

"Sod off, Clayton."

"What did he look like?"

"Silver paint job with a yellow nose and tail."

Clayton frowned, took his cap off, and smoothed back his thinning hair. This was his habitual gesture of deep thought. Ever since Boom Trenchard had appointed 100 Wing to hunt down Richthofen, it was the adjutant's job to know everything about Richthofen's *Jagdgeschwader* 1, irreverently called "the Circus" by the British pilots because of its multicoloured planes.

Clayton clicked his fingers. "Sounds like Werner Voss, the new German *wunderkind*. He's only twenty and has been fired from commanding three different Jasta in two months. Nobody wants him as a leader despite his thirty kills. Pilots we've captured tell us the word is that he's been sent to Richthofen to learn some Prussian discipline from the one man he respects."

Lance pulled a face. "He may be a lousy leader, but he's one hell of a pilot. Bloody humiliating being schooled like that."

Lance had duelled with Manfred von Richthofen's blood-red Albatross while piloting an outdated but agile Sopwith Pup. Fighting Richthofen was like facing a more experienced boxer in the ring. The man knew all the tricks of the trade and executed everything with relentless precision, cutting down your options with the remorseless accumulation of tiny advantages in every unfussy manoeuvre. Richthofen had been inexorable but today had been more humiliating. It was a grim reminder. *Keep improving. Or die. Practice, practice, more practice...*

"Don't be so morbid, old boy. We'll splice the main brace

for you in the officers' Mess tonight." Clayton shook his head in wonder. "Four on one patrol!"

"Cock of the walk one day, feather duster the next," Lance murmured.

Clayton glanced at him. "Who, you or Voss?"

Lance rubbed his forehead to ease the throbbing. "Excellent question. Ask me again in another few months...if I'm still around."

"Don't talk tosh. Of course you'll be around. You survived Bloody April in an underpowered, under-armed Pup. Why would the Huns nail you now that you have a decent plane with two guns? Four kills in one day and you are talking like a doomed man?"

Lance shrugged. "I met a better pilot today."

"And yet here you are, still hale and hearty while Voss's wingman and the plane he was escorting lie buried in the mud."

"True," Lance allowed, "but I'm a workman, a damn good one who knows his craft inside out. Voss is an artist. I could no more fly like him than I could fly to the moon. Doesn't mean I can't kill him, but I need to be cunning. Dogfighting with Voss is as smart as wrestling with a leopard."

"And how many leopards have you killed?"

"Three man-eaters. None of them easy, and all of them because I had a gun, and they didn't. Voss has two machine guns."

"Piffle. Voss could have cannons and you'd still sink him. By all accounts, Voss is a fun-loving bloke who loves champagne and a good party. He's only got talent. Whereas you're a revenge-fuelled, devious and driven bastard."

2
Blood In the Snow

One day later - 18 June 1917.
Ypres Sector, near Menin.

Tracer lanced from Richthofen's red Albatross. The formation of khaki planes ahead scattered like a covey of startled pheasants. One banked hard across Richthofen's nose, who fired and missed the ninety-degree deflection shot.

Hans, following his leader, nailed the enemy with two quick bursts. The first chewed the propeller to stumps. The second chopped the pilot into a welter of blood.

The stricken two-seater banked into a sliding dive, trailing white smoke, its useless propeller windmilling. Hans followed it, grunting with satisfaction as it headed lower and deeper into German territory. The pilot had to be mortally wounded because the plane made no attempt to pull out. Hans watched, dry-throated and excited, as the observer tried to reach back towards the cockpit to correct the steep dive, even though he must have known the attempt doomed.

The plane slammed nose first into a field, and the wings splintered into fragments of flying parts among yellow flowers.

Hans smiled. At the end of the patrol, he would commandeer a car and go claim a souvenir or two from his victim.

As he climbed back to re-join the *Jasta*, Hans savoured that he'd made the shot that the great Richthofen had missed. That tasted extra sweet. The rest of *Jasta* 11 would never love Hans whatever he did, but they would respect his marksmanship. Not that Hans cared. *Fuck 'em all.*

Not just that, but this was his tenth kill—the magical number that ushered him into the legendary brotherhood of aces. Let the rest of the *Jasta* 11 pilots pick the bones out of that. *Too bad, arseholes, I'm an ace.*

Ten kills should also get him the Iron Cross, First Class. Max Immelmann, the first ever ace in the German air force, had won the Blue Max—Germany's highest award for bravery—for eight kills, but as the war progressed such a score became commonplace. Nowadays ten kills, the tally that denoted an ace, earned "only" an Iron Cross First Class, still a mighty prestigious award.

Hans basked in the thought of the heavy medal bumping on his chest, proclaiming him a true hero of Germany. Not bad for an incompetent flier.

That was Richthofen's label, but even Hans couldn't argue with the verdict. He had heard the commander of *Jasta* 2, Erwin Bohme, saying that the Albatross flew like a living being that understood its master's wishes. Hans snorted. Maybe for the gifted pilots like the Richthofen brothers, or Manfred's baby-faced prodigy Wolff. But for Hans, aircraft were disobedient carthorses he wrestled into some sort of submission. Hans was probably—no, make that a racing certainty—the most ham-fisted pilot in Richthofen's elite *Jagdgeschwader* [JG] 1. In fact, the *only* ham-fisted pilot. Given that four *Jasta* comprised JG1, with nine pilots in each squadron, that meant he ranked a long way down. But by God, he could shoot better than any of them! And so Richthofen kept him, without ever hiding his distaste.

A drop of scalding water splashed his cheek and he jerked. His plane skidded too close to the experienced Allmenröder, who glared at him and gestured rudely. *"Küss meinen Arsch!"* Hans growled. It wasn't his fault his radiator was leaking. His mechanics should have checked. Hans would nail Korporal Muller's ball-sack to the hangar walls when he landed. With a big hammer and rusty nails. The water might scald when it left the radiator, but his soaked flying coat would turn to ice at three thousand metres—resulting in scalding and incipient frostbite on the same patrol, thanks to Muller. Hans wedged himself the far side of the cockpit to escape the drips, but they seemed to follow him. He would make sure that sloppy bastard Muller suffered worse.

~

Hans Schmettow climbed out of the car, his palms sweaty with anticipation, and hurried over to the wreck of the FE2. The glow of achievement warmed his belly, an unfamiliar sensation. The last time he'd experienced such pleasure was the day he lost his virginity to a stable girl. Even more unexpectedly, his new ace status kindled a furnace of ambition. The next hurdle after an Iron Cross First Class? Ten more kills would take him to twenty and qualification for the most prestigious medal available to a fighting officer, the Pour le Mérite, the so-called "Blue Max." A Blue Max made you a god in Germany. Could Hans Schmettow, unloved whelp and social outcast, attain such lofty heights?

Hans frowned, wary of the trap. The black fortune that had dogged him from conception had taught him to get his disappointment in first before someone else rammed it past his clenched teeth. He understood that good times were just the momentary pauses between life kicking him in the balls with steel-capped boots. He'd learned to leave ambition to those whom the gods loved, like Manfred Richthofen.

No doubt Richthofen was a prickly bastard and a self-righteous preacher, but no-one—not Boelke, not Hans, and not the British—ever doubted the man's genius as a pilot and as a tactician. He would be pleased with Hans's ace status. Not for Hans, but because turning the clodhopper into an ace would confirm Richthofen's reputation as a *Menschen Fänger*—a maestro who can coax impossible feats from those he leads. Neither could Hans deny that the pickings were bounteous when you hunted with the maestro, which Hans had done more often since Lothar Richthofen, Manfred's brother, picked up a bullet in the hip and was invalided back to Germany. Perhaps Richthofen owned so much of the gods' regard that some was rubbing off on Hans? For the first time in his life Hans allowed himself ambitions—a royal-blue Maltese cross with gold edging, fame, and revenge.

He burped. Too many oysters for lunch. Bodenschatz had somehow conjured up crates of fresh shellfish and the pilots had stuffed themselves like rats in a dugout. The adjutant was another military prig, with a posture so rigid that Hans reckoned his parents must have stuck a broom up his ass when he was a child. But he had a genius for provisioning. A supply of autographed photos of Manfred von Richthofen helped. "Dedicated to my esteemed fighting companion," read the inscriptions. The corrupt army commissars sold them for a fortune to the bullshit artists back in Germany. No doubt they opened the Fräuleins' legs.

Hans smirked. He didn't need such aids when he was in Berlin. His tailored flier's uniform showed off his tall erect figure, while his soulful blue eyes, blond lashes, and baby face melted women's hearts and unlaced their corsets.

The crashed plane dragged his thoughts from frolicking sluts. It lay crumpled in a corner of a field covered in buttercup flowers. The wings lay strewn haphazardly with their blue-white-red British roundels like incongruous clown faces in a sea of yellow flowers. Hans stood and gloated. There it was—hard proof of kill number ten. No-one could take this away from him.

The bodies of the pilot and the observer still lay twisted in the wreck. Ground troops had looted the crash as usual, but they had left the dead men's remains untouched. Not surprising. The impact of the crash had driven the huge engine forward to crush the two men into a stinking red pulp that now buzzed thick with flies. Two ravens, Odin's birds, flapped away from the cockpit as Hans approached. Here and there white bone stuck through the morass, and the only recognisable body part was the observer's face, frozen in a rictus of terror, with eyes staring wide above an open mouth. This one had died screaming.

Not even the hardened troops, inured to death itself, had wanted to reach into the sickly mess. Hans did not hesitate, thrusting his hand into where he thought he might locate a wrist, and groped, hoping to find a watch. The gooey mess felt warm. Must be the heat from the engine block. His fingers closed around bone. He pulled. The pulp surrendered a forearm with an obscene sucking noise and a putrid belch. Hans unfastened the watch, its leather strap soaked in blood, guts, and engine oil. He wrapped it in his white handkerchief and placed it in his jacket pocket.

Then he squatted to get closer to the observer. He reached out and tilted the face so he could see it more easily. His fingers left five red streaks across the pale cheeks that had remained curiously uncoloured by the surrounding gore.

Hans communed there for a few minutes, etching the details deep into his memory. The welcome magic seeped its warm glow from his throat into his chest, and charged his heart into a deeper thudding beat, every pulse distinct and sonorous like the heavy tread of death itself.

As far back as Hans could remember, he had a fascination with death. When he was twelve, he first beat the hedgerows for the New Year's pheasant hunt. As the birds rocketed from their cover and the booming shotguns broke them into tumbling carcases, he scampered to collect the blood-streaked bodies before the dogs. He heard the praise awarded to the most successful shooters and noticed how the hierarchy of skill overcame even the hierarchy of social standing. A lesser nobleman with outstanding shooting skills could be the king of the hunt. Most of all, he remembered one of the gruff old counts, breath steaming from his bearded mouth like the smoke still swirling around the shotgun barrels, saying, "There is a beauty about rich arterial blood in the snow on a Sunday morning." From that day on, Hans understood death had a special significance to some.

Watching the old die from disease was ugly, but seeing something young and vital plucked from the prime of life was to understand the awesome power of death. Life might play favourites, but the Grim Reaper treated all as equal. Death didn't care a fig if you died a hero in battle or went mad with the pox, whether you went to the grave as a cardinal of the church or hung from the scaffold as a murderer. All were equal, just meat for the worms. In death Hans would not have to look up to anybody, not even the likes of the high and mighty Manfred Richthofen.

The first time Hans held a dying doe's head in his lap and gazed into her liquid eyes, an epiphany surged through him. The closest connection he felt to other living things was sharing the instant of death, that unique moment of the last exhalation when life fled to parts unknown and the body on earth changed state.

No other experience matched those moments. Until he became a fighter pilot. He came to crave the godlike rush as a human died under Hans's guns. When a doomed pilot jumped, empathy jolted Hans's heart and dried his mouth. Only in wartime could you murder men and be a hero. War might kill and maim a lot of men, but it opened opportunities for a certain few.

"Sir? Sir? Are you alright?"

He snapped out of his reverie to find his driver staring at him, puzzled. Hans still crouched beside the crash with his hand cradling the dead man's chin. He straightened up, letting the white bloodless face fall into the gore. "Of course I am, you idiot. I told you to stay with the car."

The driver's expression moved from concern to cold neutrality. He snapped to attention and clicked his heels. "*Jawohl, Herr Leutnant!*"

"Get a bayonet and cut me out the roundel with the British markings from the left wing. Then take me back to the airfield."

"*Jawohl, Herr Leutnant.*"

Hans stomped back to the car and sat in the rear seat. The buttercups had painted his flying boots with golden pollen. He wiped them clean with the driver's scarf, which the disobedient asshole had left on the front seat. Let that be a lesson.

He relaxed as he waited for the driver and his prize. In the full history of the Schmettow family, a history littered with military heroes, no-one had ever won a Blue Max since Frederick the Great created it in 1740. Hans would be the first. *Then my grandparents, my aunts and uncles, my cousins, who have ground me into the shit all my life, they will fawn over me for bringing glory to the family name.* Hans would invite them to watch the Kaiser hang the medal around his neck, and then use his fame to destroy them. The bitterness against those who had killed his parents tasted like copper coins.

I must reach twenty kills. Whatever the cost.

3
The Best Teacher

Same day - 18 June 1917.
RFC, Bailleul Airfield, near Ypres.

Lance closed his eyes and waited.

"Pull up, man!" shouted Arthur Wolsey, Wing Commander of 100 Wing.

"Oh, Christ!" Clayton exclaimed.

The screaming yowl of the stressed rotary engine of a Sopwith Camel in full dive was cut short with a deep thud, shocking in its abruptness. Lance opened his eyes. A plume of black smoke slowly coiled upwards, marking the pilot's death at the target range on the far side of the Asylum airfield. The senior officers of 100 Wing stood beside the airstrip in silence.

"Silly sod," said Thompson, the commander of 333 Camel Squadron. Anger emphasised his Canadian twang and his granite jaw jutted in disgust. "I told him not to focus too hard on shooting the targets when he was diving on them. Eighteen years old, straight out of school, straight into the RFC, and straight into the ground. Waste of a good plane and now I have to find another replacement."

Clayton rolled his eyes at Lance. If the Thompson Admiration Society membership extended beyond one, and that was a big if in 100 Wing, Lance judged the adjutant wouldn't be the other.

"You are too harsh, Thommo," Arthur said. "Trying too

hard is not the biggest sin."

"Being stupid is," Lance said in a harsh voice. "He almost killed himself yesterday the same way. I heard Thommo warn him."

"Shame. He was a rapid fast bowler," Rod Andrews said, one hand clutching a large glass of whisky. The handsome Australian who commanded 222 Squadron had, before the war, terrorised the English batting with his ferocious bowling in cricket matches, and no-one had ever heard Rod admit that another bowler was "fast," never mind "rapid fast."

"It's true," Andrews said. "We had a game yesterday. He hit me on the noggin with a bouncer. Only tennis ball cricket, but still...hell of a bowler." Andrews saluted the pillar of oily black smoke with his glass and slugged back the whisky.

There was silence for a while as they digested the epitaph. The drifting smoke from the crash left a bitter tang in the nose.

When Boom Trenchard, general in charge of the RFC in France, appointed Lord Arthur Wolsey as commander of the new elite anti-Richthofen wing, Arthur had promised he would raid other squadrons only once for their aces. After that, he pledged, 100 Wing would train their own. Now that promise had come back to haunt him.

In their worst nightmares, no-one had expected the elite unit to lose half of their men in a single day. There again, when hunting Richthofen's Circus was your raison d'être, there was a fine line between hunter and hunted—as the deaths of 100 Wing's three famous Victoria Cross holders, Lanoe Hawker, Albert Ball, and Leefe Robinson, had shown.

Lance, who had finally accepted Arthur's wish that he command Ball's 111 Squadron, had been told he could request a few experienced pilots. But HQ had also insisted that 100 Wing accept and train novices like other squadrons. These newcomers possessed frighteningly few flying hours, never mind combat training. Now late in the evening, with their own flying done for the day, the squadron commanders were trying to rectify the lack of training for their four new novices. *And now there are three...*

Arthur fired a green flare to recall the other trainees back to the airfield. The commanders waited in silence and watched the majestic golden rays of the dying sun arc between the towering cumulus clouds. Gorgeous orange and blue pastels streaked the sky with an abandon that the most drunken artist would never have dared use for fear of overkill. It was a thing of beauty, much more so than the novices' landings.

Lance winced as an SE5 kangaroo-hopped across the field with three large bounces.

"That's Lieutenant Terry. Thirteen hours total flying, only two on SE5s," Clayton remarked.

Arthur turned to his adjutant in disbelief. "They are sending them out on thirteen hours? They may as well put them in front of a firing squad. We cannot afford to lose SE5s in landing prangs. Send him back."

Clayton shook his head. "After Bloody April, the RFC is so short of pilots, twelve hours is par for the course. I'm told Terry was the best of his monthly intake at the Joyce Green training field. Keen as blazes. Captain in the artillery and took a demotion to join the Flying Corps. Brave too. Military Cross and Bar."

"Brave is good," Arthur muttered, "But it would be useful if he could fly."

"That wasn't such a bad landing," Lance said, "for a man with two hours on the type. I'll make sure he gets twenty hours on SE5s before he crosses the lines. Otherwise, I'd feel like a murderer."

"Nice plan," Arthur said. "But with Haig planning his big new attack and the Huns trying to find out where he will launch it, that might not be possible. It will be all hands to the pump soon."

Another SE5 crunched into its landing. The creak of its wooden undercarriage as it took the strain was audible to the watchers thirty yards away.

"That's your nephew, Budd," Lance murmured to Arthur.

Arthur winced. "How is he doing?"

"About average on flying and shooting for someone with his lack of experience. Which means he's borderline. But unlike the others, he thinks he already knows it all and won't listen to any advice."

"He always had a gift for saying the wrong thing at the wrong time," Arthur said. "My sister swore he had improved. Does not sound like it. It will be hard to keep him alive."

"Hard to *want* to keep the snotty-nosed brat alive," Rod Andrews added sotto voce.

Arthur glared at the Australian, but then Lance saw him grimace in acknowledgement of the accuracy of the remark. "I cannot say I wanted him in this outfit, but Megan pulled strings and by the time I found out it was too late. So, we will have to make the best of having him on board. What about the other new man?"

"Newby shows promise," Lance replied. "He flew earlier and is on the ground over at the target range now."

"Gentlemen," Clayton interrupted, "allow me to introduce lieutenants Terry and Budd. This is Wing Commander Wolsey, in charge of 100 Wing."

The senior officers turned to meet the newcomers. Terry was in his late twenties, stocky and compact with dark tousled hair and a heavy five o'clock shadow burgeoning on a rugged face. His salute was as correct as his weathered Artillery Regiment tunic.

In contrast, the younger Morgan Budd shone in his custom-tailored RFC uniform. Dark eyes gleamed from a pale face under slicked-back hair, black as a crow's wing. He carried his chin high with a bold gaze, and the hint of petulance around the mouth only lightly marred his lean handsomeness. It was hard to believe that he was Arthur's nephew. Arthur's broad-shouldered physique, wavy blond hair, and pleasant open face contrasted with Budd's slim darkness.

Budd did not bother with a salute. "Hello, Uncle," he said, a brilliant white smile transforming his face from spoilt to dashingly handsome. The extraordinary voice was a shock even to Lance, who had heard it before. Thompson, who had not met Budd, looked startled.

The voice was incongruent with the young dandy. It was deep and authoritative—the sort of timbre with which God would have imparted the Ten Commandments.

Arthur ignored his nephew and returned Terry's salute. "At ease, gentlemen. Welcome to 100 Wing. You know our mission— to hunt down the Circus. But you have a duty to yourselves and to us to stay alive for the first month. You will not be of much use in that period, but you will learn faster than you ever thought possible. Soon you will be a danger to the Huns rather than to yourselves. So, no heroics until you have mastered air fighting. Listen to your commanders. Clear?"

"Yes, sir," Terry answered in a terse Yorkshire accent. Budd smiled in a superior manner as if he had a mysterious insight. That smile, which Lance had seen too often in the last few days, grated on him. Perhaps it was Lance's innate colonial inferiority complex rubbing up against Budd's aristocratic privilege. Yet neither Megan nor Arthur showed such arrogance, so where the hell did Budd get it? Megan had begged Lance to look after her son when he arrived at 100 Wing, and Lance had agreed before he'd met Budd. When Lance had volunteered to take Budd into his squadron, Arthur had looked surprised but grateful.

Lance wasn't sure how much longer he could hide from Arthur that Lance and Megan were lovers, but lovers or not, Lance was regretting taking on the role of nursemaid to the haughty prat.

Arbuthnot's severed tongue sizzled in its own blood on the glowing engine cylinder. Newly minted Second Lieutenant Newby could see, hear, and smell it. He heaved. When his stomach finished its rebellion, he wiped his chin with his sleeve. He'd been with the armourers at the target range when the crash occurred. The Camel had tunnelled nose first into the ground at more than 100 mph, mashing Arbuthnot into a jellied red mess against the engine block. Somehow, in the shattering crash, Arbuthnot had bitten his own tongue off. It was a sight Newby suspected he would never forget.

He'd walked away on shaky legs as Sergeant Major Smythe organised the tidy up of the remains. The thought made Newby want to throw up again, but if anyone could handle that job it would be the imperturbable Smythe. The man was built like one of those new-fangled tanks, six foot three yet so broad of shoulder and deep of chest and belly he almost looked squat. All topped off with an outstanding handlebar monstrosity on his upper lip that put Lord Kitchener's moustache on the famous recruiting poster to shame.

Newby walked back to the target butts to regain his poise. He had taken the airborne strafing practice at the ground targets as a sporting challenge, but Arbuthnot's death had brought home the dangers of war flying, even when it was just training. Newby closed his eyes and prayed for the poor man.

When he opened his eyes, he found Smythe waiting beside him.

"Sorry, sir, the butts are closing for the day."

"How many hits did I get?" Newby asked, trying to take his mind off the horror.

"Four, sir."

"Only four? You're joking?"

Newby walked closer to the target, where four red rings

marked the successful shots. He looked at the edges of the target, then at the back.

"But I fired hundreds of rounds. Where did they all go?"

"Somewhere else, sir. A lot near where the men were having lunch by that beech tree. Scattered them like a shoal of sardines."

"Over there? That's impossible!" Newby protested.

"Maybe, sir. But you managed it."

"Oh God, Sergeant Major, you must think I am a frightful duffer."

"No, sir, yer the shooting champ for the day."

"No need to be sarcastic, I'm doing my best."

"I was not being sarcastic, sir," the veteran said. "You are the only one who hit the targets at all. Mr Arbuthnot, God bless his departed soul, even killed two horses in the next-door field before his accident."

"Really? Then I did well."

Before the sergeant could answer, Major Fitch appeared. "Sergeant Major Smythe, why are you wasting precious minutes chatting with Lieutenant Newby?"

"Giving the lieutenant his shooting score, sir."

"He had a score? Wonders will never cease." Fitch walked round the target.

Newby studied him. At first glance Fitch did not look unusual, standing of average height with brown hair and the lithe build of an athlete. A second glance took in the face and its curious immobility of expression, the muscles locked in a grim mask of ingrained certainty that was as intimidating as hell. A two-inch white scar across the left cheek gave him a mildly piratical look, but the eyes...

Newby shuffled his feet as Fitch looked up and pinned him with those glacial green eyes flecked with bronze. That unblinking gaze seemed to go right through him, so much so he had to fight a compunction to look behind to see what was there. Newby shivered despite himself. He wouldn't want those eyes behind a gunsight and on his tail.

"So how would you rate your shooting, Newby?"

"I got the highest score of the day, sir."

"Mmm," Fitch mused, turning over the target. "Four hits from two hundred rounds. On a stationary target that isn't returning fire. Ever do any shooting before—shotgun, rifle, revolver?"

"No, sir, I was more of a cricket man myself. And I play the trumpet."

"That would explain a lot." Fitch stabbed Newby in the chest with a forefinger that felt like a rod of iron. "You are absolutely pathetic. What are you, Newby?"

"Pathetic, sir," Newby mumbled, his face getting hotter.

"No Newby, not just pathetic but ab-so-lute-ly path-etic. Say it."

"Ab-so-lute-ly path-etic, sir."

"Good. Now we both understand. If you scored four runs and everyone else on your absolutely pathetic cricket team scored zero, does that make your paltry four runs something to brag about?"

"No, sir. But I did my best."

"What you believe is your best isn't good enough, Newby. In this war you will either die or find that your best lies far beyond your current estimation. His Majesty spends hundreds of pounds training you to fly the most modern fighting machines in the world. He houses you, feeds you, transports you to France, gives you a batman and fitters to look after you, and fills up your plane with fuel and ammunition. Then you—the apex of all this effort—get a grand total of four hits on a stationary target with no-one firing at you. So, what will happen when you go over the lines, Newby?"

"Er, I'm not sure, sir."

"Well, I'm sure. You will be as dangerous to the enemy as

a bleating lamb in an abattoir. And if you are not a danger to the enemy, you are a total waste of time. My time, Newby. Time when I could be killing His Majesty's enemies instead of babysitting you."

"Sorry, sir, I will try to be less pathetic."

"Do you know the root of 'pathetic'?"

"Pathos, sir."

"Correct, Newby. Sorrow, sadness, suffering, tragedy, misery and grief. You, however, won't be feeling any of these things. Because a Hun assassin who *can* shoot straight will have spattered your brains across your instrument panel. There will be no return game the next week where you might score a century to redeem yourself, no team discussion over tea and crumpets to talk over what went wrong. Because you will be dead, Newby. Either a charred corpse or just mashed into the mud. But your mother, your father, the girlfriend, who all waved you off while wiping away their tears, they will feel the grief, the sorrow, the suffering, the tragedy, the misery. You will feel nothing. Nothing, Newby, 'cos you will be six feet under the sod."

Newby winced, but his commanding officer drove on remorselessly. "And the worst of it, Newby, is that because you are now dead, I have to go through the whole thing again with your replacement. The whole bloody cycle happens again. The next fresh-faced Newby comes in, sprays bullets everywhere except the target, and chuckles, 'Oh dear me, I did my best.'

"I will not waste my time training cannon fodder for the Huns when I could be killing those same Huns instead. For you to stay in my squadron, you must change from a bleating lamb into a slavering wolf. What will you be, Newby, lamb or wolf?"

"A wolf, sir."

"Shout it man, shout 'I am a wolf.'"

"I am a wolf."

"Louder! Much louder!"

"I am a wolf!" The cry echoed around the firing range. Was there anyone to see him making a spectacle of himself?

"Better," Fitch said. "Now since you can fly but can't shoot, and you certainly can't yet fly *and* shoot at the same time, we will teach you deflection shooting on the ground. I have two shotguns. We will do what wolves do, some killing."

"Sir?" Newby blanched at visions of unleashing a killing spree upon the French peasantry.

"Only pigeons, but they act more like Hun aircraft than the target butts. They fly, they jink, they dart. To kill them you need reflexes, and to fire not where they are, but where they will be when your bullets reach them—just like shooting at Huns. With the not-so-insignificant exceptions that the pigeons are as quarter as fast and are not trying to kill you in return. When the Huns come at you, they'll be travelling at hundred mph minimum. That means they will be fifty yards on your left one moment, and then one second later, fifty yards on your right. Calculating that and leading the target is deflection shooting—the basic skill of a fighter pilot."

Fitch strode away. "Come on. It will be dark in three hours, and we won't stop until you have killed twenty pigeons."

"Gosh," Newby said faintly, "I've never killed anything. From a model citizen to a mass killer in three hours."

"Worthy cause. The officers' Mess gets pigeon pie for a week."

"What happens if we don't kill twenty before nightfall?"

"We stay hunting until we do. Whatever it takes to get the job done."

"But we could be out here all night and still not kill enough," Newby moaned.

"True." Fitch pursed his lips. "Alright, I will allow owls as well as pigeons but I'm not sure the Mess would thank you for owl meat. It's quite stringy. One way or the other, if it takes until tomorrow, we stay out until you kill twenty birds. So, you'd better hit your targets sooner rather than later."

Fitch tossed Newby a shotgun and a box of shells and nodded as Newby deftly caught them. "You have a sportsman's hand-eye coordination. You just need to practise. And by God, you will practise 'til your trigger finger bleeds."

Newby traipsed after the lithe squadron commander as he loped into the dark woods. From behind, Newby noticed an oddity. Fitch's footfalls were silent, and he trod so lightly he left no tracks. Newby recalled the stories that Fitch had been a hunter back in Africa. That might explain it.

As they entered the woods, Fitch stopped so abruptly that Newby bumped into him.

"Get killing," Fitch commanded.

"Where?" Newby asked, looking around, his eyes still adjusting to the shadows.

Fitch leaned against a slim birch tree and crossed his arms and legs. "You want me to pull out a nipple so you can suckle on it?"

The scorn rankled. Newby drew himself to his full height. "My headmaster always said that good teachers can impart knowledge without resorting to scorn."

Fitch bared his teeth. "Ah, the suckling babe can bite. That's good. Trouble is, Newby, when you head into Hunland, there is an excellent chance the last teacher you will ever meet will be fifty yards behind you. His name is Richthofen, and he will impart his knowledge with a pair of Spandau firing lead bullets. His lesson will be that killers use their brains as well as bullets. So, use your noggin, find pigeons, and get killing."

Newby took the point. Fitch's rants were scalding but at last someone was training him to shoot. Newby pulled the shotgun to his shoulder and stalked deeper into the gloom, slitted eyes ready behind the raised barrels and a forefinger poised on the trigger. "I'm a killer," he muttered.

"It sometimes helps," Fitch sighed, "if you load the gun."

~

It was Fifi's fault. "Some piple zay," Fifi had murmured in her charming accent, slitting her sloe eyes suggestively at Elliot Springs, "Zat it eez an aphrodisiaque." And now he was broke. Pater's allowance was a generous one, but Springs had blown it all. He pondered how to recoup his losses as he waited for the gathering of the newly founded Mess Procurement Committee.

The trouble had started in Paris, as it often did in Springs's experience. He had been passing through on the way to his new posting to fly Sopwith Camels in 333 Squadron and was persuaded to visit the Moulin Rouge cabaret club. There he met Fifi, an elfin actress who pined for a drink called absinthe. She waxed lyrical that this was the drink of the Belle Époque in Paris, a romantic world of bohemian musicians and writers, struggling artists and glittering courtesans, all swirling in the cafes of Montmartre. Yet no matter how vigorously Springs flashed his wads of notes, the Moulin Rouge would not supply absinthe. Given Fifi's inspirational performance later that night, Springs reckoned a further aphrodisiac would have been wasted on her. Three bottles of Veuve Clicquot champagne seemed to do a perfectly good job.

However, that intriguing introduction ignited his interest in absinthe. His curiosity became an irresistible attraction when he heard that the French government had prohibited the drink in 1915, declaring that its consumption was detrimental to the war effort. The rebel and the romantic in him allied together, not for the first time in his life, to produce a compulsive need.

Romantic dreams had inspired Springs to leave South

Carolina and volunteer to fight for the British while America was still neutral. Those dreams were long gone. Honestly, a graduate in philosophy from Princeton should have known better. Early in his flying career, he realised that he was unlikely to survive the war. So, he determined to experience everything exotic, erotic, or forbidden that he could before he departed to the pearly gates.

Absinthe ticked most of those boxes, and he tracked down the elusive nectar in a dusty, cobwebbed cellar. The smuggler insisted on a minimum of twelve cases of Pernod Absinthe, and after a fearsome weight of French francs changed hands, Springs drove off with his loot. Unfortunately, he had spent his father's monthly allowance with that single purchase, which left him a pauper for a whole month. Even worse, he discovered that the Pernod was virtually undrinkable.

Earlier tonight, at dinner in the Mess, Clayton had asked for volunteers for the Mess Procurement Committee.

"I'm looking," Clayton said, "for two Mess officers, one to take charge of the booze and one to assist with the food. I've always found that these posts are best filled by officers who take a keen interest in such things."

Arthur spoke first. "Weston eats enough for three men and will be an excellent candidate on the food side. I can also help you somewhat on the alcohol. My ancestors pillaged France, Portugal, and Scotland for centuries with sword and coin. They always brought home piles of wine, brandy, port, and whisky. So much so that even the alcoholics in the family haven't run the cellars dry. There is no better cause than the pilots, so I'll get a regular shipment organised from the estate. That should help your budget, but I can't assist you on the new-fangled cocktail spirits that I gather are all the rage."

"I have the answer for that," Thompson said. "If the Royal Navy sank German ships at a tenth of the rate Elliot Springs sinks cocktails, they would have been sailing up the Rhine by now."

Springs opened his mouth to protest but paused, struck by Thommo's pale grey stare that dared him to disagree. Thommo was a generous boss in the bar but not a good man to cross. The easy smile could deceive you. More truthful was the chin that jutted below a cropped moustache like a ramming prow under the bow-wave of a Roman war galley. Even Thommo's short ginger hair bristled.

"Delighted to aid the war effort," Springs murmured. Perhaps he could peddle the Pernod onto the Mess?

Now, close to midnight, the 100 Wing Procurement Committee was in its inaugural session at the dining table of the Mess. Springs and the bar orderly were concocting cocktails for the committee members.

The only other people in the Mess were two of the new 111 Squadron pilots, Stokes and Kerrigan, who were playing a game of snap in the lounge chairs in the far corner.

"Snap!" Stokes bellowed, but a good second behind Kerrigan. "Stuff this!" the burly Australian declared, jumping to his feet. "It's no fun losing all the time."

"Teach you to play cards with a professor," Clayton said.

"A professor of what?" Springs asked.

Kerrigan inclined his head with a small smile as he also stood to leave. "Mathematics. Doesn't help much with a game of snap, though. It's just that Stokes is so much taller than me, it takes longer for the thoughts to get from his brain to his mouth."

"Cheeky bugger." Stokes slapped Kerrigan on the back, a fond tap that sent the smaller man staggering. The two left the Mess laughing.

Springs handed each of the Procurement Committee a wine glass full of a yellowy green liquid with a cloudy swirl. When Springs put his on the table, Clayton made shooing gestures at him.

"Oi, put the glass on a drinks mat, not on the wood. This is French walnut from the 1700s, a valuable antique, and I don't want rings on it. I had to bribe the local chateau owner with two crates of whisky for this, so we had a decent dining table for the Mess. Look at that shine—two hundred years of polishing to get a patina like that."

Springs peered at his reflection in the table. Damn, his face had gained a lot of lines. Either that or the table had seen better days. Maybe both, he decided. He didn't want to be unfair to the table. Clayton was a cultured man and if he'd parted with two crates of Scotland's finest, the table must've had something to commend it.

Springs sniffed his glass and gagged at the pungent scent of anise. As recommended by Fifi, he'd mixed five parts water to one part Pernod, plus a sugar lump. "Viola!" he declared. "This will be 100 Wing's signature cocktail. Quite unique. We are lucky that I acquired some Pernod Absinthe; it is like gold dust at present."

The committee members accepted his offering without enthusiasm.

"The colour of mustard gas," Weston said dubiously. In his massive hands, the wine glass looked like a fairy goblet. The farmer's blond thatch and affable face topped six feet and three inches of rough-hewn muscle, and a dray horse's depth of chest and weight of limb.

"Smells as dangerous as mustard gas," Clayton said, his nose wrinkling in distaste. "And it is illegal in France. However, as you have generously donated it to the Mess, I accept the offering provided it does not actually poison anyone."

"Er...I was hoping the Mess Committee would consider reimbursement for my selfless act of initiative on behalf of the wing." Springs slid an invoice in the adjutant's direction.

Clayton's eyebrows climbed as he read it. "Lieutenant Springs, if we repaid you for your unauthorised purchase, the entire alcohol budget for the year would be gone."

Springs blinked in shock. "There is a budget? For booze?"

"Springs, your patriotism is beyond reproach. But I do feel your grasp of the realities of war in the British Army are somewhat tenuous to say the least."

"I'd never have joined up if I'd have known. There are only two essentials in war—booze and bullets. The government pays for bullets. They should pay for booze for the fighting men so we can keep firing the bullets."

"No, and that's final," Clayton said in a manner too dictatorial for Springs's liking.

The rest of the committee put their glasses down and hastily reverted to the topic of the moment before Springs could force them to drink the concoction. That topic was not procurement but rather disposal. With over seven hundred men to feed, the wing generated so much waste from the kitchens that the garbage dump overflowed, and rats were running amok. The pilots complained about the stench, and the medical officer muttered about the dangers of a bubonic plague.

To help cull the rat population, officers sat in deckchairs near the kitchen when they finished flying for the day, with drinks in one hand and pistols in the other. They greeted the appearance of a single rat with volleys of gunfire that Springs claimed would not have disgraced the Last Stand at the Alamo. The medical officer changed his complaint and stated that the rat hunting was more of an immediate danger to health than the plague. Arthur could ignore the medical officer, but when the kitchen staff went on strike because of the deadly threat from flying bullets, the wing commander told Clayton to solve the problem. Clayton passed on the dilemma to the Procurement Committee.

"Pigs," Weston said.

"What?" Clayton asked with a puzzled frown.

"Pigs," Weston repeated. "Buy piglets and put them in a pen just outside the kitchens. They'll hoover up the waste.

They eat anything, and when they are fully grown, you slaughter them and have cheap pork and bacon for the Mess. Then buy more piglets and do the whole thing over again. Costs you nothing to feed the pigs, and nothing to get rid of all the garbage. And imagine that lovely pork crackling!" The big man's eyes grew dreamy, and he swallowed to avoid drooling.

Springs shuddered delicately at the prospect of so much pork fat and made a retching noise. The rest of the committee looked at him in surprise. To cleanse his palette of the imagined fat, he took his first gulp of his creation. This time, his shudder was far from delicate and left his eyes bulging in their sockets.

The others watched with interest. Springs put the drink down with care, looked defiantly at the others through his watering eyes, and said, "Quite possibly an acquired taste."

"You've done enough acquiring, young man," Clayton said. "We have twelve cases of this contraband and going by your reaction, we will still have twelve cases when we finally win the war in 1924."

"If this stuff has an effect like that on an experienced boozer like Springs, perhaps we should just drop these bottles on the Huns instead of bombs?" Weston suggested.

"Going back to pigs," Springs said in a hasty attempt to divert the subject, "are we are in danger of replacing the reek of rotting garbage with the sweet aroma of pig shit? Do they eat their own shit as well?"

Weston looked pained. "Of course not. You start a manure pile and use it to grow your own vegetables. And if we don't want to do that, the local farmers will help themselves to all the manure they can get."

"Alright, chaps," Clayton said. "We will give the piglets a go. Weston, you buy them from a local farmer, and I will sign off on the funds to repay you. That is all the agenda items for today. Thank you for your time, gentlemen."

Weston levered his considerable bulk out of his chair and left the Mess. Springs remained. He hadn't surrendered his hopes of persuading the adjutant. "Adj, about that Pernod. Doesn't it seem to you very uncivilised for the Mess to be paying for pigs but not for absinthe, the apogee of French liquors? I mean—"

Newby burst into the Mess, his boyish form shivering and bedraggled. "Barman, for the love of God, a cuppa tea to warm me up, please!"

The bar orderly raised an eyebrow but left to get tea from the kitchens.

"Whisky is the usual warmer upper around here," Springs said.

"Gosh, no! Can't stand the taste."

The bar orderly reappeared with a steaming tin mug of tea, and Newby cupped it with shivering hands and slurped a mouthful.

"Aha! Just the ticket! Thank you." Newby wiped the back of his hand across his mouth and looked around the Mess, an errant schoolboy checking for teachers.

"Evening, Major Clayton, sorry, sir. Didn't see you there. I'm in danger of pneumonia. As adjutant, you must know that Major Fitch is certifiable."

"Perhaps a trifle unorthodox," Clayton demurred, "but His Majesty does not award medals to people who don't get the job done."

"Aargh! That phrase again. Barman, any chance of more tea, please?"

Reinforced with another cuppa, Newby threw himself into one of the deep chairs. "He's a psychopath. Had me murdering pigeons with a shotgun all evening. Wouldn't stop until I had twenty. Still—" Newby brightened at the recollection— "I got my own back."

"You did?" Clayton sounded dubious.

"Yes, sir. It was about half-past eight and I had just eighteen dead pigeons. So Fitch said my only hope of getting the job done tonight was to bag a couple of owls. We stole into a farmyard to see if there were any hanging around in the barns. Fat chance. He must have cleaned out the entire owl barn population with some other trainee mug. By then it's eleven o'clock and raining to boot. Bloody sopping, freezing, miserable wet I am, when suddenly two chickens run out from underfoot. Before I knew what I was doing, I blew them both to bits—bam, bam! Fitch looks at me like I'm mad, but I had suffered enough. I said, 'You wanted twenty dead birds, now I've got twenty. The chickens are birds, and they were on the run. You wanted quick reactions, ruthlessness, and deflection shooting. Well, I got the job done—think of the chickens as a couple of Bertha bombers.'" Newby paused for a long slurp of tea.

Springs clapped. "What did Fitch say to that?"

"He laughed, but not for long. There were feathers everywhere, the farmyard was going mad with squawking chickens, barking dogs, honking geese, and the farmer, his wife, and daughter all shrieking. They were afraid the stinking Boche were attacking them. Total nuthouse," mused Newby with a smile of fond recollection. "A very irate, very large farmer's wife in her nightgown was screaming at Fitch, who was waving lots of francs at her to shush her up. I snuck out of the yard and here I am. Serves him right, I say!" He took another gulp of tea, peered at his mug, and seemed surprised to find it empty.

The door crashed open. Fitch strode in, carrying a shotgun in the crook of his arm.

"Evening all," Fitch said. "Newby been telling you about our night?"

"Why don't you hang around the piano and sing songs like the rest of us?" Springs asked.

"What? And miss all the fun? I had farmer de Croisset's daughter out in the cold with a wet nightie. What a sight. Breasts like pears."

"That's not how Newby tells it," Springs remonstrated. "He had you shelling out fistfuls of francs to a very large lady who was so terrifying that Newby took flight."

"As a wingman, Newby leaves a lot to be desired. He fled at the first sign of trouble, but if he had hung around, he could have enjoyed the sights. I was stretching out the bargaining with old man de Croisset while young Mams'elle Croisset was enjoying me enjoying her. Quite a flirty little baggage, that one. Then Madame Croisset noticed us ogling each other, and the price soared so fast I wasn't sure what I was buying. I thought maybe it included the daughter too, but sadly not. Still, I got two chickens for the Mess, although the cook will need to take the pellets out first."

"It sounds." Springs said, "as though you also got an eyeful of Mams'elle's charms in a wet nightie, for a price less than a drink and a gawp at the girls over at No.10 in Amiens."

"I bow to your expertise in that arena," Fitch said as he turned to leave. "Newby, be at the shooting butts tomorrow morning, 0700 sharp, for the next stage of your education." The door banged behind the major as he left.

Newby looked over at Clayton. "Why is he picking on me?"

"He said you had good potential as a pilot if you learned to shoot and developed a mean streak."

"Oh." Newby looked pleased. "He hasn't shown me that he thinks I am any good at anything, other than getting farmer's daughters out in their nightwear."

"Yes, well," Clayton said, rising from his chair. "Don't let it go to your head. It doesn't matter what you or he thinks, it is what the Huns do that counts. His last trainee went down in flames on his first patrol. He was a damn good shot, but he never even saw the Albatross that got him. I'm off to bed."

"Good night," a dazed-looking Newby replied. "Why did he tell me that?" he asked Springs. "It won't help me sleep."

"Just count your blessings that Fitch is training you. I've never seen a commanding officer devote so much time into training pilots."

"But isn't that his job?"

Springs snorted. "Most majors don't even fly over the lines. I like my commander, Major Thompson. He's generous in the Mess bar, which is more than most majors, but he's far more interested in increasing his own score than keeping me alive. And frankly, given our respective abilities, it's a better use of his time. Eighty percent of kills probably go to the top twenty percent of pilots. But enough depressing shop talk…" Springs pushed one of the rejected cocktails towards Newby. "If you want to sleep, try this."

"Jolly interesting colour. What's it called?"

"Maiden's Slumber," Springs extemporised.

"And it helps you sleep? Smells like medicine."

"That's just it. All the benefits of a medicine to help you into a dreamless slumber, wrapped up in the delightful flavour of a modern, sophisticated cocktail."

"Can't say I've ever had a cocktail before. Mother didn't approve and Father said they were barbaric mixtures."

"That's just old school talking. This is the latest thing in New York and Paris."

Newby knocked back half the glass in one gulp. He gagged and turned deathly pale. "Ye gods!"

"Yes, it is nectar for the gods, isn't it?"

"Well, I suppose it might taste better than cod liver oil. It makes me feel frightfully grown up—drinking cocktails, I mean."

"Yup. Cocktails do that, and a lot more besides."

Newby finished his drink in another gulp and shook his head to clear it. "What did you say the name was? Maiden's Prayer?"

Springs pushed his own glass over to the Englishman. "Exactly. Have another."

"Jolly decent of you. What's the No.10 you mentioned to Major Fitch, something about ogling girls?"

"Best officer's brothel in Amiens. Ask for Angelique when you go. She's the tops. When you leave, even your toenails are limp."

Newby choked and sprayed Pernod all over his trousers. "Bedtime, I think," he said and left the Mess without looking Springs in the eye.

Springs shook his head. These English schoolboy innocents drank like sailors, fought like devils, died like martyrs, but went puce at the mention of a working gal. Ten to one Newby would be in a brothel inside a month—if he lived that long.

Anger stabbed through Springs at the thought. He was older than Newby, and he had a degree in philosophy from Princeton. Fat lot of good it had done him. He'd come into this war with his own naïve conceptions. Perhaps it was the alcohol hitting, but he felt the black dog of depression stalking him. What a waste of young men. There was nothing he could do to save Newby; it was as much as he could manage to look after himself. He looked at the last surviving glass of Pernod. Drinking alone was always a danger signal, but what the hell. He knocked it down in one and headed for bed with tears in his eyes.

Of course, it was the Pernod.

4
Ashes

Lance lay awake in his cot, listening to the thudding guns in the darkness, his mind fluttering like a moth round a gas lantern. He'd gone to his tent chuckling at memories of the chaos in the barnyard—the daughter's sloe eyes and her sly smile at his admiring glance, hens and the mother clucking in panic, a garlic-infused hug from the farmer when he realised he wasn't being invaded by the Boche.

But then he'd read the letter from Pa that the mail orderly had left on his bed. Now, no matter how hard he sought and failed to find refuge in sleep, his mind and guts churned with Pa's words.

Distant flashes from the explosions at the front flickered through the flaps of his tent. Twelve miles to the east the war raged as usual, but the guns were not what kept sleep away. Words from Pa had pierced his core worse than anything the enemy could achieve.

Lance swung his legs out of bed, clutching the rough serge blanket around him, and padded over to the tentpole where his clothes hung. The cold duckboards under his bare feet made him shiver.

The barbed hooks of guilt had first snagged him when Ma died of a snake bite when she rescued the young Lance from a cobra. Those barbs sunk in deeper the day Lance led his safari into a German ambush while visiting his then fiancée in German East Africa. Lance had no way of knowing Germany had declared war, but he held himself accountable for Hamisi's immolation and the crippling of his youngest brother, Francis. As a skilled hunter experienced in bushcraft, Lance should never have been ambushed. And later, when Lance led his company into an artillery barrage that killed his brother Will, he blamed himself again. Yet all that self-recrimination had been self-generated, and the barbs of guilt he'd endured were no more than pinpricks compared to the wounds Pa's letter had inflicted.

He lit the hurricane lamp and dressed. Gooseflesh puckered his skin as he pulled on his serge uniform, still damp with the morning chill. He shivered and took Pa's letter from his jacket pocket. He sat in the folding canvas chair under the hissing yellow light and unfolded the crinkled paper. For a while he waited there, staring at the tent walls but seeing only regrets that chained him to the past.

Outside his tent, a faint cry sounded, someone else's nightmare. A familiar sound.

He sucked in a deep breath and turned his eyes to the letter, to the words that he could barely comprehend when he first read them.

Lance, there is no easy way to say this, so I will just come out with it. Francis shot himself. After you took ship for France, the agony from the knee got worse and worse. He was bed-bound and addicted to the laudanum the doctor gave him for the pain. I never told you as I knew you were going through enough. He was fading, and when the Doc tried to wean him off the opium, it all became too much. He left a note that said he could not carry on living like this—better to end it

now than become an incoherent husk. He asked me to
pass on a message to you. Hosea 8:7.

Lance shut his eyes. Now Francis had joined Ma and Will across the great divide; Pa was the last.

And now I must tell you that I lied when I wrote that I did not hold you responsible for what happened to your brothers. I was trying to protect you from such thoughts. I know, beyond doubt, that you would have laid down your own life to prevent such events, but somewhere in my darkest mind, resentment built. When I opened the bedroom door and saw Francis with his brains blown out, that resentment broke through all restraint. I cursed you.

Your mother died saving you from a snake, and I blamed you. Now Francis is dead, after being crippled when you were in charge, and I blamed you. Will went to war with you and won't be coming back, and I blamed you.

Yet why should I blame you for any of them? Intellectually, I know you are not responsible for the acts of snakes, or rabid dogs like Kapitän Peters. And Will had a burning desire to march to war that nobody could have stopped. But the dark thoughts did not listen to reason. I drank for two whole days and nights and there was not an hour when I did not curse you.

A tear dropped onto the page and the ink smudged. Lance raised his head and wiped his eyes with the back of his hand. Pa's words reminded him of Kathy, Will's widow. She had accused him of being a curse on everyone around him, a Jonah. Since then, he'd told himself the same many times. It was his cross to bear, and revenge against the Huns was the only thing that made it bearable.

A rumble of guns in the distance agreed. Wind moaned past the guy ropes, shivered the tent, and made the poles creak. A squall of raindrops pattered on the canvas. He bent his head again.

*When I sobered up, all the curses had run dry. I
wish I could say the boil had festered, burst, and lanced
itself—but it hasn't. I was angry with the world, with
you, and mostly with the Germans. Having watched
my youngest son die a little every day over the last two
years, I too want revenge.*

"No Pa! Please, not you too," Lance whispered. His guilt
for Francis and Will was an open sore in his soul, but if Pa died
too...

And Pa did not realise the half of it. He did not know how
Lance had dithered at the crossroads under the artillery-
spotting Hun aircraft when Will died; that Lance had been
daydreaming of Heidi's kisses when the German askaris
ambushed them; and most of all that Lance had provoked the
cobra attack that killed Ma. If Pa knew those things...Lance
sighed. Like a slave to the galley oar, he bent his head, knowing he would not escape more lashes from this letter.

*A few short years ago I had a wife and a family, a
farm, and a hunting safari business—all I ever desired.
I counted myself among the most blessed of men. Now
all is ash. I have no reason to stay in Africa with Will
and Francis dead, and you facing death every day. All I
had left in Africa was a house full of ghosts.*

*So now, I am writing this in England where I have
re-joined my previous Regiment. They said I am on the
old side for active service but the scale of our officer
losses, and my experience as an officer in the Boer War,
means they are keen to use me at the Front. I'm told the
Army's private mail is slow so by the time this letter
finds you, I might be in France.*

*When you left Africa, I counselled you against suc-
cumbing to a quest for revenge. Yet now I find myself*

following the same path. Soon I hope to join you in paying back the Prussians for what they have done to our family, in the only coin those bastards understand. The world seems a bitter place. Revenge, and you, are all I have. When I reach the front lines in France, maybe I will search for you.

Your Pa.

Lance crumpled the letter in his fist. Damn him! Pa and life back in Africa remained Lance's true North, the only sane path he could see through this hellish war. If he lost Pa, he would lose the only future he could imagine—if by some freakish chance he lived. Damn and blast Pa!

He straightened out the letter on his thigh, smoothed out the wrinkles. Then he raised the chimney of the hurricane lamp and pushed the paper to the flame. It flared brightly and shadows danced like evil sprites on the canvas walls. When his fingers burned he let go, and the flames fluttered to the floor. Wind swirled the black ashes around the tent, breaking them into ever smaller pieces until the air was clear again.

5
Esprit De Corps

Later than morning, groggy from a night of tossing and turning, Lance wafted an ineffectual hand against the clouds of cigar smoke fugging the office that Arthur and Clayton shared. Rods of rain lanced down from the low-flying clouds and drummed against the windows and on the roof. HQ had declared the day as a washout.

"Who says it's not good enough?" he asked.

Arthur puffed on his cigar from behind his foldable campaign desk, apparently a recent present from his wife, and shrugged. "Who do you think? Boom Trenchard, of course."

"For Christ's sake! It's only been six days since we lost over half the squadron when it was commanded by Albert Ball. I've only been in charge for five days."

"What is your strength right now?" Arthur asked.

"There's five of us left of the original squadron. Two replacements, Kerrigan and Stokes have war flying experience in Sopwith Pups, but they are still learning the SE5. And the two tyros, Budd and Newby. That's nine in theory. But the tyros are lambs to the slaughter at present, and one of the old hands, Cecil Lewis, has an ear infection. He's in hospital having it drained and will be out for a week. So that's six operational pilots. Half strength. Besides, I thought it was

HQ's job to get us replacements."

"If you wait for HQ to do anything other than complain, you'll need to change your name to Rip Van Winkle," Clayton said from the other side of the office, waving a battered tin kettle in one hand.

At one stage this hut must have been a farm kitchen because an ancient wood-fired stove took up one wall. Clayton kept a kettle bubbling there all day so the pilots could always call in for tea. He raised an eyebrow at Lance as an invitation for a cuppa and Lance shook his head. Too hot and humid for tea. Clayton shrugged and went back to his makeshift desk— an unhinged wooden door laid flat across two packing cases— that lay submerged under waves of memos and army acquisition forms.

Lance turned on the adjutant. "You're the paper pusher here, the Mr. Fixit. Can't you arrange replacements?"

"No, I can't. You need to do it."

"Me?" Lance glared at Clayton. "When I agreed to command a squadron, Arthur promised you'd do all the paperwork."

"I did," Arthur conceded, "but here's the reality, Lance. HQ sends out an order telling other squadrons to volunteer their best pilots for a posting to an elite anti-Richthofen Wing. The 'elite' tag gets up the noses of the other commanders, as does the demand to hand over their best men, so they recommend their troublemakers. That's human nature. I would do the same. Which is why I will only take volunteers, or we will end up with the dross instead of the crème de la crème."

"Therein lies another problem," Clayton said. "Lanoe Hawker, Leefe Robinson, and Albert Ball all died fighting the Circus in the last few months. Two of them among the best fighter pilots in the RFC, and the other one the most famous. All three of them awarded the Victoria Cross. So, the scuttlebutt says 100 Wing is a suicide job and our supply of volunteers has dried up."

Lance stared at them in disbelief. "You're saying the RFC is full of cowards?"

Arthur shook his head. "No. We are saying it takes a certain kind of warrior to volunteer to fight the Circus every day, and even such die-hard fighters need to believe in their leader."

Clayton looked at his fingernails. "What Arthur is trying to tell you in his diplomatic way, is that you need to inspire potential volunteers to join. You must paint a picture of what they and the squadron can achieve, and how you can make it happen. Show them what success looks like, how they will be part of something greater than themselves. Henry V's Agincourt speech. That sort of thing."

"I'm a sodding pilot, not a snake oil salesman flogging fame and glory to gullible fools."

Clayton looked pained. "Shakespeare is not a snake oil salesman, and it's called inspiring, not selling. Albert Ball was inspirational with his actions, and they would have volunteered for him. But they won't volunteer for a chippy colonial obsessed with his personal score—which for some strange reason is the reputation you have. You need to show them that is not who you are. If you can."

"Sod the two of you. You're the bastards who persuaded me to become a commander. 'Be the British Boelke, you said.' Now you're saying I'm the problem. Talk about changing your tune!"

Arthur knocked ash off his cigar end. "Stop trying to escape. We never said you are the problem. What I am telling you is that if you do not take charge of life, life takes charge of you. Call it what you like, snake oil salesman or inspiration, but take charge of the process. Leaders influence events and people. Be a leader."

"There was nothing like that in my officer's training. Never heard of an army officer having to sell a vision. Officers order, men obey."

"True enough, that is the British Army training," Arthur

conceded. "Good infantry are moulded into a single organism that obeys orders. They beat individuality out of their men on purpose. But every pilot in the RFC is a volunteer and such men are a whole different breed, who tend toward the adventurous or romantic or rebellious. The champions in their ranks will not drop in your lap courtesy of the army bureaucracy."

A long silence filled the room. Pa had taught Lance to solve his own problems and asking for help rankled. He ran his fingers through his hair and sighed. Still the silence stretched on. Lance wanted to punch that small smile off Clayton's face. Damn them both! "Help me," he growled.

Arthur leaned forward. "What sort of men do you want in your squadron?"

Lance frowned. "Pilots who can fly and shoot, of course."

"No. That is what men do. It is not their character. Decide what type of characters you want. Then find a couple and entice them to join your squadron. They will persuade others who are similar, and then you have a snowball rolling downhill."

Lance threw up his hands. "You and Clayton know loads of pilots in the RFC. Why don't you recruit the best?"

"Because," Arthur said as he leaned back, "this is your squadron, and it will only work as a reflection of your beliefs. Does Manfred von Richthofen accept anyone his HQ gives them? Heck, no! We know from prisoners that he scouts talent personally and uses his charisma to obtain volunteers. That is leadership. You need to do the same according to your beliefs. Not mine or Clayton's. You are the hunter, the ace from Africa as the London papers trumpet. 100 Wing may have put dents in the Circus—most of them courtesy of you and Albert Ball, bless his soul—but they have damaged us worse. That might change if you become the leader you could be."

Lance blew out a ragged sigh. "This is too complicated for me. I don't have a clue about the things you two are talking about."

"Bollocks," Clayton said. "Arthur just sold you a vision, and you bought it. So did I, because Arthur meant it. If you tried to say the words Arthur said, I wouldn't believe you. But if Lance Fitch told me he knew how to kill more Huns while losing fewer men, then I'd believe him. And if Arthur, a dilettante retarded by centuries of aristocratic interbreeding, can inspire people, then so can you."

Arthur laughed and puffed out a perfect smoke ring. They watched it float to the ceiling.

"When you put it like that," Lance said with a twisted smile, "it sounds almost feasible."

~

"Clayton, why am I wasting my time here?" Lance asked. The miasma of slopped alcohol and cigarette smoke that clouded the officers' Mess ranked high among Lance's least favourite ambiences. "I've better things to do after dinner than be a barfly."

Clayton perched on a high wooden barstool in the middle of the long bar and took a sip of red wine. The previous plywood bar had disintegrated during a particularly violent binge and Clayton had arranged a novel replacement by harvesting timber sleepers from a railway track shattered by Hun artillery. Heavy thick beams laid on aircraft trestles served as a bar top that ran almost the length of one wall, long enough for twenty men to stand shoulder to shoulder.

Lance tapped the solid oak. "This isn't your most elegant acquisition. It looks more like a bridge than a bar."

"But one thing is for sure," Clayton said. "If the pilots break anything in another binge, it won't be this bar."

"I'd rather my pilots broke the bar than their bones."

"Then keep your men under control. It's not my bar assaulting the pilots."

At least someone had shaved off the oil-stained outer

layers, leaving a woodgrain with characterful swirls, knots, and cracks. Clayton traced a vein with his finger and smiled winningly at Lance, who narrowed his eyes and took a pace back. That smile reminded him of the toothy leer on the face of a crocodile. "What do you want, Clayton?"

"I asked you here for two reasons," Clayton said. "First, I want to show you leadership styles in action."

"Here in a bar?"

"In every squadron or wing, the commander's office should be the brain, but the bar is its beating heart." Clayton nodded at the far end of the railway sleepers where Thommo was holding court with his Camel pilots. "Exhibit A. Watch and listen carefully and tell me what you learn about leadership."

"From Thommo? You'll be telling me next that Colonel Custer was a genius cavalry commander."

Clayton scowled. "I'm trying to help you here."

Lance stared at him, but eventually turned to eavesdrop through the buzz of drunken youths.

"It takes a real man to be a Camel jockey," Thommo pontificated, his chin leading as his grey eyes swept his men for challengers. "The Camel is a wild stallion of a plane that needs skill and guts to fly. Compared to a Camel, the SE5 is a placid gelding, and the Bristol is a carthorse. Also, us Camel humpers gotta have cast-iron livers to handle the booze we need to bind our stomachs after the rotary engine sprays castor oil over us. We are men's men. Down the hatch boys! Keep the shits away!"

"Up the Humpers, down the hatch!" the Camel pilots cheered before knocking back their drinks. Lance rolled his eyes at Clayton.

Clayton shrugged. "The man is a bullshit artist, but there is a method in his madness. See what he's doing?"

"Getting drunk," Lance said, sipping his lemonade.

"He's creating an esprit de corps in his own image. Chippy,

angry, 'us against all comers.' You read the motto Elliot Springs pinned to the noticeboard?"

Lance snorted. "I was there when Arthur tore it down. He reminded Thommo that officers are supposed to be gentlemen."

"We happy Humpers, we happy few, we feed, fly, fight, and fornicate as one," the Camel pilots chanted on cue.

"Thommo obviously has taken the ticking off to heart," Lance said. "At least it's 'fornicate' now."

Clayton was less impressed. "You colonials have degraded standards. We never used to hear such language in the officers' Mess."

"Sorry about that. Next time we will leave the mother country alone with her high-falutin' decorum. Then you can tell us if the German manners are better while you are serving them their breakfast sausage and sauerkraut."

The adjutant shuddered at the thought. "Colonials might be the lesser of two evils," he conceded. "I mean, sauerkraut first thing in the morning?"

A raucous baying with a vague resemblance to song erupted from the other end of the Mess. Rod Andrews leapt onto the piano with a full pint mug of beer in one hand. Froth flew as he conducted vigorously.

Waltzing Matilda, Waltzing Matilda
You'll come a waltzing Matilda with me.

"Ah," Clayton said. "Exhibit B."

"You can't be serious," Lance said. "Prancing on a piano is leadership?"

"No? Did you know Rod Andrew's captained Australia at cricket?"

Lance felt his eyebrows climb.

Clayton nodded. "1912. Australia toured England and Rod captained the team for one game. I met one of the Australian players, and he told me the story. Twelve players tried to take the field. When the opposition complained, Rod turned to his teammates and said, 'One of you jokers get lost'. That took them a while to sort out, and then the other ten waited for Rod to say where he wanted them to field. 'I'll bowl,' Rod said, 'The rest of you, scatter.' The Australian manager was apoplectic, but somehow the team excelled and steamrollered the game in record time. 'Why?' you may ask.

"The great American Civil War general, Sherman, said every leader needs to command the souls of his men as well as their bodies and legs. Look around you, Lance. To your left, Camel pilots crowded around their commander. To your right, the Bristol Misfits in a circle around Rod Andrews. Now where exactly is the crowd of adoring SE5 pilots from your squadron?"

Lance looked around. His pilots were scattered through the Mess, never in more than pairs, most talking quietly. As he watched, some drifted towards Rod Andrews's singalong.

"So," Clayton said in satisfaction. "Who are the leaders in this room?"

"Humph," Lance said. "But you said every leader needed a vision. Damned if I can see what vision Rod Andrews is selling his men."

"Ah, that's a subtle one. He's selling the 'no vision' vision."

"And you said Thommo was full of bullshit!"

"It's a very Aussie form of inspiration. 'We're all equal; why should my view be better than anyone else's? Have fun anyway you like, for tomorrow you might die.' He doesn't say the words because he doesn't need to as he lives them convincingly. I'd say he—"

"Bastard!" Thompson howled. "Son of a bitch Taggart cut me!"

Lance turned to see Thommo nursing his right hand, which dripped blood onto the floor. Opposite him stood one of his flight commanders, Taggart, a thickset Scotsman in a kilt with a formidable set of Victorian mutton-chop whiskers. He clutched his Black Watch bonnet in his right hand, peak facing forward, waving it threateningly.

"Aye, razor blades sown in the peak, an' I'll cut yer more if ye try lifting ma kilt again."

"I was just having fun, for Chrissakes," Thompson said in a fury. "Everyone wants to know what Scotsmen wear under their kilt."

"It's no respectful," Taggart growled. "Would ye lift yer wife's skirt in public?"

"You bloody moron! Where's your sense of humour?"

Clayton and Lance shouldered their way between the men. "Thommo," Clayton said. "Why don't you get that seen to by the medic. Get some stitches and stick a bandage on it."

"You can put your cap away," Lance said to Taggart. "I think we have the message you don't want people lifting your kilt."

Thommo left, clutching his hand and cursing. The slamming door thudded like a howitzer firing.

Taggart looked around the pilots, who were regarding him with wide-eyed disbelief. "Och aye, it's just a scratch I gave him. He's lucky I dinnae give him a Glasgow kiss." Taggart put his bonnet on and mimed a head-butt. "Then he could'na see for blood pouring aff his forehead."

Lance empathised with the hurt pride of a warrior, the butt of a crude joke in an alien world. On the other hand, Lance himself had laughed the first time he noticed Taggart striding to his Camel, with woollen long johns under his kilt to protect his nether regions against frostbite at high altitude. Lance smeared the drops of blood into the dark floor planks with the toe of his boot.

"As a matter of interest," he said to Taggart. "Why *do* you wear a kilt when you fly? It's damn impractical."

The Scotsman picked up his whisky glass and turned it in his hands, looking into its amber depths. "The first battle of the war wuz near Polygon Wood at Ypres. Me an' the lads, First Battalion Black Watch, we pushed back the Prussian Guard, seventeen thousand strong. Some said the Prussian Guards hadn'a lost a battle fra Waterloo onwards. Well, they lost that day at Ypres, but at the end we was down to one hundred men frae one thousand."

He looked up and his eyes were moist, but he stood tall with pride. "We swore, us what survived, we'd wear the Black Watch kilt proud inta battle til we won the war. I may've left the Watch, but I'm no breaking my oath and taking the kilt off."

He drained the glass in a swift motion. "I'm the only one of 'em lads still alive today, the last o' that bonny group o' men, all warriors. This kilt honours them." He slammed his upended empty glass on the bar and stalked out of a hushed Mess.

Lance looked at Clayton. "Explain again how Thommo builds esprit de corps in his own image? I obviously didn't grasp it the first time."

"Touché, but there's more to that little spat than meets the eye. Which reminds me of the second reason I asked you here—I wanted to ask you if you would take Taggart into your squadron. He handed in a transfer request this morning."

Lance frowned and thought through what he knew of Taggart. By reputation the pilot possessed bags of fighting spirit but was shrewd and hard and not disposed to die through needless recklessness. Lance knew why. The Scotsman always carried with him a dog-eared photo of his wife and two children. Sometimes Taggart would stare at that photo for ten minutes or longer, shaking his head and muttering about what a lucky man he was. He had showed Lance the photo once and although the woman in it was broad and homely, her smile lit up the black and white paper like a firework. On either side were the children, a son and a daughter aged between three and five. Their fair hair shone blond and their cheeky grins echoed their mother's. Lance had felt a pang of jealousy that shocked him. It was such a simple picture of happiness that it cut him to the soul.

"Before I decide, tell me why Taggart asked for a transfer."

"Yesterday the Humpers had a shindig with some Huns. At the debriefing, Thommo claimed a kill to be shared between himself and Taggart. Taggart said he never put in for a kill unless he saw the plane crash, so Thommo claimed sole credit. Of course, he needed a second pilot to confirm the kill and tried to bully Taggart into changing his story. When Taggart refused, Thommo stomped off muttering, 'Blind Scottish twat. You might have better eyesight if you didn't spend so much time wanking over the photo of your ugly wife.'

"You know the little knife that the Scots wear down their long socks with the kilt? Taggart turned white with fury and tried to stab Thommo with his knife. I pulled him away and told he'd go to jail for murder if he killed Thommo, and his children would be ashamed of him. I promised a transfer to another squadron inside the wing. Otherwise, one dark night we will trip over a dead body, and it sure as hell won't be the butler who did it."

Lance grimaced. "I'd whip a man who was that rude about a wife of mine. I'll take Taggart, but you square it away with Thommo. I'm not doing your dirty work. He and I need to fight together, and I'd rather not be on bad terms with him."

"I was under the impression that ship sailed the first time you met."

"I'm trying to be a better man."

"A better man *and* leadership? Plenty to work on, then. Are you sure this quixotic impulse to tax your brain after so many years of under-use might not over-rev the poor thing?"

~

The rain had ceased when Lance escaped to his tent around 2200 hours, and the earth smelled clean and new-born.

Another letter lay on his camp bed. He hesitated, still feeling the lash of the last one, but then he breathed in its gentle lavender fragrance. Definitely not from Pa.

When he opened it, the paper was stiff and high quality, and the heading proclaimed it the stationary of Lady Megan Exenrude.

Darling! Good news! Lance smiled. Megan was fond of exclamations. *I have become a patron of Queen Alexandra's Imperial Military Nursing Service. It is my bit for the war effort. After all, if the Maharajah of Somewhere or other can fund a squadron of the RFC (who I gather paint Tigers on their planes as an expression of thanks!) the least I can do is fund a nursing effort. They are setting up a hospital in St. Omer and as one of the largest patrons I wangled an invitation to do the ribbon cutting when they open the hospital on 20th June. So, make sure you get a night's leave for then! I will contact you closer to the day, but I will be staying at the Hotel du Commerce.*

Love, Megan.

PS do not tell Arthur! He will not give you leave if you do!! He is such a virtuous prig!!!

For a second Lance thought of his ex-fiancée, Heidi. Bad idea. He slammed shut the door on that memory. When war had broken out, Lance lost all trace of her. Revenge became the primary emotion in his life, not love, but even so the only way Lance could cope was to accept that Heidi was lost to him. She'd existed in a past life. Best keep it that way.

St. Omer was only twenty miles away and the pilots often visited when bad weather washed out flying. It was also the RFC supply depot for the region, so there was always an excuse of getting necessary spare parts for the SE5. It was faster to drive to the depot and pick up parts than wait for the supply trucks to deliver them.

Lance's heart picked up a beat as he thought about their last meeting, in Paris after the ceremonial award of his Croix de Guerre. She had been like a pagan goddess that night, wild and uninhibited, naked except for her long tresses black as midnight, and her silver bracelets that jangled with the urgency of their loving.

Yes, he would find a way to St. Omer—by hook or by crook. Jangling the bracelets with Megan was the only antidote he had found to the soul-sucking strain of the war and his flame-filled nightmares. And now he must worry about Pa too. He prayed that Megan's magic still worked....

6
At The Hour of Death

Lieutenant Neil Middleton floated four thousand feet above the battle-scarred hellscape of Ypres, His plane, an FE2b two-seater, featured an antiquated pusher design where the pilot sat in front of the engine, and the observer sat in front of the pilot, right in the nose, giving the latter an unparalleled view from his shallow cockpit. Nothing except a wood and fabric framework, only knee high, sat between Neil and the carnage thousands of feet below. Neil's pilot, Captain Warner, was inclined to unexpected manoeuvres and several times had almost tipped Neil overboard. If that happened, Neil's life would hang on the three-foot safety cord with one end snapped onto his waist belt and the other onto a ring screwed into the wooden frame. Although no-one had ever satisfactorily explained to Neil how to clamber back into the cockpit in the face of a seventy-mph gale while hanging on the end of a cord. Assuming the harness didn't break...

Neil pushed such cheerful thoughts to the back of his mind as he tapped out his Morse code correction to the British heavy artillery battery. Their target for today was a German pillbox near St. Julien. It squatted below him, gray and ominous in the sea of brown mud that surrounded it. The last shell had landed close to the target. Soon they would blow the blasted pillbox to hell. His squadron had lost so many planes and men while artillery-spotting on this target, they had begun to think it was cursed. But two more corrections at most, and Neil would be the toast of the infantry below and his own squadron.

While he waited for the guns to make the corrections before they fired again, he savoured the glow of incipient success. Rose would be proud of him. He fingered the un-familiar engagement ring on his finger, still unable to believe his good fortune. He had proposed on his last leave, more in hope than expectation, and been startled into silent, unbreath-ing awe when she accepted. Rose was the catch of his Surrey village, with flowing russet hair, a small nose, a laughing mouth, generous curves and eyes bluer than the summer sky.

He sighed and turned once again to peer through his bino-culars at the scabrous concrete pillbox far below, ready to spot the fall of the next artillery shell. Three months to his next leave, when they would marry on his twenty-third birthday. Best to focus on the job until then. But it wasn't easy...

~

Four thousand feet below, Major Stan Fitch, commander of the First Battalion of the King's Own Regiment, inched his trench periscope above the sandbags, keeping it slow so as not to attract the eye of an enemy sniper. He twisted a knob until the shell-blasted morass south-east of St. Julien sharpened into focus. Even through the powerful magnification he couldn't see any sign of the pillbox. Only four shattered tree stumps poked above the bare mud, crooked skeleton fingers reaching towards the washed blue heavens.

"Don't worry, Major. This time we'll nail the bastard," Captain Dodds said with the confidence of a seasoned artillery observation officer.

Stan grunted, unimpressed. "Best that you do. Soon my battalion will go over the top at that pillbox. My boys will die if you don't pulverise it. Where is the bloody pillbox?"

"You won't see it sir, not from ground level," Dodds said. "The Huns are damn good at concealment and—"

A godlike thud interrupted him. Stan's ribcage reverberated, even though the massive 9.2-inch siege howitzer had fired from two miles behind them. The reinforced concrete pillboxes were impervious to regular artillery, so Stan had called in the heaviest guns in the British armoury. Even still, it required a direct hit to destroy one.

He waited; eyes glued to the periscope. Howitzers fired their three hundred-pound shells with a high arc and a long hang time.

There!

Through the magnified scope, earth fountained a hundred feet high in eerie silence. Debris rained down, seemingly in slow motion, raising splashes in the mud. Seconds later, the sound waves arrived with a thunderclap that pummelled Stan's ears.

The massive shell-burst impressed Stan, but he couldn't tell whether it had landed close to the enemy pillbox. No matter—the spotting aircraft, hovering four thousand feet over the target, would send corrections to Dodds' Morse operator. But the process took time. *Not that it matters. That pillbox isn't going anywhere—until we blow it to hell.*

He turned to Dodds, who was staring upwards into the sky.

"Bugger, blast, and hell!" Dodds said.

~

Neil Middleton scowled from his perch in the sky. Damn. His last correction had dropped the shell two hundred yards west of the pillbox. Close, but no cigar.

A thump on his shoulder made him turn back to his pilot, Captain Walters, who pumped his fist up and down. "Hurry!"

Neil turned back. "Not helpful," he muttered. As if Neil needed reminding that Richthofen's Circus prowled these skies like ravenous wolves. The FE2b was a sheep but at least they had an escort, a Sopwith Camel fighter—perhaps the most potent dogfighter in the skies today—that hovered protectively above them.

Neil did a quick computation. The code for artillery spotting was simple but effective. The alphabet letter indicated yardage in hundreds, so two hundred was "B." The numeral worked off a clock face with the target at the centre, so twelve o'clock was due north of the target and six o'clock due south. So "B9" would inform the gunners the shell landed two hundred yards west of the target. Of course, the yardage was all the observer's guesstimate and therein lay the skill. Neil had a gift for it, he was one of the best. He'd get it right this time and they could go home. He bent over his key.

"What the dickens ..." Neil swore as his pilot bashed him from behind, jolting his fingers from his Morse keys. He turned to abuse his pilot, but then followed the latter's pointing arm.

"Oh, Jesus!"

Dots diving in a V formation from nine thousand feet. With the arrowhead pointed at his heart.

Huns! Nine of 'em! Neil's heart thumped against his ribcage like a panicked animal trying to escape. They were doomed, especially if those planes were Albatross—the Germans' best fighter. He dropped the Morse key and grabbed the spade handle of the Lewis machine gun. His lips moved of their own volition.

"Hail Mary, full of grace. Our Lord is with thee. Blessed art thou among women, and blessed is the fruit of thy womb, Jesus."

Walters banged him on the arm again and gesticulated urgently downwards.

"Hell and damnation!" Neil swore.

He had forgotten about the wire cable dangling below the plane that transmitted the Morse signal. Until Neil retrieved all 150 feet, the pilot could not manoeuvre or the wire might foul the propeller. Neil grabbed the reel and wound in a frenzy. His lungs heaved and his muscles burned but he kept his arm pumping. Their chances were slim, but slim beat none. Which were their odds until he wound in that damned cable.

The single Sopwith Camel, bravely flung himself in front of the avalanche of Huns. God bless him! Tracers sparkled both ways. The Camel exploded in a fireball and the Albatross charge swept onwards.

Neil dropped the reel, despite the fifty feet of wire left, and grabbed his machine gun. Clumsy in his terror, he missed his first grab at the cocking handle. Machine guns crackled, and Neil winced as tracers flashed just past his shoulder, the pungent phosphorous smell searing his nostrils. The FE2b lurched as he fired, and almost threw him over-board. His tracers soared wide into the empty sky.

An Albatross roared past, so close the black crosses loomed huge against the glistening red wings. Another Hun came at them. Neil fired, shoulders shaking as the gun hammered and spent cases flew. Then the FE2b skidded and pitchforked him face-first against the machine gun. His nose and lips smacked into the hot metal and the tang of blood flooded his mouth.

Clinging to the Lewis gun handles, Neil shot a look backwards at his pilot. Captain Walters was slumped back in his cockpit, blood dribbling from his slack mouth, his desperate eyes protruding from a pale face. A bullet hole, neat as you like, had punched through his flying coat at lung height. But one hand still clutched the joystick.

"Holy Mary," Neil croaked, "mother of God ..."

Guns hammered again and Captain Walters jerked sideways. The nose of the plane dropped. Wind shrieked through the wires as the dive steepened.

Neil closed his eyes, strangely unafraid but flooded with regrets for what might have been. Him and Rose—the dreams had been so beautiful, but now they were less than smoke in the wind. "Pray for us sinners, now and at the hour of death..."

~

Leutnant Hans von Schmettow howled in triumph as the FE2b pilot crumpled under his bullets. The British aircraft spiralled downwards, heading deeper behind German lines. He pulled back on the stick, and his red-and-white Albatross soared upwards.

He followed the red Albatross of Manfred Richthofen, who led the nine planes of *Jasta* 11 back up towards the safer heights at 3,000 metres, from where they could plunge like a falcon on their victims. Speed was the god of a fighter pilot, and altitude plus gravity granted speed. Not that the puissant Albatross needed much help. The power of Hans's 170hp Mercedes Benz engine pulled the Albatross upwards on angel's wings, beautiful in form and function. His streamlined red fuselage curved with a graceful nose like a cigar cylinder, and the white wings swept back in harmony with the rounded rudder and tail plane.

The exposed mechanism of the engine hypnotised Hans as they climbed. The valves, springs, and rockers hammered in a frenzy at full rpm, dripping hot oil and grease that the slipstream smeared all over his face. But it was a tiny price to pay for flying one of the deadliest fighting machines in the sky. The sinister black cylinders of the twin Spandau machine guns crouched at either side of the engine, ready to dole out steel-jacketed death at eight rounds a second. If the British were stupid enough to send up yet more sacrificial lambs, Manfred Richthofen's *Jasta* 11 would be delighted to feast upon them.

~

"Hun bastards!" Stan lowered his binoculars as the doomed British plane spun earthwards, flicking over and over like an autumn leaf, trailing a banner of thick grey smoke.

Dismay washed over him. That was the second spotter aircraft shot down today and together they'd only directed four artillery shots. Every time they had to start afresh. That bloody pillbox would never get nailed until the Royal Flying Corps could protect their spotter aircraft better.

Stan gestured at the phone. "Order another spotter plane."

Dodds shook his head. "I can't. It's murder up there—we've lost four spotter planes and three escorts in two days on this pillbox. Eleven men."

Stan glared at Captain Dodds, keeping his face hard. "Listen, Captain, if your guns don't knock out that pillbox before the main assault, thousands of infantrymen will die and the whole attack will stall. It's a harsh world, but the cost of a few more pilots versus thousands of troops is simple mathematics. Suggest a larger escort but order the spotting plane. Now!"

Dodds stared back with a stubborn frown. "I won't have more deaths on my conscience."

Stan wheeled on Dodds' Morse operator. "Did the plane get off another correction?"

The operator grimaced and shook his head. "Nothing that makes sense, sir."

Stan stared into the sky where a dogfight now raged above him. But whoever had waded into the Huns had done so too late for the FE2b, which meant the pillbox still ruled all powerful. He rubbed his forehead, feeling the onset of a raging headache.

Artillery was a mighty powerful thing, no doubt, but where you stood—whether you were doing the killing or the dying—determined your reality. For those who aimed and fired the guns, they ruled as precise tools of destruction, a science that hurled the maximum tonnage of high explosives onto a target in the minimum possible time, constrained only by the limits of human muscle and mechanical realities.

For those on the guns' receiving end, its thunder fell like Thor's hammer, awesome and relentless.

But for those troops who had to fix their bayonets and charge the artillery's "destroyed targets," such monster barrages too often proved merely expensive landscape rearrangement. As the troops charged forward, the battered but intact concrete pillboxes would loom, phoenix-like, from the sulphurous grey smoke and mow down the attackers with interlocking fields of machine gun fire.

Put Stan Fitch in the sceptic's camp, for when the assault came, he would lead the First Battalion of the King's Own Regiment over the top. At the thought, a strong fist gripped his stomach and squeezed.

He pulled a folded reconnaissance photograph, 8x12 inches, out of his blouse pocket, and smoothed it on an ammunition crate. "Look at this," he said to Dodds. He jabbed a dirty finger on two roughly parallel lines that zig-zagged across the page like scars from a mad razor slasher. "Those are the Germans' first two lines of trenches. On the day of the attack, your guns preliminary bombardment is due to blow those apart. But when that bombardment starts, we know from experience that the Huns will slip away to the third line of trenches, where less artillery can reach them. They will make their stand there." Stan pointed at a third scar, darker and thicker than the others, the line broken by an ominous round black blob "And here is the pillbox we are trying to destroy. You can't see it on the photo, but there will be roll upon roll of razor-sharp barbed wire to funnel my battalion's thousand men into a concentrated kill zone in front of the pillbox. That fortress, impregnable to infantrymen, will be bristling with nests of machine guns—each gun firing five hundred rounds a minute. That pillbox will pin down my men, and the Hun artillery counter-barrage will massacre them in the open. The attack will founder right there. Unless we destroy that pillbox before the attack starts."

Stan picked up a trench phone and held it out to Dodds. "So make that phone call now, ordering another spotter plane, or I'll have you cashiered and find someone else who will do it."

Dodds' shoulders slumped and he took the handset. Stan turned away and walked towards his command post. He heard Dodds mutter "ruthless bastard," but Stan didn't turn back. He knew secrets that Dodds did not.

The capture of Messines Ridge a few weeks ago had drawn the Germans' attention into Flanders and away from the mutiny-riddled French. Now another crisis had erupted. Germany's U-boat campaign was sinking more Allied merchant vessels every week, tightening like a tourniquet on the lifeblood of men and raw materials flooding into Britain by sea from her Empire and the rest of the world. Without these supplies, the island nation's capacity to fight was withering.

So General Gough's Fifth Army would attack through Passchendaele Ridge and cut the railway supplying the German garrisons from Ypres to the Belgian coast. The Fourth Army would then launch an assault on the coast to destroy the Germans' main submarine bases at Ostend and Zeebrugge. Then the British Empire's maritime lifeblood would resume its flow.

The date of the attack was still secret, but the briefing by Stan's commanding officer had been emphatic. For Gough's attack to succeed, Stan's battalion had to take that pillbox on the first day and push on towards Passchendaele, an impossible task if the howitzers didn't pulverise the pillbox.

To do that, the guns needed an artillery spotter plane and the spotter plane needed fighter escorts. Otherwise, the guns would be firing blind and hoping for the best. Three years of war and millions of dead infantrymen provided overwhelming evidence that Hope was a lousy artillery aimer. So sitting ducks or not, the RFC crews must fly.

But as Major Stan Fitch strode away after ordering up fresh cannon fodder, he prayed that his son Lance, a captain in the Royal Flying Corps and based at Bailleul Airfield nearby, would not be one of them.

7
Christians To the Lions

Five minutes earlier,
same day - 20 June 1917.
Ypres Sector.

Lance lined his Aldis sights on the Hun thirty yards ahead. An incongruous yellow scarf fluttered from the Hun pilot's neck. *Yellow? Must be from a girlfriend. Too bad. You should have looked behind you.*

When the crosshairs bisected the yellow scarf, Lance thumbed the gun paddles on the joystick. The machine guns hammered. Recoil shuddered the SE5, and tracers arced into the Hun's back. The Albatross jerked and spun into the dirty grey cloud below. For a second, Lance imagined a German girlfriend now bereft, but the thought blew away in the slipstream. Doling out death and destruction to the enemy tasted as good as ever. "For they shall reap the whirlwind," he vowed in tribute to those he revenged.

Lance had stalked this solo Albatross, a rare sight as the Huns flew in packs these days, as he led an evening patrol between Ypres and Armentieres. He took the kill as a good omen on his first patrol as flight leader since Ball's death.

The incomparable Ball had been only one of the casualties on that ill-fated fight. His squadron had fragmented in the fractured weather, and Manfred Richthofen's Circus, hunting as a pack, had used the heavy cloud cover to pick off pilots who flew alone. Only five of eleven SE5s returned, and one of those five had been Lance. That was the day Lance reluctantly accepted command of Ball's squadron.

Lance looked behind him as he climbed back towards fourteen thousand feet. The square snouts of five khaki coloured SE5 fighters followed him in a V-shape. Arthur Rhys-Davids flew closest on his left. The nineteen-year-old scholar from Eton showed rare promise as an air fighter, albeit a reckless one. He copied Albert Ball's gung-ho style, chock full of bravery but bereft of common sense.

Behind Rhys-Davids on the left, flew the flame-haired Stokes and the professorial Kerrigan. Both had been flying since 1916 but were new to the squadron and SE5s. On Lance's right, the closest SE5 swayed from side to side in the formation. That would be Newby. Lance sighed. The boy had so much to learn. Weston's plane floated behind Newby, the giant farmer's head and shoulders sticking incongruously high out of the cockpit. But Weston could fly, and he could fight, and he was protecting Newby's back.

Traditionally in the RFC, the most junior pilots flew at the back of the standard V formation so they would not crash into anyone. Lance disliked that logic. The "Tail End Charlie" was the most vulnerable position in a formation and giving the role to a novice weighted the odds of his survival even further against him. Lance had tucked Newby in the middle, surrounded by experienced hands. But they all gave Newby a wide berth as his SE5 strayed.

Lance searched the full arc of the sky, using his thumb to block the glare of the sun, now sinking low. Richthofen's favourite tactic was a surprise attack out of the sun. Best to be wary.

If hunting the Circus and its leader was the wing's official mission, Lance also had a personal scab to pick with Richthofen and his blood-red Albatross. The German had shot down Lanoe Hawker, Arthur's predecessor as wing commander, while Lance raged helpless on the ground below. It had been a fair fight and Lance would not have held it against Richthofen had he not boasted to the German press that he had awarded himself a silver cup and mounted Hawker's machine gun above his door like a stag's head. Lance ground his teeth at the thought.

And in every encounter with Richthofen's Circus, no matter how hectic, a corner of Lance's mind searched for an Albatross with a red fuselage and white wings. Lance carried grudges against Huns like an ox towed a heavy cart, impossible to imagine one without the other, but the bulk of the load served as his penance for the dead. However, Lance granted himself one self-indulgent vendetta. Herr White Wing had strafed Lance on the ground after Lance had crash-landed with a dud engine in no-man's land. Such strafing was universally condemned as a coward's act. It breached the unwritten code that pilots duelled to the death in the air but did not murder foes who reached the earth safely.

Every pilot carried a forlorn hope he might still cheat death if he were shot down. And if you were skilled enough, or beloved enough by the gods, to dodge the cuts of the Grim Reaper's triple-bladed scythe of bullets, flames, and gravity to reach terra firma alive, then damn it, you bloody well deserved to live whether you spoke German, English, or gibberish. In this lousy war where a thousand rules told how to kill, a man needed one rule that preserved his humanity. Lance would never break this pilot's code and had never seen it broken.

Except once, by the murderous Herr White Wings. A special place in Hell waited for that man and Lance yearned to make the introduction.

Movement on the edge of his vision caught his eye, and he peered eastwards towards Menin. A cluster of dots diving earthwards over St. Julien. Dogfight! Lance triggered a one-second burst to catch his flight's attention and pointed a gloved hand at the specks. He turned towards them, careful to move in a wide arc so Newby would not fly into anyone.

Lance made sense of the dots as the distance closed.

Nine Albatross diving to attack an FE2b and a Camel around 4,000 feet. At that low altitude, it could only be a gunnery spotter plane and its escort. Lance cursed and checked his throttle was wide open, muttering encouragement to the poor bastards below.

Lance searched above and behind to ensure that no-one would ambush his flight as they bounced the Huns below. All clear. He signalled to his flight by chopping his hand downwards twice, and half-rolled into an arcing dive, making sure the sun was behind them. As always, the rising snarl of the engine and the shrill whistling of the wind through the wires were the urgent fanfare of bugles summoning him into the headlong charge. Blood pounded in his ears and sang through his veins. His thumb stroked the trigger paddles as the Huns grew larger, but he was still far out of range.

Tracers lanced out below from the cavalcade of German planes. A vivid flash as the Camel exploded and the Albatross swept onwards to the FE2b. Seconds later the big two-seater rolled tiredly into a spin, trailing thick gray smoke. *Christ! These Huns were good.* Five seconds, two kills. The lead Albatross soared into a climb, followed by his comrades, apparently still unaware of the SE5s hurtling towards them.

Lance's plane jittered and jolted as it barrelled downwards at 150 mph. That made the Aldis telescopic sight useless. Lance placed his Vickers gun ring and bead sight on the lead Albatross's red nose. Red? Lance flicked a glance over the rest of the plane. All red. *Richthofen.* Lance's guts tightened and he ran his tongue over his dry lips.

Wait. Wait. At two hundred feet from the Albatross, he eased back on the control column to lead the target. At the last second the Albatross pilot seemed to sense his danger.

Instantly, it banked hard, sliding away under Lance's nose. Impossible for Lance to follow. Lance kicked the right rudder bar to find another target before he flashed past.

A red and green Albatross filled his sight. He corrected the skid and mashed his thumb onto the triggers. Both machine guns pounded. His tracers sawed off the tail plane which whirled away, sending the Albatross into wild gyrations.

Lance howled in triumph and pulled back into a soaring climb to keep his height advantage. Centrifugal force drained blood from his head, blurring his vision. He sucked in his gut, as tight to his backbone as he could. Ball had taught him that trick to help prevent a blackout. Before his speed bled away, Lance banked hard to clear his tail of any potential attackers. When he checked behind, only the faithful Weston followed him. *Where the hell are the others?*

He searched below. The Hun planes had scattered like a startled shoal of sardines. His own victim was plummeting earthwards, and another Albatross on fire raged like a meteor across the sky.

But the rest of the Albatross had embroiled the rest of his flight in a dogfight.

Lance cursed. He'd told them before the patrol to use the SE5's strengths—speed and dive robustness—to dive, shoot, and zoom rather than get dragged into a messy brawl. Only Weston had obeyed. The problem was not the dogfight itself—six SE5s against seven Albatross were not bad odds—but dogfights attracted other planes like flies to manure. With the Germans flying in larger formations than the British, things could turn nasty in a heartbeat. Dirty grey thunderclouds cluttered the sky, and large formations of enemy planes could materialise like magic in such conditions.

Lance turned to see five dots climbing towards the dogfight from the east. From that direction, they would be Huns. Lance eased behind a large cloud and worked his way to intercept the newcomers, so he and Weston could bounce them from above as they joined the dogfight.

Lance hugged the cloud contours, his prop wash shredding the grey cumulus into banners. When he emerged from behind the cloud, he was in a perfect position to ambush what he could now see were five Pfalz.

Lance looked back at the dogfight and stared in disbelief. From nowhere, six more Albatross had already waded into the mael-strom. Lance grabbed the Very gun and fired a green flare—the signal to disengage. It gave away his ambush on the Pfalz, but his men needed to escape while they could.

As the green flare trailed across the sky, it led Lance's eye to a greasy finger of smoke pointing towards a flaming comet with the square wingtips of an SE5. *One of mine.* The executioner, an Albatross, was climbing away from the top of the column of dark smoke.

Rage surged inside Lance. He signalled for Weston to follow and threw his plane into a howling dive towards the Hun. As he did so, he saw elsewhere in the dogfight, two Albatross swooping on a lone SE5.

Lance wavered. He could rescue the lone SE5 or avenge the dead one. But he could not do both. The rage and need for revenge that seared through Lance was a physical yearning so deep it constricted his throat. He drew deep shuddering breaths to get oxygen into his lungs. *Breathe, for God's sake!* He forced the rage away, pushed it deep, and locked it away somewhere. It hurt, God it hurt, but at last sanity prevailed.

He swore and wrenched his plane away from the climbing Albatross to rescue the lone SE5. His plane dived faster than any Albatross, and Lance gained on the two German ambushers. But he still wouldn't be in time to prevent the Huns' first fusillade. He fired at extreme long range, hoping to distract them, but the tracers died well short.

Now he was close enough to see that the lone SE5 was

Newby's plane. No-one else in his flight flew with the same jerkiness. *Look behind, you silly sod!* It was as if Newby heard him. The flash of a pink face tilted upwards towards the diving Huns on his right quarter. *Good man. Now do as I told you and break towards the attack. You'll be clear and I'll nail at least one Hun before we run for home.*

Newby should bank to his right. Lance positioned himself to intercept the Huns as they tried to follow. He watched their rudders, waiting for the first swing. Then he would strike. The Hun was as good as dead.

The German's guns flickered, and Newby banked—*The wrong bloody way!*

And dived. Gifting the chasing Albatross an easy non-deflection shot from directly behind

Bloody idiot! I told him many times. Never dive away from an attack from above. Bullets are faster than planes.

Aided by their extra speed from their dive, the Huns closed on Newby. Lines of white tracer bullets streaked from the two Huns. Newby swerved out of one glowing spear of tracers and directly into the other Hun's line of fire. Despairingly, Lance fired again. Too far out to be accurate. But his tracers snaked past the left-hand Hun, who broke away with a startled swerve.

Lance turned his attention to the remaining Albatross, whose blood-red fuselage glistened between angel-white wings. Recognition jolted him. This was the murdering savage who had strafed Lance on the ground the day Lanoe Hawker died. A savage glee surged through Lance. Fickle Lady Luck was smiling on him today—which didn't happen too often, so best take advantage. This time he would nail the bastard.

The Hun had tunnel focus on his victim. He would never see the avenging SE5 until Lance closed to a hundred feet and flensed the Hun's ribcage with lead. Lance's trigger finger itched. Eight hundred yards to go.

While Lance narrowed the gap, the Albatross fired at

Newby again. Twin tracer lines streaked into the SE5, which jerked. A flap of torn fabric fluttered from the rudder. This Hun could shoot. A novice like Newby didn't stand a chance.

Lance was still too far away for accurate shooting. If he fired now, he would alert White Wings to his presence and the bugger would escape. If Lance waited until he was a hundred feet behind, the German was as good as roasting in Hell.

But by then, Newby would also be dead.

Lance growled in frustration. Of all the Huns in French skies, this was the pilot he most hungered to kill. Lady Luck had tossed him the bone he craved. Then as his jaws closed on the prize, she unveiled her exquisitely vicious price.

Lance must choose—both Newby and the Hun would die, or neither. A coldness settled in his guts. He would kill White Wings. If that meant Newby died first, so be it. The kid had ignored his training and would have to take his chances.

Lance threw a quick look behind. Weston was still glued to his tail—*Good man!* Behind Weston, a pack of pursuing Albatross. They wouldn't catch the SE5s in a dive. He ignored them.

Lance barrelled towards his prey, his gloved thumb poised over the twin trigger paddles on his control stick. *Wait for it.* Four hundred yards...

White Wings fired again. A thin banner of black smoke unfurled behind Newby's SE5.

Lance's thumb quivered in frustration. "Wait," he cajoled himself. Three hundred yards. Still too far for accurate shooting. *If Newby is still alive when I reach one hundred yards, I'll fire. If the Hun kills Newby before then, I'll nail the bastard from thirty yards.*

Perhaps Lance's plane jolted in a pocket of air and jogged his thumb. His Vickers gun hammered, surprising him. Tracers streaked past the Albatross. Alerted, the Hun reefed into a tight climbing turn.

Lance's right arm twitched on the joystick to follow but he

jerked it back. A pack of Huns had to be on his tail. If he chased White Wings, then he, Newby, and Weston would likely all die. If Lance continued their dive away, the superior speed of the SE5 would leave the Huns behind.

Lance's guts twisted as his eyes followed the soaring white wings of the Hun. "Next time," he vowed.

He overtook the still diving Newby and with his left hand he stabbed towards the Allied lines. Newby nodded, and the three of them dived for home. Lance looked behind and sure enough, a chasing line of Huns stretched after them. *No shame in running. Even a leopard runs from a troop of baboons.*

As he watched, the Huns gave up and turned back. Lance led Newby and Weston in a dive through a large cumulous cloud, just to throw off any stubborn Huns. He shivered in the clammy wetness. The sweat that had pooled in his crotch and armpits during the dogfight was cooling.

Underneath the cloud he found another SE5, who tagged onto their group. Lance recognised Rhys-Davids, who waved and waggled two fingers. *Two kills! How the hell did he manage two in that brawl? The boy has talent.*

Lance grew warmer as they bled off height. The adrenalin leached from his bloodstream, leaving the familiar mixture of euphoria and exhaustion.

As they flew homewards, the sun dropped and fiery fingers of flame began to streak the western horizon. Above it all, the beautiful blue-grey heavens of another dying day.

~

When they reached the airfield, Lance lingered above as the other planes landed. He wanted to watch as the sun slipped below the far-away boundaries of the rolling earth, the last curtain call of Nature's greatest daily show.

Earthbound men never saw this sight. Whatever foul

things happened on this earth, at least you could rely on sunsets. Lance had stopped praying to God after seeing the carnage of the artillery barrage on his company and his dead brother. Nothing like seeing family blasted into raw red meat, speckled with yellow guts and grey brains, to suck the faith from your soul. But even after that hideous experience, it was hard to behold a sunset like this and not ascribe its aching beauty to some divine hand.

When the last crescent of gold shimmered below the horizon, Lance throttled back, floated his plane over the trees, and flared into a perfect three-point landing. He switched off the engine and climbed out stiffly, resting on Digby's steady hand. Lance tugged off his leather helmet and gloves and gave them to his fitter. He stood still for a while, letting the solid earth absorb the slight trembling of his knees.

"I saw one of ours go down," Lance said. "Do we know yet who it was?"

"Lieutenants Kerrigan and Stokes are missing, sir." Digby shouted the news, aware of a pilot's post-flight deafness after the hours of thundering engine and rapid altitude changes.

"Two of them? Damn." Depression settled on him, dank and gloomy as the slate-grey drift of a winter's squall. He'd lost a third of his pilots on his first patrol as commander—a ratio as bad as his predecessors'. And Lance had been scathing of those predecessors' tactics.

"You alright, sir?"

Lance opened his eyes to see his fitter's weathered and concerned face. He gave a bloodthirsty grin to maintain appearances. "Right as rain. Chalk two more Huns to the tally, Digby."

"That's the ticket, sir! How many kills do you have now?"

Lance frowned. Somewhere along the road he'd lost count. "No idea. Two more is the important thing. Check the wire to the right aileron, would you? It feels slack."

Lance stamped his feet on terra firma, trying to get the circulation going after the cold. But questions worried at him like jackals fighting over marrow bones. What had he done wrong? He could not have been clearer in his pre-flight briefing. *Do not get dragged into a dogfight. Follow me and dive, shoot, zoom.* Yet most of his pilots did exactly what he had warned them against.

Now two, almost three, were dead. How had he failed to get the message across? He had explained the logic behind the tactics, and they had all nodded. Were they stupid? Unlikely. Kerrigan was a bloody professor, for God's sake.

Perhaps all orders and logic evaporated in the heat and stress of battle? That would explain Newby but not the experienced Stokes and Kerrigan. Lance scratched his head.

Then the answer hit him. They had both been Sopwith Pup pilots before joining 100 Wing. When the Albatross and Pfalz appeared over the front in early 1917, they outclassed the older Pup. Faced with enemies better armed and faster, a Pup pilot's best hope was to turn and keep turning until the Huns got giddy.

In battle, Kerrigan and Stokes's ingrained habits had swamped Lance's advice, and they reverted to what they knew. Lance had spent all his spare time training Newby, figuring that the experienced men would be fine. He should have taken up the two pilots and trained them over and over in dive-shoot-zoom until he embedded the new habit in them. Words were not enough. Actions, repeated ad nauseam until their muscle memory became second nature, were the only way to teach war flying.

He had failed Stokes and Kerrigan. Lance had learned a lesson, and when Richthofen was the teacher, you paid the price in blood. More deaths because of Lance's mistakes. You'd think the guilt would be easier to take when you got so much practice.

"Lance! Did you hear me?"

Lance turned to see Arthur Rhys-Davids, his angelic face and ruffled hair making him look younger than his nineteen years. "What?" Lance gestured towards his still-ringing ears.

The slender Etonian leaned towards Lance and spoke louder: "The flamer was Stokes. I saw a red Albatross nail him."

Lance grimaced. The burly Stokes was—had been—a good pilot with ten kills or so and couple of medals. So keen and now so dead, just another bloody statistic. Lance shrugged and started for the debriefing hut.

Rhys-Davids fell in step with him, smiling, and declaimed,

The Curfew tolls the knell of parting day,
The lowing herd wind slowly o'er the lea,
The ploughman homeward plods his weary way,
And leaves the world to darkness and to me.

Lance looked at the beaming face of this most English of youths and marvelled at his innocent joy amidst the thunder of this war. Apparently forgotten was the savage scrap with the Huns and his two kills. Never mind the flaming death of a squadron mate, Rhys-Davids was beaming as though he had discovered gravity. "Gray's Elegy, written in 1750 and still apposite. Marvellous!"

Lance didn't know what apposite meant but he got the gist. He felt a hundred years old. It seemed that at nineteen, even in the middle of the bloodiest war in history, you could still believe. Whatever life hurled at you, your brain could dream of happy endings. He draped a protective arm around the youngster as the magic of the sun's final show melted over them.

Then Lance stopped short as he saw Newby's plane. The SE5 sagged, one wing drooping low from sliced bracing wires, fuselage and wings trailing strips of torn fabric. The weight of command dropped on Lance's shoulders like a lead cloak, and the balm of the sunset vanished. He withdrew his arm from

Rhys-Davids's shoulders and faced him.

"You disobeyed my instructions to stick with me and dive and zoom. Why?" Lance asked.

Rhys-Davids looked shamefaced. "I'm sorry, Lance, it's just that when we dive on Huns, I feel like the devil incarnate bursting with the dazzling thrill of playing the best game God ever created, mad after Huns and just forgetting everything else. I will try to not let it happen again."

Lance grabbed him by the shoulders and shook him hard, staring into his eyes. "Never again, y'hear! It won't be the best game God created when the Huns fill you full of lead."

Rhys-Davids nodded. Lance waved him away, towards the debrief with Clayton. Rhys-Davids looked hurt but trudged away, peeling out of the last of his flying gear.

Lance watched Newby. The youngster bobbed in animated discussion with his fitter, who wore the lugubrious expression of someone who would spend the night repairing hundreds of bullet holes. Newby was poking the holes in fascination, trying to work out how there could be so many without the bullets hitting anything essential.

Back in Africa, Ma had planted a hedge of Christ's thorns around her flowerbeds to keep antelope away from the tender shoots. If you fell into the bushes, the tips of the thorn broke off inside your flesh. There, they festered and went septic unless you dug the tips out and bathed the wounds in antiseptic. Newby's smiling face reminded Lance of his choice a scant thirty minutes ago, and the thorns of guilt stabbed deep. Lance had been Newby's commander and yet he had been willing to sacrifice the boy to kill Herr White Wings. Even though chance or some subconscious thought had sabotaged Lance's decision not to open fire from so far away, he could not deny that he had first made the conscious verdict that Newby was expendable. In the cool aftermath, Lance despised himself for his decision made in the heat of battle. This wound would fester, and deservedly so. What sort of monster had he become?

Newby turned and saw Lance. His open youthful face lit up. "Sir! You saved my bacon, no mistake. It was like the cavalry riding to the rescue!"

"You're a bloody idiot," Lance said.

"Sir?" Newby's eyes grew wide. His fitter coughed and beat a hasty retreat.

Lance stabbed a forefinger into Newby's sternum, forcefully enough to make Newby take a pace backwards. "I missed killing the bastard who shot down Stokes in order to save your sorry little arse. You nearly got yourself killed because you forgot everything I told you about *never* breaking away from an attack. Even worse, when you broke the wrong way you stopped me from nailing at least one of the Huns attacking you. So, because you are incapable of remembering your training, three Huns are still alive and your plane is almost a write-off. In short, you are a hindrance to His Majesty's Royal Flying Corps. Which means you are a help to the Kaiser. Understand?"

Newby squirmed. "I'm doing my best, sir."

"The lament of a moron. If that is your best, we are all better off without it. What did I tell you, repeatedly, about diving away from an attack?"

Newby frowned as he tried to remember. "Er... to never do it, sir?"

"Why not?"

"Because a bullet is faster than a plane, sir."

"You do have a brain. How come you didn't do what I told you to do?"

"Um, 'cos I guess I forgot in the excitement, sir."

Lance shook his head in despair and stared at his pilot for half a minute, wondering how to solve the problem. Newby fidgeted and chewed at his lips under the gaze. Eventually Lance snapped his fingers. "Someone told me you are a sprinter?"

Newby beamed. "English schoolboys' hundred-yard dash champion last year, sir."

"Mmm. How do they start the race?"

"Starter's gun, sir. Bang, and off you go."

Lance smiled, which seemed to worry Newby, who shifted from foot to foot. Lance slid his hand down to his flying boot and pulled out his Webley revolver—standard officer issue. Some pilots carried the gun to shoot themselves if their plane caught fire in the air. Lance carried his to shoot Germans if he crash-landed on their side of the lines.

Lance raised the revolver and aimed it at Newby's left foot. "What would you do if I told you I am going to fire a bullet into the ground under your foot?"

"Er, move my foot, sir?"

"Clever lad. I will fire on the count of three. One, two, three..."

Newby was pale faced, but he stood his ground and hastily raised his foot. Lance fired into the ground where the foot had been, and the report echoed around the airfield. Faces turned towards their peculiar tableau. Lance's revolver smoked while Newby balanced on one leg, shaking and making little flapping motions. The onlookers remained frozen.

"Good, you can follow simple instructions," Lance said. "No! Keep that foot up!"

Lance turned his pistol to aim at the foot still on the earth. Newby's arms flapped with agitation. "Now tell me—the next time the Huns attack you, which way will you break?"

"Towards the attacker, sir!"

"Sure? I could just shoot your foot now. Nice little wound that would send you back to Blighty? Save the RFC an aircraft and save me writing a death letter to Mumsy?"

"No, sir! I mean, yes, sir. I am sure I will turn into the attack, sir!"

"Look at me," Lance ordered, still aiming the revolver at Newby's right foot, the one planted on the ground. Newby stared back with eyes nervous as a rabbit, eyelids twitching in fear. Still holding Newby's gaze, Lance fired again.

Newby collapsed. The shot sent crows cawing in flight from the trees. A medic ran towards Newby. The nearest mechanics edged even further away from Lance's pistol.

They all stopped when Newby staggered to his feet unhurt. The bullet had drilled the earth a few inches from his foot, but the nervous shock of the gun going off had turned his leg into jelly.

Lance waved his smoking revolver under Newby's nose. "If I can't alter the way your tiny brain thinks, I'll alter your instincts. You will get four friends to stand around you in a circle and they will take random turns to fire near to your feet. Whoever fires, you will turn towards them instantly, run towards them, touch them over the heart, and say 'You are mine.' Then you will run back to the centre of the circle and wait for the next man to fire at you. You will do it all over again, and again, and again. For twenty minutes. You will do it in full flying gear so you will be sweating from the running and the fear. Just like a proper dogfight. This way we will bypass your brain and hone your reflexes. Just like the starter gun and your sprinting. You will practise this every morning first thing for the next five days. Understand?"

Newby nodded, ashen faced.

"Get to it! Now!"

As Newby stumbled away, Lance's mouth tasted sour. He felt as though he balanced on a knife edge—dangerous not only to his enemies but to his countrymen.

~

As always when a patrol returned, Clayton came outside to count them. He watched Lance's drama with Newby from a distance and rubbed his small moustache. Lance had been commander of his new squadron for six days and already he was shooting at his own men. A tad unconventional, to say the least.

Clayton propped himself against the doorframe of his office and frowned. How could he help Lance? Answers came as willingly as a kicked cat. Maybe he should suggest to Arthur that he should send Lance on leave?

When Lance appeared to make his flight report, Clayton waved his friend into the office where the ever-present kettle bubbled. Lance threw his gauntlets onto one of the five rickety farm chairs that littered the office and plonked himself on another. He reeked of castor oil, gunpowder, and sweat.

"Richthofen's crew caught a gunnery spotter team at four thousand feet over St.Julien. We were too late to help but got embroiled in a revenge scrap. Then loads more Huns waded in, and we lost Stokes. Kerrigan is missing."

Clayton wrote down the details and avoided looking at Lance. "Kerrigan won't be coming back. I took a call from the artillery spotters. He crash-landed on our side of the lines and survived the landing, but the Hun artillery bracketed him. Just enough left of him to identify him from his papers."

Lance sighed and his shoulders slumped. "Rotten way to die. Survive an air battle and a crash just so the blasted shells can turn you into tomato paste. I loathe those ruddy guns."

"Rhys-Davids says he shot down two, but only one is confirmed by others, so one it is. Weston confirmed your two kills, and he got one confirmed by Rhys-Davids. So, you downed at least four of the bastards. It may not seem like it, but on the day, it's a win. Glad you didn't kill Newby—that would have evened out the maths. Care to tell me why you were shooting at him?"

"Silly sod forgot his training. Almost got himself killed."

"And him having failed, you decided you would do it for him?"

"I wanted him to remember his training next time." Lance shifted in his seat, his voice low. Clayton strained to hear him. "Sometimes I loathe the newcomers. Their only sin is they aren't Leefe Robinson with his practical jokes, or Albert Ball with his quiet sense of belonging, or the rest of the ghosts since I got into this game."

"Tea?" Clayton asked.

Lance nodded. "Humans must have a finite number of face shapes. When enough squadron mates have died, every new face reminds you of an old one. Your brain puts a name to the first one of each type, and the door revolves so fast you don't get time to re-train it. I keep calling newcomers by the names of ghosts, and everyone looks at me like I'm mad. It's exhausting learning the new names and then finding they've gone before their names even stick in your mind. So bloody tiring..."

Clayton offered Lance a mug of piping hot tea. As usual Lance took it without wincing at the scalding heat. He seemed to have hands of asbestos.

The adjutant peered at Lance. His green eyes, always so striking, had shrunk into eye sockets bruised the colour of plums by stress and exhaustion. The scar on his left cheek contrasted as a white streak between black powder and castor oil stains. Sweaty hair stuck to his forehead. Clayton had never seen him so haggard. Back in the days when Lance relied only on himself and didn't worry about anyone else, he came across as an unconquerable rock. Clayton had long ago paid Arthur the sovereign over their bet on whether Lance could be a leader, but now he thought he may have conceded too early. The pendulum had swung from caring too little for others to caring too much.

"Lance, there's a reason every trade has apprentices. It takes time to learn. Flying is a more difficult profession than most, and war flying the hardest."

"They don't have time. You get it right or die when the

Huns mark your papers. Newby seems promising—intelligent and keen but not stupid about it. There's something of my younger brother about him—the quirk of the mouth and the goodhearted earnestness of him—which makes me want to protect him. The world is a better place with him in it. Then the silly idiot reminds me that he'll kill himself anyway, and I'd be better off not liking him. Or anybody else."

"Mmm. How is your sinus infection? The medical officer says he grounded you but you refused. He reckons you'll do lasting damage to yourself. How do you feel?"

"Exhausted. I have a permanent low-grade headache grinding above my eyes, and horrible green grunge comes out of my nose."

"Well, maybe fly less for a while until you get better?"

Lance grunted. He didn't sound impressed with the idea.

"What's the matter? Worried the Huns will win the war while you take it easy? Or concerned Thommo will overtake your number of kills?"

Lance snorted.

"Did I say something funny?" Clayton asked sourly.

"You really don't like Thommo, do you?"

"If he says 'Mama Thompson's boy' one more time, I'll borrow your revolver and shoot him."

"Give him a break. I know he's a glory hound, but by all accounts, he gets Huns."

"Does he? You mean by *his* accounts he gets Huns."

Lance shrugged. "I'm too tired to argue. I just want a shower to wash away the sweat, the whale grease, and the castor oil. And then to drop into a lovely dreamless sleep."

Lance's voice ached with longing, and he seemed to go into a trance. When he spoke next, his eyes gazed into the far distance and he murmured more to himself: "Washing is easy, the dreamless sleep is harder. Always the nightmares—the fire blowing back in the slipstream towards my face, the agony and stench of my bubbling flesh, the roar of the flames..."

Clayton said nothing, pretending he had not heard. Some things were too private.

Lance continued, his voice quiet and ruminative: "In the air, everything takes place so fast yet I feel like I have an element of control, that I can influence events. In my nightmares, it all happens so slowly and yet I am helpless. That makes it so excruciating, the inexorability as the fire reaches towards me..." His words trailed off into silence. He rose and shook himself like a labrador leaving a river.

"I'm off for a shower before the others burn all the wood for the hot water."

Clayton wagged a finger at Lance. "Don't forget to give me the names of the officers you want as replacements."

"No chance. It rips me apart inside, feeling responsible for people I get killed. Men I barely know. If I picked my pilots myself, I'd feel like a Roman emperor choosing which Christians to feed to the lions. I'd go mad with guilt. Hell, I'm already going mad with guilt!"

"Lance, we've been through this. You need to pick your men if your squadron is to succeed."

Lance strode to the door. "Get whoever you can. I'm off to St. Omer for a dinner. I'll be back for the morning patrol."

The door slammed on his way out and rebounded open. Clayton sighed. The ancient adage said you could lead a horse to water, but you couldn't make it drink. The authors of that piece of advice never had to deal with a hammerhead mule like Lance. Try leading him to water.

8
Light And Shadow

Evening the same day - 20 June 1917.
Hotel du Commerce, St. Omer, France.

"Isn't Arthur wonderful?" Megan asked as Lance caressed her curvy bits with a fluffy white towel. The hot bath tinted her buttocks a glowing pink and she smelled of lavender soap.

"Certainly is," Lance murmured as he dried her cracks and crevices. He had borrowed the squadron motorbike for the hour-long ride to St. Omer. It was the fastest mode of transport, able to wriggle past military convoys and marching columns. There had been a plethora of both tonight, and a resulting pall of heavy dust. He would have to leave Megan before sunrise, so it had been a long ride for a short night, but not for one second of the slow and bum-breaking journey had he doubted it would be worth it. To lose himself in Megan's warmth and then sink into the dreamless sleep that such loving gifted him, this was a magician's boon and Megan was the only such magician he knew.

Now he wasn't so sure as she strung his lust along. It had taken him two hours to get her naked in the hotel room and the signs were that she wasn't finished spinning it out yet. At this rate he would be loving and leaving, reaching the aerodrome with zero sleep. It was a very Megan form of punishment.

He had arrived at her hotel late, coated in dust with a

throat as parched as the Tsavo plain. Megan had been holding court in the palm-potted lobby, surrounded by young French officers—a queen with fawning courtiers. Her hair, black as midnight, cascaded to her slim waist and her silver silk dress shimmered around her shapely body.

She saw him enter, waved her champagne glass, and said something to her admirers. The officers turned to look at Lance and laughed. He ploughed through them, a Roman war galley on a ramming mission. He grabbed her arm and dragged her outside to a table on the terrace.

"Feeling masterful, are we?" she asked. "I imagine the caveman approach works in Africa. You're late."

"What a bunch of popinjays. From the look of their pristine uniforms, none of them has done battle with anything more lethal than a champagne cork."

"An appreciated skill, as they kept my glass full while I waited for you. I'm not in the habit of dallying. Next time I won't wait."

"Blame the Huns, not me." Lance was in no mood to kowtow. Today's losses still rode him hard.

A throat cleared behind them. *"Excusez-moi, Mam'selle. Avec les compliments des officiers."* The waiter flourished a chilled bottle of champagne and poured two glasses with great élan before melting away.

Megan raised her glass towards her admirers, who returned the toast. Lance glared and knocked back the whole glass in one. The bubbles sizzled on their way down his parched throat.

Fortunately, the chilled champagne had worked its magic on them. At dinner at Treille d'Or, the best restaurant in town, Megan had served him a starter of sultry glances, a main course of gentle touches skin to skin, and a dessert of whispered promises. All had roused Lance to fever pitch over an hour ago. Now, back in her hotel room, she was naked but still drawing out the flirtation.

She wiggled her buttocks against his hardening length. "It's amazing how well Arthur has done despite all his disadvantages."

"Strewth, woman! What disadvantages? The man is handsome, rich, and intelligent. We should all be so lucky!"

She turned, her breasts swinging. "You mean you don't know?"

"Know what?" Lance cupped one breast and ran his thumb over a nipple that hardened in response.

Megan purred but eased his hand away. "You really don't know?"

Lance sighed. Lust raged through him, but he'd learned that the rewards for playing her games were wondrous, so he settled down for conversation. "Obviously not. Seems like he is rich, powerful, good looking and well liked. So tell me, what are his disadvantages?"

Megan picked up a hairbrush from the bedside table and pulled her long black curtain of hair to one side. Then she brushed it methodically, silver bracelets jangling, Lance admired the play of her muscles and the contrast with her smooth roundness, which changed elliptically and changed again. She watched him watching her for a while, a small smile on her lips, before asking, "How can you spend so much time with Arthur and know so little about him?"

"Well, I don't know what I don't know. But it's probably irrelevant to life in the RFC."

"Men! Women in such a situation would find out everything about each other. How else could we work together?"

"It's war. What counts is not the man's background, or what plays he likes, or what party he votes for. The only thing that matters is whether his mates can rely on him in battle. Any time we aren't fighting, we are organising the war or trying to forget it."

There was silence for a while, except for the swishing of her mesmeric brushing.

"Megan, tell me but don't waste your breath badmouthing Arthur. I won't believe you."

"No, I would never say bad things about Arthur. This is the opposite. But unfortunate things happened to Arthur, and to me. Maybe I shouldn't prattle, but it's well known in society, and I'd rather tell you before you found out from someone else."

"I'm listening."

"In a minute." Megan put the brush down and clipped her long hair back into a single flowing dark mane. Then she took her glass of champagne to the bedside table. She pushed him onto the bed, crawled between his legs, and leaned back against him. Her head rested under his chin, and she grasped his hands and placed them on her breasts. He cupped them, revelling in their smooth heft.

"Arthur is a bastard," she said.

"What!" His hands started to drop away from her breasts, but her hands pinned them to her.

"I don't mean he behaves like one, but that he was born out of wedlock. Our father was a virile man who behaved much as an old-fashioned lord with the *droit du seigneur*. Arthur's mother was a lady's maid who had the misfortune to catch his lordship's eye.

"When she became pregnant, Lord Wolsey moved her from the house before it became obvious, and into a cottage on the estate, supposedly to be a seamstress. The mother died delivering Arthur, and he was given to foster parents on the estate. They knew who his father was, but no-one else did. Not even Arthur."

Megan paused and took a sip of champagne. She offered Lance the glass, and he shook his head.

"A month after the seamstress died, Lord Wolsey married my mother. It wasn't a union created in heaven. My mother was an earl's daughter who Lord Wolsey seduced and made pregnant with me only a few months after he'd conceived Arthur. My mother's family was aristocracy and could not be bullied like a lady's maid, so they forced a marriage. My father believed my mother had got pregnant deliberately to trap him into marriage, and he resented it. He exiled her to a London apartment and did not even make a pretence of any relationship. I grew up with my mother, both of us abandoned and betrayed.

"Meanwhile Lord Wolsey continued to seduce any young woman he could, quite publicly. My humiliated mother cursed him daily. She died when I was sixteen, a sad alcoholic in her final years. I was left on my own, not financially, but in every other way."

Lance nuzzled her neck. "Must've been tough," he said.

She rewarded him with an intense kiss. For a few moments Lance lost himself in their duelling tongues. He hardened and pushed against her rounded buttocks. She murmured in pleasure but broke off the kiss. "Down, boy! Let me finish the story." She took a long gulp of champagne and continued.

"Later, my father married a second time, but they never had children. Then days before the war, both Lord and Lady Wolsey died in a fire at their London home. There had a dire shortage of males in the Wolsey line for almost five generations, and everyone thought my son was in line to be the heir. Stop wriggling!"

"I've got a dead leg; I need to move."

"I hope it's not the middle one! We can't have that one dying." She sat up and turned to sit cross-legged facing him.

"In his will, Lord Wolsey included a marriage certificate to Arthur's mother. So Arthur, who for most of his life had been unaware he was a Wolsey bastard, never mind a legitimate heir, became Lord Wolsey.

"Arthur was as shocked as anyone. My father had made

sure Arthur was well brought up and educated, but as a commoner. He'd never been trained to be an aristocrat and heir to one of England's largest land holdings. Meanwhile my dead husband was a baron so my son had noble lineage on every side and I raised Morgan appropriately. But my father got his way—as he always did—and the title went to Arthur."

Megan's tone had hardened and her eyes blazed. Lance sneaked a look at his watch and sighed. Just three hours until he would have to leave, and Megan's mind seemed more on family history than romance.

"So, considering Arthur's disadvantages," she continued, "he has done wonderfully."

This discussion seemed loaded with potential pitfalls, so Lance stuck to the banal. "How old was Morgan?"

"Twenty back then."

"Impossible! You are too young!"

"Oh, thank you, Lance." She stroked his cheek. "So gallant!"

"Wait a moment. What age are you now?"

This time her smile came lightly chilled "How fast laurels fall..."

"Come on, Megan. This makes no sense to me."

"Let's just agree I am over thirty, had a child young, and leave it there, shall we?"

"You said Arthur has done incredibly well. What does that mean?"

"When Arthur inherited, he found the entire Wolsey Estate mortgaged to banks who were clamouring for repayment. Also, these new-fangled death duty taxes meant that the robbers in the Tax Department were demanding a huge amount of cash. The entire worth of the estate would not have paid off a quarter of the debts. While he was alive, none of the banks dared to demand that my father pay back his debts, but after his death the vultures came to roost. It looked as though the

Wolsey family would end in ruin and ignominy. After five hundred years. Then Arthur wangled a marriage to the daughter of an American industrialist. The father wanted a serious title in his family, and Arthur needed serious money in his, so from both their perspectives it was a winning match."

"Wait—you're saying Arthur's wife is through an arranged marriage?"

"He's not the first or the last peer of the realm to marry for money. Are you shocked?"

"It doesn't seem like Arthur."

"I presume you haven't met her?"

"No, what's she like?"

"Very...exotic."

"Exotic? *You* are calling someone else exotic?"

"I have Celtic blood, which is not so exotic for the British, but she's a dago of some sort. Her father was American Irish businessman who made a fortune building railways in South America. He married an Argentinian woman, supposedly descended from Spanish royalty. Their daughter, Arthur's wife, has an American accent but the looks and temper of a dago blue blood. She is spoilt and wilful beyond belief. Her American upbringing has led her to try to persuade Arthur that the British aristocracy needs to modernise and 'free' their tenants. What a bizarre idea!"

Megan took a longer swig of champagne. Lance smiled to see this worldly woman flushed with indignation. He guessed Arthur's wife was no ugly harridan. Megan noticed the smile and tossed her mane of hair.

"Anyway, what matters, despite her bizarre ideas, is that her father died and left his money to Arthur. Now the Wolsey Estates are not merely out of hock, but fabulously wealthy again. Who knew that grubby things like railways could be worth so much lucre? The Wolseys remain a power in the land, and Arthur has chased the banks and the taxman back into their kennels. *That* is why Arthur has done wonderfully."

The tawdry history perturbed Lance. Colonials thought of England as the cradle of civilised and urbane behaviour, with the aristocrats as the apogee. Yet after this tale, English high society sounded rife with behaviour that would get officers banned by their regiments. By comparison, the more prosaic society in Africa appeared more honest and elevated.

Megan seemed to sense his confusion. She reached for his groin and tickled him with her long nails. "But enough about Arthur—we need life here again. The Wolsey scandals seem to have bored it. Aha! The flames of passion have not smouldered out entirely!"

He laughed at her mockery. *At last...*

He leaned forward to kiss her, but she fended him away. "Wait! I have a present for you." She bounded off the bed and came back clutching a parcel wrapped with string. "Open it," she said.

The present Lance wanted was Megan, but he unwrapped the parcel to find a honey-coloured leather helmet. He fingered it in amazement. Never had he felt a leather so soft. "It's amazing."

Megan smiled. "It's made by Rolls Royce, who claim it is the most comfortable driving helmet in the world. Made from the skin of a chamois mountain goat. I thought it might work for flying too. Will it?"

Lance pulled it on. Compared to the stiff leather of the RFC standard issue, this was satin versus sandpaper. Perfect for summer flying and medium altitude patrols but too thin for high altitude flights in winter. But he could wear it as a liner to a sheepskin helmet for those types of flight. "It's perfect. What a thoughtful gift."

That won a kiss from Megan, so he wrapped his arms around her, and soon the kissing turned into mutual urgency. Rolling onto her back, she urged him to mount her in a voice husky with need. He slipped into her and built his rhythm. Her hoarse cries told him that she too was riding towards orgasm. She dug her long nails deep into his flanks and raked them upwards.

Lance bellowed in pain, and his desire shrivelled. "Christ! What the hell are you doing?"

"Sorry darling," she whispered, cupping her palms around his face. "Most men fancy it."

"Well not this man! Jesus! Megan, that was painful," he growled.

"It was stupid of me, darling. I'm sorry." Megan dipped a long forefinger in the blood drops and licked it. Her tongue showed crimson, and she purred like a cat. Then she clenched herself around his shaft, laved her pointed tongue deep into his ear, and swirled it around the sensitive skin. Lance moaned with pleasure despite himself.

She whispered into his ear. "Forgive me?"

"Mmm." But his tone was still grudging.

She pulled his mouth down and kissed him, deep and long, rocking her pelvis languidly and murmuring with satisfaction. As he relaxed into the sex again, she stroked his cheek and whispered, "I was trying to give you pleasure, darling. Everyone likes some sort of pain—we'll find your pleasure-pain."

Lance did not answer, focusing on the sensations as he picked up the pace to a canter again.

"Perhaps it's here," she murmured, almost to herself, as she took his right nipple between her nails and squeezed hard.

"God!" Lance exclaimed, but this time the pain sent a jolt of electricity sparking to his groin and he bucked between her thighs. Instead of stopping, he drove into her even harder and faster.

"Aha! We've found it!" she taunted, then lifted her head and clamped her teeth onto his nipple. The exquisite agony galvanised him and a part of him wanted to shake her away, but only part. She clung to him like a limpet using arms, hands, mouth, and teeth, goading him mercilessly with her pelvis until he shuddered and shot inside her, hard and deep.

After he had recovered his breath, he rolled off her and rubbed his nipple. "That hurt too!"

Megan chuckled huskily. "Is that a complaint?" She rolled next to him and pillowed his head on her breasts. He snuggled between them and listened to her still-racing heartbeat.

"Yes...and no."

"You will ask me to do it again."

"I don't think so."

Her laugh was pure, silvery amusement. "Oh Lance, you are so staid. Look into your shadow side for a moment."

"My what?"

"Everyone has a shadow side that we carry inside us, even if we are unaware of it most of the time." She traced the ridged muscles of his flanks with a forefinger. "You must have a strong one, or someone so conventional and idealistic could not have killed so many people."

Lance tried to change the subject. "What's that got to do with lovemaking?"

She raised herself onto an elbow and looked at him. "Light and shadow. Love and hatred. Ying and yang. Pain and pleasure are the opposite sides of the same coin. You can't have one without the other."

"That's nuts. I never hurt lovers."

Megan snorted. "Lance, please! When you lick me down there, that extreme pleasure you give me is a form of pain. Why else would the French call the orgasm *la petite mort*? Let yourself go beyond the conventional boundaries of behaviour. It can be exhilarating to unleash yourself."

She dug a forefinger into his ribs so hard he grunted. "For example, you use your strong hunting instincts to be a sneaky killer in the skies. Yet Society says that hunting urges should not be used against humans. So the public school boys, the ultimate slaves to convention, pretend it is a game. That is why they don't want to sneak up and shoot people in the back. It doesn't worry you because you ruthlessly extend your hunting mindset to humans in a way that most men can't. Your willingness to regard other men as dangerous animals that can legitimately be shot without warning, that is your shadow side."

Lance did not care for the analogy. "I don't hunt humans, I hunt aircraft."

She chuckled. "Believe whatever helps you. It doesn't worry me. I find it exciting."

To escape the talk of killing, he steered the conversation to a lighter tone. "I am the very model of a colonial gentleman. How could I have a dark side?"

"Faugh! A colonial, you say? Disgusting! Only one level above savages!"

"Sorry, we can't all be English aristocrats."

"Darling, we are the worst. Lord Acton once said that 'Power corrupts, and absolute power corrupts absolutely.' Our aristocracy is a living example of that."

"Does that apply to you too?"

The laugh came late and with a hint of falseness. "Oh, I am but a mere woman. I only observe."

"Well, you seem to have observed a lot."

"I'm a Wolsey. As I've told you, we have our history. I just look after me and mine."

"No. You have looked after me too, and I have revelled in it. I'm sorry it is only for one night but that makes it even more precious."

"Ah, you are adorable." She snuggled back into his arms, spooning against him. "Dear Lance, feel free to give me a little pain when we make love again. You may enjoy it. I know I will enjoy receiving it. Go to sleep now, but wake me before you go, and we'll try it then."

Lance wrinkled his nose and did not reply. Hurting a woman was anathema to him. He caressed her hip, sliding his hand over her soft skin. Megan's breathing settled into a soft cadence, and his eyes closed.

A memory drifted into his thoughts as he slipped towards sleep. He was a child in Africa, watching an agama lizard sunning itself on a flat rock, warming its cold blood in the sun. Its head glowed red and its body glittered iridescent in green hues with metallic shafts of blue sparkling in the bright light. It was a magnificent jewel contrasting with the drab tones of earth and stone. He bent to pick it up and it hissed at him. He jumped back as he noticed the needle-sharp teeth, the flickering forked tongue, and the void onyx-coloured eyes and their obsidian pupils.

His father grabbed his arm. "Careful, Lance! Agama bites are nasty. Sometimes beautiful things are the most dangerous. It's nature's warning."

9
Stress Is a Hun on Your Tail

Three days later - 23 June 1917.
Bailleul Airfield.

The next few days summoned raging summer storms and, Clayton thought, a febrile quality to the camp. The orders from GHQ became more strident, their demands for patrols more frequent. Haig's latest attack must be imminent. But the weather frustrated all plans.

A storm ripped apart 111 Squadron's tents and left possessions strewn in the mud like debris from a campsite massacre. A lightning bolt gouged a four-foot trench in the Camels' airstrip, and the Town airfield became so waterlogged that 222 Squadron's Bristol fighters sank into the mud up to their axles. Broken telephone wires draped forlornly from the poles at the edges of the aerodrome.

The pilots, penned in the Mess or anteroom but on permanent standby for a break in the weather, grew tetchy. Arthur arranged a rugby match to relieve the pent-up frustrations but abandoned the game after several players almost drowned in the bottom of a ruck.

Clayton reckoned that had been a good decision as he splashed through the darkness on his way to the Mess, where most of the pilots were waiting for dinner. But it left the men simmering—with so many strong characters in the wing, an argy-bargy of some sort was a racing certainty. Clayton's money rode on Thompson or Elliot Springs being the instigator. Arthur expected his adjutant to keep the order, but Clayton had no such plans. Some violent horseplay would be a catharsis. He would intervene only if it came to fisticuffs; otherwise, he would enjoy the theatre.

When Clayton reached the Mess, he shook the rain off his coat, hung it on a peg near the door, and strolled over to an empty stool halfway down the railway sleepers. The barman limped over with a glass of burgundy from Arthur's cellar. Clayton smiled his thanks and took stock of the room.

The atmosphere reeked of wet clothes and the haze of stale cigarette smoke trapped by the low ceiling. A puddle under the coat hooks was busy merging with the lake leaking under the main door. At one end, the gramophone croaked out a scratchy version of *The Robbers' March* from one of the latest London musicals, *Chu Chin Chow*. Thompson and Springs started an off-key rendition of the catchy chorus, but shouts and boos reduced them to sulky silence.

But if the stage was drab, at least tonight's cast looked promising. Rod Andrews was perfect as the rough-edged Aussie, Thompson believable as the chippy Canadian bantamweight boxer, Elliot Springs convincing as an irreverent Yank, and Rhys-Davids a ringer as the teenage Eton public school boy. Not to mention Taggart playing himself as a stroppy Glaswegian. Last week Clayton might have put Taggart on the list of potential trouble starters, but now the other pilots gave him a wide berth for fear of offending him inadvertently.

Oddly enough it was the ever-polite Newby who inadvertently kicked off the evening's entertainment.

"According to the *Times*," he announced, "a new MP who had to make his maiden speech to the House found the experience deeply stressful."

"Pah!" Morgan Budd objected in his deep voice. "Stress is an Albatross on your tail."

An awkward silence hung in the air and Budd looked around. A few pilots turned their back on him. "What?" he asked, hunching his shoulders.

Clayton explained the gaffe, but it came out more harshly than he intended. "Perhaps you could wait until you have been across the lines and experienced an Albatross on your tail before you offer such opinions."

A deep shade of pink suffused Budd's pale face. He opened his mouth to reply but Newby rescued him.

"It must be stressful batting on a dodgy wicket against a lightning-fast bowler," Newby said. "What do you say, Rod? You played against England and Bill Hitch, who they say was the fastest bowler in the history of the game. Did you feel stressed?"

Rod Andrews, ensconced in one of the comfy chairs, turned a page of the *Illustrated London News* but did not look up. "Nah, mate. Fast bowlers never worried me. Faster they come, faster they go. The buggers I hated were those crafty Bosie leg spinner blokes. You think the ball is going one way, but it spins the other. Made me look bloody stupid when I tried to hit them into the Swan River."

"That magazine," Thommo said, pointing to the *Illustrated London News*, "says stress is when you are Lady La-di-da and no-one arrives at your daughter's coming-out ball."

"You are all wrong," Arthur pontificated from beside the doorway where he was hanging his wet coat. "Stress is when you are flying an FE2b with Lance in the front gunner seat. He has a Hun in his sights and is firing over your head. The Hun dives away behind you, and Lance traverses the machine gun, still firing, towards you. It is obvious he really, really does not want to let that Hun go, and you can see in his eyes he is calculating what will happen if he keeps firing. You know he would sell his soul for a kill and you are hoping he remembers he will die if he kills his pilot. All of this takes place in two seconds, and you watch the barrels swing towards you, still firing, and you pray to God that he will lift that trigger finger before he shoots you. Now that is stress!"

The pilots hooted with laughter, which doubled when Arthur finished: "It is why I put him forward for pilot training, because I knew one day he would be unable to resist!"

Lance chose that moment to barge into the Mess. The mirth rose even further, with several pilots laughing so hard they choked. Clayton saw Lance was too focused to notice the laughter, never mind understand that he was part of the joke. Rain ran off his sodden coat in rivulets as his gaze searched the room.

"Is Budd here? Good. I've been over your engine with your mechanic. He couldn't find the cause of those mysterious drops in revs that you reported, but the engine is fine now. Meet me in the hangars in ten minutes and we'll sort your ammunition links bullet by bullet so we can be sure they won't jam again tomorrow."

Lance left as abruptly as he had arrived. Arthur grabbed his coat and followed him out. "Lance, hang on. There's something I need to show you."

Budd had stood up uncertainly when Lance entered but became truculent as soon as Lance and Arthur left. His usual deep baritone voice sounded whiney. "What about my dinner? I don't understand this insistence on loading our own guns. The armourers are experts. They do nothing else all day. Why the hell shouldn't they do it?"

Clayton put his head in his hands. He had to give Budd his due—the kid had a real talent for aggravating folk. Loading your own ammunition was non-negotiable in Fitch's squadron. He drummed his mantra into every pilot—"If you're too lazy to load your own bullets, you're too lazy to live." A novice pilot challenging his commander's pet hobbyhorse promised a volcanic response. Slow grins spread among the other pilots at that thought. As Arthur's nephew, Budd had enjoyed some slack—not because Arthur was a lord, but because the pilots liked and admired their wing commander. Clayton reckoned Budd's grace period had just reached the knacker's yard.

Elliot Springs took pity on Budd, surprising Clayton. The American's pugilist's face and amusing cynicism apparently harboured a hitherto undemonstrated diplomatic capability. "It's nice to have a leader who invests time in keeping you alive," he drawled. "Some of us might be grateful that our commander spent the afternoon checking our engine and would miss his own dinner to help check our ammunition. Would you do that for me, Thommo?"

Thommo laughed. "I wouldn't miss a cup of tea to keep *you* alive."

"See? I'd thank the Lord every minute for a leader who cared. But all that Mr Budd worries about is his dinner. Fearless, he is. I wish I were so fearless."

Budd ignored the American. "My friend Chalmers in 24 Squadron says their pilots carry a hammer. If their guns jam, they clear them by whacking them with it."

Rod Andrews turned the page of his magazine. "Next time you get a gun jam, whatever means you use to fix it is fine, so long as it works. You need to cross the lines one of these days."

Budd's dark eyes blinked under the attack. "It's not my fault if my engine keeps getting wonky or the guns keep jamming. Fitch always tells us not to cross the lines if there is something wrong with our plane."

"Aye, dinnae fash the poor wee laddie so," Taggart said.

"You gotta love this war," Elliot Springs said. "It brings all sorts together. Britain used to be so class-conscious. Now you have working-class Glaswegians standing up for English aristocrats?"

"He's a young laddie. War flying's tough on all of us. I've my own wee lad, and one day I'd hope someone wae stick up for him when folk gang ap on him."

Springs's eyebrows climbed. "He's in your flight; it's you he leaves in the lurch when he turns back."

"Aye, it's because he's in mae flight Ah'm sticking up for him. One for all and all for one, and all that claptrap."

The big Cornish farmer, Weston, as usual unaware or unperturbed by the simmering undercurrents, took up the conversation. "I had a friend who took a hammer in his plane to fix gun jams."

"There you go," Budd said, looking around for approbation.

"The hammer never cleared a jam, but he certainly felt better whacking the gun. Unfortunately, the hammer killed him in the end."

"That's ridiculous," Budd scoffed. "Hammers don't kill people."

"This one did. My friend kept the hammer in the cockpit sleeve. One day he came into land, not realising that his hammer had come loose in a dogfight and fallen on the floor of the cockpit. He banked into his landing pattern and the hammer fell into the slot next to the control stick. It jammed the stick, so the plane kept on banking. He went smack into the trees. Same thing almost happened to me with my sandwiches one day. My Ma always said my gluttony would be the death of me."

"That's just bad luck. Lightning won't strike twice." Budd blustered. "My friend has never had a problem."

"Yeah, mate?" Rod Andrews drawled. "How many kills has this cobber of yours got?"

"None yet, but he's been across the lines plenty."

"That's good enough for me. In the blue corner is Lance Fitch, currently the heavyweight champion, the highest-scoring living ace in the RFC. And in the red corner, a total nonentity in his first fight. Who shall we bet on? Yup, it makes sense to bet on Chalmers. Definitely. Especially as we are only betting with our lives. Smart thinking, sonny."

Budd looked at Andrews and his mouth twisted into a sulk. "I prefer my thinking to that of a crude colonial from the land of convicts, thank you. No wonder Leefe Robinson and the rest went west."

Uh-oh. Clayton sensed that this silence had a different quality, the charged stillness that prickles the air just before the storm hits. *Hope Budd has enough sense to reverse out of that one.* The pilots nearest Budd edged away from him, but he did not seem to notice in his righteous anger.

Rod Andrews lowered his magazine and sighed. "What does that mean, mate?"

"Means that people say you ran away and left Leefe Robinson to die."

Clayton eased his weight forward on his bar stool, prepared to intervene if it turned nasty. But Rod Andrews remained seated and continued leafing through his magazine.

"Care to come closer and say that again, sport?" The words were challenging, but the Australian's voice sounded bored. He rolled up the magazine and smiled at Budd. Clayton relaxed back onto his stool. Whatever Rod was planning, the kid deserved it.

Budd hesitated. Clayton read his mind. *Andrews is a tough nut, but how much damage can he do from the depths of a saggy armchair? Besides, even a colonial wouldn't dare start a fight in the officers' Mess.* So, Budd stepped closer until he towered over the seated Australian. "Certainly. People say you abandoned Leefe Robinson, and that's why you got back, and he didn't. They say you are yellow."

Andrews grabbed Budd's sleeve and pulled him off balance towards the chair. Simultaneously he thrust the solid end of the rolled-up magazine hard into the youngster's Adam's apple. Budd collapsed as though shot. He rolled on the floor in agony, clutching his throat and gasping for breath. The sheer effectiveness of the casual assault shocked Clayton. Nobody had yet moved when Arthur strolled back into the Mess to find his nephew writhing on the ground.

"What the hell is going on here?"

"Mr. Budd seems to be choking on his digestive biscuit," Andrews said.

"So why is no-one helping him?" Arthur asked in disbelief.

"Goodness me!" Andrews exclaimed. "Where are our manners? Here mate, let me give you a pat on the back." The Australian sprang out of the chair and strode towards Budd, who scuttled away on his knees like an escaping crab, wheezing, with one hand clutched around his throat. Arthur moved to help his nephew, but Budd crabbed towards the door, struggled to his feet, and staggered out of the Mess.

"That man has the manners of a c c c cockroach and the morals of a Whitechapel c c cur," Rhys-Davids opined.

Clayton took a sip of his wine. Budd certainly created unanimity. He'd never heard Rhys-Davids say a bad word about anybody before and he only stammered when he felt strongly about something.

Arthur raised an interrogative eyebrow at his adjutant, who gave a little shake of his head. It was better that Arthur did not get involved. The wing commander shrugged and left.

~

A few hours later, Clayton asked Andrews to come to Arthur's office and escorted him inside. Clayton had never seen the Australian look so unsure of himself. Not surprising. An assault on a fellow officer in the Mess was grounds for disciplinary action. Neither did it improve things when the victim was a baron and the commanding officer's nephew. Rod Andrews did not give a fig for social etiquette, but he wasn't stupid. He'd crossed several lines: military, social, and common sense.

"You wanted to see me, sir?" The harsh yellow light behind Andrews cast a giant shadow over Arthur as the commanding officer sat behind his desk. A match flared as Arthur lit his cigar and puffed it into life with pungent clouds of smoke. Clayton moved closer to the door where a draft eddied the smoke away.

"Thank you for coming, Andrews," Arthur said with formal courtesy. "I appreciate it is after dinner and I have dragged you away from the comforts of the Mess."

"No worries, sir. An early night might do me good."

"Do us all good, I expect. Especially those who try to keep up with you ..."

"Er, yes, sir, but you can't blame me if the Poms can't hold their drink."

"Indeed."

Arthur picked up a letter on his desk and waved it at the Australian. "Lieutenant Budd alleges that you assaulted him in the Mess."

"Ha!" Andrews's voice radiated scorn. "I never touched him."

Arthur raised an eyebrow at Clayton. The adjutant shrugged. "Strictly speaking that is true, only his sleeve. Who ever heard of anyone assaulted by the *London Illustrated News*?"

"Mmm," Arthur responded. He turned back to Andrews. "Were you a lawyer in your previous life?"

"No, sir. Stockman on a ranch in the outback. But I played cricket with a lot of lawyers."

"Obviously they taught you how to split legal hairs. Must be a rugged life as a stockman?"

Andrews's voice warmed. "No, sir, best job on God's earth—just yer mates, the wind, the sky, and the stars at night. The occasional snake, but not as many as I found when I moved into the offices in the Big Smoke."

"Big Smoke?"

"City, sir."

"Who taught you to use a magazine as a weapon? I would not have thought many cattlemen carried magazines around with them on bar crawls. Or was it the lawyers who taught you that too?"

"Just a stockman's talent for making do with what's at hand."

"Useful trait in a war too. Although I'd prefer you use your talents on the Huns rather than on our side. Do you have an issue with Lieutenant Budd?"

"No, sir, no more than with grit in my underwear."

Clayton suffered a coughing fit. A flash of irritation passed across Arthur's face before he spoke. "Then I have a request, which I will need to put in language even an Australian can understand."

Arthur paused, and Andrews's face hardened. Clayton could read his mind. *Here comes the priggish Pommie lecture, just because Budd is an officer and a toff and the nephew.*

But then Arthur offered a smile. "The next time a junior officer impugns the courage of another officer in this wing, I want you to insert a magazine into an orifice of your choice. Could you do that for me? As a personal favour?"

The big man's face split into a startled grin. "I can only try, sir. Mind you some of them have right tight arses, I'm not sure if the *Illustrated London Times* will fit."

10
Needs Must When the Devil Drives

The 200hp Hispano-Suiza engine bellowed as Lance opened the throttle. His big-bladed propeller blurred into a brown haze and the wheels bumped over the soaked ground as he led A Flight into their take-off.

Yesterday's savage weather had relented but periodic showers still drenched the airfield. Moisture soaked the air, and a watery sun glistened silver off the dripping trees and puddles.

As the SE5 accelerated, the tips of his propellers conjured rainbow-coloured halos. Lance's tyres kissed the earth good-bye, and as he climbed away, he checked behind. Three khaki planes followed him. Their wheels sprayed plumes of surface water that the slipstreams whipped away, so the aircraft seemed to trail smoke as they lifted off the sodden grass. Lance's goggles misted. He pushed them up onto his forehead and slunk behind his tiny windscreen. His eyes watered against the rushing wind as he climbed into the sky.

Twenty minutes later, he levelled out at fifteen thousand feet on a heading towards Menin. At this altitude, shafts of dazzling sun stabbed between the sodden grey clouds that cluttered the sky. For a few seconds Lance revelled in the glory of the bright sunshine after the soggy world of recent days. Then he bent his mind to the mission briefing, such as it was.

Clayton had run into the Mess, the door slamming open. "Ahoy, Lance! HQ wants your squadron in the air, *immediatement.*"

Lance gestured around him. "What squadron? B and C Flights are already up on assigned patrols. I only have A Flight here. Ask Thommo or Rod."

"Nope. HQ has given the Bristols a bombing mission with Thommo's Camels as escort. Whatever planes you have, get 'em airborne chop-chop. A squadron of Sopwith 1½ Strutter bombers should be on their way back from Courtrai. They are on a photographic mission to locate the Hun's reserve deployments near where Haig's big attack will take place. But in order not to alert the Huns, HQ disguised it as a bombing run. Their escort got lost in the clouds and have just landed short of fuel. The Sopwiths are out there alone."

Lance winced. "A target near the Circus's home airfield and no escort? Poor bastards."

The adjutant nodded. "HQ says it's imperative the photos get back and we are the closest fighter airfield. Fly due east to Ploegsteert and then steer towards Menin. Try to find them and help them home."

Now Lance and the escort were on the way. He checked his flight tucked in a V shape behind him. The two tyros, Newby and Budd, floated on either side, with Taggart weaving behind them to provide cover. *Some escort. Just four planes, two piloted by novices. But I can't mollycoddle them any longer now the offensive is about to start.*

At least Budd had made it over the lines for the first time, although ironically in circumstances more dangerous than any of his aborted sorties. Newby's skills were growing and he was razor keen, but he would be a bunny in a fight against the

Circus. And Budd? Well, Budd was Budd. Lance had tried, in honour of his promise to Megan, to train her son but Budd always found a way to screw up.

Lance diverted around an ominous black cumulonimbus cloud. As they rounded it, a lone Rumpler emerged ahead of them and a thousand feet below. Quick pickings, and a fat target that would blood the youngsters and boost their morale.

Lance led them in a curving dive towards the dappled purple and green enemy. As they drew closer, Lance signalled Budd to lead the attack. The Hun observer had his head down, probably tinkering with a camera. This would be an easy kill.

Budd proved him wrong. Lance had trained him to slide into the blind spot under an enemy's tail plane so he could take a short-range, low-deflection shot against an unaware enemy. Instead, Budd opened fire from above and from a ridiculous distance. Lance's lips compressed. Why did he bother training the idiot? Did nothing stick in his mind?

The observer jerked in alarm as tracer streaked fifty yards past his left wing. Black smoked poured from the high exhaust stack as the pilot rammed on the power. Futile. A Rumpler couldn't outrun an SE5 at this altitude. Lance drew level with Budd and motioned him closer to the enemy. Budd's goggled face nodded and he shortened the range, but not by much, before firing again. His tracers shot well wide of the target. Lance stabbed a gloved hand towards the Hun. This time Budd closed to two hundred feet before firing. Not great but better. The improvement was short lived. The observer's machine gun flickered. Although the tracers missed, the SE5 flinched and broke off the attack.

For Christ's sake. What Lance had envisaged as a quick kill to boost morale was now chewing up time, fuel, and bullets. But he couldn't let the Rumpler escape. It might have key reconnaissance photos.

Lance checked to confirm that the surrounding airspace

was still empty. Then he dived under the Hun and swooped up under its tail, close enough to see the oil streaks on the fabric beneath the fuselage. His first burst shattered the observer's right elbow. The German fell back into his cockpit hunched in agony and the barrels of his machine gun swivelled heavenwards.

Lance gestured for Newby to complete the kill. Before Newby could do so, Budd's SE5 cut in front and Newby had to rear his plane away to prevent a collision.

Now the gunner was out of action, Budd's aggression was obvious. He closed to within fifty feet and fired long bursts. It was lousy shooting, but at that range the two machine guns hosed the Hun with a torrent of lead. The observer jerked and slid down out of sight. A strip of fabric ripped from the top left wing. Still the plane flew onwards, Budd's guns hammering at it.

Lance shook his head. In Africa he'd once seen a young Maasai tribesman botch the ritual slaughter of a bullock. It should have been a single clean thrust to the heart. But the nervous youngster had missed his killing stroke and left the bullock bellowing its agony. The panicked boy leapt at the sacrifice, hacking and stabbing while the victim brayed in anguish. When the bullock finally died, the elders hummed their disapproval and the boy hung his head in shame. Budd's efforts on the Rumpler made for equally painful watching.

The end finally came with a thin stream of oil, thickened into a plume of black smoke, and then the dreaded red flames bloomed from the engine. *Another flamer. Poor bugger!*

The pilot swatted at the rising flames with his gloved hands as the slipstream pushed the searching fingers of fire towards his face. He side-slipped to blow the fire to one side, but to no avail. The bonfire surged over the cockpit. *End it, man! Jump, for Christ's sake!*

As if he had heard, the flailing figure rolled the burning plane and launched his body into the void. His dark flying coat billowed between his outstretched arms as he faded into a dwindling speck.

Lance retched onto his boots. Wiping his chin with his heavy gauntlets, he looked over at Budd, who took both hands off the controls and clasped them above his head like a victorious boxer. The aircraft skidded and Budd had to grab the joystick again, but nothing shook his broad grin beneath the soulless, goggled eyes. Lance glared at him, the bad taste in his mouth only partly from the vomit. It took a real hero to knock down a slow reconnaissance plane when the observer was out of action. The Huns were the ones with guts, flying that old crate across the lines.

Lance shook his head to clear the insidious thought and signalled for his pilots to regroup. He turned the nose of his SE5 back onto a heading for Menin and pulled into a climb to regain their lost height.

Five minutes later he spotted a swarm of black dots in the distance, like a cluster of gnats. Dogfight! He turned towards the gaggle, still straining for altitude.

As they got closer, he worked out the details. Fifteen Albatross were swarming over a squadron of Sopwith 1½ Strutters like hornets over an open jam pot. The ragged formation of slow two-seaters were easy prey and two black columns of smoke led earthwards. Fifteen crack Hun fighters against nine obsolete two-seaters and four SE5 with two novice pilots. Lance shifted in his seat. This would be a tough scrap even if his whole flight were full strength and packed with veterans.

He scanned the sky and noticed a dozen planes heading to join the fray from the west. They would reach the dogfight before Lance. At least that would even the odds.

Then he saw the curved wing tips. *Albatross! More of the bastards! How many do they need to shoot down a few bombers?*

Lance's brain churned. If he joined this melee, he would most likely add his pilots to the slaughter while achieving nothing. Cold logic argued that they should avoid this fight. Or was that cowardice talking? Should he abandon eighteen men? Besides, Clayton had said the Sopwiths might have key reconnaissance photos.

He turned his flight thirty degrees and slid behind wispy clouds to escape detection as the SE5s continued to claw their way towards and above the massacre. Whatever he decided, they would need the extra height.

And what about his responsibility to his own pilots—not to fritter away their lives on a lost cause? He shook his head, baffled, and wished Arthur was here to solve the riddle.

The Sopwiths tightened their circle, trying to cover each other, but the Huns were hacking them out of the sky, and now only seven remained. Maybe the Huns would end his dilemma by shooting down all the Sopwiths before A Flight reached them? His lip curled with self-contempt at the thought. *Get behind me, Satan.*

Lance checked behind him. All present and correct. He signalled them to tighten their formation. They would plunge through the Huns in a solid arrow to shatter the ring of Albatross around the Sopwiths and allow their countrymen to escape.

They were almost above the fight now. The Germans were tripping over each other in their haste to complete the massacre. A Sopwith shuddered under a dual attack. The top wing peeled from its struts and fluttered away. The lower wing folded and plunged earthwards. *And then there were six green bottles left sitting on the wall...* twelve men to save.

A machine gun stuttered on his left. Lance looked back at Taggart, who jabbed his finger to the right. Budd had banked hard and was heading away from the fight. Lance grunted in shock. As he watched, Newby peeled off to follow. They were running away!

Lance had never imagined such a scenario. It was unheard of—RFC pilots deserting their leader in the face of the enemy. He shifted in his seat in disbelief, muscles twitching, icy cold shivers running over his body. Fearful, he checked his left again, half expecting to find no-one there. But Taggart's SE5 had tucked behind him, thank God. The Scotsman gazed at Lance through the whirling propeller and gave an ironic salute. A rush of admiration surged through Lance.

Then he looked at the sheer number of the Huns and licked his dry lips. Two SE5s and six Sopwiths matched against twenty-five German fighters, probably all from Richthofen's Circus—the cream of the German air force. Lance would not, could not, flee. But neither could he see a way to make this attack more than a suicidal gesture. No good choices left, the nightmare of a hunter. This was a futile charge into oblivion.

Fury boiled inside him. Damn the Fates for mocking him with this dilemma. Almost alone in the RFC, he'd preached against the RFC's "Charge of the Light Brigade" mentality and noble but useless deaths. Yet faced with the choice of fleeing while others died, he too preferred death to living with the corrosive self-doubt of cowardice

He'd always known it would end one day. A final fight. But he'd never thought his final act would be suicidal charge through a ragged sky into the massed ranks of the enemy. Who'd have thought it? Lance Fitch, a hero of lost causes.

He rubbed his gloves along his thighs and rolled his shoulders like a boxer stepping into the ring. He'd take a lot of the bastards with him across the big divide. *But, please God, give me a bullet through the heart. No flames.*

He slid out from the final cloud, placing the weak sun behind them. Below, the brightly coloured Huns darted among the drab Sopwiths in a silent ballet of death. Lance took a deep breath. He looked over at Taggart, whose expressionless goggles gazed back. Lance's guts spasmed and his left knee jerked continuously.

Before his nerves could unman him any further, Lance half-rolled into a slashing dive. As his plane plunged like a stooping hawk, the engine roar rose to a banshee howl and the wind shrieked through the bracing wires. The wild charge sent battle lust surging through his veins. *Bugger the odds, just kill the bastards!*

His plane juddered as his speedometer needle jammed off the dial. Aiming was impossible at such speed. Lance gave the top Hun formation a cursory squirt of tracers as he plunged past, just to panic them. A startled Albatross swerved away from Lance's tracers and smashed into a Pfalz, blossoming into a ball of fire. *Bonus!*

The SE5s hurtled onwards to the Albatross hacking at the tattered Sopwith survivors.

Guns hammering, Lance charged into the Huns, who scattered like a shoal of pilchards from a great white shark. A yellow Albatross broke apart under Lance's guns. An Albatross banked away from Taggart's tracers but exposed his belly to the Sopwith's gunners. They sawed off the Hun's left wings and the plane flipped wildly as it tore apart.

Lance and Taggart shattered the ring of attackers and the Sopwith crews waved their thanks as they fled through the gaps. Lance pulled the stick back and the SE5 soared upwards. His stomach heaved and the wings creaked as he strained to regain height.

Three Albatross dived from head on. The lead Hun opened fire, twin Spandau flickering. Lance snarled and kicked the rudder bar to hose all three approaching planes. He couldn't shoot accurately like this, but he would sure as hell give them a fright.

Splinters flew from his centre strut. He ducked as the red underside of the nearest Hun flashed over him. Elated, he saw his bullets stitch fuselage and then he was soaring high with his momentum.

But now the surprise at the SE5's sudden ambush was over. The Germans settled to hunt down the interlopers. Guns sounded close behind him, and he skidded right, then left. He ducked as a bullet whined off the gun mount in front of him, leaving a smear of silver. Christ! These Huns were good.

Only the SE5's speed was keeping them alive—for the moment. Albatross blocked them from above; Pfalz to the west cut them off from home. The Huns had them boxed.

Tracers flashed past. Close enough to sniff. His speedometer exploded and a glass fragment slashed his cheek. The shatterproof windscreen starred opaque. *Bank harder, for Chrissakes! Don't you want to live?* The horizon wheeled horizontal, the world losing its axis. His heart hammered. *Black painted bastard in front! Kill him! Missed.*

Something struck his right heel, a hammer blow. Burning pain. Wetness in his boot. Tearing sounds—a line of holes at the edge of the cockpit, leather coaming ripped ragged. *Break, you silly sod!*

More bullets thwacked into his fuselage. Lance cringed. Where the hell was that coming from? He glanced behind; nobody was in range. *There!* A red Albatross was beneath him, standing on his prop. *Heck of a shot!*

A purple and green Pfalz crossed his bows. He let fly on reflex. It jerked into a stall and fell away.

A shadow out of the corner of his eye. He yanked the SE5 into a steep turn towards it, ready to fire. *Whoa! It's Taggart!*

Something plucked his sleeve at his wrist. A red-hot iron burned across his shoulder blades. The airframe juddered; he was about to stall. Feet and hands quick to control. More bullets laced his fuselage. *Turn into the bastard!*

Tracers smoked past his eyes. Sweat stung his eyes. His shoulder burned and blood trickled down his shirt.

Turn! Rudder! Fire—TURN! Right rudder...straighten. Fire! Missed the bastard. An Albatross screamed past, undercarriage raking feet above his head.

127

The German guns hammered incessantly. Lance's arms ached as he wrenched into yet another turn. Someone had tied lead weights to his feet and they no longer danced on the rudder bar. Sluggish now, the SE5 wallowed. A white Albatross blocked left, a mottled Pfalz attacked from his right. Another Albatross behind. Bullets shredded fabric off his upper wing; wooden spars showed like ribs. *Christ, he's good! Can't shake him. This is it...*

Taggart plummeted like an avenging angel on the red Albatross, which broke off its attack on Lance to face the new threat. It feinted left, and as Taggart dived past, the pilot turned smoothly and riddled the SE5 prop to tail. The SE5 ripped apart. A small body rotated as it fell.

An image flashed in Lance's mind—Taggart's wife and bairns smiling into the camera.

A berserker's blood lust rampaged through him, and he bellowed an inchoate howl of revenge into the slipstream. His enemies' death became his sole focus, living now an irrelevancy. Planes swirled around him, thick as leaves in an autumn storm.

His eyes, stinging with sweat, turned onto the nearest Hun. *Who's next? I'll ram the bugger. Let us die together, you and I...*

~

Rod Andrews seethed. *Me, a bloody bomber pilot?*

What was the point of creating an elite anti-Richthofen unit, equipping it with the latest fighter planes, cherry-picking the finest fighter pilots, and then sending them on a bombing mission? Only those Pommie idiots in HQ could come up with such a moronic plan.

Just because the Bristols were two-seaters was no reason to treat them as bombers. The plane was designed as a fighter and the pilots were trained as fighter pilots. When Rod found out which drongo in HQ was responsible, he would give him a piece of his mind.

Rod led his squadron eastwards, climbing sluggishly up to ten thousand feet through the scattered clouds. His plane handled like a pig with four Mills bombs clustered under its wings. He had total confidence that he and his men would miss their target, a railway yard near Courtrai. Train yards were big buggers but none of Bristol pilots had ever dropped a bomb—due to the short notice and bad weather, they hadn't managed a single practice run.

Worse still, Thommo's Camels were the official fighter escort, twelve of 'em stacked above the Bristols. The Bristol crews had not appreciated the resulting mockery from the wing's Camel pilots. Elliot Springs had sidled up to Rod, put a hand on his shoulder, and said with deep insincerity, "I feel your pain, *mon frère*," before wandering off, giggling. It was bloody humiliating, fighter aircraft like Bristols being "escorted" by slower planes.

Rod frowned and peered through the disc of his propeller. There seemed to be black dots all over his windscreen. He swore at his fitter's laziness. Why couldn't the man clean his windshield properly? But the dots were moving. He stuck his head out the side, squinting through his goggles against the slipstream. Still lots of dots. Too many to be planes, surely. But what else could they be?

He grinned mirthlessly. This was just the excuse he needed. Rod checked below to confirm that they had reached the German lines, then signalled to his squadron to drop their bombs. It wasn't exactly precision bombing, but what the hell, they were dropping bombs on Germans. He hoped.

Either way, he wasn't about to carry Mills bombs into a dogfight and the Huns wouldn't ring HQ and complain that the railway yard hadn't been bombed.

He waited until the last Mills bombs had disappeared, then turned his squadron towards the swarm of planes. He opened the throttle to maximum and his Rolls Royce Falcon engine bellowed its approval. The Camels followed, panting in the Bristols' wake like short-legged beagles after hunting hounds.

His puzzlement grew as they flew closer. There were none of the swirling loose patterns that characterised massive dogfights. Yet neither were there the neat formations and staggered levels of a large enemy formation. Was this a trap? Were the Huns impersonating a dogfight to lure them in? If so, they were doing a damn poor job. In Rod's experience when the Huns laid a trap, they were fiendishly clever about it. So, what the flippin' heck was going on?

A dot flared bright like a struck match, then fell leaving a smudge of dark smoke. Rod Andrews grimaced. *Sure as hell, that's a dogfight!*

The picture became clearer as they approached. Five Sopwith 1½ Strutters sliding away from the main gaggle of planes, heading east without pursuit. His frown deepened. Why would the Huns let easy prey escape?

Drawing closer still, he saw the reason. A single SE5 was rampaging through the Huns like a dingo through a flock of sheep. Beyond question the British pilot was unhinged. Whenever a Hun attacked the SE5, it turned to ram the attacker. The Hun planes clustered around the madman, wheeling and plunging in chaos as they dodged his suicidal charges, and each other, while trying to shoot him down. White tracer trails criss-crossed the sky but always the SE5 emerged to rampage onwards.

"Some nutter has declared war on the whole German air force," Rod muttered. "Let's see if we can't even the odds." A few kills would remind the wombats in HQ that 222 Squadron was a fighter outfit.

~

Perched above the swirling chaos of the dogfight, Hans Schmettow watched white tracer-smoke lace the sky as JG1 hunted the lone SE5.

When Richthofen had shot down his wingman, the Britisher went berserk. Hans had never seen such a suicidal display of ferocity and skill. If anyone tried to chase the remaining Sopwith two-seaters, the SE5 pursued with the clear intent to ram. The result was airborne anarchy—twenty matadors tripping over each other as they attempted to stab the rampaging bull at the same time.

Hans watched as Richthofen tried sneaking up on the SE5, but every attempt ended with him swerving away from a collision with a comrade. Boelke, Richthofen's predecessor as prince of the *Luftstreitkräfte,* had died when he collided with a fellow pilot as they both chased the same plane. Richthofen was one of Boelke's wingmen that day, and he often lectured his pilots not to repeat his mentor's mistake. Not that any of them seemed to recall the warnings today.

No surprise then when Richthofen climbed above the mayhem to keep an eye out for Allied fighters. Hans followed. The sheer number of German planes concentrated in one place would soon attract British attention like flies to a shithouse. If all the Germans focused on one plane, they could easily be ambushed.

Below Hans, Kurt Wolff's red and green Albatross weaved onto the SE5's tail. The British plane had absorbed plenty of punishment and trailed a thin banner of grey smoke. Its reactions had slowed. *He's punch-drunk. Now will be the end.* The baby assassin, second only to Manfred Richthofen in his number of kills, would be too good for the tiring Englishman.

Hans searched the sky. In the distance, more aircraft were already heading this way. It looked like a mixture of big-winged Bristols and some stumpy Camels.

He looked back to see if Wolff had finished the Englishman, and blinked. Somehow the Tommy had reversed their roles and glued himself fifty feet behind Wolff, firing in short bursts. The Albatross jerked. Hans held his breath, but a Pfalz slid into the attack and hammered the Englishman off Wolff's tail. Wolff turned gingerly for home, his plane wobbling.

The madman shook the Pfalz off by diving straight at a nearest mass of Germans on a suicidal collision course. The Pfalz wisely did not follow. On his way through the scattering German formation, the Tommy put a burst into an Albatross, which rolled over and spun earthwards.

It was ridiculous, but the sole Britisher was terrifying JG1 with his madness. Time to leave before the other enemy planes arrived. Hans knew Richthofen's mantra. God knows he said it often enough: "If enemy fighters, without bombs or cameras, want to fill empty sky, that is no concern of the German air force. Let them do it." For sure, when they got back to the airfield, Richthofen would scold his pilots over their loss of discipline and allowing one enemy plane to make fools of them. Hans pulled a face. More tiresome lectures from the professor.

Sure enough, a flare soared from Richthofen's Albatross as he signalled to his commanders to gather their flock and start eastwards before the Allied planes reached them. Richthofen spiralled down to usher Wolff's crippled plane home, giving the damaged Albatross leeway as it weaved drunkenly.

~

Sheer exhaustion had thinned Lance's red mist. A berserker's battle frenzy was a forest fire—the fiercer the flames, the shorter the burn. The Huns would get him soon, but he would take a few more with him. *Shadow!* He flung his plane into a turn towards it and fired, but his ammunition belt had run dry.

This was the end. He'd fought for a thousand years, and he was spent.

He picked another aircraft and pursued it, determined to ram this one. Foggily he wondered why the Albatross looked like a Bristol. The plane ahead jinked this way and that to escape but Lance inexorably closed the gap. *You and me, we go to Hell together!* The swirling disc of his prop edged ever closer to the tail plane ahead.

He jerked as a red flare exploded in front of him. Huge spots danced in Lance's vision. He shook his head. His mind seemed as clouded as his eyesight, as though he was fighting his way up through layers of deep sleep. He blinked as his eyesight returned, albeit blurry. Camels and Bristols surrounded him but kept a wary distance. Where the hell did they come from? Where were the Huns?

Another flare arced towards him, but this time green and farther away He followed the flare to its source and saw a Bristol with Rod Andrews's markings, a yellow kangaroo on the fuselage. The Bristol cautiously edged closer.

"Okay?" the Australian signalled.

Lance could barely lift his arm to wave. Rod stabbed a finger towards the Allied lines. Lance nodded. *What's going on? Why are they babysitting me?*

The exhaustion, physical and mental, crushed him. His brain had turned to mush, and his arms and legs to lead weights. His mouth was full of ash. Sodden with weariness, he slumped in the cockpit.

Then from deep inside a voice sang, "I'm alive!" His acceptance of his imminent death had been so complete he found it hard to believe that he was still part of this world. He mouthed, "I am alive," testing each syllable. As he spoke the words, their reality seeped into him.

God, it felt good.

Lance banked for home, and as he did so the memories hit him. *I killed Taggart by leading him into that fight. He saved my life and lost his. And the cowards ran. No doubt they are in the Mess already while Taggart is a broken body in the mud.*

The shell-shock relapse struck, a roaring white chaos tumbling inside his head, powerful as ocean breakers in a winter storm. His body shook as he fought to anchor his mind against the raging surf's surge. He jammed his eyes shut to keep the madness away, so hard the inside of his eyelids showed the colour of blood. *Not again! Never again!*

He clutched his sanity to him with sinews of hate while the great white waves roiled inside him. For an eternity he struggled, grunting and twitching. Finally, the roar relented, became a whisper as he slid into calmer waters. He opened his eyes. Reality surrounded him: a thundering engine, wind whipping his cheeks through his bullet-starred windshield, a ragged sky—never more beautiful—and an escort of Bristols.

Nothing remained from the near breakdown except the diamond-hard purity of his hate. *I will see justice done. For Taggart, for his wife and bairns.*

~

Hans slid into his position behind Richthofen as *Jasta* 11 escorted Wolff's Albatross homewards. Wolff must be wounded, as his plane was wobbling all over the sky. Hans chortled with glee. If Wolff was incapacitated, then Richthofen might promote Hans to be his permanent wingman, with kills galore guaranteed.

Hans did not pretend to understand the bond between the two men. Some said it was because Wolff was the living embodiment of the Richthofen's genius at spotting and nurturing talent. Reputedly, Wolff had crashed and killed his instructor on his first flight. Somehow, he had passed the tests to join *Jasta* 11. He'd scored zero kills for four months while Richthofen and the other pilots built the *Jasta* into the preeminent killing machine. Richthofen ruthlessly fired other kill-less pilots, but not Kurt Wolff. Then something clicked for Wolff, and he became a killing fiend, rising to one of Germany's premier aces in a few short months.

And I have more kills at this stage than Wolff ever did. Yet Richthofen still treats me like shit that won't leave his boots. If Wolff disappears, maybe I'll become the new Wunderkind. The longing that surged through Hans at that thought shocked him. He was less surprised by the accompanying intense ill will for Wolff. Not that Hans had anything against Wolff. He was one of the few pilots who had not shown disdain for Hans, but Hans needed more kills for his Blue Max, and he'd get them faster if Wolff wasn't around.

Jasta tittle-tattle said Kurt Wolff had been raised in a Prussian orphanage, and now in his early twenties he still looked like he belonged in one. His cherubic baby face with its big ears, his waif physique, and his extreme shyness all contributed to his nickname—*die zarte Blume* or "Delicate Flower." The juvenile idiot insisted on flying in an oversized leather flying coat with a woollen nightcap that increased the impression of a kindergarten runaway.

Yet that infant wore a Blue Max dangling around his throat, Germany's highest decoration. During Bloody April alone, the Delicate Flower shot down twenty-three Allied planes, the single largest haul of kills in the *Luftstreitkräfte* that month. That month he eclipsed both the Richthofen brothers, and the fast-rising Werner Voss. As an ace, Wolff was right up there with the best of them. Hans smirked. *Not as good as the mad Englishman, though!*

Even through the goggles and coat, Hans could see Wolff's hunched shoulders and pain-twisted face. The youngster tried to smile at Richthofen as he waved his left hand, which was wrapped in his silly nightcap, now soaked scarlet with blood. The boy winced as the slipstream tore at the wounded hand, and he hastily retracted it inside the cockpit. *A hand wound, that's not so bad. Shame. Not worth a fuss, although I'm sure Richthofen will make one over his favourite.*

Hans stewed on that thought until they arrived at Marcke Airfield, *Jasta* 10's base. Wolff flew with *Jasta* 11 and his airfield lay just across the Courtrai railway line at Marckebeeke, but Wolff couldn't wait. His red and green Albatross sank into its final approach, but when he flared out to land, the plane floated and floated onwards. *He's still got some power on. He can't handle the throttle and the stick at the same time with that hand...*

The Albatross throttle lever was small and on the left side of the joystick. Wolff would be flying with his right hand and struggling to manage the lever with his wounded left. *With that fucking stupid nightcap wrapped round his hand, no wonder! He's going to land too far down the strip. Here comes a doozy of a crash!* Hans felt his face split into a gleeful grin.

At last the wheels touched. Too late. Hans licked his lips as the landing Albatross rocketed towards the railway lines. Suddenly the Mercedes engine bellowed into life again as Wolff tried to lift his Albatross over the twin rails.

And failed.

"Gesundheit!" Hans murmured, without meaning it. The railway lines sheared off Wolff's wheels and crumpled the undercarriage. The heavy nose pitched into the earth, and the Albatross somersaulted onto its back. It careered across the grass upside down, gouging a muddy gash into the turf and strewing wreckage behind it. Eventually it ploughed into a fence and slammed to a halt. *That is the Delicate Flower plucked. Such a shame.*

Richthofen slammed his plane down as close to the crash as he could, jumped out, and ran towards the wreck. Hans followed more sedately. By the time he reached the scene, the ground crew had pulled Wolff out of the cockpit. But instead of the corpse Hans expected, the dazed pilot was sitting cross-legged in the middle of a crowd. How the hell did he survive that crash in one piece? The smell of spilt benzene hung heavy in the air and the hot engine metal ticked, yet no fire. Hans shook his head in disbelief. Un-bloody-believable.

Richthofen knelt beside his friend. "Alright, Kurt?"

The boyish face looked up, mouth grimacing. He was clutching his left hand in pain. "That mad bastard shot me through the wrist. Hurts like hell but I'll live. But talk about lucky—look!" Richthofen's protégé nodded at his leather helmet on the ground. It had a shredded hole torn in it, right in the middle. While the plane was upside down, the top of Wolff's head had dragged along the earth. Miraculously, only a long shallow graze showed on his scalp.

Hans turned and trudged away, his boots too heavy and his coat too hot. If the Delicate Flower were five millimetres taller, he would have scalped himself. Ten millimetres and he would have snapped his neck. Never had the margins of destiny seemed so fine. *God's turds! Why does nothing ever turn out the way I want?*

11
With Noble Birth

Same day, 24 July 1917.
Bailleul Airfield.

100 Wing's fire engine clanged its alarm bell.

Sergeant majors never compromise their dignity by running, but Smythe strode out of the hangars at Rifle Regiment double time. He took a sharp breath as an SE5 whistled over the hedgerow, trailing fabric, wires, and a thick banner of grey smoke. The fire engine clattered into action and headed for the landing strip, ready for a disaster.

But the damaged plane touched down as lightly as thistle-down. Smythe nodded his approval. Watch enough landings and you learn everything about a pilot. Only a gifted few made the transition from sky to earth seem natural and no-one made landings look as effortless as Major Fitch.

The SE5 taxied to its home in front of A Flight hangar and the sergeant major. The engine cut and the propeller blurred and clunked to a standstill. Usually, Major Fitch leapt from the cockpit. This time he didn't move.

Smythe grabbed a stepladder and strode forward. Major Fitch sat motionless with his goggles perched on his head. Gunpowder painted his face black, except where his goggles had covered his eyes. A fragment of glass stuck from one cheek and underneath ran a long streak of dried blood.

"Sir! Sir! Are you wounded?" There was no answer, so

Smythe shook the major's shoulder.

"Huh?" Fitch's glazed eyes returned to this world and peered at the sergeant major.

Knowing the post-flight deafness, Smythe bellowed into the major's ear. "Are you wounded, sir?"

"Not sure. Help me out, Smythe."

Smythe's huge arms babied the pilot from the cockpit, supported him to the ground, and held him as he swayed. Digby produced a canvas chair, and Smythe eased Fitch into it. The pilot peeled his leather helmet from his sodden hair, accepted a towel from Digby and wiped the grime, sweat, and blood off his face. He winced at the glass sliver, pulled it out, and tossed it away. Drops of blood trickled down his cheek. His hands shook, and he hid them under the towel. Then he stared into the distance for a while, sucking in deep breaths.

Smythe, who over the past two years had seen many pilots return with torn bodies and discombobulated minds, guarded the pilot like a large St. Bernard dog. He could read the tale of what had transpired in the air from the state of the pilot and the plane when they landed. He assessed Lance—pale, with a thin shallow gash down one cheek, a single bullet hole through his sleeve, a long bloody tear across the back of his flying jacket, the blank gaze and shaking hands. This was a man returning to this world having made a journey somewhere beyond most men's ken.

Then Smythe turned his inventory on the plane—the starred hole in the windscreen, a leather cockpit coaming that looked like an angry bear had mauled it, the speedometer a tangled mess. Silver smears ran along a twisted gun mounting and an aileron hung on a single hinge. Must have been one hell of a scrap.

Major Fitch seldom returned with his plane riddled with bullets. And if he did, he remained self-possessed, no matter how severe others thought the fight. Yes, he was sick at every flamer but that was a minor foible, and the ground crews warmed to him for this sign of human weakness.

"Sergeant Major." Fitch's voice roused Smythe from his reverie.

"Sir!"

"Please ask lieutenants Budd and Newby to join me. Keep others away, but you stay here with us."

"Sir."

When Smythe returned five minutes later with the two officers in tow, Major Fitch had peeled off his coat and was examining one of his flying boots, where the heel had been shot off. Dark sweat stains pooled under the armpits and across the shoulders of the major's khaki shirt. A single streak of red slashed diagonally across his back where the shirt had been sliced as if by a knife.

Smythe heard the sharp intake of breath from Newby as he saw the state of the major and the plane.

"So glad you made it, sir! Hell of a show!" Budd said as the pair stopped in front of Fitch. The major looked at them, eyes hard and bright.

"Lieutenant Budd. Why did you turn back before we attacked the enemy?"

"My guns, sir. Jammed."

"You tried to clear them before returning?"

"Yes, sir. I wanted to stay and help you." Budd's deep voice resonated with regret and sincerity. "But I remembered that you always teach us to return home when our guns jam rather than play the hero."

"Yes...I'd hate you to play the hero. One last chance—you swear your guns jammed. Both guns?" The major stared at him with those gleaming tawny eyes, the left one weeping a few slow tears. Smythe winced. He knew from experience that such tears from the major's damaged eye came like lava flows, a warning just before the volcano blew. Best to be far away when that happened.

Budd didn't seem worried. "Yes, sir! On my oath as an officer and a gentleman." His voice was confident and strong.

"Very well. Lieutenant Newby?"

Newby was pale, almost as pale as the major. "Sir, I was scared witless. I admit I was in one hell of a funk, but I only turned back when my engine overheated badly. It started running rough when we tangled with the two-seater and got worse and worse."

"Mmm. Sergeant Major. I want Lieutenant Budd's guns out here on a trestle. Get them yourself, make sure that no-one alters them or has fiddled with them since he landed. Check the situation on Lieutenant Newby's engine and report back."

"Sah!" Smythe saluted and strode off again. He bristled with outrage at the thought his ground crews could have jeopardised the major with their carelessness. Gun jams and engine trouble were not totally avoidable, but often they resulted from sloppy work by the ground crew.

When he returned five minutes later, he knew his weathered face was red with suppressed fury. He directed two ground staff to set up the Vickers and the Lewis gun on a trestle, facing the trees at the end of the aerodrome. He then waved his men away.

"Sah! Lieutenant Budd reported multiple jams when he landed but the armourers have not yet found a defect in either gun." Smythe took a deep breath. "Lieutenant Newby's engine has a split oil line. It overheated, the metal has distorted, and the mechanics will need to put in a complete replacement."

Smythe heard Newby exhale in relief, but the sergeant major kept his eyes on Fitch.

"Thank you, Sergeant Major. Lieutenant Newby, we were all scared going into that scrap. There is no shame in that. Remember it is what you do that counts, not what you feel. Go now."

"Thank you, sir. And sir...I am sorry about Captain Taggart."

"Go!" The youngster saluted and scampered away like a whipped puppy. "Sergeant Major," Fitch said in a hoarse voice. "Beg Wing Commander Wolsey's pardon and ask him to join us as a matter of urgency."

Budd started at the mention of the wing commander. "Why bother Uncle Arthur?" he asked.

Lance waved a hand at Smythe to carry out the request. When Smythe returned, Major Fitch was striding around in a circle behind Budd, who was standing at attention.

Wing Commander Wolsey frowned. "Lance, what is happening? You are bleeding. Are you alright?"

The major responded formally. "Sir, I wish you to hear and bear witness to the following events."

The wing commander winced at the formal tone. "Is it to do with Lieutenant Budd's behaviour? And if so, is it appropriate for the sergeant major to be here?"

"Yes, sir. It is to do with events around Lieutenant Budd's conduct today. And he has made assertions that make the sergeant major's presence relevant."

"Very well, Major Fitch. Proceed." Wing Commander Wolsey stood straight as a ramrod and placed his hands behind his back.

Major Fitch spoke in a monotone. "Today I took A Flight to escort home a Squadron of Sopwith 1½ Strutters. When we found them, they were under attack from the Circus. When I turned to rescue the Sopwiths, lieutenants Budd and Newby left the formation and returned home."

Smythe saw the wing commander stare at Budd in astonishment, but he said nothing as Major Fitch continued.

"Captain Taggart was shot down and I was rescued by 222 and 333 squadrons. On my return, I asked both lieutenants to explain their actions. Lieutenant Newby said his engine had overheated, and he barely made it home. The sergeant major checked and confirmed this story. I have dismissed Newby and hold him blameless in this case. Lieutenant Budd reported that his machine guns jammed but the armourers have not found a reason."

"Both guns, belt and drum fed?" the wing commander asked, frowning at Budd.

Two red spots burned on Budd's cheeks, but he replied firmly enough. "I swear as an officer and a gentleman that both guns jammed, but not at the same time. The Lewis gun jammed during my first attack on the Rumpler I shot down, and the Vickers on my final attack. Fortunately, the Hun was on fire by then. I stayed with the flight while I tried to clear the jams. When I realised I could not solve the problem, I followed Major Fitch's standing orders to return home if guns jam. I would like to add that the major and Captain Taggart attacked about forty German aircraft to rescue the Sopwiths. They deserve the very highest recommendation for bravery for their selfless actions." Budd's deep sonorous voice sounded so wise it was a weapon of truth.

The wing commander opened his mouth to say something, but Major Fitch spoke first. "I would like Sergeant Major Smythe to examine the guns in front of you, sir,"

"Uncle," Budd protested, "I have sworn as an officer and a gentleman that they jammed. That should be sufficient."

Wing Commander Wolsey frowned. "In normal circumstances, it would be. Major Fitch, do I understand you are refusing to take the oath of an officer of this wing?"

"Yes."

The wing commander rubbed his nose. "That is unusual."

"Lieutenant Budd is an unusual officer," Major Fitch said.

"Dammit, Uncle! That's intolerable. I may only be a junior officer, but I am a Wolsey. This man is impugning the family honour. It would have meant pistols at dawn not so long ago."

"That would be satisfactory," the major said with relish.

Budd flushed. His mouth opened and closed like a goldfish's.

"If I'm accusing him of being a liar and a coward," the major said, "why would I take his word on anything? I'm only a Blackie colonial but I thought we had passed the days when it was assumed that the nobility could not tell a lie?"

The wing commander sighed. "We may be past those days, Lance, but I have to say it is a passing that I regret. I do not wish to impugn an officer's word lightly."

"Lightly?" the major whispered. Tears rolled down his left cheek and his lips were a bloodless thin line. "Taggart is dead because he did his duty, and this cowardly cur is alive because he ran away from the enemy."

"Uncle," Budd said, "Major Fitch is distraught at the loss of his friend. It is understandable, but perhaps you should allow him to rest until he regains his senses."

"Shut up, both of you!" Wing Commander Wolsey barked.

Smythe saw a shudder ripple through Major Fitch as he fought to regain his self-control. The major took a deep breath. "Very well. Let's try a different way." He strode over to the Lewis gun on the trestle table and swivelled it until the blank eye of the muzzle faced Budd. "No need for anyone to inspect the weapon. We can check if this gun is jammed by pulling the trigger."

"I don't think—" the wing commander started, but the major's trigger finger was already whitening.

"No!" Budd cried as he flung himself to the side. The muzzle of the Lewis gun tracked him, but no shot followed.

Budd regained his composure. "Uncle. Major Fitch. Guns can jam and unjam. It would be a shame to cut me off in the prime of life—" he smiled winningly— "and have to tell Mother that you killed me by mistake because of a miscreant bullet."

"Guns don't jam without reason. Equally they don't unjam without reason." The major's trigger finger tightened again.

The wing commander moved forward to intervene. Budd grabbed him and used him as a shield against the Lewis gun. "Stop him, Uncle!" The shout of desperation scattered the crows in the trees. "He's mad. He'll kill us both!"

Smythe stood frozen, unable to believe the madhouse. These were his commanding officers for God's sake!

The major dropped the Lewis gun and strode towards Budd, who let go of his human shield and ran. The major was on him in an instant. Budd swung wildly. Major Fitch brushed past the flailing arms and punched the lieutenant in the gut. Budd collapsed into a wheezing heap, and the major kicked his backside. "Confess, you gutless coward."

Budd curled in a foetus position, arms protecting his head. The major kept kicking him.

"Sergeant Major, stop him!" Arthur ordered.

Smythe broke the spell that had held him immobile, and bear-hugged Major Fitch from behind, holding him off the ground as the major wildly kicked at the air. There were advantages to being over six feet and built like a brick shithouse.

Budd uncurled to sneer at Major Fitch. "So I'm a coward. And you have proved it. Congratulations. But I am alive, and where is your noble Taggart? He's dead 'cos you led him there against forty Huns." Budd staggered to his feet and wiped blood from his lip. "You killed him, Fitch. I will sleep like a baby tonight, but you, you honourable sap, you will twist and turn while thinking of Taggart."

The major tried to hurl himself at Budd, but Smythe held him as he cursed.

"Oh yes, Fitch," Budd taunted, wiping his mouth with the back of his hand. "Nothing bad will happen to me. Dear old Uncle can't afford the family disgrace. Neither can the government." Budd's voice lifted in parody, "'We can't afford to have the plebs thinking the aristos are not cutting the mustard, eh what!'

"I'm alive and Taggart is dead, and I won't even be disgraced. Shame there is no justice in the world. Oh wait, maybe there is. You won't be able to fuck Mummy anymore. Ah!

Uncle, dear Uncle...I see from your face that you didn't know your wonderful Major Fitch is fucking my Mummy. Surprise, huh?"

Smythe wished he'd heard none of this. It was too much insight into a murky world. He liked his world full of simple truths and simple trusts. Major Fitch had stopped struggling and Smythe released him.

Wing Commander Wolsey turned to his nephew. "Is nothing sacred to you?"

Budd was brushing dirt from his uniform. "Sacred? Yes, my life for starters."

"Your life is worthless!" Major Fitch snarled.

Budd turned to him. "You win the point, but I will win the game. Poor sap, you don't even know the rules. The ones where the great and the good decide what will happen in England. Didn't Mumsy tell you the Exenrude motto? *'Generositate nil sister contra,'* or for uneducated colonials, 'With noble birth nothing shall stand against me.'"

Major Fitch glowered at him blank-faced for a second, then dropped his right hand to his flying boot, drawing a Webley revolver. Budd gaped—from a yard away the muzzle must have looked as big as a cannon. But the wing commander placed his hand on top of Major Fitch's. He made no move to press the pistol away. The major ignored the hand and cocked the revolver. "Arthur, move aside. I can't let this snake live while Taggart is dead."

"I understand, Lance, but his life is not worth yours. Dozens of men are watching us right now. Kill him and whatever the rights and wrongs, you will stand trial for murder."

"It is my debt to Taggart." The major pulled the trigger. The firing hammer dropped with soggy thunk. Budd's legs folded like a new-born calf's, and he slumped to the ground, white-faced and trembling. Major Fitch looked down to see why the revolver had not fired. The firing pin had snapped hard on the webbing between the wing commander's thumb and forefinger, and blood welled down his hand. He did not flinch, just kept his hand there. Smythe stepped forward but the wing commander waved him away with his other hand.

"You want to save this worthless trash?" Major Fitch asked, incredulous.

"I want to save you, my friend and Britain's most successful living ace. That seems to me to be worth saving. A court martial will look after Budd. Have faith in the process. The Army doesn't like cowards and liars any more than you do."

The major snorted as he searched Lord Wolsey's face. "You won't protect him?"

"I swear that I will not protect him in any way. Whatever happens in a court martial, even a death sentence, I will not aid him."

They all ignored the choking noises from Budd.

"As an officer and a gentleman?" Fitch's voice rang with the steely conviction of an executioner.

The wing commander's eyes remained steady. "As your friend."

Major Fitch's eyelids flickered, and he frowned. Long seconds passed. The angry buzz of a Camel rotary engine started in the distance. Smythe held his breath. A nerve in Major Fitch's cheek ticked repeatedly. A crack of thunder made Smythe jump, and the first raindrops hit him on the face.

"Damn you, Arthur, you always find the words." Irritation thickened the major's voice. He pulled back the hammer, allowed the wing commander to pull his hand away, uncocked the weapon, and slid it into his boot again. "I don't need oaths. You looked me in the eye, and that's good enough for me."

He strode off and Smythe inhaled a deep breath. Drizzle slanted across the airfield, the advance guard of a rain squall that set tent flaps snapping.

The wing commander sucked the bleeding webbing of his

thumb hand and scowled at his nephew with deep contempt. "I never thought you amounted to much, but I never dreamed you would fall so low. Sergeant Major, escort Lieutenant Budd to his quarters pending his departure to England for a court martial for cowardice in the face of the enemy."

"Sah!" Smythe saluted. He wished he hadn't been part of today's events. In thirty years in the British Army, he'd seen acts of cowardice, some in the colonies against hordes of charging natives, some in Belgium against the massed machine guns of Mons. He understood the fear, and in some cases he had hushed up the incidents to give a man another chance. But in every case Smythe had seen, hidden or court-martialled, the man involved had shown shame and remorse. Until today. Smythe slitted his eyes against the driving rain and looked down at the lieutenant, still snivelling in the dust that was rapidly turning into mud. The man was a disgrace to the uniform.

Smythe schooled his features into an impassive mask. "Sir, when you are ready."

~

Three days later - 27 July 1917.
Ypres Sector, Bailleul Airfield.

Clayton hunted for Lance. The time had come for some strong medicine. Medicine that would be as bitter for Clayton to give as for Lance to swallow.

In the dark of a moonless night, he tripped over a guy rope outside Lance's tent and swore. He stuck his nose into the tent, but Lance wasn't in his quarters either.

It had been three days since Taggart died. Military police had marched Budd away to England for court martial, and Lance had submitted a letter of resignation from squadron commander of 111 Squadron. Arthur tore it up.

Clayton had not seen Fitch in the Mess during all that time. Lance flew solo patrols and then disappeared until the next one. Crowe had taken over de facto leadership of the squadron while refusing Lance's request to do so officially. Arthur, Clayton, and the men of 111 Squadron watched with concern and prayed the storm would pass.

Clayton found his friend at the far end of a dark hangar, a pool of dirty yellow from a hurricane lamp the only light in the cavernous space. Lance sat on a battered wooden stool in front of three tin buckets, checking ammunition with a bullet clamp. A squadron of moths circled the hissing hurricane lamp beside him. Occasionally one of the insects would fly too close to the lamp and perish with a flare of flame and a pungent burning smell.

Clayton pulled up another stool. Lance did not even look up as he pushed a bullet into the clamp. It fitted, and the pilot threw the bullet into the "good" bucket and selected another bullet to test. A slight distortion in the metal jacket, imperceptible to the naked eye, caused the next bullet to bulge and the clamp rejected it. Lance threw it into the "bad" bucket with a grunt of dissatisfaction. The originating factory and the local ground crew would have done this check already. But the sometimes-fatal fact was that everyone found it a mind-bogglingly boring task, and too many bad bullets made it into the pilots' machine guns. A careful pilot checked his own—no-one had as big a stake in the task as the man taking those bullets into battle. Clayton picked up another clamp and joined his friend sorting the ammunition. They worked without speaking for a while.

Lance broke the silence, speaking in a monotone, as he continued to test the bullets. "You know what I like about weapons? The certainty of the steel in your hands—the hard and definite shapes, the predictable way the parts assemble, the comfort of their simplicity. You don't have to think when you work with them. Treat a weapon right, clean it, oil it, care for it, and it will look after you. You can rely on it to do what it is supposed to do. No more, no less."

Clayton sighed. "Ah my friend, you are not the first to compare humans adversely to other things. And you will find no greater cynic about human nature than I. But the Clayton acid tests are these: can you snuggle up to this other thing like you can a woman and feel the same delicious desire to lose yourself deep in her depths? Or can it make you belly laugh aloud like a good friend? Or can it write prose and poetry that makes you weep with pity or cry with joy? If the answer to any of these is no, then—despite all the shams and brutalities of humanity—I must vote for it over anything else."

Clayton shuffled his bottom like a chicken laying an egg, trying to get comfortable on the hard stool. "Now this is the sort of abstract conversation I adore. But the real reason I came is to tell you the commander of those Sopwith 1½ Strutters has put you in for a Victoria Cross. Said he and the survivors owe their life to you, and it was the single bravest act he has seen in the air. He wrote that you could have escaped with honour many times, but you refused to abandon the Sopwiths. Boom has supported the nomination. Army HQ is popping champagne corks that the Sopwiths got critical photographs of a previously unknown gun battery and a reserve ammunition dump, both in line with the main assault area. Those photos allowed DH4 bombers to obliterate both. Even General Gough, no lover of the RFC, has written a letter of commendation to Haig saying the RFC is doing a hell of a job. You are flavour of the month."

"Yet," Lance said without looking up. "Taggart is dead, his wife a widow, and his wee bairns fatherless."

"True, and nothing will change that. But unlike so many of our deaths, at least we can see a credit in the ledger. Taggart did not die in vain. He helped save lives, not only those of the Sopwith crews but also the infantrymen who will launch the attack. The successful bombing was due to you and him. Hell, if Gough is giving *any* credit to the RFC, then a heck of a lot of credit must be due."

"I'd rather have Taggart alive."

"I didn't realise you were so close to him."

"I wasn't, but I dare say his wife and children were. That didn't stop me from getting him killed. You told me the Sopwiths' leader said we might have escaped with honour. I could have led Taggart out of that fight. While I stayed, he stayed. It's my fault he died. Now I can't sleep for guilt, as that bastard Budd predicted. Jesus! The nightmares ..."

Lance sighed and straightened his back with an audible crack. "If I stay as squadron commander, I will go stark raving mad. I've too many lives on my conscience already. Getting medals for leading Taggart to his death makes it worse."

"For God's sake, Lance, stop being maudlin and melodramatic. In war, people die because of command decisions all the time. You saved five Sopwiths, that's ten men directly on the credit side. One lost and ten saved. You also helped get critical photos that will save thousands more. So, honour Taggart and move on. He is another casualty of the war, but one who died for a reason and whose dying deeds made a difference."

Clayton paused as Lance rose, collected a Lewis gun drum, and started loading it with bullets from the "good" bucket.

"And, Lance, as for your guilt, every good war leader from Alexander the Great onwards has agonised over the deaths of his men. Some glory-seeking commanders don't care enough and too many of their men die without reason. Some leaders care too much and don't risk enough casualties to win battles. But when you lose battles, you lose wars. When you lose wars, the deaths on your side are in vain. Only the great commanders care, but still risk themselves and their men to win.

"Don't delude yourself, Lance. You aren't unique in your suffering. So, buck up and stop feeling sorry for yourself. Be a man. Be the man you are. If you won't, then men like Thommo who don't give a hoot about their men will become the leaders by default. That would be more lives on your conscience. You are a good squadron commander. You owe it to your men to provide them with that leadership."

Lance looked up directly at Clayton for the first time, his dark eyes sunk into the drawn hollow cheeks. In a few days Lance seemed to have wasted into a gaunt shell of himself. Clayton grimaced. Maybe he'd gone too far with his lecture.

When Lance spoke, his tone, although tired, remained measured. "I won't forget Taggart. He was my wingman, and I should have protected him. He died shooting a Hun off me, and my debt is always to remember. Intellectually you are right, of course. I've told myself the same thing a dozen times. But I just can't convince myself of it. It doesn't ring as true as something that snake Budd told me. Taggart is dead 'cos he trusted me, and Budd is alive 'cos he didn't." Lance took a deep breath and his voice gusted with emotion. "That's a bloody hard pill to swallow."

"Budd will get his just deserts, and everyone who spends enough time in the air out here will lose a wingman. Hell, Thommo loses one almost every week."

"Yes, well, I try hard not to be Thommo."

Clayton found another dud bullet and flung it in disgust into its bucket. "You have a point there. I was out of order. Sorry."

"Apology accepted. When I took command of 111 Squadron, Arthur promised that if I wanted to opt out, I could do so with no questions asked. I've done that. Don't bother trying to talk me out of it."

Clayton shrugged. "By the way, the Sopwiths' leader said you and Taggart downed at least four Huns. You never claimed any in your report."

"I can't remember much, to be honest. It's all a blur. Give them all to Taggart. I don't want any glory out of his death."

Silence took over again, punctuated by the odd clang. Guns rumbled in the distance as a shout of laughter and a volley of curses floated through the hangar door. A hiss announced that another moth had misjudged the flame.

"Lance, do you know how I got my DSO?"

"I heard you won the medal for a fracas on the Indian North-West Frontier before the war and you got your gammy leg at the same time. Rumour says after your platoon was ambushed, you went back alone to rescue one of your wounded troopers. They say you got shot in the process but refused to leave him. Then you crawled all the way to the rest of the platoon, dragging him with one hand and shooting a revolver with the other."

"Something like that. What you need to understand is how vicious the Pathans were. They had a charming habit of skinning their captives alive and forcing us to listen to their screaming all night. When the victim couldn't scream any more, the tribesmen would jam the man's jaws wide open with a twig so he couldn't swallow. Then their women would piss in the poor sod's mouth 'til he drowned. For the Pathans, it was the cruellest, most humiliating, and most painful death they could devise. And believe me, they had vivid imaginations in such matters. In short, getting captured was a seriously bad idea."

Lance had stopped loading the Lewis gun drum. Clayton nodded at his shocked expression. "Imagine how I felt when I got back to the ambush site and found two wounded men. I could save only one. So, I played God, chose one, and he ended up living."

"The other one got flayed alive?"

"Nope. I shot him in the head. The sad thing? The man I rescued was a shifty worthless son of a bitch and the one I shot was a friend of mine. I'd been the best man at his wedding. He was too badly wounded to fight and he would die soon. But if he didn't die soon enough, the tribesmen would torture him. He begged me to shoot him. As I took aim to kill my friend, he looked me in the eye, clutched my arm, and thanked me."

"Jesus! I never knew these little wars in India were so savage."

Clayton laughed without amusement. "Funny how the *Times* never published the atrocities of the Pathans. Anyway, the man I rescued couldn't walk, but he would live and could still shoot even if he wasn't mobile. We only had ten unwounded men. So for the good of the platoon, to help us all survive, I rescued a man I disliked rather than my friend."

Clayton clanged another bullet into a bucket. This one went into the "good" bucket, but the adjutant hurled it with venom.

"The even sadder thing? A unit of Hobson's Horse rescued us ten minutes later. I had no idea the cavalry was around. If I'd rescued my friend instead, the platoon would not have suffered. He would have died in my arms, not by my hand. But the saddest thing of all is how I am often reminded about this whole sorry story. Because my friend's wife was pregnant with my goddaughter, Isabella. I love her dearly, but every time I see her, I have a vision of her father smiling at me as I shot him."

Clayton saw Lance wince. He opened his mouth and closed it again without saying anything. Clayton knew the feeling. *There aren't the words.*

"But at least I'd saved *someone's* life, right? That was a useful sop to my conscience for a while. Until three months later, when the man I rescued raped a fourteen-year-old Indian girl and the judges sent him to jail.

"You'd think God would be satisfied with one message I'd got it wrong, wouldn't you? But He just kept on ramming it home. That's when I stopped believing in Him. I tell myself every day that from time immemorial men at war have been trying to make the 'right' decisions and often failing. But we did our best with the information we had. And that is all we can hope to do."

Clayton hurled a bullet into the bucket with enough force to almost knock it over. "I did learn something though," he continued in his conversational voice. "Never narrow your mind and life down to a single impulse like revenge or guilt. If you do, that extreme focus becomes a demon riding you so intensely that you stop noticing the wonders of the world. You're left indifferent by the sway of a pretty girl walking on a sunny day, the rich notes of a nightingale in full song, or the scent of a wild rose. When you fish the riverbanks, you lose your wonder at the kingfishers swooping in flashes of iridescent blue and red across the shadow-dappled waters. When you sail, you no longer whoop with joy when the white spray leaps from your bow into rainbow arcs. Don't let that happen to you, Lance. It's a form of death."

Clayton stood and stretched, arching backwards with his hands on his hips. "Here endeth the lesson. I'm too old to sit on stools. This sorting of bullets is like shelling whelks—harder work than it looks—and you have enough ammunition to win the war tomorrow. What do you say we head to the Mess and get a nightcap? I know you rarely drink, but I need one after waking those old ghosts. I've not told anyone before and it ain't easy telling."

Lance blew out his cheeks. "Christ! I'll take a drink myself after that story." He rose, his shadow looming against the hangar walls. "Thanks for telling me. It does help put things into perspective."

"So you'll stay as a squadron commander?"

"I didn't say that, but your story puts my problems in perspective and that helps. You must have had bloodcurdling nightmares and a lifetime of second-guessing yourself. How do you manage?"

Clayton shrugged. "You survive. Any fool can sail on a sunny day; it's surviving the night storms that counts. You bury all your shame, guilt, and regrets six fathoms deep, and you sail on, accepting the winds and weather and setting your sails accordingly. Do the things that keep you afloat and if you manage that for long enough, you eventually win through to a sunrise that makes the dawn sing."

Clayton took a gusting breath. "And that moment is a blessing beyond compare."

12
A Good Dream

28 June 1917.
Ypres, British trenches, King's Own Regiment.

The next day, horizontal rods of rain stung Lance's face as he splashed along the river at the bottom of the trench, shoulders hunched against the torrential downpour that swept in vast curtains across the flat Flanders gloom. Glutinous mud and an ankle-deep flood sucked at his boots. A sodden and sullen sentry marked the entrance to an underground bunker.

The storm had wiped out flying for the day, and on a whim, Lance had borrowed one of 100 Wing's tenders to hunt down Pa. If his information was correct, his search would end here.

"Major Stan Fitch?" Lance asked the man.

"Down below, sir." The sentry moved a reluctant twelve inches out of the minimal protection of the entrance, and Lance brushed past him into a log-framed doorway draped by a sodden blanket.

Lance hesitated. He could turn around and never see Pa again. That would be the easy path to avoid the painful truths that would surface in a confrontation with his father. Temptation tugged at him, but the whisper that had brought him here would not cease. A reconciliation with Pa, all that remained of his family, was worth any price.

Any price? My own sanity? I'll not risk that.

Lance turned to leave. He bumped into the sentry.

"Down below, sir," the man prodded, not bothering to hide his annoyance that the dithering Lance was occupying his shelter. The soldier blocking Lance's escape seemed like a message from on high, so he turned back.

He ducked through the coarse blanket that served as a door and stepped into a gloom dimly lit by hurricane lamps hanging from nails embedded in log walls. The line of lamps swung in the draft, knocking against the timber as they threw their washed-out glow onto crude wooden steps that lurched downwards towards a Stygian gloom. If ever there was an entrance to the underworld, this was it. Lance stumbled down the uneven steps to find another hanging blanket, this one even more threadbare. He pulled it open, slipped on the muddy bottom step, and almost tore the blanket down.

A man sat alone, facing away from Lance, his profile backlit by a lamp as he hunched over a map spread on an upturned barrel that served as a desk. The musty air stank of fresh earth, wet wool, and rum. The broad-shouldered figure did not turn. Drops of water pattered off Lance's coat onto the duckboards. A gust swirled past him and set the map fluttering. A hand thumped it back into obedience. "Come in or get out but close the bloody blanket one way or the other," the man growled, his voice more gravelly than it used to be.

Lance took a deep breath. "Pa, you're an idiot."

The figure froze, then turned. Lance fought to hide his shock. Pa's eye sockets had sunk into a gaunt face while craggy cheekbones and a lean jaw thrust into prominence under sallow, drum-tight skin. Angry lines as deep as dried-up river-beds cracked his forehead and flowed down either side of the prow of his nose. The shaggy eyebrows still rode thick and wild but were now full of iron grey that matched his tousled hair.

His eyes, steady as ever, appraised Lance. "I've seen you look better."

"I could say the same." Lance sat on a crude stool across the barrel. "All our flights are washed out. So I took the opportunity to find you, as it seemed you weren't coming to visit me."

Pa pulled a face. "I didn't have the guts after I sent that letter. Thought you wouldn't want to see me."

"I'm not sure I do."

Pa lifted his eyebrows in resignation. "I know it's irrational of me to blame you. Anger at the survivor, I guess. I should never have told you. It was my burden to carry, not yours." He scratched his goatee with a dirty forefinger. "Who was it that said we can never call back four things—the spoken word, the fired arrow, the past, and the neglected opportunity? A wise saying, valid for written words too once they are read."

"You didn't tell me anything I don't tell myself. But it hurt more from you."

Pa winced and said nothing.

"But" Lance said, "I'm learning to forgive a lot in this war."

Relief washed across Pa's gaunt face. "In that case..." He stood and fetched a bottle and two small, chipped glasses from the far recess of the dugout. The cork came out with a plop and the pungent aroma of dark rum filled the stale air. Pa splashed tots into the chipped glasses and handed one to Lance. "Cheers. Death and confusion to the enemy." He offered to clink glasses.

Lance pushed his glass away. "I don't drink."

Pa raised his eyebrows and sank both in quick succession. The glasses thunked onto the table, some drops staining the maps. "Care to tell me why I'm an idiot?"

"You lost two sons, but you had a life and things you should be proud of—the farm, the hunting business, friends, the community in Taveta, and the school and the church. You helped build all those from scratch; you invested part of you into them. You should have stayed there, not come here."

Pa snorted. "The Huns burned the farm, remember? Besides, those things didn't keep you in Taveta. The words pot, kettle, and black come to mind." That searching gaze was as uncomfortable as ever.

"Did you sell the farm?" Even the words hurt.

"No. I left a manager in charge. My will says you inherit."

"Thank God. Why didn't you leave Uncle Frederick in charge?"

"Ah." Pa refilled his glass to the rim with exaggerated care. "The old bugger signed up for the Frontiersmen Battalion to scout for them around Rufiji."

"But he's past sixty. Why would the Army take him?"

"If you were General Smuts, who would you rather have? Frederick Selous, the most famous hunter alive, who knows every foot of the country, or some snot-nosed youngster?"

"Point taken."

"He won a DSO," Pa said and knocked back his rum. "Then a sniper shot him through the head."

"Christ!" Lance closed his eyes. The walls of the dugout seemed to close around him. It was hard to breathe. Selous had been his godfather and had taught Lance much of his bush skills. His bushy silver beard and magnetic blue eyes were an indelible part of Lance's youth.

Pa poured Lance a glass of rum and this time Lance gulped it down. As he did so, there was a massive explosion, and its shockwaves punched Lance's ears and ribs. He jumped up as the bunker shook. Dirt fell from the roof. More explosions. Then the shellfire turned into one long rolling thunder that rocked the room. Pa put his hands over their rattling rum glasses as the roof logs creaked and the earthfall became a shower. A whistle blew, shrill and urgent. Shouts echoed outside.

"A Hun attack?" Lance shouted.

Pa checked his watch, shook his head, and held up two fingers. "Wait two," he mouthed.

Sure enough, the barrage abruptly stopped two minutes later.

Pa shook the earth off the maps. "Just their usual five o'clock two-minute strafe. You can't say the Huns aren't punctual." He pointed at the single crown sewn onto Lance's epaulette. "I see you're a major now. Last I heard you were a captain."

"Apparently they are making every Tom, Dick, and Stan majors now."

"Indeed." A quirk of the mouth, more like the Pa of old.

"Just acting major," Lance said, "And I've resigned."

Pa put the maps down and sat up ramrod straight. "First time I've known you quit on something."

Lance frowned. "I haven't quit. I'm just not good at it. It makes sense to let someone else do it."

"When I first let you fire a rifle, you couldn't even hit the sky. Now the papers say you can shoot the fillings out of a Hun pilot's mouth from a thousand yards while upside down in a spin. If you want to go back to being a captain, that's fine. Just don't fool yourself. You're quitting, surrendering. I didn't raise you to run up the white flag at the first setback."

"No? Then why did you give up on your life's work and come here?"

Now it was Pa's turn to be silent. Lance raised a hand in apology. He searched for the right words but could not find them. He tried anyway, his tongue clumsy.

"Pa, I've spent every flying minute chasing revenge for events past. But now and then I dream of a future that might just possibly exist. You and I sitting on the porch on our farm, watching a flaming sunset silhouette Mt. Kilimanjaro." Lance took a deep breath. "I find peace and serenity in that picture. Even though I will probably die and not be part of that scene, I still want you to experience it. That's why I am fighting to win this war. So you, and maybe me, can enjoy what you built. Without fearing that Germans will rampage across the border to burn and kill. That's a war worth winning, whether or not I am alive to see it. And now you are here. Just as liable to die as me. And if you die, that murders my dream—my only dream of a future."

Pa's voice was rough. "It's a good dream, Lance, but it's yours, not mine. If you make it through, you'd best find a soulmate to share sunsets with rather than a crotchety old geezer."

Lance leapt to his feet, his stool falling over. "Damn you, Pa, go home! Don't be so bloody stubborn. Live! One of us has to live. You're almost fifty. You shouldn't be on the front line any more than Uncle Frederick. I made mistakes I have to atone for. You weren't responsible for crippling Francis and getting Will blown to smithereens. I am.

"And I can make a difference in this war, Pa. All those hunting skills you and Uncle Frederick taught me, those are unique in the sky. I may be a lousy commander, but I'm gifted at war flying. If anyone can shoot down Richthofen, I can. All due respect, Pa, but you're an over-the-hill infantry major. When you go over the top and the machine guns start, you will be one more shredded body. For nothing Pa, nothing."

Lance was panting, both fists planted on the barrel. He straightened, embarrassed by his naked emotion. "Get a desk job," he muttered. "Get a rear echelon billet. Anything. Just get the hell out of here."

Pa looked at him, steady as you like. "Finished?"

Lance glared at him but nodded. Pa poured more rum for them both. He looked into the depths of the glass. "There's something I haven't told you. I wasn't going to tell you, but I don't want us to end this way."

His tone chilled Lance. The air seemed thicker.

Pa still didn't look at him. "You may only have a slim chance of surviving this war, Lance, but you have a chance. I have none. I have a malignant growth inside my guts. The docs in Africa gave me less than a year. A good chunk of that year has gone." He slugged back the rum.

The news hit Lance like a punch. He'd watched hundreds of men die and had built his defences strong, but Pa's news cut through his barriers like a bullet through paper. "Are you sure?"

"I'm afraid so. Why do you think I look like a walking cadaver already?"

"I don't believe you." Lance shook his head, his voice growing stronger as he convinced himself. "The army wouldn't have accepted you for the front line if that were true." He despised himself for the plaintiveness in his voice. A child pleading for confirmation that Father Christmas was not a lie.

Pa's half-smile was both sad and contemptuous. "You think they examined me closely? Those poor Army docs, they know the Huns will most likely kill you within a year, so why bother examining your health? They keep their eyes averted so they don't see the human inside the men they certify as fit to die. I told them I was fit for the front lines, and I wanted to go. They ticked the boxes in a heartbeat."

"You here for revenge or to die?"

Pa looked at him steadily. "Both. I watched chronic, consistent pain turn Francis from a man into a gibbering wreck. That is my future. The disease consumes me from the inside. I can dull the pain with rum or laudanum. Rum flows freely in the British Army, and I saw what laudanum did to Francis. I considered blowing my brains out, but I didn't want to exit the world that way. I'd rather go out like old man Selous.

"All my life, I've told myself I control my own destiny. I taught you that too. Deep down we both know there's an element of that credo that's bollocks. In our river of life, who knows if it is God, fate, or chance that carves out the channel? But carved it is, and we can only choose how we swim in that flow. Still, there's power in that choice. I can't defeat this disease, but I'm buggered if I'll let it dictate my exit. I'm going out proud, not a whimpering husk."

Pa gave a lopsided smile that tunnelled the crevice lines even deeper into his gaunt cheeks. "Turns out I have a use for the Huns after all. They ruined the last years of my life and earned my vengeance. Now they owe me a good death."

Lance hung his head and blew out a gusty breath. It was a lousy hand that Pa had been dealt. Lance felt he should cry, but he had no tears left in him. He sagged onto a stool.

"It's alright, Lance," Pa said. "I've accepted it. You must too. But I'd prefer it if my death wasn't a cause for more revenge but instead motivated you to live. Win the war, then go home, find Heidi if she is still alive or someone like her, and build a life together on our farm. Hell, even have children if you feel brave. That's my dream for you. One that is possible, unlike yours."

Lance stumbled off his stool and hugged his father—for the first time since Lance was ten and Ma died.

Pa pushed him away after a second and held him at arm's length to gaze into Lance's eyes. "I've had a good life, Lance, no regrets. Make sure you can say the same. Don't die wishing. Be a leader. Take your revenge and then let go of it." Pa's voice was steady, and he held Lance's gaze, his eyes cool and level. This was a man at peace with his life and fate. Lance forced the muscles of his face into a small smile and nodded slowly.

"Have you heard any news of Heidi or Herr Schumacher?" Lance was afraid to hear the answer, but he had to ask.

"Nothing." Pa's voice was gruff. "I don't know if the German Army found out he helped you escape, or they were caught by the typhoid epidemic, or it's just the fog of war. Certainly, there's no working mail left in our part of Africa." He frowned. "I'm not hopeful. Before the war, it was a land of savage beauty but harsh and unforgiving. The war added chaos—famine, disease, and breakdowns in transportation and law and order. A lot of folks have gone missing."

Voices echoed from the stairs and the blanket was pulled aside by three soaked officers. "New orders from HQ, sir," said one, looking curiously at Lance. "We need to respond."

Pa nodded acknowledgement but did not break eye contact with Lance. "There is one thing you can do, Lance. Opposite us, south of St. Julien, is a sodding big Hun pillbox. We've shelled the bejesus out of it, but it seems that nothing short of a direct hit will knock it out. Unfortunately, we can't keep an artillery spotter aircraft over it for long enough. They get shot down, even with an escort. It must be a priority with the Huns, as it is with us. If you could liaise with the spotter squadron and give one of their planes a royal escort, maybe we could nail the bastard. That'd give my boys a chance when we go over the top."

Lance nodded. "Consider it done."

Pa clapped him on the shoulder. "Good man! Come and see me again before the attack."

Lance shrugged into his coat as the officers questioned their major. He took one last look at Pa, a rock of certainty surrounded by an eddy of younger men. This was the man Lance would remember.

He strode up the stairs towards the gloomy grey light. His greatcoat, sodden and heavy, felt damp and chill even on the inside. But he was glad for its protection when he pushed into the spiteful rain and bitter wind that raged in the world outside. It was better than nothing, that was for sure, and these days Lance took any comfort he could find.

13
Wolves Wanted

Lance woke with a start. He lay on his cot under the coarse serge blankets as rain drummed on the tent and gusts of wind caused the guy ropes to creak. The deluge muted even the habitual thunder of artillery from the front, but that was not the reason for his surprise. A glance at his watch told him it was past nine o'clock in the morning. Since he'd joined the RFC, he'd never slept so well.

Perhaps it was because he'd finally made up his mind. He knew what he wanted. He just did not know how to achieve it.

He ran a hand along his stubble and thought back to yesterday. After the visit to Pa, Lance had returned to Bailleul covered in mud and soaked through. For the second consecutive night Clayton persuaded him to down two glasses of red wine in the Mess, where pilots tactfully pretended they had not noticed his recent absence. When he went to bed he couldn't sleep, his brain churning with Pa's revelations. But after a few hours he made his decision, and then slept like a dead man until now. The twin burdens of guilt and exhaustion lightened from a crippling cross to a bearable burden. Even his sinus headache had eased. The world seemed a more cheerful place despite the rain drumming on the canvas.

His batman, Sykes, sidled into the tent with a blast of

damp air. "Morning, Sykes," Lance greeted him.

The corporal grunted, slopped a shaving bowl of hot water down on the wooden nightstand, and handed Lance a piping hot tin mug. Lance sipped the bitter tea with a grimace. "Christ, Sykes. I know the British Army likes its tea strong as gunpowder and I can't change that, but you usually give me sugar at least."

Sykes said nothing, just stuck his calloused and nicotine-stained forefinger into the mug and stirred it. When he finished, Lance sipped again. The sweetness flooded his taste buds. He closed his eyes. "Delicious!"

"Let yer sleep 'cos flights are all washed out. Snoring like a pig you was, sir. Good to hear."

Half an hour later, shaved, booted, and braced in his uniform, Lance felt physically and mentally energised. For the first time since Taggart's death, he could see his path forward. He would withdraw his resignation letter. Clayton's parable of self-pity and Pa's jibes had pointed the way. But he had to discover how to do a better job with his squadron and break the cycle of losses to the Circus. He had to embed a new culture and create a new breed of pilot in tune with his philosophies of war flying. But how? This was his Gordian knot, and he had no clue of how to unravel it.

He shrugged into his greatcoat and braved the rain and mud with a dash into the Mess. As he hung his sopping coat, he saw Rod Andrews and Springs huddled together, secretively muttering over a large map. Intrigued, Lance pricked up his ears. Despite the plotters' low voices, he overheard phrases including "daylight raid," "worthwhile targets," and "get out of Dodge City once we have achieved the objective, because sure as hell they'll be chasing after us."

Lance wandered over to their table. Rod watched him coming and nudged Springs. They two of them waited for him to approach with broad grins.

"Alright, you two," Lance said, "if you're planning a good raid, I want in on it."

The plotters looked at each other with delight. "Are you sure?" Rod asked. "We need three people to make it work, and we can't have any snitches. Once you say you are in, you can't withdraw once you know what the raid is. And you can't tell anyone else. You promise?"

"I promise," Lance replied, nettled that they thought his nerve was less than theirs.

"Okay," Springs drawled. "Take a chair. We have two possible raids planned. My Aussie friend here and I are having a difference of opinion. You can help us choose which raid we go for. One is high risk with a lower probability of success, but if we succeed..." The American leaned back in his chair and kissed his pursed fingertips in the Gallic appreciation of something spectacular.

"The other raid," Rod added, "is closer and easier, and the odds are better, but I have to admit that Springs is right—the payoff will not be so rewarding. Which would you choose, Lance?"

They looked at him expectantly.

"Which might end the war sooner?" Lance asked.

The two plotters glanced at each other.

"Mate, to be honest the easy one won't have any impact," Rod answered. "The riskier one—well, that's harder to call. If the raid is a success, then the generals' morale might collapse if they can't obtain suitable replacements."

"Let's go for that one then."

"Alright!" Springs said. "I like the man's style."

Rod stabbed a finger at a red circle drawn in crayon on the map. "Then this is the objective."

Lance frowned. "But that's behind our lines."

"Damn right." Springs said gleefully. "That is the chateau where a bunch of Frog generals keep their mistresses. What's the collective for mistresses? A bounce?" He giggled and re-filled his glass of wine.

Lance stared. "Springs, it's only just eleven o'clock and you're drinking already?"

"My father always advised me to start the day as you intended to carry on. Relax, Lance. The weathermen forecast we'll be socked in with rain clouds all day."

"We reckon," Rod said, "that the Frog generals must get the crème de la crème of mistresses, right? I mean, if they take all the trouble to put them up in this chateau, they've got to be right bonza sheilas. It stands to reason that some of these young, gorgeous mistresses must be tired of pot-bellied, garlic-eating old men and may fancy a bounce with a real man o' war. Either a rich Yank flashing cash, or a rugged Aussie oozing manliness, even a boring Blackie with some medals. But we need a driver to stay in the car for a quick getaway while Springs and I persuade three willing females to desert for a night. That'll be your job."

Lance felt his cheeks flame. "Bastards!"

Rod and Springs cackled with delight and toasted each other: "To our chauffeur!"

"As a matter of interest," Lance asked, "what was the other plan?"

"Raid the nearest nurses' quarters after lights out," Rod said. "I was in favour of this one—a sure-fire certainty with the possibility of many willing escapees. But you and Springs want quality not quantity, and for once I thought I'd try the idea."

"Aussie dingbat! You got me on false pretences, I'm not—"

"You promised!" the other two chorused.

Lance shook his head. "Only because I'm a man of my word."

Springs hooted with laughter. "If we can fly four-poster beds like we can fly planes..."

Despite himself, Lance felt an unfamiliar smile tug at the

corner of his mouth. After Arthur and Clayton, these were the two men whose company he most enjoyed. Their indomitable lust for life was an antidote to the cancer of the war and its politics.

He was about to let the smile bloom when Ball's memory reminded Lance of his oath. Never again would he allow another pilot inside his defences. Friends die on you. Feelings make you weak. To stay sane, it was better to keep your distance.

He pushed his chair back and made his voice cold and clipped. "No. I won't be part of your juvenile pranks."

Rod shrugged. "Each to his own."

Rod looked indifferent, but Springs' battered pugilist's face looked as forlorn as a whipped spaniel's. Lance felt like a cad. Perhaps he could row a course between friendship and rudeness? He hadn't enjoyed the ostracism he'd endured in 13 Squadron. He took a deep breath.

"Listen, you blokes are the straightest shooters in the wing. I've decided to stay on as leader of 111 Squadron. I don't want the job and I'm not so hot at it. Getting my pilots killed is eating away at me. I want to resign but nobody else thinks it's a good idea. Not my father, not Arthur, not Clayton, and not..." He paused, unsure how to describe Megan. "Anyway, any advice?"

"Take up drink," Springs said. "*In vino veritas,* as the Romans used to say. Booze is a fine companion. It never judges you, never whines at you. I guarantee that after a half-bottle of wine, your crippling sense of responsibility will wash away, and you can convince yourself you are the best war leader since Napoleon."

"Honestly, Springs, is there a question to which your answer isn't booze?"

"Ask a juvenile, get a juvenile answer." Apparently whipped spaniels could carry a grudge.

"Rod?" Lance asked.

The Australian shrugged. "Booze works for me. But if you don't like that wicket, try this one for size. No matter how lousy you are, you are probably better than your replacement would be. Hell, I'd say you are a better flying leader than Thommo or me."

"You set the bar so high," Springs murmured.

"But I do have one rule for my squadron that I recommend," Rod continued. "No pricks allowed. Whereas you permitted Budd, that bull's pizzle, to screw you and your squadron."

Lance rubbed his forehead. "I never guessed Arthur's nephew would be such a bastard."

Rod pulled a face. "Fair enough, but when it was clear that he was a prick, you weren't ruthless. One bad apple rots a whole barrel in a hurry. This war is tough enough without dealing with pricks. Do everyone a favour next time—if you make a mistake, fix it fast."

Lance scratched his head and remembered trying to honour his promise to Megan that he would look after her son. He nodded in recognition—he'd been thinking with the wrong part of his anatomy.

"I agree with Rod but only up to a point," Springs said. "Avoid recruiting pricks, but don't get choirboys either. You ain't the cuddliest of creatures, Lance. You're a wolf, so get wolves around you. That way you won't have to change yourself. Wolves don't want sheep leading them, any more than sheep want wolves. Me, I wouldn't want to be part of your squadron. Liable to be too grim for me, and you'd always be lecturing about cutting down on the booze."

"If we follow our learned Yank's logic," Rod said, "when you are a prick yourself, you need to recruit other pricks. Look at that prick Thommo. He recruits pricks like Springs."

"I couldn't have illustrated my point better myself," Springs said.

Lance nodded. "No pricks, recruit wolves. That's easier to understand than some of that high-falutin' leadership stuff from Arthur and Clayton about owning souls and inspirational visions" He scratched his neck. "Who'd have guessed? Wisdom out of the mouths of babes and boozers."

~

"Arthur," Lance begged, "help me."

He had to raise his voice above the dirge of the wind that moaned under the door and the dismal racket of the rain on the tin roof of Arthur's office hut. Since his discussion with Springs and Andrews this morning, ideas had come thick and fast. Problem was, they churned in his mind like a witch's brew. His head throbbed.

Arthur dashed off another signature on a pile of papers without looking up. If he had heard Lance, he disguised it well. Since the Budd affair, Arthur had been cold and distant. Lance had a sneaking suspicion that this was less to do with Budd and more about the revelation that Lance and Megan were lovers. But Lance didn't dare pick that scab, so they talked war and nothing else.

Lance slapped his hand down on the next piece of paper.

Arthur stared at him, his eyes hard. "You are out of order."

Lance left his hand flat on the papers. "You begged me to command a squadron, and I am struggling and begging for advice. At least pretend to be interested."

"Fitch asking for advice? That is a first." Arthur sat back. "What do you want from me?"

"I have to replace half a squadron of pilots. I want a different breed. The trouble with you Brits is that you have a surfeit of physical courage, but a shortage of mental courage. Most Brits would rather die than have anyone wonder if they were cowards. You know what one of 13 Squadron told me?

'Dying happens only once. Cowardice lives forever in the minds of your friends.'"

"Do not knock it. That fear of your mates' contempt is sometimes the only thing that gets men into battle."

Lance gave a nod of acknowledgement. "I understand that, but the Germans have the right approach. They don't award their top medal for bravery. They give it purely on results—the number of enemies killed. If a Circus pilot charged over-whelming odds and got shot down, I'm certain Richthofen would only give a Dummkopf award."

"I thought you were fighting to avoid doing things the German way? Next, you will be voting for Kaiser Bill. It sounds as though you have chosen what you want, so what exactly are you asking me?"

"Help me get a new breed of pilots for my squadron. No more daring heroes. No more Hawkers, Leefe Robinsons, or Albert Balls. I want cold-hearted assassins who stab the enemy in the back. Lots of them. A pack of wolves like your Kipling books. What do you think?"

"I think you have mixed metaphors. Wolves or assassins? Make up your mind. You want your pilots to be loners or hunting in packs?"

Lance considered this. "Both. Wolves when we fly in for-mation. Assassins when they fly alone."

"Choose. Complex messages are lost messages."

"Alright. Assassins then."

"Hardly a rousing recruitment pitch. 'Cold-hearted assas-sins wanted.'"

"Help me then." Lance said through gritted teeth.

Arthur put down his pen and picked up his cigar case. He drew one out, cut the end, and searched for his matches. "Pilots will not find the idea of being assassins motivating. It is not in the British psyche. And I cannot get a mental picture of assassins flying in formation. Go with wolves. They hunt together a lot but are also good solo hunters. Words are not your forte, but you can quote Kipling: 'The strength of the pack is the wolf, and the strength of the wolf is the pack.' That is simple, memorable imagery. Run with it."

Lance rubbed his chin. "And how do I find these people? I don't know where to start."

Arthur's cigar lit with a cloud of smoke, and he spoke around it as he puffed. "Ask Bill Franks, commander of the Depot Airfield at St. Omer. He sees just about every pilot when they either arrive or leave France, or when they collect a new plane. Go pick his brains tomorrow."

~

30 June 1917.
St. Omer Airfield, RFC Depot.

"I want pilots who use their brains before their balls," Lance said, warming himself in the filtered sunlight that forced itself through the filthy windowpanes of Bill Franks' threadbare office. Yesterday's savage weather had relented, and a blue sky shone outside the gloomy Nissen hut.

"Mmm, not the usual request," Franks said, slurping on a steaming cup of tea. His office squatted next to the airstrip, and they often had to pause for the snarl of aero engines to pass. "Most commanding officers want the fire-breathing types."

"I don't object to fire breathing; it's the Charge of the Light Brigade types I want to avoid. Gung-ho with brains would be ideal."

"Let me see if I have this straight. You want dedicated Hun killers, but ones prepared to run away to live another day if the odds are against them?"

Lance nodded.

Franks sucked noisily on his tea. "Tough job you boys in 100 Wing have. I'm not sure I'd recommend any friends because hunting the Circus seems like a job with a short lifespan. Most men who want to take on the Circus are the type who believe they are immortal."

Franks gazed out through the window for a while. "But you might be in luck. I think I have someone who would bite your hand off for a chance to fly SE5s against the Circus. Just arrived in France after a spell instructing in England, just gagging to kill Huns."

Franks leaned to shout out his office door, "Corporal, get me Lieutenant McCudden. He should be on the flight line if he hasn't left already. And fetch three teas while you are about it."

Lance opened his mouth to say that he did not want tea, but the angry buzz of an unleashed rotary engine forestalled him. Franks strode to the window and cocked his head to watch. Lance turned just in time to see a Sopwith Pup soar off the runway straight into a 360-degree loop.

"Idiot," Lance said. Most pilots lost height on a loop. To do so on take-off meant death. A good pilot able to gain altitude in a loop was a rarity, and even then an engine hiccup, or a miscalculation by a yard, would lead to a smoking hole in the ground. This pilot completed the loop successfully, and Lance started to turn away. "Someone should ground that man before he kills himself," he told Franks. As Lance finished the sentence the Pup howled seamlessly into another loop. "What the...one loop is dangerous, two is certifiable!"

Franks grinned. "You haven't seen anything yet."

Lance tensed as the Pup rolled through the top of its second loop and swooped towards the earth. A crash seemed certain. But miraculously the Pup bellowed over the huts, making the tin roof rattle. Lance relaxed, then froze as the plane's nose screamed upwards into a third loop. His jaw fell open. Three loops on take-off were impossible.

When the Pup half rolled off the top of the loop and droned off, Lance shut his jaw with a snap. He turned and found Franks laughing at him. "I felt the same way the first time I saw that."

"He's done that before? Who the hell is it?"

"That's Jimmy McCudden, the man I recommended to you. Does it all the time; it's his signature move."

"Bloody hell! Does gravity take the day off when he flies?"

"Apparently."

Lance shook his head, half in admiration and half in admonishment. "Show-off, but a heck of a good one. What's his story?"

"Son of an Irish career ranker, joined the engineers as a bugle boy back in 1910, became one of the best engine fitters in the RFC. I was his commanding officer for a while. When he told me he wanted to become a pilot, I refused. Told him any fool could fly but a man with his gift for engines was irreplaceable. As you can see, I have a talent for wonky predictions. Probably explains why I'm commanding the aircraft depot."

"Not sure you were so wrong. I don't think I want a show-off like that, no matter how good a pilot he is."

"You should meet him," Franks said, "He's a quiet man, careful and calculating in most things. This stunting is the exception."

Lance sighed. "You really think he'll be worth it?"

Franks knocked the ash out of his pipe into his waste basket and ticked off his fingers. "Number one, he's experienced. Been through the Fokker scourge and not only survived but became an ace. The only reason his score is still low is he's been instructing for six months. Two, to go from Irish bugle boy to officer pilot in this class-conscious army is a hell of an achievement. That takes a man of exceptional character. Three, he wants to score kills so badly he can taste it. Four, you may want cool calculating pilots, but this is still war flying.

A bunch of accountants assessing probabilities won't beat the Circus. You need a certain amount of daredevil and McCudden is ready to blossom. But then again, we've established I'm not the best judge of men!"

~

When Jimmy McCudden arrived at Bailleul two days later, his looks reminded Lance somewhat of Albert Ball. McCudden possessed the same slight build and dark handsomeness and the same brooding intensity. But there the similarities ended. Where Ball flaunted rebellious long hair and an oil-streaked uniform, McCudden was neatness personified. He slicked back his brown hair and gelled it in place, his parting ruler straight, his uniform impeccable. The only flamboyance McCudden allowed himself was his artfully crumpled officer's cap, which proclaimed that its owner had been around the block.

A short discussion later, Lance was celebrating a kindred spirit. McCudden had never hunted and considered war flying to be a science learned from keen observation and applied intelligence. Where Lance talked of stealth and stalking, Mc-Cudden rattled on about angles of attack, degrees of turn, and arcs of fire. But their different approaches led to the same conclusion. War flying should involve fanatical shooting practice, meticulous care of equipment, and a canny style of fighting that ensured that wherever possible surprise, numbers, and the physical elements were firmly on your side. If Lance could find a few more men like this, his squadron would be lethal.

Once ensconced at Bailleul, McCudden donned overalls and huddled in the hangars with his fitters. He spent hours with his mechanics talking about compression ratios, horsepower, cylinder heads, rocking levers—most of which was gobbledegook to Lance. Albert Ball had been a talented amateur mechanic who could converse meaningfully with his ground crew. McCudden was a gifted career professional who taught his ground crew tricks they did not know. A McCudden-tuned engine would be several mph faster and leagues more reliable than the factory model.

When Lance asked McCudden for pilot recommendations, McCudden suggested Mick Mannock, an older Irishman he had instructed at Joyce Green.

"Lance, from your description of the type of person you want, Mannock will be ideal."

"If you say he's good, that's enough for me."

McCudden shied like a beaten colt. "Whoa, Lance—you should meet him first."

"Why? You said he would be ideal. Let's not waste time."

"Well, you may not agree with me. For starters he is thirty years old."

"What? This is a young man's game."

"He's as keen as mustard, but he's also a...socialist." McCudden's voice trailed off as if he had used a foul word. "A vocal and opinionated socialist."

"If he's a Hun-getter, I don't care if he is green with pink spots. But if he is an-over-the hill socialist, what exactly has he got going for him?"

"He loathes Germans as much as you. Also he's intelligent, full of smart questions, keen to learn, a good flyer, and he practices shooting every single day."

"Then we'll take him."

McCudden grunted dubiously. "Don't say I didn't warn you."

~

When Mannock arrived two days later, he fitted Lance's ideal of an archetypal Irishman—tall with an angular brooding face under floppy dark hair, an intense gaze, and big hands waving as words spilled out with the passion of an orator and the polemics of a politician. And those words were music to Lance's ears.

"Air fighting is a science, and I'm here to learn it," Mick said.

Lance smiled. "Then you've come to the right place, just so long as you know that the purpose of that science is to kill Germans while staying alive yourself."

"Count on me for both of those," Mick said. "I want to kill the bastards as much as anyone, but an excess of courage is stupidity."

Lance's smile broadened. "Do me a favour and air those views, will you? There are too many potential martyrs in this outfit."

It turned out that encouraging Mick to share his opinions was like inviting a pyromaniac to a firework festival. His arrival coincided with the award of a bar to Rhys-Davids's Military Cross, and a binge developed in the Mess to celebrate the medal. Rhys-Davids deflected the praise pushed his way. "I'm just doing a job, a job I don't enjoy, but like all of us I'm trying to do it well. My only hope is that, come the peace, we shall do even better." Murmurs of agreement followed his words.

Mannock, leaning against the bar with ankles crossed to display yellow socks, gleefully sledge-hammered the mood of high idealism.

"In the meantime, killing Huns by any means, fair or foul, is a duty to a nobler mankind. The bastards are best cooked alive. Sizzle, sizzle, wonk, wonk, flamerinoes."

"That's a bit bloodthirsty," Clayton said.

"I agree that the bully Junker mentality must be stopped at all costs," Lance said. "We need to kill our enemy as fast as possible, so we can end the war and go home. But I would never wish flames on anyone."

"Bloodthirsty?" Mick asked, his voice rising. "These bastards are evil! Too many folk talk as if a dead Hun is an unfortunate consequence, like an opponent breaking his neck in a sporting game of polo."

The Irishman pushed his forelock back away from his eyes and stabbed his finger at the adjutant. "In 1915, Germany violated every rule of the Hague Convention on the rules of warfare, a treaty they had signed only eight years before. In April of the same year, they launched the first-ever poison gas attack, an atrocity that killed over fifty thousand men in the most horrific agony. Fifty thousand men! If you stacked those poor souls on top of each other, the pile would tower over Mount Everest and half as high again."

"I was there," Lieutenant Terry said. "And I saw the poor bastards who were gassed. I don't mind telling you it made me piss myself in fright. Lads' eyes were streaming yellow stuff and they were coughing up bits of lungs. Blood and froth everywhere. It's diabolic, that gas, and it's true the Huns started it."

Clayton waved a hand to concede defeat, but Mick wouldn't let him go so easily.

"A few weeks after the gas attack, a Hun submarine sank the *Lusitania* and killed over a thousand innocent civilians, including over a hundred Americans. How stupid are the Huns? We all know, because torpedoing the *Lusitania* brought the Americans into the war. It was a monstrous act that is illegal under international law, yet they couldn't help them-selves."

"I had friends on that ship," Elliot Springs said, swirling his wine glass. "Two girls, one twenty, one eighteen. No-one ever saw them again. Crying shame; they were great gals."

Mick had won his argument, but he continued to press his case, a barrister in high dudgeon. "Just weeks after sinking the *Lusitania*, the German zeppelin air ships dropped bombs on undefended civilians in London, killing old men and women. Again, wilful murder of non-combatants which is illegal under international law. Three obscene deeds of infamy within two months, all abominations against the laws and mankind itself. The militarists who run Germany these days are bloody inventive in using new technology to commit mass murder by air, sea, and land, in ways outlawed throughout the civilised world. I don't give a damn if an archduke gets assassinated in Sarajevo or anywhere else—the fewer dukes the better, in my opinion—but those ruthless bastards in Germany must be ground into a red paste."

"At least our departed pal Leefe shot down one of the airships," Clayton muttered.

Mick ignored him. "I read that the wife of the scientist responsible for developing the gas was also a scientist, and she had seen the horrific suffering when her husband tested his gas on pigs. When she heard of the German gas attack at Ypres, she committed suicide. Kaiser Wilhelm, on the other hand, the man who ordered the attack, opened pink champagne for the officers involved. Obscene. A woman with a conscience, and an emperor and a military with none."

"Dead is dead," Thommo said in his Canadian twang. "There ain't much difference between blowing a man apart with a shell or gassing him. The only rule in war is to win."

"Bollocks!" Lance slammed his glass on the bar. "Might doesn't justify the slaughter of innocent civilians or vile forms of killing to spread terror." As always when hot rage seized him, tears trickled from his damaged eye duct, a memento of a brutal German beating back in Africa. Lance ignored the tears as they rolled down his cheek and glared at Thommo. "If you really think that, you're fighting for the wrong side. We'd be no better than the bastards we're fighting."

Clayton brushed past Lance and eased between them. "Thommo is just being provocative. You didn't mean it, did you, Thommo?"

Thommo bared his teeth, slid off his barstool, and bounced

on the balls of his feet like a boxer. Elliot Springs grabbed his arm. "Another drink, Major?" he asked and muttered something under his breath to his commanding officer. Thommo scowled at Springs but then flicked on that inner charm switch of his, relaxing into a lazy smile as he accepted a foaming champagne glass from the American. "Jeez, there are some touchy folks around here. 'Course Huns are evil bastards."

~

Now Lance had to divvy his squadron into flights with equal blends of experienced pilots and novices. He took A Flight for himself with Rhys-Davids, the Etonian Hun killer par excellence; Weston, the giant Devon farmer; and the tyro Newby.

Lance awarded command of B Flight to Jimmy McCudden, and gave him Mick Mannock and Cecil Lewis, a tall youngster who was already a veteran after joining the RFC at sixteen in 1915. Terry, the new man, rounded out the mix. Despite his medals earned in the artillery, the rugged Yorkshireman remained a novice in the air.

C Flight went to the sole surviving flight commander from Ball's last mission, Cyril "Billy" Crowe. Since Ball died and during Lance's command funk after Taggart's death, Crowe had led patrol after patrol to keep the squadron in the fray despite the loss of so many pilots. In the air, he'd been a rock in a difficult time.

On the ground...less so. His whisky intake might have been marginally less than Rod Andrews's, but even the Australian didn't wander around the airfield all day in pyjamas and slippers.

Clayton dragged Lance into the office one morning. "I'm not a stickler for the King's Regulations," Clayton complained, "but there are limits. I saw him talking to the mechanics in a dressing gown."

Lance shrugged. "If the Grim Reaper touched you like that—you can't get closer than the Huns shooting your goggles off—you might be a tad eccentric. I admire his courage and resilience."

"What if everyone dressed like him? This isn't a theatre full of bloody luvvies; it's the Army. He's your officer—rein him in."

"Not me. He's a battle-hardened flight commander with a good blend of aggression and prudence. He uses dive and zoom tactics to perfection—exactly what the Wolfpack needs. As far as I'm concerned, if he wants to parade around in slippers before he shuffles off this mortal coil, he's earned the right to be an exception. Anyone else who gets his goggles shot off and keeps killing Huns can do the same."

Crowe cherry-picked some veteran mates of his from 56 Squadron, much to the fury of their commander, Major Blomfield, but Boom Trenchard backed 100 Wing. As a result, C Flight was full of experience but formed a clique. Lance struggled to remember their names. He didn't press himself on them; he kind of liked the remoteness. Crowe was on board with Lance's tactics and was a mighty experienced, mighty capable flight commander. Let him handle his men on the ground the way he wanted. The less Lance knew about those men, the less guilt he would feel when they died.

Besides, Crowe's flight boasted a ratio of seven kills for every loss, a feat that put Lance's record to shame. Perhaps Crowe should command 111 Squadron?

Lance picked at a hangnail on his left thumb, worrying at it until blood welled. Doubts scoured his mind like thorns. *What if I'm still a Jonah?*

14
Three Gifts

5 July 1917.
Jasta 11 near Courtrai.

Hans Schmettow hummed a little Wagner to himself as *Jasta* 11 approached their airfield at Marckebeeke at the end of an uneventful patrol.

He jerked in shock as guns stuttered. Whipping his head around, he saw Richthofen firing his guns in warning and stabbing a gloved hand upwards.

Three planes diving from high left! Damn close! Snub fuselage. Round rotary engine cowling. Sopwith Camels. Twin tracers stabbed from the attackers.

Richthofen turned into the attack. Hans followed, heart pumping, guts wrenched by the force of the turn. Camels could out-turn Albatross in all circumstances, except one— when the Camels were barrelling down in a dive. The speed of their plunge pushed them wide and the lead flight of three Albatross slid below and behind the Camels. In a heartbeat the roles were reversed.

Crazy English bastards. Camels were exceptional in a dogfight but three attacking nine Albatross over their own airfield? Hans cocked his Spandau machine guns and licked dry lips. *Jasta* 11 would punish their arrogance.

Hans waited for the skidding Camel to fill his ring sight. His guns pounded. Tracers chewed the roundel on the Camel's rudder. The tailplane broke away. The Camel flipped wildly and gyrated earthwards. One gone. A flaming comet on his right. Richthofen's opponent. Two down.

The second flight of three Albatross had spread to the west to block the Camels' route home. The last flight had climbed so they would have height on the dogfight and pursue any enemy that looked to escape. Everyone in the *Jasta* knew the drill.

The surviving Camel reversed and came for them. Richthofen, leading the flight, fired first. The nose of the Camel sparkled and tracer lines arced both ways. The Camel broke towards Hans. He fired. Full deflection. Missed. Turned to follow. An Albatross diving from above cut in front of Hans, who swerved and cursed.

From nowhere, a French SPAD appeared, pursued by two Albatross. A long trail of black smoke puffed from the SPAD, a lick of flame, a fiery explosion.

Hans blinked as three Sopwith Triplanes careened through the melee towards him, painted black as coal. *Where did they come from?* Rods of tracers reached for him. He jerked the joystick left and kicked left rudder. A Triplane followed him effortlessly, strafing his Albatross. *More turn!* The nose juddered, warning of a stall. He rolled the nose down and fled. Tracers flashed between his wings. He banked again, full power, and made the tightest turn of his life. He held the turn, his calf cramping. Gravity wrenched at him.

The sky rotated in crazy circles. Vignettes flicked past his eyes: tracer lines gashing a spider's web of white across a blue sky, an Albatross and Triplane colliding, plummeting, locked together like lovers, a column of black smoke, and at the bottom, the Camel falling. Richthofen waggling his wings in victory.

No more tracers chased Hans. He looked back. Two black Triplanes soared above them all. They were out of reach. You couldn't catch a climbing Triplane in an Albatross.

Sweat stung his eyes. He tilted his head so the beads from

his forehead ran down the side of his nose. Around him, order returned. Planes fell into formation behind Richthofen.

He blew out a breath and looked at his clock. Only three minutes since the Camels first attacked. Hans had never felt so alive, and his heart was pounding in his ears. The downed Camel brought his score to twelve. Any day now and his Iron Cross First Class should arrive. When it did, Hans would visit his beloved family for the first time since he'd won his Iron Cross Second Class back in 1916. He smiled at the thought. Soon the serpent would nest in the bosom of the family.

He slotted into formation at the tail, content to be the last one to land while he enjoyed his dream of revenge on his least favourite family member.

~

"Your father was a wastrel." Aunt Hilda had always started Hans's humiliation with the same phrase, her sharp eyes boring at him over her big beaked nose. Hans would nod, not because he agreed but because he had learned that opinions were a luxury he could not afford.

Hans had been too young to truly remember his parents, but Aunt Hilda, his guardian, was always ready to tell the heart-warming tale over and over. Whenever Hans was summoned to the main house, he was scrubbed up and brushed down before being presented to his aunt. The unfamiliar high starched collar would itch his neck while she told the story.

His father, Friedrich, first son of the Count von Schmettow, had been a delicate boy with a love of literature and art and a strong romantic streak, none of which had equipped him well for life as a Prussian count in a martial age. In his twenty-first year, he was sent to travel Europe and compounded his character sins by eloping with Eva, an eighteen-year-old Austrian-Hungarian snitch of common stock.

At this point in the story, Aunt Hilda's knitting needles would click faster and faster, reminding Hans of the clacking beak of an angry crow. "Your mother might have been acceptable as a quick tumble, but not as a mistress who might breed bastards, and certainly not for marriage into Prussian aristocracy. There was so much Hungarian blood in the girl that she was practically a gypsy. No doubt she used all those sluttish tricks to ensnare Friedrich, but a firstborn should have known better. The hot blood those gypsy women have, and those dark smouldering looks. She turned his head. After all the family did for Friedrich, that is how he repaid us."

The family rewarded Friedrich's betrayal with ostracism. The rebellious couple settled in Budapest with little means. Some years later, after the glow of early love had faded and the realities of an impoverished, disowned son had bitten, Friedrich visited his family and grovelled for forgiveness.

Aunt Hilda was there. And she had told Hans the story on his eighth birthday—and every year since— with great relish.

Friedrich begged his parents. He had no money, no loyal friends, and no means of support. His wife and child were starving. "On all that is holy, please take pity, give me *something! Anything! Please! I beg of you. If only for the child's sake. He is your blood."

After a family consultation, they were sufficiently moved to give Friedrich three things—an empty room, a loaded shotgun, and a curt instruction to do the decent thing. For once, he did. Aunt Hilda would sniff at this point in the story, as if surprised.

When Friedrich's wife, Eva, heard the news in Budapest, it had the desired effect. Hans would never forget that part. He was four when he opened the bedroom door to find his mother and the bedsheets covered in crimson and the cloying stench of blood. He crawled onto the bed, saw the gaping slashes at her wrists, and hugged her, crying for her to wake up.

Their landlady discovered him there two days later when she broke down the door to evict them for lack of rent. The Schmettow family swept Hans under the carpet with brutal efficiency, hiding the dirty secret with the gamekeeper's family in a remote hunting lodge on the vast estate. Fallen nobility he may have been, but he was still nobility and the gamekeeper and his wife did not presume to provide the softer part of parenting. Their job was simple—beat into the boy the Prussian obedience, fortitude, and stoicism that his father had so signally lacked.

"Never forget how much you owe this family," Aunt Hilda would say, stabbing a knitting needle in his direction. In later years Hans would see that same steely eyed look over a bayonet and rifle as a British soldier charged his trench.

The only saving grace for Hans was that game hunting with a rifle or shotgun was high on the list of desired Prussian virtues. He was a gawky and uncoordinated boy, except when it came to that ineffable ability to marry the vectors of time, distance, and velocity that distinguish the best of game shots. To the young Hans, this skill was as natural as breathing and neither the pheasant jinking against the sky nor the deer bounding through the forest could escape his deadly aim.

As soon as possible the count sent Hans to a Prussian military academy where brutal beatings became merely tedious and the unbearable turned into routine. And that was for the outstanding cadets. For an outcast like Hans with the social skills of a Silesian peasant (as fellow cadets told him to his face), life was a tad less pleasant.

The war rescued him. Wars kill a lot of people, no doubt, but it provides some with second chances and Hans was one of these happy few. As an officer in the 3rd Brandenburg Regiment, he was not a stellar success, but neither was he the conspicuous failure that seemed his default role.

He won an Iron Cross Second Class at Ypres in 1915. After

his company repulsed a British attack that had reached the German trenches, his commanding officer found him, panting and wild-eyed, standing over four dead Tommies he had hacked to death with a sharpened trench spade. Their blood drenched Hans from his helmet to his steel-shod boots. Impressed by the heroic image, his commander recommended him for a medal.

On his next leave, Hans headed home for the first time since the war started so he could flaunt his medal. "Second-class Iron Crosses are as common as Portuguese whores," his grandfather, the count, sneered. Deflated, Hans did some research on the Schmettow military men. Sadly, his grand-father was correct. Second-class Iron Crosses were two a pfennig in their family. It was a minimum acceptable stan-dard. Even the Iron Cross First Class was not uncommon. Such an award would qualify him for a middling place in the family pantheon. But no member of the Schmettow family had ever won a Pour le Mérite in the seventy-seven years since Frederick the Great founded the nation's highest award for military officers. A family failing that stung the count.

When Hans discovered the *Luftstreikrafte* in 1916, his fortunes changed. As an infantry officer, being an expert shot was not an advantage. But as a gunner in a two-seater plane and later as a scout pilot, Hans found his vocation. Here, his uncanny ability at deflection shooting was a rare and appre-ciated talent. Here, his ravenous appetite for kills was a virtue. The rise of Hans Schmettow had begun.

An Iron Cross First Class would be just a stepping-stone. If he reached the giddy heights of twenty kills, he could expect a Blue Max. Then he could slither back into that nest of vipers that called themselves his family. And he would strike—for his parents.

Hans had planned his revenge already, and in exquisite detail. *Never fear, Aunt Hilda; I will never forget what I owe this family.* He had only known his father as a haggard and drawn figure, and his mother's smile had gone missing before Hans's memory arrived. But when Hans wreaked revenge against the Schmettow family, they would sleep easier in their graves.

But first, the Blue Max. Only eight more kills ...

15
Wolfpack

"Loners die."

Harsh words spoken in a harsh tone. Lance let them hang in the air, heavier than the tendrils of cigarette smoke that fugged the officers' Mess.

Within two days of Mick Mannock's arrival, Lance's squadron finally possessed a full complement of pilots. Those men now shuffled their bums in their seats. One coughed, others puffed harder, and more smoke curled into the air. The fumes scratched Lance's throat. He stared around the pilots, holding their gazes for a few seconds each.

"Albert Ball was the finest solo pilot in the RFC, and he's dead. When he was our commander, we nicknamed our squadron Ball's Bulls because, we bragged, we charged the enemy with the balls of a bull and the brains of a gnat. That was true. And so, on the day that Ball died, sixty percent of our squadron died as well."

Again, Lance let silence fill the room. This time no-one so much as twitched. Lance leaned forwards and put his knuckles on the long table "From this day on, the Bulls are no more."

He smashed the table with his fist. Pilots jerked in shock.

"No more mindless attacks. The last anyone saw of Ball, he was charging alone after an enemy into clouds. Ditto

Chatsworth-Muster. Ditto 'Warbaby' Harmison. They all died. The squadron scattered to the four winds, and the Circus picked us off one by one.

"I read the combat reports of the survivors. Crowe, you had the goggles shot off your face. Rhys-Davids, you said you were 'jolly lucky to escape.' That right?"

Rhys-Davids shrugged. "Lady Luck was looking after me."

"Lady Luck is a two-timing bitch." Lance glared around the room. "Rely on her and she'll slip a stiletto between your ribs while she smiles at you. From now on, we rely not on luck, religion, superstition, or fate, but on the three most reliable supports a man can ever have—yourself, your teammates, and your training.

"The Circus are flying in larger formations. They culled us that day because they stuck together while we fragmented into individuals. Going forward, we fight in a pack and we look after each other, either as a flight or as a squadron.

"111 Squadron will use wolfpack tactics and adopt the law of the wolfpack in Kipling's *Jungle Book*: *the strength of the pack is the wolf, and the strength of the wolf is the pack.* Any questions so far?"

Most shook their heads, though one or two stared back, hard men in their own right who didn't take kindly to being told how to fight. Lance didn't blame them. Until recently he would have been on their side. But at least Jimmy McCudden and Billy Crowe gave Lance nods of agreement. Weston was gazing out of the window, excavating a hairy nostril. But the big man would not be a problem; he followed orders to the letter. Unlike Rhys-Davids, whose youthful face carried a frown. When it came to reckless charges, the youngster could make a snorting bull look like a dithering dowager. Lance stared directly at him as he continued.

"There are three wolfpack laws: Law one. The brain is a weapon. Use it like one. Law two. We fight in teams whenever possible. Alone, you can chase the high-flying reconnaissance aircraft which come over our lines, but no solo offensive patrols into Hunland. If your flight or the squadron fragment, your first duty is to find your comrades—for your protection and theirs.

"Law three. You and your machinery must be properly prepared to fly and fight. If your own life doesn't motivate you to do that, then know that your teammates are relying on you. You all owe it to each other to be functioning at your best.

"That means you don't get drunk within twelve hours of flying. All of you will check your own ammunition and your sights and harmonise your own guns. When you take off, I want you confident in your machinery, your mind and body, and your teammates. When you are not flying within twelve hours, you can blow off steam anyway you like. Questions?"

Mannock rubbed his hands with glee. "The Huns are due a pasting, and we are just the chaps to do it. When do we start?"

"Soon. But first we train. From now on, training will be your life for every minute of every day, until we are the finest fighting force in the sky. It will hard, damned hard; your muscles will ache, your bellies will grumble from the castor oil, you'll be soggy with weariness and the only easy day will be yesterday. If you don't fancy that, best leave now."

In the long silence, not a man moved. Lance nodded in grim satisfaction.

~

Two days later - 8 July 1917.
Ypres Sector, Bailleul Airfield.

Arthur sighed as he heard, through his office window, Lance berating Smythe once again. "It's not good enough, Sergeant Major. I'm fed up with engine failures. Two planes out of five turned back today."

Arthur couldn't make out Smythe's reply, only the deep rumble that sounded like a volcano about to explode. He rose from his chair—time to keep the peace.

Lance on terra firma had been a pain in the posterior ever since he first joined Arthur's 13 Squadron back in 1916. But now, with a command that he took seriously, Lance was morphing from an irritant to his fellow pilots to a sizable drain on the morale of 100 Wing's ground crew.

Lance had earned enough respect from his pilots that they accepted his whipping them into shape over the past two days. It might keep them alive. The ground crews proved more resentful. The wing orchestra became the first casualty. Arthur had told Clayton to recruit ground crew who were good at their primary jobs but who also played musical instruments. The resulting orchestra played in the Mess most evenings.

Until Lance drove his ground crews so hard that they deputised Sergeant Major Smythe to inform Lance he must decide whether they were mechanics or Mozarts—they could no longer do both. The ultimatum outraged Smythe, who told the mutineers to get their idle arses back to work before he lost his temper. But he delivered the message and Lance, unsurprisingly, said they could down their violins but not their tools.

Lance threw tantrums at every gun stoppage, fuel leak, or engine trouble. Tension grew between Lance and Sergeant Major Smythe. In Arthur's view, Smythe was a marvel of efficiency. If Smythe could not make it happen, then it must be impossible. Lance didn't agree.

Lance was still ranting when Arthur reached the bickering couple. Smythe towered half a foot taller and a foot wider than Lance—a Brobdingnagian taunted by a Lilliputian. His granite face glowered with suppressed rage as he listened to Lance's tirade.

"You think the Huns give a fig that the new 200 hp engines

haven't been bedded in yet? And if they don't care, I don't care. Because it is my pilots who will die. You said your men had improved the carburettors and the air intake drain, so why the heck aren't the engines working faultlessly?"

Smythe kept his voice civil, just. "Sah, when the planes fly through rain or clouds, moisture can enter the intake pipes and ruin the petrol mixture so the engine sputters. It's not possible for the mechanics to control moisture levels in the sky."

"Find a way. Impossible is a cop-out. Problems always surrender to better thinking or harder work. I don't care if you put a gun to their heads, just fix it!"

"Ah, there you are, Sergeant Major," Arthur modulated his voice to imply that this was a chance meeting and a delightful surprise. He eased himself between Lance and Smythe. A vein throbbed in Smythe's temple, and he shuffled his feet at Arthur's presence. Lance frowned at the interruption. Arthur ignored their discomfort.

"Thank you for bringing the strain on your men to our attention," he continued. "They do a wonderful job as the Mess orchestra and keep up morale. But of course, the ground crew must give priority to their machines and the music will play second fiddle for a while. However, I look forward to their musical return shortly when Major Fitch is happy with his planes, and I will arrange a rum ration for those nights when they play."

Smythe scowled. "Thankee, sir. Right decent of you. Army ain't what it used to be. They're trade unionists these days."

"Quite, Sergeant Major. Artists are so temperamental. I understand that it is a stressful for you, providing them with the incessant mollycoddling and praise that artists expect for merely doing their job. Lance, can you come to my office, please?"

Smythe saluted and left.

"What in hell's name was that about?" Lance complained as he followed.

"That, my dear Lance, is known as the carrot. You are flogging your horses too hard—they need a carrot occasionally."

"All I'm asking is for them to do their bloody job."

Arthur stopped so abruptly that Lance bumped into him. "Lance, they're human. The army pays them a pittance for working in cold and dark tents. Your problem is that you think everyone should be as driven as you. That is not the real world. A tot of rum for men who toil all day and play music at night is a worthwhile investment."

"Bribing soldiers with rum wasn't in the manual for my officer course."

Arthur snorted. "That manual is useless in wartime. The Royal Navy started a tradition of giving their men a daily tot of grog in the 1700s and they have hardly lost a battle since. You told me once that to be a hunter you need to get into the mind of your prey. Isn't it worth doing the same for the men who make your planes fly?"

Lance said nothing, but he cocked his head on the side. Maybe, just maybe, Arthur thought, some advice was penetrating that stubborn skull for once.

~

After dinner that night, Clayton tried to fill the musical void with his piano playing, but the audience bitched and moaned. They used to love Clayton's somewhat clunky chords and limited repertoire in the days before Arthur arranged for the orchestra, but now the ingrates were spoiled. The trouble with casting pearls before these particular swine was not that the pearls were wasted. Far worse—the swine now wanted nothing else.

Clayton slammed the lid of the piano down. "See if any of you bastards can do better. It's not my fault. Complain to the person who drove the orchestra to strike."

"I'll have a go on the violin," Mick Mannock volunteered. Clayton, who remembered Albert Ball's excruciating violin playing, was expecting the same from Mannock, but the Irishman astonished the whole Mess. To Clayton's practised ear, Mannock's *Caprice Viennois* contained not just skill but also haunting emotional depth. His rendering of Schubert's *Ave Maria* reduced the pilots to a sniffling, stunned silence as it transported them to a different world.

The conductor of the London Palace Orchestra had once told Clayton that to play with great emotional depth you needed to have experienced life and have something to say. It was clear that Mannock had both. After he finished playing, Clayton waved him over to the barstools, pushed a glass of wine into his hand, and extracted the Irishman's story.

"I was an army brat in India, which damn near killed me. I got malaria and the doctors told me I spent some time knocking on death's door. I recovered but it left me sickly, so my mum was relieved when the Army sent us back to Britain. But when we got there, my alcoholic father left the Army and ran away with what little money we had." Mannock grimaced. "That was an end to my schooling. I needed to earn money so the family could eat."

"Tough start to life," Clayton said. "But you are clearly an educated man now. How did you manage that?"

"Self-taught. When you are at the bottom of the pile, there's plenty of folk ready to kick you when you're down. That's why I developed a love of the underdog and became a socialist. I saw that without education I would always be one of the victims, and maybe end up like my father—a sad loser."

"I'd say you've absorbed more learning than most of the public-school boys in the squadron. More wine?"

Mannock pushed his glass towards Clayton and nodded. "Perhaps because I'm ten years older than most of them. But isn't that the way? When you don't have something, you want it more. When it is force fed to you, you resent it." He took a long sip and cocked his head in appreciation. "Damn, that's good stuff. Arthur's private cellar, I presume?"

Clayton smiled. "The Mess funds certainly couldn't afford it! So how did you end up in the RFC?"

Mannock let out a bitter laugh. "The hard way, that's for sure. I was too dumb to see the war coming and when it broke out, I was working as a telegraph engineer in Turkey. When the Ottomans joined on Germany's side, I was arrested and thrown into a prison camp. I escaped, but they recaptured me and locked me in a tiny concrete box for weeks. By the time the bastards had finished with me, I was three-quarters dead."

Mannock slid off his stool and turned half away from Clayton, hunched over the bar. "They didn't want the embarrassment of a dead prisoner on their hands, so they gave me to the Red Cross to repatriate me home. They figured that even if I survived, I was a broken man."

He paused. A game of ping-pong on the other side of the Mess filled the silence with cracks of paddle on ball and cries of glee and despair. Mannock straightened and gave a savage smile. "They didn't reckon on how powerful a motivation they'd given me. I wanted payback. The Red Cross got me back to England and I joined the Army as soon as I was well enough. Then I saw an article on Albert Ball, which inspired me to join the RFC. So here I am."

"Hell of a story, Mick," Clayton said. "But none of that explains how you come to play the violin so well."

"As part of my self-education, I had lessons with Clara Novello, mother of the famous composer Ivor Novello. Then I listened all I could to Fritz Kreisler, the Austrian violinist. He plays like a god, best violinist in the world."

Clayton shrugged. "Have you heard the new Russian teenage prodigy, Jascha Heifetz? It's possible he is even better."

"Never in a thousand years."

"But Mick, even Kreisler said that after hearing Heifetz, all other violinists should break their instruments across their knees."

"Enough!" Mannock leapt to his feet, peeled off his jacket, and rolled up his sleeves. "Outside now. We'll settle this with boxing gloves."

Clayton stared at Mannock in shock and shook his head. "I only said Heifetz might be better than Kreisler."

"I know what you said," Mannock growled, "and I won't allow such piffle."

Lance, reading in a nearby armchair, intervened. "Mick, you're picking on an old man with a gammy leg. Go box Weston if you need a round or two."

Once reminded of his love of the underdog, Mannock was contrite. "Sorry, Clayton, I forgot. I can't agree with your twaddle, but it was wrong of me to challenge you."

"Quite alright, Mick. You weren't going to get me out of my chair!"

A shadow loomed across them both, and they looked around to see Weston standing next to them, waving a sandwich in one hand and mumbling.

"What?" Mannock asked.

Weston chewed his latest mouthful, gulped painfully, and said, "Just let me finish my sandwich Mick, and then we can box."

"Good idea. Let's go get gloves. Clack clack, tickets please, all turn up for the show!"

The pair marched out of the Mess, followed by a gaggle of pilots who wanted to watch the fun. Clayton looked over at Lance. "Well, I suppose that a thank you is in order, although I would prefer you didn't refer to me as an old man. But are you sure that setting man-mountain Weston against our last decent musician is a good idea?"

"No worries. Weston is enormously strong, but this is boxing. Mick has reach on him and will paint his face for a few minutes until the big man lands a decent punch. That will be an end to it. Mick has a masochistic streak, so when he can stand again, they will both be happy. When he has indulged in his introspective creative side, he needs to unleash some Celtic destruction to reassert his masculinity. Better he does so on Weston than you."

For the second time that night Clayton was surprised by hidden depths. So much so that he couldn't summon one of his habitual quick ripostes.

~

Five days after his wolfpack announcement, Lance's thighs and calves ached from kicking the rudder bars in constant dogfighting drills that filled his time from sunrise to sunset. His right arm throbbed, and his neck grew so stiff that he had to turn his shoulders rather than his head. He woke every night, twitching and grunting as he fought the fights again in his sleep. He was sodden with weariness, yet filled with a strange exhilaration, for he had won the battle for the muscles and minds of the wolfpack.

The pilots' muscle memory bypassed their brains. Countless iterations ingrained instinctive reactions to attack and counter-attack, both individual and collective. Sun and clouds cloaked their ambushes, and their deflection shooting shredded the targets.

Lance, McCudden and Crowe drilled the pilots in the air, but in the officers' Mess Mick Mannock became the most effective evangelist for Lance's desired culture. Where Lance and Jimmy McCudden used quiet logic, Mick Mannock was St. Paul, seeking converts through fire and brimstone. He was not in any position of leadership in the squadron, but he engaged in the battle for the minds of the wolfpack at the Mess bar and the anteroom, where the diehards gathered for their drinking and games of cards. When there was someone willing to debate something, or anything, Mick marshalled words like swords and sent them into battle with joyful glee. If no-one wanted a debate, then Mick set out to provoke one.

Gradually the new credo took root in the squadron. Killing Huns became a noble aim, with keenness, constant practice, and the black arts of cunning evolving into virtues rather than something to mock. If you were on dawn patrol the next day, leaving a binge before you became blotto morphed from being wimpish to common sense. Because fighting the Circus was tough enough without fighting a hangover as well.

The wolfpack was coming together. Tomorrow they would hunt.

16
Bait

Lance had put his head in a noose.

His SE5 circled five thousand feet over Hunland. A thousand feet below him, an antiquated FE2b did lazy figure eights, artillery spotting over Pa's target pillbox. The two of them made a tempting bait for any German planes.

He peered downwards. The trench systems of both armies stretched approximately north-south, snaking through the shell-pocked morass. The rubble of Ypres, currently in British hands, lay strewn to the west. Jagged remnants of the cathedral and Cloth Hall jutted towards heaven, oddly majestic in their forlorn splendour. To the east, Passchendaele ridge loomed over the low-lying mudscape and blocked any British breakout from Ypres. From Lance's perch above, it didn't need a military genius to see why Passchendaele ridge was critical. No wonder the Hun planes were protecting the pillbox with such zeal.

Lance's neck tingled, his senses razor sharp. He'd spent his air-fighting career avoiding perilous positions where he would be at a disadvantage if ambushed. Now he flaunted himself, inviting attack, in a sky with scattered cumulous clouds that could hide a lot of aircraft. Vulnerable was a mighty long word but didn't do justice to the intensity of the goose bumps that prickled his arms.

He'd first experienced this feeling when hunting man-eating lions. Man-eaters, wise in the way of humans and knowing that their feline sense of smell and night vision were superior, killed most often on moonless nights. That's when they were the most dangerous, yet it was paradoxically the best time to hunt them as the man-eaters came looking for human prey. At dusk, the village that had lost men to a lion would tether a white goat as bait, downwind from a suitable tree, and you, the hunter, would wedge yourself in that tree. Then you waited, motionless and stiff, as fears shivered you in the darkness, praying the wind would not change and drift your scent towards the lion. If it did, the hunter would turn into the hunted.

Some nights passed uneventfully, but if the goat bleated in terror, the manslayer was afoot. When the bleating stopped, the lion had killed. Soon the crunch of bones would disturb the still night. Then you sighted through the darkness to the white blur, guessed where the lion was gorging itself, took a long slow breath, and gently squeezed the trigger.

The rifle flash ripped away your night vision. The roar of an enraged lion sent chills up your neck and turned your stomach into a churning pit. You had no idea if you'd hit or not and cowered in the tree for the rest of the long night, hoping you hadn't missed and provoked one of the rare lions that could climb trees.

When dawn came, if you were skilful and lucky, you would spot a dead lion. If you were skilful and unlucky, you had wounded the beast and now had the unenviable task of tracking it. If you lacked skill and luck and had missed altogether, savage growls would rumble beneath you until dawn's light, when the beast would disappear. Worst of all, you'd just alerted a canny lion to your best trick, and the hunt would become a potentially lethal duel of wits over the coming weeks. But whichever of these outcomes resulted, one thing was always a certainty. The goat—the bait—lay dead.

And today Lance was the bait.

The first planes to come sniffing were a flight of British SPADs. They fell in with Lance, offering to provide extra protection for the SE5 and the gunnery spotting FE2b. Lance waved them away. They were ruining his role as irresistible bait. He saw the puzzled shrug from the SPAD flight commander and read his mind. "Silly twit has a death wish." Lance wasn't so sure the man was wrong as the SPADs swung away to resume their own patrol.

Soon afterwards, faint dots in the distance rose from the depths of the east towards Courtrai. They climbed above the lone SE5, placed themselves in the eye of the sun, and crept closer. Sleek round fuselages and curved wingtips—six Albatross! Lance ran his tongue around his suddenly dry mouth, but forced himself to carry on patrolling like a dummy that hadn't noticed the hunters who stalked him. His eyes watered as he tracked the Huns against the sun, using his thumb to block the blinding orb.

Just as Lance judged the Albatross were perfectly placed to dive into their attack, they swerved like a shoal of nervous fish and dived away eastwards.

Despite the sense of anti-climax, relief surged through Lance. Those Albatross looked like experts. Everything about their approach smacked of professionalism. Probably best not to tangle with such a crew while the Wolfpack were still learning their tactics.

He settled back to his plodding patrol. Less than ten minutes later a flight of three Pfalz approached from the direction of Lille. As soon as they noticed him, they nosed his way.

His mouth dried as he watched the slim planes knife towards him. He licked his lips and wiggled his feet on the rudder bars. Muscles tense, he waited, judging the moment to break into the attack.

The Pfalz never reached Lance.

The Wolfpack hit them from behind in a diving attack out of the sun. Jimmy McCudden riddled the leader, who plunged into a steeper dive until his wings ripped off. Rhys-Davids flamed a second that exploded in mid-air, the savage blast rocking Lance's plane. Mick Mannock sent the third into a spiralling spin, trailing a thin spume of black smoke with the pilot slumped lifelessly in the cockpit. When it merged with the earth, a pinprick of flame blossomed.

A hollow feeling dogged Lance. He had done nothing. Yet in less than one minute three Pfalz pilots died because of him.

With Lance as the bait, the rest of the Wolfpack, led by McCudden, had lurked above and behind the clouds, four thousand feet above him.

McCudden had faced a delicate juggling act. The closer he stayed to Lance, the more likely the potential victims were to spot the trap. But if McCudden strayed too far, Lance would have to survive on his own for longer before the trap was sprung. But if there was someone Lance trusted to get that balance right, it was Jimmy McCudden. He had read the Pfalz's intentions with ease and manoeuvred the Wolfpack so they remained hidden behind the far side of the cloud. Then he had sprung the trap perfectly.

But almost too perfectly for Lance's tastes. His hot-blooded hunter's instincts felt cheated, robbed of a kill by the efficiency of his squadron. The adrenalin surging through his body remained unused, frustrated. Yet his cold intellect rejoiced that he had learned how to leverage his cunning. Using the Wolfpack, he'd engineered the deaths of a greater number of the enemy than he could have managed on his own. They might not be his kills strictly speaking, but either way three Huns went to hell in a few heartbeats. He shook his head, awed by the newfound power of doling out death and destruction by proxy.

A green flare exploded below. Lance glanced down. The gunnery spotting FE2b was turning for home, so the artillery must have finished pulverising the pillbox. Pa would be happy.

But Lance wasn't finished. He stayed at five thousand feet and signalled for Jimmy McCudden to reset the trap. The SE5s climbed upwards again. Lance watched his wolfpack with pride and turned hungry eyes to search for more prey.

~

Three days later - 14 July 1917.

Lance cut his engine and jumped out of his SE5. He tousled his sweat-drenched hair and stretched. Another rewarding patrol. In the three days since the first Wolfpack ambush, the squadron had knocked down ten more enemy for no losses. Chalk up two more today.

"I'll be bait next time," Mick Mannock offered. "You need to get kills for yourself. Thommo is catching you."

"Thanks, but I'm not competing with Thommo," Lance replied. "And I'd loathe myself if something went wrong and you got downed."

"I can look after myself."

"No doubt, but I prefer this way. One day you can do the same for your squadron."

When Lance landed, his bloodthirsty ground crew no longer asked for his personal kills, just the squadron tally. He held up two fingers. The news generated muted enthusiasm from his fitter, Digby, and a distinct downward curl of the lips from Murray, his grouchy armourer from Ulster. There was no keeping some people happy. The extraordinary rate of kills was becoming mundane—although to be fair, it was not the kill rate that was exceptional so much as the kill/loss ratio. The Wolfpack had not lost a man. Not even a single SE5 had needed patching up while they destroyed the equivalent of a whole *Jasta*.

The only fault with the tactic lay with the identity of the victims. None of them belonged to Richthofen's Circus. The Wolfpack was catching lion cubs while the canny man-eaters watched from the long grass.

Lance strode over to Sergeant Major Smythe, who presided over the returning planes like a concerned mother hen. Lance scowled at him. "Sergeant Major, we need to talk. See me outside the wing commander's office at 1830 hours tonight."

Smythe looked worried. "Sah!"

~

When the sergeant major presented himself at the required time, Lance and Arthur were waiting for him.

Lance smiled, and Smythe frowned suspiciously. Lance held up five fingers. "A record today, Sergeant Major!"

"Record, sir?"

"Five days in a row without gun jams, fuel line issues, or engine problems. A record for the Wolfpack ground crews. Outstanding."

"Sah." Smythe's lugubrious face twitched in what might have been a smile.

"Now, Sergeant Major, I have come up with a reward for the ground crews. Major Thompson tells me a little bistro nearby is looking for a small orchestra to accompany an elite troop of travelling burlesque artistes."

Smythe frowned. "Burlack artists, sir?"

"A polite French phrase for ladies who cavort in lingerie, Sergeant Major. It occurred to me that this might be a chance for your men to show their musical talents to a wider audience. Of course, all these innocent musicians would need chaperoning among such potential licentiousness. That is where you come in—just the man to keep them on the straight and narrow. The musicians are in the squadron tender, ready to go, but they may leave you behind if you stay here nattering."

Smythe's eyes, which had gleamed at the prospect of ladies in lingerie, became panicked. He flung an immaculate salute and turned to run.

"Not yet, Sergeant! One more thing. This little arrangement will continue once a week only so long as our engines and guns are trouble free, *and* there are no complaints from the bistro, *and* you all keep your mouths shut so HQ doesn't hear about this. *Comprendes,* Sergeant Major?"

"Sir!" Smythe beamed, his face split by a big gap-toothed grin, the first Lance had seen from him. "You are a Solomon and a gentleman, sir!"

"The former maybe, the latter debatable. Dismissed, Sergeant Major."

Smythe hastily recomposed his visage into its customary scowl, saluted, and ran with the grace of a lumbering walrus toward the squadron tender that was tooting impatiently "Sharrup, yer idle buggers, or I'll have yer all I will!"

"Now that is what I call a carrot," Arthur said. "Of course, you found that idea in the officer's manual?"

"Absolutely," Lance confirmed. "In the index under 'strippers, uses of.'"

17
Warriors All

Lance's head throbbed and the overdone roast beef, followed by toffee pudding with custard, sat in his stomach like a cannonball. Words, so many words—only the wine flowed more freely than the verbiage. Words ostensibly spoken to salute their guest of honour, Major Fitch. But to Lance, it seemed their praise was for themselves, the worshipful companies of London.

The Guildhall glittered with candles, velvet robes, gold chains, and glistening bald heads. Fat city cats made fatter by a long war. The room hummed with self-approbation and the satisfaction of a job well done. Most guests were well past fighting age, but a good few looked like prime candidates for the armed forces. Lance brooded on that as the interminable words washed over him. He clutched a cigar, if only for something to do while the words battered him like an unceasing artillery barrage.

The unaccustomed harshness of the smoke scratched his throat raw, yet in his boredom he didn't stub it out. From time to time, he took a hesitant puff and followed it with a swig of warm red wine that made his mouth pucker. Lance ran a finger under his restrictive collar. Maybe he could pretend to go to the toilets and escape out the kitchen door? But the guest of honour disappearing would cause a hell of a stink.

The prime minister, Lloyd George, had demanded that the top aces come to England to appear at dinners designed to raise funds through war bonds. When Arthur told him, Lance had protested. "I'm a pilot, not a speech merchant."

Arthur shrugged. "What can I do, Lance? They want our top aces. As of today, that's you. Ergo, you must go. Prime minister's orders."

"Send Thommo—he'll love it."

"Thompson will do a separate round of war bond dinners."

Lance seethed, but the die was cast. He flew to Dunkirk and then caught a ship and train to London. That way he could ferry a new SE5 back to Bailleul and get something out of this nightmare. Also, he'd bullied the Army into allowing him a half-day to pay his respects to Taggart's widow.

So, this morning, he'd taken off at dawn and flown to Glasgow. The less said about that visit the better. She had listened politely, her face a wooden mask, as he related how Taggart had saved Lance's life at the cost of his own, but her eyes portrayed more eloquently than words how she wished the reverse were true. He shook his head to banish the memories and the guilt.

Lance wiped his mouth. His headache pounded with the stuffy heat, the heavy food, the dull speeches.

Bugger it! He pushed back his seat to leave.

But at that moment the man on his left, the master of the Worshipful Company of Mercers, stood to give the keynote speech. Lance belched discretely and sat back. At least this would be the last speech, but probably the longest. He cringed at the coming salvo of more words.

The room quieted for the master, a powerful figure, barrel-chested with a thick silver mane brushed back over a leonine forehead. "My lords and members of the Guilds of London." The master's sonorous voice carried into the cavernous corners of the vast assembly, and his bushy eyebrows waggled in emphasis of his points. "In these dark and dangerous times for us all, our brave troops fight in the fields of France and Belgium and earn honour and glory. Our sailors risk the perils of the deep to keep the German U-boats and their navy at bay. Our valiant knights of the air, like Major Fitch, our notable guest of honour, joust daily to sweep the Huns from the sky. It is appropriate that we praise their efforts." The master smiled down at Lance, whose face flushed at the unwanted roar of applause.

The master wiped his brow with an elegant blue and silver handkerchief. Speeches were hard work in the stifling hot room. He pointed a large hand into the air and stabbed it at the guests. "But gentlemen, I say to you that we must not delude ourselves as to the real heartbeat of this great nation of ours in its hour of need. It is commerce, gentlemen, which is the heartbeat of our great empire. Trade and shipping are the sinews which bind our global dominions. Our shipping companies bring us manpower and material from Africa, India, Australasia, and the Americas. Our great trading companies buy metals for our weapons from Australia; wool for uniforms from New Zealand; timber from Canada for our airplanes; castor oil from India for food, and medicine, and engine and brake lubricants; rubber from the East Indies and Malaysia for tyres; sugar and rum from the Caribbean. It is commerce that keeps our fleets at sea; it is commerce that equips our armies in the field; it is commerce that keeps our airmen aloft. It is commerce that gives this island nation the ramparts that can never be taken."

Another pause, and more applause. The master drank deeply to refresh himself as the raucous shouts of "Hear, hear!" rang around the hall. One deep breath and he renewed the barrage. "And who drives the commerce?"

Silence weighed the hall for a few seconds as the honourable gentlemen pondered the question. The speaker raised both arms in an enveloping gesture, embracing the whole room, Moses welcoming the faithful to the Promised Land. "You do, gentlemen! I say again, it is you!"

Knives tapped wine glasses in appreciation and the tinkling notes soared to the rafters. Lance recognised the well-bred Englishman's response to praise that he was too confident to need and too well-mannered to claim, but knew full well that he deserved.

"The world's trade passes through this great city. The goods themselves may land perchance in some minor port like Liverpool, but the ships are insured here, the contracts negotiated and bartered here. It is this city and the men who run the commerce in it who are an indispensable cog in the machine of an empire in peace, and even more so in war. Gentlemen, you too are warriors for this nation!"

Lance almost choked on his cigar at that hyperbole. Surely he didn't expect them to swallow that? But the master knew his audience better than Lance. After a brief pause, the pudgy warriors in their dinner jackets rose to their feet, hooting and hollering.

"And yet I ask you, where is the appreciation?" Another roar, even greater than the first, soared to the carved rafters. "Our prime minister speaks of war profiteering and threatens reprisals. But we say to him, commerce cannot continue unless money is made. Not too much of course, only the just rewards for the hard work and risks entailed in keeping this great empire at war. Money is needed to pay the miners, the farmers, the stevedores, the workers, and the merchant seamen. Investment is needed in machinery to make the planes, cars, tanks, and ships. Duties on our goods pay the salaries of our troops—and let it be whispered softly, even of our politicians!"

Hearty boos replaced the cheers.

"None of this can happen without money, without commerce, without trade. Tonight, I want you to send a message to our prime minister and his government. A clear and unambiguous message: let us run our business, and we will let the government run the war. So gentlemen, despite these dark days of deprivation, personal hardship, and suffering, I need you to buy our government's war bonds. I need this great city of London to prove tonight that we are the indispensable centre of commerce, trade, and finance. I ask you to dig deep into your pockets and remind the government that only through us can they hope to raise the millions of pounds sterling needed to fight this war. Perhaps then we will hear the appreciation that we deserve, and the government will come not to bury us, but to praise us. Thank you."

The speaker collapsed in his chair, his face now florid and flushed, as roars of appreciation and support rang around the hall. Lance's lip curled at the frenzy of men baying their power and influence at the walls. It was like an African tribal dance at the full moon, except here the men were fat and soft. His mouth tasted of ash and his throat burned.

Warriors? Hardship? Deprivation? Suffering? Give them a day in the trenches and they would understand just a smidgen of what the troops suffered to keep these men in their comfortable homes. *I have more in common with Boelke and Voss, great flyers and true warriors and decent men by all accounts, than with these parasites.* Lance knew he was fighting against Prussian militarism, but what was he fighting *for*? If these people were the heartbeat of the British Empire, then Lance could think of better causes.

Lance turned to find the master's leonine head regarding him with shrewdness. "A bit rich for you, Major Fitch?"

Lance thought of Clayton and reached for a noncommittal response that the latter might use on one of his tactful days. "A tad."

"I don't blame you. I was in the Army as a lad, fought in the Second Boer War at Spion Kop. Biggest cock-up I ever saw.

If you have not fought, you have no concept of the experience of battle. It is indeed hell. It teaches you that a warrior is not just someone who takes part in a battle, but one who fights well. Most of these men have no conception of what it is like to be a warrior, to be like you. They may envy you, but they could not do what you do in a million years."

"I respect your war service and understanding, but I feel you belittled the men doing the fighting."

"If I did so, it was in a good cause. These men here tonight are genuinely among the best in the world at what they do, trade and finance. In that field, they have nerve and judgement to go with their greed and rapaciousness. The purpose of tonight's dinner was to raise money for His Majesty's Treasury via the war bonds. Great Britain already owes the United States alone about half a billion pounds. Other nations on our side owe us over one and a half billion pounds. They will never repay us. Great Britain, on the other hand, will scrupulously pay its debts. Despite the size of our empire, this war is bleeding our nation dry. We desperately need money to keep going. It is not only a modern or a British problem. As Cicero said around the time of Julius Caesar, 'Money forms the sinews of war.'"

"Men too. You need men—even if troops dying in droves every single day at least saves on wages."

The master flinched at the sarcasm. "You have the right to be bitter and I won't argue with you. But know that I have lost both my sons on the Somme, and too many godchildren and relatives to count. I can no longer fight for my country physically, but I can contribute in my way. If it takes white lies and flattery with a trowel to do that, then I will. I don't want my sons' sacrifices to be in vain. They are dead and I can do nothing that will bring them back. But I can make sure that the underlying cause of this war, the untrammelled spread of Prussian Junkerism, is slammed back in its box so that this truly is the war to end all wars."

Lance looked at the man with grudging respect. He could not extend that esteem to most of the men in the room, but he realised now that they had a function in this war. He reached out and shook the master's hand with a firm grip. "Sir, that is a worthy aim. If you can, make sure that most of that money goes to better equipment for the men in the field, and does not just line pockets on the way."

"That I will, as well I can. And Major, give those Huns hell."

Lance smiled for the first time that night. "That you can rely on, sir." But he knew, as he thought of his Wolfpack, that his smile was more predatory than mirthful, and the master looked at him askance.

~

Lance's foul mood still rode him as he strode along the Thames embankment, trying to walk off his headache and the black dog of his depression. The grim, grey clouds scudding low over the Thames did not help his temper, although he welcomed the wind slapping his face in wet gusts. It blew the fug of the dinner away and calmed his throbbing head and roiling stomach. Petrol rationing had cut traffic and only the occasional car swished past, yellow beams gleaming off the wet road.

He stopped to watch a tugboat pulling a barge upriver. Spray exploded against the blunt bow of the tug and the wind whipped it away, while the dark water below its stern churned into white with the mighty effort of the huge screws. Its stubby funnel stained the dark skyline with blacker smoke and the dull throb of its straining diesels reverberated in Lance's chest cavity. All of nature, the wind and tide, fought the progress of the leashed barge, but it ploughed onwards behind the slow but inexorable force of the tug. When nature battled man, man won most of the time.

Lance snuggled deeper into his greatcoat and continued the walk to the Savoy Hotel. Waterloo Bridge loomed on the right, and he turned into the dark narrow lane of Savoy Hill. At the top, he entered once again the gaiety of London at its most frenetic. *H.M.S. Pinafore* was playing at the Savoy Theatre, and the last performance must have just ended as braying groups spilled out onto the streets.

Lance shook his head, disgusted by how the West End teemed with well-fed folk enjoying their comfortable lives. The contrasts with the men fighting in France left a sour taste in his mouth, ranker even than the cigar.

And the crowds. People, people, everywhere and not a drop of solitude. People jostling, people shouting, people busy ignoring people. It reminded Lance of the anthills of Africa. As a child he had often kicked at these dusty red clay cones, exposing a hidden city of thousands of ants, scurrying hither and thither with no apparent purpose.

Mountains, oceans, and vast plains connected Lance to a grand scheme of nature so magnificent it awakened a holy awe. London made him feel insignificant too, but in a demeaning way. When he had first seen London on his arrival from Africa, its grandeur thrilled him. Now it was just depressing.

Drab uniforms and brightly coloured dresses crowded the Savoy Hotel lobby, even at eleven P.M. The female cast of *H.M.S. Pinafore* were entertaining tonight's collection of men in uniform. Lance pushed through the noisy throng, his nose wrinkling at the wafts of a multitude of warring perfumes. He jostled a few champagne glasses by accident, but no-one protested.

The desk manager seemed particularly oily tonight as Lance picked up his key. Arthur maintained a permanent suite at the Savoy and had persuaded Lance to use the otherwise empty rooms. The downside of this arrangement was the grovelling servitude of the staff once they established that he was a friend of Lord Wolsey.

Lance kicked open the door to the suite, threw his damp overcoat onto the sofa, and marched through into the bedroom, ripping off his constricting tie. As he entered the bedroom, he froze, tie halfway off his neck.

The room lay in velvet darkness, a familiar scent infusing the air. On the far side, a single lamp shone a pool of low light on a woman sitting in an armchair. A purple satin dress clung to her figure. Shadows hid her face, but light gleamed off her crossed, stockinged legs. One high-heeled shoe rested on the floor. The other swung ominously, like a lioness's tail lashing before it charged.

~

Megan scrutinised Lance. He had lost weight, his jaw had grown leaner, his cheekbones were more prominent, and the crows' feet around his eyes had deepened. His hair showed traces of grey at the sides. What was he now? Twenty-two? Twenty-three? Yet a stranger would guess over thirty. A tender part of her that she thought she had lost forever winced at what he must have been through to suffer such changes.

He leaned against the wall with that unnatural stillness of his, hoarding the coiled energy of a dangerous man as he allowed the silence to build between them.

A small voice reminded her to not underestimate him. She always felt she had his measure in cities and in the boudoir, as those places were her natural habitat. Less so for him. However, a wolf on a leash was still a wolf—unpredictable and with sharp fangs.

Megan had staged the room to intimidate him, but he didn't show any trace of nerves as he waited. She pitched her voice low but enunciated each word precisely, leaning on every syllable. "Leading my son into hordes of the enemy elite was not exactly what I meant when I begged you to look after him."

Lance stared back, unblinking. "It was our job."

"And the court martial?" Despite herself, this emerged as more of a hiss.

"He didn't do his job. He ran away. A good man got killed as a result."

She managed to bite back her thought before it reached her lips. *As if I care about good men!*

In the street outside, a car drove past and its headlights swirled briefly around the room. The sound of its gear change grated in the quiet room.

"I didn't expect to see you again. Do you hate me for what I did?" Lance asked.

Megan picked up the glass of whisky from the side table and took a slow sip, keeping her face in the darkness while she considered. Her scarlet-painted fingernails tapped chimes on the half-empty crystal glass.

She still needed him. His punishment could wait.

She softened her voice. "Yes...and no. Morgan forgot his responsibilities and was seduced by the glamour of being a pilot and a hero. That is not his destiny. Any fool can do those things. Not everyone can be Lord Wolsey."

Lance crossed his arms. "I thought Arthur is Lord Wolsey?"

"And if—God forbid— Arthur dies with no heir, Morgan will be."

"I see," Lance said in a tone that said he did not much care.

"I forbade Morgan to join the RFC, but he can be stubborn. God knows flying is dangerous enough, but then fighting the Germans too? His chances of survival as a pilot must have been low—"

"Make that zero," Lance grunted.

Megan ducked her head in acknowledgement. "So anything, and I mean anything, that removed him from danger is welcome. You achieved what I could not and scared him away from being a pilot. When I first heard what you had done, I wanted to scratch your eyes out, but now I confess I am happy with the outcome."

"And his court martial? He may face the firing squad for desertion in the face of the enemy."

"Oh, that!" She wagged a long forefinger at him "That would never happen, dear. I would not allow it. Whatever his sins, he is my son, and there will be no court martial. It is decided."

"What?" Lance took a pace forward and his voice rose. "How in God's name can you influence the Military High Command over a court martial in wartime?"

"Please, Lance, don't pretend to be so naive. I gave you the benefit of the doubt and assumed that when you demanded his court martial, you knew Arthur and I would get it squashed. Our family is one of the oldest and most powerful in the land. Breeding and influence still count in England, and it is a better place for it."

She leaned forward into the light and took another sip, giving him a glimpse of her décolletage. Sure enough, his eyes dropped. It excited her, this power she had to draw men into her sensual web.

As he stood rooted to the floor, she rose and swayed towards him. She made her voice husky. "Did you really think the famous war hero could sneak into London and stay in Arthur's suite without me finding out?" She leaned against his body, her face cuddling into his chest.

He stood rigid, arms by his side, and said nothing.

She raised her face to his and looked into his eyes. "I'll be honest. I was disappointed with your actions, but I want my lover in my arms and bed." That at least was no lie. He was a lean and deadly animal and Megan revelled in his toned body, his stamina, and his willingness to please and learn. That such a dominant herd bull found her irresistible fed her own lust. She took his arms and folded them around her, placing his hand on her buttocks.

"Did I do right?" Her hips oscillated against him as she spoke, and his body responded to the memories and her evident desire. "Aha! Someone is glad I came."

~

Lance's shook himself, trying to throw off the foul mood that lingered from the banquet. Her generous peace offering was more than he had expected. He would never understand women, he knew that much, and instinct warned him that hidden reefs lay under the smooth-flowing words. But if there were complications ahead, they were for another day.

He sighed and allowed his hands to stroke the flare of her hips as he kissed her. "I am glad you came," he murmured between kisses.

He shivered as she licked his neck. "Mmm," she murmured. "A distinctive bouquet—salty, which I like, but with light overtones of cigar, which is not my favourite."

"There shouldn't be any cigar aroma lower down."

"Are you sure? Perhaps I should check before I order a case?"

"Please do, mam'selle, but I am afraid there is a no return policy once you have uncorked the bottle."

She gurgled with laughter and bent to her knees. For a while he rode an endless ribbon of pleasure before he pulled her up and kissed her. His primal desire subsumed all his anger at the smugness of civilian life. They fell onto the bed together, her kisses as deep and urgent as his. Her slippery mouth and tongue slid against his and sucked him into a driving vortex of lust. His father's illness, the fat cat war profiteers, and the London gloom all disappeared in the age-old rhythm and the jingle of her silver bracelets.

Afterwards, his headache cured, he fell asleep for a short while. When he awoke, the light was still on and Megan sat upright in bed beside him, sipping from a glass. Her bracelets jangled and her left breast lifted as she offered him the drink. He demurred. "No thanks, I can't stand Scotch."

Megan placed the glass on the bedside table, lay down beside him, and caressed a lingering forefinger across his lips. "Kiss me."

He obeyed, stroking her smooth, curvaceous hip. She tasted of Scotch and peat smoke and her musky scent made his senses reel. When she ended the kiss, she rolled on top of him. "I read in the press that you have killed more enemy pilots than anyone else. Tell me what it is like when you kill someone." Her slanted eyes glinted as they searched his, a half-smile playing on her lips.

His romantic mood shattered, and his voice became rough with irritation. "This is not a usual conversation, Megan. Suppose I ask you as a loving lead in—have you killed many men?"

She smiled brilliantly. "Only with pleasure, Lance, and now I am going to work on one more!" Her hand slipped lower and teased him to life again.

As always with Megan, it was a riot of the senses, a titillating carousel of pleasure.

After the sweat dried, he spooned behind her and drifted towards the gentle eddies of dreamless sleep. Only sex with Megan granted him that gift: a sleep without nightmares, a night without flames.

~

Megan stretched her long legs and admired her supple skin, golden in the warmth of the morning sunlight streaming through the half-open curtains. Her belly growled and made her think of breakfast. Lance's lovemaking always gave her an appetite.

With Morgan no longer in Arthur's 100 Wing, Megan needed someone to feed her information, however unwittingly. Lance was perfect, privy to Arthur's innermost plans and naïve enough to pass them on to her. Also, if she could drive a wedge between them, Arthur would lose his most capable protector in the air. Which was vital to her plans. If Morgan was to inherit the Wolsey Estate, Arthur must die before he could impregnate that dago slut of a wife with a son.

The Huns had done a damn poor job of killing Arthur so far, but his luck could not last forever. The odds against his survival were remorseless, especially when 100 Wing faced the enemy's elite every day. Morgan said that Lanoe Hawker, Leefe Robinson, and Albert Ball were all better fliers than Arthur, and all of them were killed by Richthofen's Circus. But the way Morgan told it, Arthur's odds plummeted further if Lance protected him less in the air.

Lance might even be useful in the longer term. If he survived the war and if she could train him to accept a bridle, he could make for a dashing consort. A famous war hero could open doors still closed to a mere woman, even if she was a Wolsey. She would walk the great halls of the royal and rich with him beside her—handsome in his youth, haughty in his stiff-necked pride, dripping in glory from the spilled blood of his country's enemies. The Victoria Cross, England's supreme medal for valour, forged in bronze from the cannons of the Crimea, would flaunt itself on his chest, and post-war high society would fall at the feet of such a good-looking and gallant couple.

And though Megan wasn't keeping Lance for his lovemaking, it was an added benefit. Especially after the drooling moustaches and the flabby bellies of the geriatric generals and politicians she had slept with to win Morgan's freedom. The memories were still raw—blubbery flesh wobbling beneath her, the wheezing breath that smelt of decay as she flogged ecstasy out of their ancient carcasses. She'd wondered if it might put her off sex for the rest of her life. Happily, Lance had answered that question.

But still, he must pay. She would make him suffer for every rank, enseamed bed that she endured to unravel his sanctimonious betrayal of her son.

Lance stirred and stretched out a hand. She rolled onto her stomach, naked on top of the sheets, and revelled in his touch as his hand stroked down her neck, between her shoulder blades, along her spine, and down to the curve of her hips. A rough callous on his forefinger scratched slightly on her soft skin. Was that the trigger finger that killed all the Germans? A frisson shuddered through her. She grew wet again and murmured approval.

His voice surprised her. "I can't believe you have forgiven me for Morgan."

Megan stiffened. She rolled over onto her back. "After last night, what more do I have to do to convince you?"

Lance's green and bronze-flecked eyes bored into hers. She looked away and waved a hand. "I should warn you. You have given Morgan a strong sense of purpose—he wants revenge on you. You have shown him that life is serious, that even my son will have to fight for some things. Suddenly he is listening to me. I am polishing his skills and training him how to dissemble, hide motives, and influence people so he will learn how to suborn generals and politicians. I have to say he is showing a natural talent in these areas. More than I had dared hope. Now he will be promoted to captain and attached to RFC HQ staff in France, where his strengths will show, and we will find him rapid promotion."

"What?" Lance sat bolt upright, the bedclothes falling off his ridged stomach. "Promoted? To the RFC staff in France?"

"Yes, didn't Arthur tell you?" she asked. *That should put the cat among the pigeons!*

Lance's lips tightened. He started to say something but snapped his mouth shut and stormed out of bed to the window, saying nothing. Megan smiled to herself. He would come back.

For a time, she had thought it would be easy to turn his lust into an obedient infatuation, as she had with many men. But his public denunciation of Morgan's cowardice had shown that would be difficult. The boring and old-fashioned virtues of honour and decency lay deep-rooted inside him. However much he lusted after her, it would be a delicate task to prise him away from his bedrock beliefs.

Megan might have given up the challenge but for the strength of his idealism. Idealism that pure could only find itself betrayed, and she would twist his idealistic zeal into anger. His disillusion at the war bonds dinner and her son's escape from court martial had already started the process.

Now she must harness the lurking beast inside his psyche, which showed in the passionate intensity of his multiple revenge quests, and his assassin's approach to killing in the air. Like a wild stallion, he needed careful handling, but disillusion and lust would be the whip and spur she could use to break him to her purpose. Then she would teach him the savage glee of galloping wild on the dark side, untamed by the reins of tired convention and the curb of stifling morality.

Megan lifted her arms and locked her hands behind her head, pulling her breasts higher and more rounded, and waited for him to turn around and enjoy the tableau. While she waited, she savoured the sight of his taut buttocks and lean waist. Deliciously, she hugged to herself the knowledge of her immediate revenge. *You are a beautiful lethal killer, my dear, but no-one plays games with me and mine without suffering.*

"Don't be sour," she said. "You must have known that

Arthur and I wouldn't let the family name be ruined."

"Don't be fucking *sour?* It's a disgrace! Taggart, the man who did his duty, is dead and his wife and child alone in the world. And your son escapes scot-free. It makes me wonder what I am fighting for."

"Don't shout at me, darling. Only losers resort to shouting, and I never thought of you as a loser, Lance. At least not until I heard you tried to resign from commanding a squadron."

Lance rounded on her. "I didn't want to be a leader. You and Arthur, you nagged me into it." His voice faded away. "And now men have died because of my leadership."

"Oh, for God's sake, Lance, stop whimpering! I told you men in wartime need hard men as leaders. I thought you were hard. You hated Germans, and it sounded as though you didn't care much for your own side either. Now that they have made you a leader, you sound like a mewling milksop. Do you think there has ever been a successful officer who didn't get men killed? Everyone else is declaring you a marvel, and all you do is whine. Grow up and do what the old Lance would do—avenge them!"

He stared at her, and she rolled her eyes. "Pff. Don't look at me like a beaten puppy." This wishy-washy Lance wasn't to her liking at all. But she'd whipped him enough, time for some honey.

Megan leaned towards him to let her breasts sway forwards, then trapped them between her arms to deepen the valley between them. His eyes slid down to follow them—like all men, looking in the wrong places for answers. She widened her eyes for him as she gazed at his hardening manhood.

"Be grateful Arthur ripped up your resignation. Get on with it. And as for Morgan, he is my son. What did you expect me to do? Lead the lynching mob?"

"The generals do a damn good job of court martialling the plebeian cowards, the shell-shocked nobodies. Shame they aren't as zealous at prosecuting craven aristocrats."

For God's sake, Lance, come fuck me before your whining turns me off. She slipped her pink tongue between her moist lips and breathed more deeply.

He strode back to the bed and kissed her hard on her uplifted mouth, and she pulled him onto the mattress with open limbs and a throaty murmur. She rode his anger, thrusts inflamed then tamed, until the dam burst and left them both quaking and shuddering.

He rolled off her onto his back, panting, and she stretched like a satisfied cat before throwing a leg over him possessively. "You rut with the vigour of an animal, Lance."

"Is that a complaint?"

She laughed. "Not from me, darling. It excites me, but you kill like an animal too. You live close to your shadow side in all your appetites."

He shifted underneath her leg. "Killing is not an appetite, Megan, not for me."

She smiled into his chest. *No? Men are so blind.* "Maybe, Lance, you are like those man-eating lions you told me about? You have killed so often now, perhaps you have a taste for killing and don't realise it."

"Rubbish!"

Methinks he doth protest too much. "Would you like some breakfast? I can get some sent up if you wish, darling?"

When the scrambled eggs and tea arrived, she slipped a pinch of buckthorn powder into the teapot. Not enough to be fatal, but enough to punish. She'd suffered as she had serviced those panting, slobbering, blubbery old men in order to save Morgan from Lance's accusations. He must suffer too.

She poured a cup, added milk, and handed him the poisoned chalice. As she did so, she kissed him, slipping her tongue between his lips.

~

Later that day
Over the English Channel

Lance grunted involuntarily as his guts spasmed again, doubling him over in pain. Cramps rocked his body and sweat rolled down his forehead despite the chill at six thousand feet. He let the SE5 fly itself. He had no choice.

Eventually those spasms waned. The next phase came with a thunderous rumble in his stomach. He groaned, his entire focus clenched against the humiliation of soiling his breeches. His plane lurched all over the sky, but he didn't care.

When, at last, that phase also eased, he took a deep breath and straightened in the cockpit. By now he knew the cycle. He had maybe five minutes before the next attack. Each cycle had grown stronger. Thank God he was flying the stable SE5. In a Sopwith Camel, which demanded constant pressure on stick and rudder, he would have already spun into the sea. But he must land the plane soon because he wouldn't survive if he ditched in the foam-flecked Channel below. He was closer to France than England but if the spasms kept getting worse, he was a dead man, even in an SE5. No aircraft could fly itself for long in this turbulent sky.

He peered forwards and through the scattered altocumulus clouds, whipped thin by the strong wind. But ahead of him, only white-capped waves rolled away endlessly into the distance. Lance checked the compass and cursed. He'd wasted precious time off course. Swinging east, he squinted with watery eyes through the haze. Was that wispy line the coast of France? Or was it cloud, conjured by hope into an illusion of land? He nosed down into a shallow dive, trading the safety of height for speed.

Below him, the grey Channel rollers grew more solid and

threatening as he lost altitude. His eyes flicked to the horizon but clouds obscured the view. He drummed his fist on the cockpit coaming, urging the plane on, desperate to beat the next wave of cramps.

Only four hours ago, Megan had been treating him to breakfast in a gilded room at the Savoy. Now he faced the ignominious death of crashing into the sea while ferrying a new SE5 from England. *Killed by a dodgy meal from London's finest hotel. At least the Huns will be laughing.*

The nose of the SE5 burst through the thin layer of cloud. There! Not just land, but a sprawling splodge of buildings. *Dunkirk, by God!* He'd lucked out. St.Pol-sur-Mer airfield lay a mile south of Dunkirk, right on the coast ahead of him. He pushed the nose down further and his spirits rose as the wind whistled louder through the wires.

He was on his final approach, forty feet up, when the cramps abruptly returned. His foot slipped from a rudder bar as he grunted and doubled over. The plane lurched into a sideslip. He corrected just in time to skid clear of the looming water tower. With his coordination of stick and rudder warped by the spasms, he over-corrected and the landing rattled his teeth, but the undercarriage held and the plane ran straight and true.

As soon as the tail skid bumped the grass, he taxied fast towards the nearest wooden latrine hut, scattering ground crew who had approached to help him. When the aircraft trundled to a halt, he wrenched himself out of the cockpit and scuttled, hunched over, into the latrine, where his bowels voided in a stinking, splashing mess.

"Jesus Christ!" came a broad Lancashire accent from the stall next door. "What's died in there? That's worse than Fritz's gas!"

Lance just groaned in response, too wretched to take offence. Outside the SE5 engine ticked over and the shouts of the ground crew grew louder. The Lancashire man fled from his stall and enlightened the men outside with coarse jokes as Lance was chained to the bog, wracked by stomach cramps while his body purged itself over the next half-hour.

After a few cups of dynamite-strong tea, he recovered enough to continue the flight. With his guts improving, it freed up his mind to churn over Budd's escape from court martial. His brain joined his bowels in turmoil. His mood was black and festering when he arrived at Bailleul after another bog break. It was late and the light was bleeding into full dusk when he landed. He handed over the plane to the mechanics and barged into Arthur's office.

Arthur and Clayton looked up at the forceful entrance. "Heard about Budd's court martial?" Lance asked without preamble.

The awkward silence told him they had. Arthur cleared his throat, and said in a neutral tone, "Welcome back. Good to see you too, Lance. It appears that the Army overruled my recommendation and squashed his court martial."

"Why?"

"HQ did not take me into their confidence. When Boom passed on the news to me, he was puce with anger. After all, he endorsed my recommendation too."

Lance glared at Arthur, then swivelled on his heel to look out the window, buying time to control the vicious responses that crowded the tip of his tongue. In the distance, a Hispano engine started up, coughed twice, and then chugged into its rhythm.

"And you, Clayton?" asked Lance, "Any clues from your moles in HQ and the Army?"

Arthur glanced at Clayton, surprised. Clayton arched an eyebrow at his commanding officer before replying. "Since you ask, little birdies whisper in my ear that Lady Exenrude spread her wings, so to speak, to protect her erring cuckoo. A ditty is doing the rounds in Westminster:

There is a certain lady from Exenrude
Who does her politics in the nude.
Lords and generals give their blessing
As her bosom is very prepossessing
While she is amorously undressing."

"Salacious garbage," Arthur growled.

Clayton bowed all round. "I apologise and stand reprimanded. Let us stick to known facts. Three jolly important personages interceded on Budd's behalf—one cabinet member with a large stomach and an equally large sphere of influence in both Parliament and the press, one portly presence in the House of Lords, and one skinny aristocratic field marshal. Between them they squashed the court martial before it started. Haig and Boom were livid, but they have more important fish to fry. So it came to pass that our young toad escaped his just deserts, which should not be a surprise. After all the family motto is '*Generositate nil sister contra*'—which for our colonial's benefit I shall translate—"

"I know," Lance said. "'With noble birth nothing shall stand against me.' I can't believe I'm fighting to keep titled parasites with mottos like that safe in their beds. If I'm around after the war, I'll be voting for whoever wants to tax 'em out of existence."

"Tut, tut," Clayton said with a wicked smile. "That would put a crimp in the Wolsey Estate."

Arthur gave his Adjutant a filthy glance.

"Know what the Army tittle-tattle back in England says?" Lance said. "An officer at the airfield had heard that Arthur and Lady Exenrude were furious when Morgan Budd, potential heir to the Wolsey title, volunteered to fight for king and country. So, they hatched a plot to court martial him to get him out of danger, safe in the knowledge they could quash the accusations once he was safely back in England. The valiant Budd is mortified that his family compromised his honour and is determined to return to active service, but his efforts are being blocked by his over-protective uncle."

"A plausible tale, no doubt spread by Budd," Clayton said. "Many will believe it."

"It is ridiculous tosh!" Arthur snapped.

"We know it's rubbish," Lance said. "But the conspiracy theorists say that if Lord Wolsey truly wanted to court martial anyone, he would have made it known far and wide. No-one would have dared stand against a Wolsey. I'm told the political and social graveyards are full of those who took on Lord Wolsey."

Lance stared at his friend and commanding officer, his eyes hot and hard. "But you didn't let it be known, did you, Arthur?"

"Of course I did not! Not because I wanted him cleared, but because I trusted the Army had enough integrity to do the right thing. Politics and the Army should not mix."

"I rather think it was the previous Lord Wolsey who buried those bodies," Clayton murmured, seeking to dissipate the storm clouds.

Lance ignored Clayton. He was still glaring at Arthur. "Why didn't you make sure they did the right thing? You owe Taggart, the whole of 100 Wing, that much."

"How the hell was I to know they would squash it?" Arthur lurched to his feet. "I promised you I would not interfere with his court martial, and I did not. What else do you want?"

"I want justice. I want Taggart's bravery rewarded with a medal, so his wife and children know he died a hero. And I want Budd's cowardice reviled and his name dragged through the mud. Anything less dishonours the RFC pilots who fight and die for their country."

"Well, I do not run the RFC, never mind the Army, so do not blame me! I put Taggart up for a medal and Budd for a court martial. I did my bit."

"Did you? Funny, 'cos Taggart didn't get a medal and Budd

didn't get court-martialled. Don't you lords have your unofficial channels to get your own way in good old England?"

"Damn you, Lance! I do not need you as my conscience. I played it by the book, so find someone else to blame. You got a blasted medal and Taggart did not, but that is not my fault. The commanding officer of the Sopwiths you rescued praised you to the sky in his report. He did not see Budd run for home, and he hardly mentioned Taggart."

Arthur turned his back on his officers and grabbed his coat and cap. Turning, he thrust his cap at Lance like a baton.

"The press got a copy of the Sopwith commander's combat report, and everybody wanted to hang a gong on you, and no-one wanted to focus on the sordid little by-story about Budd. Haig and Boom are keen to punish cowards and malingerers, but they got outranked by the war cabinet, who decided the story of an RFC hero defying the might of Richthofen's Circus should not be tainted with tales of another's cowardice. Bad for the public's morale, etc., etc. I cannot succeed where Haig and Trenchard failed, even if I am a lord. That is the truth. And the two of you—" the cap stabbed out again towards them— "can shove the gossip up the tittle-tattlers' rear ends." Arthur gave a hostile glare to his subordinates and stalked out of his office.

"Methinks he doth protest too much," Clayton muttered.

Lance was more emphatic. "He should have pushed harder. Arthur is a good man, but he would be a great one if he battled for his beliefs. How can he be so brave in war and so feeble in conviction? He has such power and influence, and so little inclination to use it for good."

"I agree, *mon frère*. But he worries that if he uses his influence, he is perpetuating the problem. He's so purist that he thinks away his ability to act. Sort of a Hamlet, I suppose."

"Where did you hear that dirty ditty about Lady Exenrude?" Lance's voice was rough.

Clayton looked at him in surprise, and then with speculation. He cleared his throat. "I was guilty of listening to my cousin, a member of Parliament, but since they are protected from slander laws while in session, they are often the worst of gossip mongers. But let's change the subject before the steam coming out of your ears blows off the top of your head. Seen this?" Clayton held out a copy of the *London Daily Mail*. "Thommo took the opportunity to brief the press on himself while he was in London."

A photo of Thommo in the cockpit of a Camel adorned the front page, immaculate in dress uniform, hair slicked back, a debonair silk scarf wrapped around his neck. Teeth dazzled in a cocksure grin under his trimmed moustache. "Daredevil Major Thompson takes on Red Baron," the headline screamed.

Lance tossed the paper back. "He's welcome to it. I don't want publicity."

"You should read the last two paragraphs. The ones that say..." Clayton raised the paper and read in a portentous tone. "The dashing Canadian is locked in a neck and neck race with Major Lance Fitch, the Ace from Africa, to be the top scoring ace of the British Empire. Asked what makes the two of them so successful, Thompson answered that they were totally different in their approach. 'War in the air is new and you have to respond by using modern ideas. Major Fitch believes in old-fashioned methods, the way people hunt in Africa. This works for him personally, but the RFC needs senior officers who look to the future as they train pilots and design tactics.' Asked if there was a spirit of competition with Major Fitch, Thompson replied that they were friends but there is a good-natured rivalry. He then added with his trademark daredevil grin, 'I fully expect to win!' It is precisely this spirit of friendly competition in downing the dastardly Huns, that in the coming months will have the likes of the Red Baron looking over their shoulder with fear."

"What tosh journalists write," Lance said tiredly. The heat and anger had drained from him and been replaced by overwhelming apathy.

"It doesn't bug you, this public implication that you are outdated?"

"I couldn't give a damn. My job is to shoot down Huns and they don't read the *London Daily Mail*. I'm sure they'll find my outdated bullets just as nasty as Thommo's. If he wants to pump himself up in the press and take a few shots at me in the process, that is his affair, not mine."

"Frightfully mature of you," the adjutant said. "Not sure I'd be so forgiving."

"I'm not bloody forgiving," Lance said, exasperated. "I'm just bloody exhausted fighting people who are supposed to be on my side." He slumped onto one of the chairs, a punch-drunk boxer reaching his corner at the end of a punishing round. Dysentery and disillusion were as potent a combination as a left hook and a right uppercut.

"God, I can't tell you how depressing London was. It's a cesspit of intrigue and avarice. I was summoned to meet various generals and politicians. Did they want to hear ideas of how we could win the air war? Or ask what we need? The hell they did! They wanted me to say what a terrible job Boom Trenchard was doing. When I said I didn't think he was doing a bad job, they told me I didn't understand. All because the prime minister thinks General Haig is a disaster, and Trenchard is a supporter of Haig. Jesus! If the generals and politicians put half that effort into the war instead of backstabbing each other, we might have won by now. I don't know what the hell I am fighting for anymore."

"What?" the adjutant asked with a mocking smile. "Not king and country? You colonials are a seditious bunch."

"Never met the king, and frankly—based on the people in charge in London—I'm not sure I like the country."

"Lance, you're wallowing in self-pity again. Ever since I've known you, this has been a personal war for you. You're here for revenge, and to win the war so you can go home and live safely in Africa without the Huns invading you. You never swallowed all the patriotic claptrap, so don't act all disillusioned when you find out we have pricks among our politicians and generals. They are still a darn sight better than the Kaiser, who even neutral observers think is cruel, bombastic, and power crazed. There is a valid reason why over twenty countries are at war with Germany. If we don't teach them a lesson now, they would overrun Europe and the colonies to the detriment of human decency in those areas. You've said all this yourself a dozen times."

Lance blinked, then nodded. He sighed and scratched his cheek. "You're right. It's just that recent events are sticking in my craw."

Clayton nodded. "It disgusts everyone when they go back to England on leave and see the fat cats at home playing while we fight the war. Still, I hope the ladies of London did their patriotic duty and made it up to you."

Lance looked up, alarmed that Clayton had heard something about his meeting with Megan, a guilty reaction that made Clayton's sardonic eyes gleam.

"Aha! A shot in the dark, but a veritable bull's eye for Clayton," the adjutant crowed.

Lance beat a retreat. "Dinner time. Coming?" He fled the office, followed by a chortling Clayton.

They took a step outside and paused. While they had been inside, a light drizzle had set in, accompanied by a nasty cutting wind. The two officers slapped on their caps, ducked their heads, and scurried towards the Mess, which rang with a sing-along in full voice.

Two German officers crossed the line
On the lookout for women and wine.
Inky pinky parlez vous.
They came to an inn on top of a rise.
A famous inn of bloody great size.
Inky pinky parlez vous.
"Oh landlord, you've a daughter fair,
With lily white bosom and golden hair."
Inky pinky parlez vous.
"Nein, nein, mein Herr, she's much too young."
"Mais non, mon père, I'm not too young;
I've often slept with the parson's son."
Inky pinky parlez vous.

Lance pushed open the door and a blanket of warm air hit him as the pilots bellowed the chorus. It felt like home.

18
The Three-Stage Cure

Five days later - 25 July 1917.
100 Wing. Bailleul, Ypres Sector.

The night was full of flames. But tonight, Lance's usual nightmares of fiery death were joined by a leering Budd, cackling in glee as he watched the fingers of fire reach for Lance's cockpit. Then the flames took Megan's form. "Pain and pleasure, two sides of the same coin," the wraith of fire whispered as she scorched his cheek with a caress.

Lance jolted awake, woken by his own thrashing which had tangled him in his bedclothes. Exhaustion crushed him, worse than when he had gone to bed. He'd been back in France for five days now, and still the dreams came. His watch showed 0415 hours. The dawn patrol would take off in an hour. B Flight was scheduled for the dawn patrol, but he might as well join them rather than toss and turn for a few more hours. Anything to occupy his hyperactive mind.

He yanked on his woollen socks to protect his feet from the cold wooden duckboards, then wriggled into his rough serge shirt and trousers, and slipped on his leather cavalry boots. He grabbed his flying gear in the crook of his elbow and strode out of the tent, deliberately underdressed, hoping the chill would snap him out of his torpor. His boots swished through the dewy grass as he hurried through the grey predawn to the hangars, where he told the fitters to prepare his plane for an early flight. The birds' dawn chorus started as he walked back. Their merry trilling did not improve his sour mood. *It's alright for you—you don't have Huns shooting at you when you fly.*

Lance was first into the dark Mess. The breakfast orderlies clattered their way in from the kitchen and began lighting lamps and laying out the breakfast.

"Morning, sir," Sergeant Williams said. "You on the dawn patrol this lovely morning, sir? Thought it was B Flight today?"

"It is, but I might join them."

"Keen as mustard you are, sir. Don't know how you blokes—begging your pardon, sir—do it day after day."

Lance grunted and said nothing. If only the sergeant knew the truth.

He forced a change of thought and wondered who would be on dawn patrol today. Several pilots were on leave, including the B Flight commander, McCudden. Lance had given the flight to Mick Mannock while McCudden was away, and today could be a chance to assess Mick as a flight commander.

"Your usual, sir?"

"Thanks, Williams. Less sugar and more salt in the porridge this time, I hope?"

"Couldn't rightfully say, sir. I passed your comments onto the cook, but we never know what the daft bugger will do. It was a grand idea by Lord Wolsey to get us a chef from the Ritz Hotel, but army porridge ain't his idea of real cooking so he's always adding summat to it."

Mick and Weston had ambled in, both bleary eyed, but catching the tail end of the conversation.

"I like porridge the way it was at school," Weston said, accepting a large portion from the sergeant. "Nice and simple, none of this fancy stuff."

"Heathen Scottish invention," Mick said. "Ought to be banned in a civilised Mess."

"Thought you were half Scottish?" Lance asked.

"My father's half, but he ran off. That's why I stick to Irish whisky."

"Good Irish logic," Lance said.

"Yuck!" Weston exclaimed. "The porridge is foul! What's he put in it this time?"

Lance took a spoonful. "Whisky and cream?"

"Mmm," Mick said. "Let me try. Lance knows nothing about spirits. Nope, I'd say brandy."

Weston flung down his spoon in disgust. "I like brandy and I like porridge, but they really don't go together."

Mick wandered over to the Decca gramophone, and soon the gentle strains of "Londonderry Air" wafted through the Mess.

Lance winced. "Do you have to play this before a dawn patrol? I feel melancholy enough at this time of the morning."

Before the Irishman could retort, Terry shuffled into the Mess looking as pale and wan as that naturally swarthy man could. "Morning all," he greeted them in a gruff voice. A few weeks ago, the Yorkshireman had gone down with a suspected case of measles, and he had been quarantined away from the squadron. As a result, today would be his first patrol over the lines.

Lance studied him, eyes narrowed. Last night in the Mess, Terry had waved a letter and announced he was the proud father of Annie, a new-born baby girl of seven pounds. The Mess lit up with whoops and insisted he pay for a round of drinks to wet the baby's head. Terry showed a photo of a mewling pug that left Lance cold, but the father glowed as he pored over the picture. Lance had watched him to ensure that he did not drink too much before his debut patrol and only saw him have one beer. So was this morning's queasy look the result of secret imbibing or just nerves?

Mick tackled the issue with his usual sensitivity. "Hung-over or nervous?"

Terry cleared his throat as though ashamed. "Nerves, I'm afraid."

Mick laughed. "Don't worry, it's natural. We were all nervous on our first time across. I still am, more often than not."

"Try the porridge," Lance offered. "It gives the stomach something to chew on during an early patrol."

"I prefer two eggs in a whisky," Mick said. "The whisky counteracts that damn castor oil, so I don't have to go to the loo all day long."

"Nothing beats good old-fashioned English fried bread, egg, and bacon, if you ask me," Weston declared.

"I think I'll choose that," Terry said, "The rest sounds a bit too exotic for my tastes this morning."

"Williams," Lance called. "The full fry-up for Mr Terry, if you please."

"Coming up, sir. Mr Mannock, your eggs in whisky."

"Thanks, Williams," Mannock replied. "What are you doing up so early?" he asked Lance. "Going on a solo patrol?"

"I thought I would tag along with your flight, if you don't mind."

"Well, you might have more joy on your own today. It's Terry's first time over the lines, so I'm settling for a cautious once-over, a familiarisation flight. But if you want to come along, you're more than welcome."

"How about I join you and help look after Terry? That way you can do a more aggressive patrol, and if you see something, you and Weston can attack while I cover him."

"That would be grand!" Mannock exclaimed. "Train Mr Terry and kill a few Huns. Two for the price of one! Alright, Terry, a few last instructions. Number one, always watch me and always obey my hand signals. Number two, no heroics. Your job in the first month is to survive, and when you've done that, you'll have the skills to be a real Hun killer. Number three, I'll do my best not to get into a real scrap, but if we do and a Hun gets on your tail, remember the following. Get into a vertical bank, pull the stick into your stomach with the engine on full, and pray hard. After a while most Germans will give up and try shooting from another angle. As soon as he starts manoeuvring, kick on full bottom rudder, do one and a half spins, and run like hell for home, kicking the rudder from side to side to make his aim more difficult. Oh, and keep praying! That and the SE5's speed should do the job."

Lance raised his eyebrows. Mick had taken all the things that Lance and McCudden had taught him and packaged them in one complete but pithy set of instructions. The man had stolen more than one kiss from the Blarney Stone. Perhaps Mick's theatrical delivery and colourful phrases might stick in pilots' minds better than Lance's hunting jargon and McCudden's scientific terms?

"Isn't life grand?" Mick asked. "You get a breakfast cooked by a Ritz chef, served at your seat, and eaten with silverware in a warm Mess. Then a maiden voyage into Hunland with the great Fitch to guard your tail. What better way to start your career as a Hun killer?"

"Beats the hell out of fighting in the trenches," Terry allowed.

Mick stood up. "Time to saddle up the cavalry. Terry, if your knees start to knock together, that's normal. Mine do it, usually after a fight but sometimes before. People think it's an old wives' tale but let me tell you it isn't."

"Isn't it?" a surprised Weston asked, grabbing a last piece of bacon off Terry's abandoned plate and stuffing it into his mouth.

Mick shook his head. "Not for those of us who don't carry our brains in our stomachs. What is it with you and food?"

"My mum told me never to die with dirty underwear or an empty stomach."

The four of them traipsed out of the Mess towards the airfield where dawn smudged the eastern horizon. On the flight line, a fitter waited for them with a tub of whale grease. The pilots lathered the foul-smelling ointment on their faces to protect against the bitter cold at high altitude.

"As a matter of interest, Weston," Lance said as he pulled on a heavy wool fisherman's sweater to go under his heavy flying coat. "What would it matter if you died with dirty underwear?"

"Mum was afraid the neighbours would think badly of her."

"The Hun burial detail wouldn't care," Mick said. "Even if there was enough of you to check."

Lance shrugged into his flying coat and peeled off towards his plane. A Hispano-Suiza engine kicked into life with its throaty roar, blue exhaust flames flickering along the cowling. The noise drowned Weston's response but Lance was sure that Mick and Weston would be bickering all the way to their planes, and he smiled faintly as he checked his wings and tailplane, paying special attention to the bracing wires and the moving parts—the ailerons, rudder, and elevators.

Lance pulled on his leather helmet, shook hands with Digby in his usual pre-flight ritual, and clambered into the frail and flammable miracle of flight.

He breathed in a heady mixture of fresh air, castor oil fumes, and whale grease, and cleansed his thoughts of everything extraneous to the hunt. Air fighting swept the mind clean, leaving no room for worry about other things. Just one bare boned imperative—kill or be killed. A puzzle less tangled than the maze of politics or the enigma that was women.

His hands darted to controls, levers and switches in the methodical flow of an experienced pilot. Radiator shutters open. Mixture rich. Starting mag switch on. Digby heaved the prop and Lance caught it on the throttle as it started first time. The engine settled into its rich chuckle at 800 rpm. Oil and air pressure good, water temperature around sixty degrees. Controls free and loose, aerilons and rudder responsive. Time to fly. "Chocks away!"

Simplicity of focus carried its own beauty.

~

Fear constricted Terry's throat. Shallow breaths rasped into his lungs, but still the lack of oxygen at twelve thousand feet made him lightheaded.

He'd fought three years on the ground and mastered fear there. But this, his first patrol across the lines, was a voyage into uncharted territory and dread clamped a harsh fist around his stomach and squeezed so hard he grunted. And now he was the father of a tiny, vulnerable bundle that needed him if she was to have a decent life. Before, he wanted to live; now, he *had* to live. He gritted his teeth and sucked in as much frigid oxygen as his lung lining would allow. *Focus on the job! The fear and other thoughts are just noise.*

Mannock had told him he would need at least ten flights before he would understand, or even see, all that was happening in the surrounding sky. His job was to survive until then, not to worry about killing Huns. Weston said a first patrol across the lines was a life-changing event, "like losing your virginity, only less fun."

He'd swathed himself in long johns, his tunic, two jerseys, and a bulky flying coat with his hands encased in clumsy sheepskin mittens. When he had pulled on all the gear on the ground, the sweat had rolled down from his armpits in torrents.

"I feel as helpless as a new-born baby in swaddling clothes. How in hell's name do I fly, never mind fight, in all of this?" he'd asked Mannock. "I need to take a layer off."

The Irishman shook his head and smiled. "When the bullets fly, the impossible becomes easy. Before then, you'll think you are dying of cold. Keep all the layers, and thirty minutes from now you'll be saying 'Thank you, Mick.'"

Terry checked his dashboard clock. *Make that twenty-five minutes, Mick.* Even his bones ached like they'd frozen to iron. If he'd ever been warm in his life, he'd forgotten the feeling.

B Flight flew in an inverted V-shape with Terry and Weston tucked fifty yards behind Mannock. The reassuring outline of Fitch's SE5 floated behind Terry's tail. Terry had practised formation flying a few days ago, but today nerves made his control shaky, and it took all his concentration to hold the correct position.

Mick's gun stuttered and Terry jumped. But Mick was just testing his guns. Terry did the same. The obedient hammering of the machine guns reassured him. As an ex-artilleryman, the familiar smell of cordite made him feel like an old war horse going to battle again. Mick jabbed his arm downwards. They were passing over the lines and Terry stared, fascinated.

It looked...odd. He knew the trenches below with the loathing of an intimate—the foul-smelling mud, the itching lice, the rusty spikes of barbed wire, the stark dead ribs of shattered trees. But from here it appeared so peaceful. A brown carpet pockmarked with black that must be the shell holes. A weird thought floated into his brain. *Like a plum pudding with lots of raisins.* Only the sporadic orange flash of artillery bursts seemed familiar.

WUFF! A huge black explosion, centred with vivid red, rocked his SE5. His heart stopped dead. Then it resumed thumping, but now in his throat. He swallowed, amazed that his plane was still flying. He looked at the rest of the flight, who carried on unperturbed. Anti-aircraft fire. *They said its bark is worse than its bite, but Jesus...*

Terry scanned the ground to find the guns firing at him, and then glanced back for Mick and the others. His heart thumped again. *Where did they go?*

WUFF! WUFF! WUFF! This time the bursts were closer. His plane rocked. *Holy Mother of Mary!* A star-shaped hole gaped in the fabric in front of his cockpit. He gulped, and searching, found the others had dropped five hundred feet.

Guiltily, he remembered Mick saying that they would alter

height every twelve seconds to fool Archie. A small change in altitude was imperceptible to the Huns on the ground thousands of feet below, yet was enough to reduce the chance of a hit. Twelve seconds was the usual interval between salvos. He side-slipped off his excess height, just as the others climbed higher. Cursing himself, he clawed after them. *"Wuff wuff wuff."* A full salvo this time, but further away.

He checked to see if Fitch still protected his back. The SE5 floated fifty feet behind. Fitch's goggled face looked like an insect's head, but he gave Terry an encouraging thumbs-up signal. Reassured, Terry returned the gesture. As they cleared the front lines the anti-aircraft fire faded out. Terry shifted to get comfortable on the thinly padded seat.

Still they climbed, the buffeting slipstream becoming even icier as they rose through ragged regiments of clouds. At fifteen thousand feet the big fluffy masses of cumulus cloud dispersed and the vast sky arched above, a dome of glacial blue ribbed with herringbone patterns of thin cirrus cloud. The glare from the rising sun burned stronger. Terry had fond memories of the friendly sun rolling back the mists on the Yorkshire moors, but this sun was a pitiless enemy that hid everything from the east. From where the enemy would come.

Terry held up his thumb to block the burning disc, as he had been taught, searching for the black specks of approaching enemy planes. His eyes watered helplessly and dots danced in his vision.

Mannock swung north, and the glare receded to the flank. It seemed unfair that the Huns would always have the sun to hide behind each morning. But at least he had Fitch and Mannock, who would spot enemy planes long before he did.

Terry focused on looking around in directions away from the insistent glare. All was clear—a few clouds still lit with the shimmering pink of dawn, and a line of barrage balloons that hung like dark sausages suspended in mid-air. Perhaps the

Huns had taken the day off.

They turned west and droned onwards. Terry noticed the others constantly twisting to search the sun's glare behind them. Their vigilance made him nervous, and the skin between his shoulder blades crawled.

To his relief, they turned south again. Still the sky seemed empty. Gradually the cold and inaction led to lassitude. Crossing the lines for the first time was supposed to be like losing your virginity, but this was like going to the dance and finding no girls. And he had to piss.

His preoccupation with his bladder almost caused him to miss Mannock's abrupt turn. He followed as they slid past white blocks of cumulus. They skirted the towering canyons, their slipstream shredding the solid-seeming clouds into wisps of vapour. His compass needle gyrated as they twisted between the ever-changing white cliffs, the thunder of their engines the only constant. Mannock banked hard around a corner of cloud and Terry pursued him. They burst from the edges of the cloud back into bright sunlight.

Terry jolted in his seat. What the heck?

Ominous black crosses floated in front of him, on wings of green, brown, and purple camouflage. An enemy DFW C.V two-seater plane, distinctive with a tall exhaust jutting above the top wing. So close. So unbelievably here.

Mannock's guns hammered, jolting Terry into reality. Poised in the Hun's blind spot, Mannock fired from underneath and only twenty yards from the German. The pencil line of tracer skewered the gunner, who was gaping open-mouthed at the apparition of B Flight. A gauzy puff of red and the man collapsed. A puppet without strings. Dark smoke poured from the exhaust as the plane dived. Flame flickered from Mick's gun muzzles in a staccato beat. Short bursts. *Always short bursts.*

A tiny answering flame appeared under the dark mottled

fuselage of the Hun. Just a trace of red, peeking shyly from under the engine at first. Then a glow. Mannock stopped firing. The flames slid along the underside of the fuselage, feeding on the doped fabric. The red tongue grew longer. Its smoke thickened and plumed behind, choking Terry as he flew through it.

The Hun pilot twisted back to look at his attackers. His mouth opened and Terry imagined he heard the scream of terror. Thirteen thousand feet above the void. Closer to hell than to earth. On fire. No escape.

Terry watched with a hammering heart. Flames reached towards the cockpit. The pilot flailed at the fire with his gloved hand. At first to some effect. Then the glove caught fire. He tore his other hand off the stick and stripped off the burning glove. But now the hungry flames had found him. His white scarf ignited. He flapped at the fiery necklace with his bare hand.

Terry puked his guts into his cockpit.

Fitch's SE5 dived across Terry and fired. The German pilot jerked upright and fell face down over his front gun. Thwarted flames raged over him. His plane rolled over and spiralled earthwards. Terry found that he had not breathed and took a huge gulp of air. As he did so, the doomed aircraft exploded in a bloom of red and yellow. Debris rained downwards from the black cloud that hung suspended; the still flaming engine fell fastest, flowed by a wheel, a body, miscellaneous debris and last a shattered wing fluttering slowly lower. Terry vomited again.

Mannock signalled to head home.

Terry had seen his share of deaths but never anything so horrifying as this. On the ground, the threat of death by shell or bullet carried its own terror, the prospect of crossing that great divide, possibly into eternal nothingness.

But in the air, they also faced burning alive—a hell beyond imagining. Planes were composed of little more than an engine and fuel tank housed in a wooden frame draped with lacquered fabric. Four or five times a day they rode these fragile, flammable miracles of flight across the skies with a tank of combustible petrol fumes sitting almost in their lap. And every fifth bullet the enemy fired at you was a tracer. Their phosphorus-filled hollow bases ignited on firing to leave a fiery trace through the air, allowing the gunner to see whether his aim was true. If your plane ignited, you made a choice. Ride the flaming vessel, screaming until the fire burned out your lungs? Or jump into the weightless void, screaming until you smashed into a shattered mess of shivered bones, blood, and guts? Either way, you screamed a lot.

When they reached the airfield, Terry's feet jittered on the rudder pedals. He jammed his thighs against the sides of the cockpit to control the violent trembling and managed to land without too many humiliating kangaroo hops.

His sympathetic ground crew must have seen it all before. They ignored his puke-stained flying coat, eased him out of the cockpit, and steadied him on terra firma until his legs obeyed him, all the time murmuring meaningless pleasantries in soothing voices. He stood, swaying, stiff and still shocked.

"Thank you," he said, his heartfelt gratitude encompassing all from his spotty-faced armourer to God. He gulped a few deep breaths, eased off his helmet and gloves, and took off his coat. Gathering his composure, he ran his hand over his face, braced himself, and walked with the others towards Clayton's office for the debriefing.

"Whoohee!" Mannock exclaimed. "Sizzle sizzle wonk wuff! What a flamerino! One less of the bastards."

Terry looked at him, shocked. Weston shrugged. Lance wiped whale grease off his cheeks with a grubby rag.

"Tell you what," Mannock continued. "They won't get me like that. I'll put a bullet in my head long before the flames reach me."

Terry bent over and retched the remnants of his breakfast

over his boots. Lance offered him the grubby cloth to wipe his mouth. The reek of whale grease triggered another bout of vomiting. This time he wiped errant dribbles with the back of his hand. He scowled around at the other pilots. "If that happens to me, do for me what Lance did for the Hun."

Mick laughed. "Won't happen if you follow my rules. But carry a revolver in your cockpit just in case, my lad!"

"Promise me," Terry pleaded to Fitch. Even to his own ears he sounded on the verge of hysteria.

Fitch nodded, eyes fixed on his. "I promise," he said.

Weston grabbed Terry by the arm. "Follow me to the Mess. I know what you need—kippers."

Terry recoiled. He was about to reply when he noticed Weston smiling at him. "Don't worry," Weston added. "We don't have any. But the thought cures most people. When you think of kippers there's no room in the mind for anything else. Don't ask me why. Dad had a three-stage cure for everything; eat a kipper, drink tea so strong your spoon stands in it, have a shag. Follow that advice, and I guarantee you will be cured of anything."

"Except syphilis," Clayton said.

"How do you know?" Weston asked indignantly. "Maybe if you dipped your dick in tea that strong, it might cure the pox? My dad said the tannin is a curative."

"Kindly keep your appendage out of the Mess teacups or I'll pour boiling water over it."

Weston smirked. "Not enough room in the teacups for my dick."

"An interesting boast considering the cups are two inches deep. Might I ask whether you managed to do anything to send the Kaiser packing in your spare time this morning, when you were not stirring your tea with your dick?"

"One confirmed DFW for Mick," Fitch said. "Three of us saw it explode. Don't know what the Huns are up to, but I've seldom seen them so busy early in the morning. They're brewing something. If we weren't nursing Terry, we could have had about a half-dozen good scraps. Mick did a great job sneaking around them to pick out his victim without getting us into a huge shindig."

Terry's jaw dropped. "The sky was empty," he blurted, and at once wished he hadn't.

Four faces smiled at him with pity. Mannock draped a long arm over his shoulders. "My boy, let's go replace your breakfast, shall we? That was a rough first patrol, and it's normal to miss things on your early flights."

"I'll come too," Weston said. "Give you some moral support."

"Thanks," Terry said, "but you can't steal my bacon again, you know."

Weston looked hurt, but then his face cleared. "Perhaps your fried bread?"

19
Feeling Fey

Two days later - 27 July 1917.
Bailleul Airfield.

Arthur winced as Thompson smashed a fist onto his desk. The table jumped, and the tin in-tray clattered onto the floor, followed by a blizzard of papers. That was the trouble with the folding campaign table his wife had given him—the designers had lived in a golden era when no-one mistook officers' desks for punching bags. Colonials had a lot going for them when it came to fighting but left something to be desired when it came to respecting furniture or officer protocols. Served him right for picking three of them as his squadron commanders.

"You bastards abandoned me and my Camels!" Thompson's sweat-damp short-cropped hair stood in spikes, and his eyes blazed hot above his jutting jaw. Arthur felt a headache starting. It was going to be one of those days.

The debrief after 100 Wing's latest clash with the Circus had turned acrimonious before the squadron commanders even sat down.

Arthur's ears still rang with the thunder of his engine, his senses still swayed with his plane's dip and float, and his brain ached for some peace and quiet. It seemed 100 Wing tried to tear itself apart every week and only Arthur stood against the tide. He felt like King Canute. Damned tiring.

"Keep your drawers on, Thommo," Rod Andrews said.

Lance Fitch crossed his arms, and looked at Thompson with a sour twist to his mouth

Thompson stabbed a finger towards Arthur. "You put my Camels on low escort with the DH4 bombers and then abandoned me when the Huns attacked us. Why the fecking hell didn't the rest of you come down to help us?"

"Because we were all waltzing with our own partners," Rod Andrews drawled. "The blighters were queuing up on the dance card. No-one had any time to nurse-maid anyone else."

"Nursemaid?" Thompson's voice rose several octaves.

"Shut up, all of you!" Arthur's bellowed outburst startled them into silence. "Sit down! That includes you, Thompson." Arthur pinched the bridge of his nose and closed his eyes for a second. When he opened them, everyone was sitting. That was good. He hadn't lost them yet. "All of you are losing sight of the key issue. Haig's ground attack is due any day now. If that assault succeeds it might end the war. It will not succeed unless we win our battles with the Circus for control of the sky, so our reconnaissance and bomber aircraft can do their job and theirs cannot. We lost that battle today. We need to find a better way. Together. If we splinter, we lose. If we lose, we die...and so will thousands of infantrymen. It's that simple."

Arthur stared at each of his men in turn, trying to catch their eyes and bring them to heel. Thompson dropped his gaze and rubbed the knuckles of one hand with the other. Andrews held Arthur's gaze as he sat sprawled with arms and ankles crossed, his lady-killer looks marred by a thunderous scowl. Lance perched on the edge of his seat, his hands on his knees, glaring at Thompson. A single tear ran down his damaged left cheek.

Arthur knew that sign only too well. Lance was a hair trigger away from one of his berserk moods. The atmosphere inside the cramped hot office reeked with the tang of suppressed violence. Arthur let the silence drift while he considered how to defuse the antagonism. When fighting teams suffered heavy losses, either they pulled together, or they ripped themselves apart. This lot were heartbeats from the latter.

Before brawling, most men gave themselves courage by posturing and mouthing threats. Not the men in this room. A fight here would arrive with the speed and violence of summer lightning. It would be the beginning of 100 Wing's breakup.

"Clayton, can we have some tea, please? And then we will discuss this in a civilised manner." Arthur eased himself from behind the desk and sat on its edge, closer to the potential combatants. The scratch of the match as he lit a cigar sounded loud. Four pairs of eyes glared at him. *Good. I have united them with hatred of my cigar.*

Lance stalked to a window and threw it open before sitting again.

A wasp buzzed in from outside, and Thompson smashed it against the wall with a flying glove. They waited in silence for the kettle to boil.

100 Wing had escorted a squadron of DH4s to bomb the railyards at Courtrai, the largest road and rail junction in the Ypres area. It was no coincidence that Richthofen's Circus were based minutes away from the town. When General Gough's Fifth Army launched their long-delayed attack, German reinforcements of men and munitions would flood through Courtrai.

This mission had involved the RFC's finest. DH4s were the latest British bombers, as fast as many fighters once they had dropped their loads. Yet the sortie had been a disaster. The Circus forced the DH4s to jettison their bombs on the Menin railroad, well short of the major yards in Courtrai, and flee for survival. 100 Wing suffered high losses too, with the Camels bearing the brunt.

For the surviving pilots, it would mean a Mess dinner with too many poignantly empty chairs around the table. Their toasts to departed friends would be a litany tonight.

Steam hissed from the kettle. Liquid gurgled as Clayton poured tea into four tin mugs and handed them out.

"Thank you," Arthur said, wincing as he took a slurp of hot tea. He put the mug down and looked at his expectant officers. "You start," he said to Thompson. "Be civil, please."

"The high cover is supposed to protect the low cover, and none of you came down to help." Thompson stared around them with those granite-coloured eyes, the muscles in his cheek twitching overtime. "Like cowards."

Lance lunged from his chair at Thompson. Arthur, expecting the move, tripped Lance, who sprawled into Clayton's legs. Both men went down in a heap. Andrews threw his tea at Thompson. Thompson ducked sideways to avoid the scalding liquid which splattered some wall maps behind him. He leapt up and advanced on Andrews, who rose to meet him, fists cocked.

Arthur stepped between them. "Thompson, throw one punch and I will block you from ever commanding the Canadian Air Force. Andrews, I will banish you to a bombing squadron in Mesopotamia."

Arthur stiff-armed them apart and pointed at their chairs. Lance was still pinned under Clayton, who had not so accidentally entangled himself round Lance. Arthur pulled them to their feet. "As for you Fitch, you will fly a desk in a Whitehall office for the rest of the war."

All three miscreants glared at Arthur who glared back, no give in him.

They sat, Thompson dusting off his chair with pointed bad grace, Rod Andrews with a sardonic smile, and Lance with the cords of his neck drawn taut. Arthur remained standing.

"Major Thompson, the next time you accuse a fellow squadron commander of cowardice, I will post you out of 100 Wing in disgrace and write on your file that you are unsuited for higher command. That will kill forever your chances of advancement in the air force. Understand?"

Thompson turned his pale eyes away but nodded. Arthur turned to the Australian. "Major Andrews. Officers do not throw things to settle arguments. This is the Army, not a school playground. Never again. Clear?"

Andrews waved an apologetic hand. "He got me a bit crook with the coward thing. Won't happen again...sir."

Arthur looked at Lance for long seconds but said nothing. Then he shook his head as if in despair at an errant child. Lance flushed.

"Good. Now we are clear about the rules." Arthur softened his voice. "Thompson, your squadron took low cover because you told us the Camels fight better below ten thousand feet. I was with Fitch with the SE5s as the top cover, and it seemed like all the Huns in the German air force came down on us. Some of the bastards stayed and fought the SE5s, and the rest kept going to attack the Bristols at middle cover, and then you and the bombers. There were enough to take on all of us, so by the time the Huns reached you Thompson, everyone above you was fighting for their lives."

"So why the hell do I lose five men and the rest of you only two?"

"Because you don't train your pilots," Lance answered before Arthur could. "They scatter all over the sky and end up alone, they break away from attacks, and do everything novices do. As a result, they get killed, so you keep getting new boys, and you don't train them either, so it's a vicious circle."

Thompson sprang to his feet, then backed down as Arthur towered over him. But the Canadian's voice rose again. "Damn you, Fitch! It's fine for you in your SE5s with all your speed and high-altitude performance. Come and fly a Camel and see how you do!"

Lance snorted pure disdain. "Seem to recall, Thommo, you

wanted us all to have Camels. Remember saying, 'Give everyone Camels and I will clear the skies in a week'?"

"Bitching at each other won't solve the problem," Clayton interjected. "You chaps have been pasting the Huns recently. What made this different?"

"Numbers," Arthur said wearily. "The Huns had more planes up there than just the Circus, yet they were all flying to the same plan. Richthofen seems to have control over even more *Jasta*. We were four squadrons including the DH4 and still they swamped us."

"It wasn't only numbers," Lance growled. "Our escort tactics were daft. We traded away our biggest advantages. Firstly, our speed. The DH4s are good at altitude and are faster than Camels and as fast as Albatross and Pfalz. We should have used just an escort of Bristols and SE5, who are also fast and better than the Albatross at height. Instead, we slowed down the whole formation so the Camels could keep up, and the bombers went over the lines at ten thousand feet, again to suit the Camels."

"Of course!" Thompson said, throwing up his hands, "It's my fault. Typical Fitch, blaming everyone but yourself!"

"We are all to blame," Arthur said. "We are learning as we go. We all know the Camel is top notch in a dogfight, but you cannot deny it is slow compared to some planes."

"Secondly," Lance continued, "we tied our fighters to the bombers, sticking close to them. We made ourselves a slow-moving and conspicuous mass while the Huns were free to attack us with height and no fear of being bounced or surprised themselves. They could break away, climb above us, then dive on our vulnerable points while we stuck to our course with no flexibility. We should have broken formation and attacked the bastards while they formed and reformed. The Huns held the initiative during the fight and we just responded to their attacks, so they dictated the tactics."

"The DH4 commander wanted us close," Arthur said. "If I were a bomber pilot, I would want the same."

"Classic Army doctrine says if you have speedy cavalry," Clayton said, "you don't tie it to the speed of the infantry."

"I know dingbat about cavalry, but Lance has got the rights of it in the air," Andrews said.

Thompson snorted, but mercifully said nothing.

"We should fly as a wing again," Lance said, "and stack our formation like we are escorting bombers. The Huns will respond with a big formation of their own to mix it with us. Only this time we won't tie ourselves to any bombers, so we will have the freedom to attack the Huns how and where we like. Meanwhile, send the DH4s in high and fast for the bombing raid, twenty minutes behind our big fighter formation. All the Huns should be engaged with us, but if not then the DH4 can out-run them at height, and certainly on the way home without bombs."

Andrews rubbed his hands with glee. "I like it mate, nice and sneaky with a potent left hook."

Thompson was less impressed. "Typical Fitch, too clever by half. The bombers will get creamed. Even Mama Thompson could tell you that."

Lance's face turned crimson. "Mama Thompson can go– "

"It is worth a try," Arthur interrupted. "Clayton, call HQ and tell them we want to redeem ourselves."

Thompson snorted in disdain and left the office, slamming the door, which bounced open again, and Arthur heard him hawk phlegm onto the mud just outside the door.

Clayton rang HQ. Arthur saw him frown, twin creases furrowing his forehead, as he explained their request for redemption to the person on the other end of the line. When he ceased talking, Arthur heard a tinny voice jabbering back. The adjutant's mouth puckered as though he were sucking on a sour lemon. He placed the handset back in place with exaggerated care, and Arthur raised an eyebrow at him.

"Our favourite officer, Budd, answered the phone. He has been promoted to captain and now serves on Brigadier General Champion's staff. He said Trenchard and Baring are away in London, and Champion is in charge in their absence. Budd promised to pass on our plan with his personal recommendation that it was hare-brained idiocy."

"Surely no-one listens to that dingo?" Andrews asked. No-one answered.

Lance rocked back on his chair and balanced it on two legs, and Arthur said nothing. The Australian rolled his eyes.

"So," Clayton said, "we wait for Champion."

The phone rang. Arthur picked it up and listened in silence for a long time. He said nothing, but he knew the others could hear the torrent of angry words from the other end. Eventually he said "Yes, sir," and dropped the handset on its cradle. It jangled in protest. "Brigadier General Champion agrees with Captain Budd. We are to reserve our strength for the launch of Haig's offensive. He believes it would be best if we focused our limited grey matter on not getting pasted by the Circus, because our losses would be an embarrassment to HQ if the press ever found out about our latest debacle."

Lance lurched from his chair and let it crash backwards as he stalked out. Andrews shook his head as though amused. "Well, mate, I'm flattered. 'He embarrassed GHQ' would be a fine epitaph on my tombstone. I'm off to the Mess for a drink." Andrews strolled to the door, where he paused. "As a matter of interest, why would you send me to Mesopotamia?"

"I understand it has a surfeit of heat, flies, and sand, together with a shortage of women and alcohol."

Andrews nodded. "Australia without the good bits. You're a clever bastard."

"You can't call your commanding officer a bastard," Clayton said. "Apologise, Rod."

Andrews looked hurt. "I meant that the Aussie way. It's a compliment."

Arthur waved a hand at Clayton. "Thank you, Andrews. I am deeply touched."

Andrews chortled on his way out and gently closed the door.

Clayton's tone remained ragged with anger. "Why didn't you argue the point with Champion?"

Arthur sighed. "He wasn't asking me for my opinion."

"Well, if the most successful wing commander in the RFC won't tell them the facts, who will?"

"Technically, I report into Champion while 100 Wing is in his sector. But ever since we moved to Bailleul, Boom has ignored Champion and has directed 100 Wing through Baring. Champion is livid. He can't attack Boom, but he busts my chops every chance he gets. Now that Boom is away, Champion is taking it out on me. Besides, you know my history with Champion and the Mess funds that got left behind in a German advance. I cannot win a battle with Champion right now. There will be another time and place."

"Seems like it's always tomorrow—"

Something snapped in Arthur. Maybe it was the draining adrenaline, or the heavy losses of the vicious battle in the skies less than an hour ago. Whatever the cause, his equanimity cracked like the crust of an erupting volcano.

"Clayton, do you realise what a cushy job you have? You do not fly or fight, send people to die, or deal with daft generals. All you do is administrate and pontificate at your long-suffering commanding officer, who puts up with more browbeating from his adjutant than he should."

Clayton stiffened and his lips thinned. "Noted, Wing Commander Wolsey." The door slammed on his way out and bounced open yet again. Arthur sighed and closed it gently—it had taken enough punishment for the day. At last, he could nurse his headache in peace. Not even an aero engine growled in the background. 100 Wing was licking its wounds in sullen silence. He delved in his desk drawer, took out two aspirin tablets and his hip flask of Glenfiddich malt whisky, and knocked back the pills with giant swig and a sigh of appreciation.

What's happening to me? Clayton was too outspoken, but my response was excessive. Arthur rubbed the side of his jaw, the stubble making a discordant raspy sound. He needed a break. But who would keep the peace between Thompson and the rest while he was away?

He slumped into his chair and looked out of the nearest window. Not that he could see much. The filthy glass filtered the low flung rays of the evening sun into a soft and dreamy light. Dust motes, disturbed by all the door slamming, floated silently in the diffused glow.

He sighed again. One of the dead Camel pilots, Kevin Vaughan, had been at school with Arthur and a close friend from the days before Arthur knew he was the Wolsey heir. A letter to the parents was the least Arthur could do. Next of kin letters were the most dreaded obligation of a commanding officer. Thompson never bothered and usually Clayton wrote them for the Camel squadron, but Arthur would do this one.

He eased off his hot flying boots and wiggled his toes with relief. He filled his fountainpen and poised it over the blank sheet of paper, waiting for the words of comfort to come to him.

His mind remained blank. He rubbed his nose and looked up for inspiration. Over in the corner of the office, between the ceiling and the wall, a spider was enlarging its web. Arthur watched its methodical work for a while. A butterfly flew into the web and fluttered helplessly in its grip. The spider's articulated legs crept towards the trapped insect. Arthur shuddered, grabbed a broom handle, and broke up the web before the butterfly became dinner. If only all problems were so easy to solve.

He picked up his pen again, but any words remained elusive. The pen, of its own volition, doodled on his blotting pad. Arthur let it flow. Sometimes doodling unblocked his mental processes. He stopped in shock. His drawings looked like tombstones in flying formation.

Arthur had not told the others the second part of Champion's monologue. The British heavy guns would unleash a hurricane of high explosive in two days' time to herald the grand Ypres offensive. Hell was coming to Passchendaele by way of Pilkem Ridge.

Champion had ordered Arthur to lead his wing over Polygon Wood the day before the assault, and to maintain command of the air at all costs. The brigadier general's thin nasal insistence had echoed down the tinny phone. "Are we clear, Wolsey? *At all costs!*" The vast swarm of aircraft that Richthofen had thrown into today's meat grinder showed that the German must have similar orders. Polygon Wood, that easily identifiable kidney-shaped forest due east of Ypres and due west of Courtrai—almost halfway between the bases of 100 Wing and the Circus—would be the killing ground for a decisive air battle.

In the two months since 100 Wing started operations, it had lost twenty-one pilots, roughly a loss every third day. One hundred and fifty-five days remained in the year. At the current rate of losses, the Grim Reaper would harvest another fifty pilots by year's end. After today's disaster, 100 Wing carried twenty-five pilots. Statistically, every man in the Mess tonight and every one of their replacements would be ghosts by the end of the year.

Arthur looked at his tombstone doodles. Who in 100 Wing would cheat the odds and be alive to sing *Auld Lang Syne* when 1918 slunk into this war-weary world?

20
Shenanigans

Two days later - 29 July 1917.
Bailleul Airfield.

As Lance watched the evening patrol land, a throat cleared behind him. "Wait," he said. He counted the returning SE5s and relaxed. Clearly the flight had been uneventful; the planes growled into their landings undamaged. He turned and found Arthur standing patiently.

Arthur scratched his cheek. "Lance, I want to make peace over Megan, and I owe you an explanation. Let us hop into my car and go to St. Omer, and I will explain over dinner?"

Lance hesitated. His SE5 engine was not pulling full revs, and he wanted to oversee the mechanics as they solved the problem. But his relationship with Arthur wasn't pulling full revs either— in fact it was spluttering worse than his engine. "Let me change out of my flying clothes. I'll be ready in a few minutes."

Arthur drove the green Bentley fast, handling the wheel with easy skill and leaving dust roiling into the pink dusk. When they reached St. Omer, he parked in front of a café with a grand facade. *Les Frères Jacques* declared the sign. They strode into a dim room where large smoky mirrors dimly reflected the crowded scene.

The patrons, the majority of them military personnel, seemed an older crowd than Lance was used to in the habitual RFC haunts. Lance did not recognise all the uniforms, but whatever the nationality they dripped with gold braid. If the Germans bombed this place tonight, they'd wipe out a swathe of the Allied top brass.

"It's full, Arthur. Let's go somewhere else."

"Nonsense. They have the best fillet of sole in France. I do not get here often, so I do not want to miss out now." He snapped his fingers and chuntered French at a doleful looking maître d'hôtel with a thin black moustache.

"Oui, oui, milord, pas de problème!" In fact, as the maître d'hôtel ushered them into a booth a few minutes later, two elderly civilians and their half-empty plates were being hustled out. Lance didn't enjoy that display of influence, but Arthur did not seem to notice.

"Lance, decide what you want and order. The chef here takes forever. *Garçon, une bouteille de Lafite Rothschild 1912, s'il vous plaît.*"

The waiter bobbed his head reverentially at the order, scurried away, and returned clutching a bottle as though it were the crown jewels. He opened the dusty bottle with much theatre and looked hurt when Arthur motioned him away. Arthur poured them both a glass. He saluted Lance and took a large mouthful, swished it around, and swallowed it with a satisfied sigh. "That is better."

"I had no idea you're such a connoisseur."

"Do not be a prig. It is for Dutch courage. I need it to tell you my family secrets." Arthur took another long pull at his wine and ran his finger underneath his uniform collar. "God, it is stuffy in here."

Lance looked around in surprise; the air seemed fresh enough to him. "A secret about what?"

"Megan."

Lance stiffened but let Arthur continue.

"You remember I acted a bit sharpish when you first told me you had met Megan? I had a reason. And after this mess

263

with Budd, you have a right to know. Even more so, if as Budd intimated, you have been Megan's lover."

Lance felt his face burn red. Arthur was not looking at him but staring at his own glass like he had never seen wine in his life. Lance locked eyes with Arthur when at last his commanding officer looked up. "Just spit it out, Arthur. We know each other well enough by now. I promise not to tell anyone."

"Jesus! You had better not!"

That needled Lance. "If you don't trust me, don't tell me."

"I have to. It is not your fault, you got caught up in it. But it is hard to air the Wolsey family's dirty laundry." Arthur took another swig of wine. "Especially to you. You are intimidating when you sit like a block of stone, never fiddling with your hands or shifting in your chair. That poker face never changes, like you are judging everything. The thought of telling you this story fills me with dread."

Lance shrugged. "I'm just listening. Why do I have to fiddle around?"

"Mmm. Alright. Here goes. It's a complicated story but I will make it as short as I can. My mother was a seamstress, not an aristocrat. What they call a commoner in England. Lord Wolsey seduced her and got her pregnant with me, but she died while she was delivering me."

"If it makes it easier for you," Lance interrupted, "Megan told me about you and her father and how you inherited."

Arthur frowned. "She did, did she? What did she say?"

"She said nothing but good things about you. The only opinion she expressed was that you had done a good job reviving the estate."

"Mmm. So, I'll focus on the bits she will have misrepresented."

Arthur took a gulp of wine and waved the waiter over to take an order. "*Deux filets de sole.*" For the first time Lance took a timid sip of the wine and his mouth puckered. He placed his glass back on the table with care.

Arthur smiled. "Lance, this is one of France's greatest wines, which by definition means the world's. If you dislike this wine, there is no hope for you."

"Get on with the story," Lance said.

"Sorry. Where were we? Ah yes, the sordid family secrets." Arthur swirled his wine and stared into its ruby depths. "So, you are aware Megan was an unwanted by-product of an unwanted marriage. Not surprisingly, Megan's mother hated Lord Wolsey and told Megan that her father had cheated and reneged on every promise he had made her. Which was probably true. My father had a talent for keeping mistresses but not for keeping promises. Anyway, Megan grew up ignored and bitter but determined to worm her way into her father's life. As she—how shall I put this?—became more wo-manly, she charmed her way into the old man's affections."

Arthur took a deep breath, and the next words came out in a rush. "Him being a randy old goat, and her being a manipulative seductress, they ended up in bed together."

"What?" Lance's exclamation made the nearby diners look at them with disproving frowns.

Arthur's face flamed red. "Ssh, for God's sake."

Lance leaned forward. "She slept with her own father? I don't believe it!"

"And got pregnant. At seventeen."

"You're joking!"

"Ssh! Sadly not. Even for my father, public knowledge of his incest would have been a scandal too far. Megan and my father lured a rich sap called Peter Budd, Baron Exenrude, to be her husband. She used her sexual allure to trap him, and my father filled his head with the glory of being part of the Wolsey family. He was the perfect mark—rich, aristocratic and stupid enough to take the bait. It seemed they had covered up their unholy crime."

Arthur paused while the waiter delivered their food. Lance tried to regather his reeling thoughts. "How sure of this are you?"

"Very sure. But wait—the tale gets worse. Exenrude might have been stupid but he could count to nine, and was surprised by how quickly Megan produced a son. He started asking questions about the early birth. Megan told my father, and he promised to bribe Exenrude to stop. Before he tried, the suspicious husband keeled over one night after dinner. Now Exenrude's doubts were silenced, Morgan would inherit his title and lands, and Megan got unfettered access to the Exenrude money.

"Unfortunately for Megan, Exenrude's death worried my father. He didn't have a problem bringing souls into the world like litters of cats but causing them to shuffle off this mortal coil early was too much for him. And if Megan had poisoned her husband, what was to stop her doing the same to him? After all, she stood to gain a lot. My father had no sons, no brothers and no male cousins, and only one daughter. Although most British peerages descend only through the male line, the older ones like the Wolseys, can descend through females if there is no qualified male."

Arthur paused for a bite of sole and shook his head in wonder. "The chef here has a genius for cooking fresh sole. This is out of this world. Amazing!"

The change of topic threw Lance. Rocked by the story, he had hardly noticed whether he was eating fish or meat. "Um, it's okay."

Arthur rolled his eyes. "Philistine. Let me finish and then I'll carry on the story."

Lance's mind churned. This was surreal on so many levels. How could Arthur talk about cooking so matter-of-factly after revealing that his sister, Lance's lover, had seduced her father?

Arthur finished his sole and sat back with a sigh. The waiter materialised to clear the plates away and Arthur revived. "*Garçon, du fromage, s'il vous plait.*

"Back to the story. By now, Lord Wolsey doubted Megan's sanity. He summoned me and told me that I was his son and heir but only a few people knew he had secretly married my mother before I was born. I was stunned. It upended my middle-class world. Then he warned me about his suspicions of Megan and how he worried she would kill him too. After all, her mother had brought her up to loathe him. Furthermore, he said, if Megan heard about me being the heir, she might come after me. So, he said we should keep the truth quiet until the time was ripe. The story gob-smacked me. Being his son and heir was unbelievable enough, never mind discovering I had a half-sister who might murder me."

Lance shook his head. "Unbelievable does not do it justice. I can't believe Megan would commit incest or murder. Maybe your father raped her, and the husband's death was a pure accident?"

They paused as the waiter set down a platter of bread and cheese. Lance's nose wrinkled. He pointed at one pockmarked with green mould. "I'd avoid that one. It's got green stuff growing in it and pongs like unwashed socks."

Arthur lifted his eyebrows. "It is Roquefort, very famous. And that mould is good for you. The country folk slap it on wounds to prevent gangrene."

"That makes my point. How the hell can you eat something when even gangrene flees from it?"

"You my friend, have your priorities wrong. You should be eating Roquefort and fleeing from Megan."

"Come on Arthur, she warned me you would be protective, but this yarn is too much."

"Protective? Ha! Let me finish. At first, I also thought my newfound father's conclusion was too far-fetched. The whole story appeared preposterous. Then a month after he visited me, he died in a fire in his London home. The blaze took hold so rapidly that no-one in the house survived. The police did not suspect foul play. My father had a history of nodding off with a lit cigarette in his mouth after a few post-prandial brandies and had burned holes in his armchair several times."

Arthur poured a refill, but the bottle gurgled empty when his glass was quarter full. He peered at the bottle in disbelief but shrugged off the disappointment. "During probate, it emerged to general surprise that I was the heir. The people whom Father had bribed to stay quiet about my birth thought of me as his bastard son, not his heir. But my father was always cunning. Among his will papers was a marriage certificate to my mother predating my birth and witnessed by a bishop who sat in the House of Lords. Father's lawyer swore on oath he'd possessed the papers since before I was born and that he had known all along that I was the rightful heir.

"For what it is worth, I do not believe them. I am certain my father invented the marriage and bribed the bishop so that he could tell Megan that killing him would not help make her or her son heir. I suspect he never got the chance to tell her. I think—"

The oily waiter hovered over them, smiling unctuously. "*Milord, voulez-vous un cognac? Peut-être un Courvoisier?*"

Arthur nodded. "*Bonne idée, deux.*" Lance noticed the gleam of avarice in the waiter's eye as he hissed something to a white-aproned underling. Arthur's bill would be a profitable piece of business, no doubt.

Arthur continued his story, oblivious. "With the Wolseys among the most powerful families in England, all the press and society wondered how I'd gone from a nobody to one of England's premier lords. When they learned the background, most of them took the view that I was a jumped-up commoner at best, and from the wrong side of the sheets at worst. You have no idea how tough it is to be thrown into an alien world where you are the outsider and where everyone seems to be against you."

Lance found it hard to be sympathetic. How hard could it be to be an English lord? But he kept his mouth shut as the cognac arrived. When the waiter tried to pour Lance a glass, he put his hand over it.

Arthur wagged a finger. "Come on, Lance, experiment. You have ignored the wine and the cheese. At least try this cognac. When Napoleon was exiled to St. Helena, this was the only drink he packed with him. That tells you something."

The waiter nodded vigorous agreement and poured the cognac before Lance could stop him.

"Try it, Lance, just a sip."

Lance raised the glass to his nose. To his surprise the aroma was rich and warm. He took a sip. The cognac slid down his throat, smooth liquid fire. Pungent, but more interesting than the wine.

"And?" Arthur asked.

Lance licked his lips. "I could acquire the taste. Perhaps a sip or two after a long cold flight?"

"Perfect!" Arthur exclaimed. "I will get you a flask of it. It should blow that sinus problem of yours right away."

"Thanks. You were saying how terrible it was to discover that you were the new Lord Wolsey..."

Arthur frowned and remained silent for a few seconds. "Maybe I deserve your sarcasm," he said. "But I found the estate hocked to the eyeballs in debt. With the old Lord Wolsey gone, and an ignorant whelp taking over, the banks and every other creditor came hunting for their money. I had never even had a bank account and suddenly I owed hundreds of thousands of pounds to car makers, banks, clubs, local shops, and anyone foolish enough to extend credit to my father. I had no training and no clue how to deal with it.

"Megan rescued me. I thought she would be angry about me inheriting. But she was the first, and for a while, the only one to give me support. She even moved into the castle and called us brother and sister. I relied on her a lot, and she taught me the ropes of running the estate. My father's fears about her appeared so wide of the mark that I forgot about them and—"

"Wolsey," barked a nasal voice. Lance looked up and saw a stick-thin brigadier general scowling at them from behind a large beaked nose. Arthur stood but Lance pretended he was pinned against the booth wall by the table. "Stand for your superior officer," the angry beanpole demanded, his bald pate glistening.

"Can't, sir. The table..." Lance gestured feebly and settled his face into its most vacuous look. The long nose turned away from him in distaste and swivelled like a gun barrel towards Arthur. "Wolsey, I am your direct superior and yet I never receive the written reports I've asked for. Why?"

"Been a bit busy fighting the Circus, sir."

"Don't get clever with me, Wolsey. You may be a lord, but I am still your superior officer. If you have time to take this officer to dinner, then you have time to write my reports. Also, Captain Budd tells me he does not recall a single formal inspection of men and equipment in 100 Wing in all his time there. Very disturbing."

Arthur frowned. "That is odd, sir, because Major Clayton holds an inspection every single Sunday. 'A day for God's Bible and the king's regulations,' he calls it." Then Arthur's face cleared. "Of course! Captain Budd must be a religious man. He must have been at the church service during the inspections."

The brigadier's peevish glare softened into a glower. "'A day for God's Bible and the king's regulations,' eh? I like that. Always thought Clayton a bit of a Bolshevik myself, but perhaps there is hope for the man." He threw Lance another suspicious glance and stalked out of the restaurant.

"That's Champion?" Lance asked.

"None other. The irreverent call him 'Hercules,' for obvious reasons."

"He looks like an affronted vulture with that long neck and huge nose."

"One that would like to feed off my carcass. He loathes 100

Wing's elite status, but he has also hated me since 1915."

"He's not all bad then. Why?"

"In one German breakthrough, I barely got my plane off the ground before the Germans arrived. Troops were shooting at me as I climbed away from the airfield. In my rush, I committed the cardinal crime of leaving behind the squadron petty cash box with eighteen shillings and sixpence in it. Hercules accused me of stealing the money under the excuse of the German advance. I was exhausted and a nervous wreck. So, I told him that eighteen shillings would not buy enough toilet rolls for a week at Wolsey Castle."

"Ouch."

"I am not proud of it. It is the only time I have ever bragged about my wealth, and I made an enemy for life."

"If, as they say, you are defined by your enemies, I am glad to be your friend. But I never realised you were such a barefaced liar. How could you keep a straight face while you spouted that inspection claptrap?"

Arthur twiddled his brandy glass. "Since this war started, I've learned how the paper-wallahs can bleed you dry with a thousand paper cuts. A few white lies are justified in the greater good. Now where was I?

"Oh, yes. Megan being my best supporter. Eventually I told her about Father's accusations. She cried a river and said it was the old man who forced himself on her, and then twisted her arm into marrying Exenrude to cover up his sins. But then, according to her, Father became jealous when she got married and stopped sleeping with him. He kept harassing her to resume their lovemaking. So much so, she wondered if he killed Exenrude in jealousy. She convinced me. I knew for a fact my father seduced everything in skirts so that part of her story rang true.

"Sometime later, my foster parents came to warn me. They told me that old Mrs Kingsbridge, a local healer who used gypsy ways for healing, herbs and suchlike, had told them that Megan had been asking the local healers for belladonna nightshade berries, which is a source for a potent poison."

Lance barked a disbelieving laugh. "Have you any idea what this sounds like? Incest, arson, poison? It's a bad mix of *King Lear* and *Hamlet* mixed in with Sherlock Holmes."

"You would not be laughing if you knew Megan."

"But I do know Megan! Don't you think I would have an inkling if I were sleeping with an incestuous, arsonist murderess? You're over-gilding the lily, Arthur—one of those would have been enough for a good story. She's never said a bad word about you or your father, and the only poisoning attempt she's made on me is with too much champagne!"

"Are you sure about that? The day you flew back from London, you said you were puking your guts out all flight."

Lance shook his head, as much to convince himself as answer Arthur. "No, that was the Savoy Hotel breakfast."

"You didn't see Megan at all? There was no chance she slipped you a little something as revenge for Morgan's court martial?"

Lance stared at him. "Arthur, if it were anyone else telling this story I'd call it bad fiction."

Arthur signalled as a cigar boy passed around the restaurant. The ritual of lighting his cigar took time but seemed to pacify him. He puffed a smoke ring and continued.

"I put that nightshade story down as scurrilous gossip and thought no more about it. Then a week later someone from Megan's estate dropped off a pheasant as an offering for dinner. When the cook gutted it, she slipped the innards to my favourite Labrador, Sally. Just before dinner, Sally had convulsions, frothing and throwing saliva everywhere. A few hours later Sally died in my arms, in agony."

Arthur blew out a ragged breath and his eyes clouded. Lance wasn't surprised. He'd heard many more Englishman say they loved their dog than confess they adored their wife.

"What did you do?" Lance prompted.

Arthur returned to the present. "I bungled it. It took me a day to recall Mrs Kingsbridge's warning. Another half day to quiz her about nightshade symptoms and to bring myself to believe that Megan might be attempting to kill me. The cook had thrown the pheasant away and although we dug up Sally for an autopsy, no-one could find traces of any poison. Apparently, a characteristic of nightshade is that the poison is untraceable after a short while. One reason poisoners like it. I had no facts to tie a murder attempt to Megan—only a dead dog that could have eaten anything, gossip about nightshade berries from someone regarded as a witch, and conjecture.

"Nevertheless, I tried to scare Megan. I told her I had a vet do tests on Sally and the pheasant, and that he had found nightshade in both. I said I had witness statements that swore she had been making enquiries about nightshade. Furthermore, I warned her I had put the proofs in a sealed letter to my lawyer with instructions for him to open it if I died in an unusual manner.

"She professed horror and claimed that one of her tenants dropped the pheasant off in her kitchen for her. As she was going to London that day, she had suggested it would be nice for me. She sobbed that the poison must have been aimed at her and thank God I had survived. I did not believe her crocodile tears or her words, but I could see I had convinced her I had proof."

The garçon appeared with more cognac. Arthur sipped and sat back in his chair with a sigh. "God, that is good stuff! I need its Dutch courage to tell you all these shameful family secrets. Anyway, since then Megan and I have been in a state of armed neutrality. As things stand, her son is the heir to the estate if I die, which gives her motive to wish me harm. But she believes I have something on her, which keeps her careful.

I suppose she is hoping that the Germans will do the job for her before my wife and I can produce an heir."

Lance looked down at the table. The story seemed too far-fetched. A light came on in his brain and he smiled.

Arthur's eyebrows arched together into a single forbidding line. "You find this amusing?"

"Megan warned me you would react badly if you found out we were lovers. If you can't handle that, just say so. Don't concoct this twisted story."

Arthur grabbed Lance's bicep with a grip like a vice. "Lance. This *is* the truth."

"Arthur, I think this is one of your 'white lies justified by the greater good' like the fib you told General Champion. If this were true, you wouldn't have allowed me to walk bliss-fully unaware into a cesspit like that."

"What?" In Arthur's anger the word came out as a growl. "I did not 'allow' you. You fornicated your own way in, re-member? And never had the decency to tell me. I even warned you."

"Bit bloody late!"

"Ha! When you said you had met her, I never dreamt you were making the beast with two backs with her. I bet she seduced you the first night you met, did she not? You poor idiot. Did you think you were God's gift to women and an attractive lady of the realm could not resist your charms for even a single night?"

That hurt, and on so many levels. That's exactly what Lance had thought, or rather taken for granted. Pain, shame, denial, and anger jostled for supremacy and left him speech-less. Something of all of that must have shown in his face.

"Sorry," Arthur muttered. "I probably should not have said that last bit."

When Lance could speak again, his voice was strained. "Your story doesn't fit with the woman I know. She even forgave me for Morgan's court martial. Few mothers would do that."

Arthur looked aghast. "Forgave you? Not a chance, Lance. If she did not punish you for Budd's court martial, then she is still finding you useful. But when you are no longer of any use to her, you'd better watch your back. She lives for Morgan and his future. When I put him up for court martial, I knew she would be spitting mad, but since she dares not attack me right now, I was not worried. But you..." Arthur shook his head. "This woman bullies when she can, seduces when she can't, and fights like a cornered snake when she feels her plans are threatened. You will be in her sights, Lance."

"Why did you accept Budd into 100 Wing if you thought all this?"

"I didn't know what type of person Morgan was. I'd hardly met him. As you can imagine, his mother and I were not exchanging Christmas cards. When his name appeared on the postings for the wing, I wanted to be fair. None of Megan's past was Morgan's fault. I thought we might wean him away from his mother and teach him to be a real man. Unfortunately, the fruit has not fallen far from the tree."

Lance scratched his head in frustration, unable to decide what to believe. "If it's true, why didn't you warn me I was wading into the hornets' nest."

"It was not me who screwed Megan and tried to shoot Morgan! You made your own bed, Lance."

Arthur threw a pile of franc notes on the table. Lance winced at the amount and made a mental note to never come back when he was paying.

"Enough of this," Arthur said. "I have told you what I wanted to tell you. You believe what you want. Let us get out of here."

A thin evening mist had descended, and Arthur drove slowly, squinting into the swirling white that smothered the headlights. They hunkered down in their seats in silence all the way to the aerodrome. When they reached Bailleul, they climbed out and faced each other.

Lance ached to mend their friendship. "Listen, Arthur, let's forget yesterday and today happened, and get back to that simple uncomplicated war we know and love."

"If you think Megan will allow that," Arthur replied in a harsh voice, "then you are thinking with the wrong part of your anatomy. As you will discover when she saws it off with a blunt knife."

He spun on his heel and stalked away, through wispy tendrils of mist and into the darkness.

21
Lower Than a Stinking Mutt

One day later - 30 July 1917.
Marckebeeke Airfield near Courtrai, Jagdgeschwader I.

Hans Schmettow's stomach clenched as Adjutant Bodenschatz made the announcement—all *Jagdgeschwader* pilots were to gather at the steps of the chateau, ready to fly. Hans followed the herd as they chattered their way towards the Chateau Marckebeeke, Richthofen's administrative headquarters. *Must be a big show. Rumour has it the big Tommy attack is coming soon. Wonder what Richthofen has up his sleeve?*

Hans had been stuck on twelve kills for three weeks. Kills had been elusive since the SE5s and Camels appeared and challenged the Albatross's easy supremacy of the air. The new Albatross DV had arrived in the past few weeks, but it turned out to be a dud. To the intense disappointment of the pilots, there was little if any improvement over the DIII. Hans's pursuit of the Blue Max had stalled, and he was determined to change that today.

A heavy rainstorm had passed over the chateau around four o'clock but the storm clouds had dispersed, although puddles still glistened in the late afternoon sun. Hans squeezed onto the crowded stone steps and by mistake trod on the foot of *Jastaführer* Althaus, who snapped an oath at him. Hans ducked his head in apology to the senior man and retreated onto the sodden grass, hiding his resentment. *Nothing worse than wet boots at four thousand metres. My feet will be blocks of ice thanks to this prick.*

Hans warmed himself with the thought that Althaus was in Richthofen's doghouse. *Jasta* 10's yellow Pfalz had suffered heavy losses in June and July and scored few kills in return. Their commander's usual pleasant demeanour had become edgy, his focus on drink, gambling, and women more fervent. Althaus wore the *Pour le Mérite* and owned an outstanding combat record from 1916, but the Camel he'd shot down a few days ago was his first success for a year. His pilots said his eyesight was going. Althaus was often the last to see the enemy, not something that bred confidence in his men. Hans, always ready to piss on someone on their way down, offered a less generous explanation: "He's lost his nerve. He's yellow, like his plane. He doesn't want to spot the enemy."

Richthofen waited until the last pilot had jostled his way close enough to hear. He stood with hands behind his back, stocky, square-jawed, and stern-faced, the collar of his flying coat turned high, and his officer's cap jammed low. Hans had seen the pose in a hundred propaganda photographs, but it still worked. The man had presence. His pale blue eyes raked the pilots, as though searching for the weak link, the skiver who might give an iota less than his best. They shuffled. No-one wanted to be that man.

"Gentlemen, our high command suspects the British offensive will take place any day now. But we still don't know where, although we believe it will be around Ypres. Which is why JG1 is here, to ensure local superiority in the air. As we have all seen, the enemy aircraft have been thick in the sky in the early evenings when the long shadows make camouflage less effective. That means prime reconnaissance photography time—for our planes and our enemy.

"The past few days, we have done an excellent job stopping the British from bombing or photographing our side of the lines. On the other hand, our reconnaissance aircraft are finding it impossible to get over their lines and discover where the British are massing their troops and guns. So, this evening we will fly in even greater strength to challenge the English lords. I have arranged for three other *Jasta* to join us over the woods near Zonnebeke, six kilometres east of Ypres. We will attract Tommy fighters like bees to honey, and the cream of the *Luftstreitkrafte* will be waiting for them. While we distract and engage the enemy fighters at altitude, our reconnaissance planes will slip past at low level on photographic missions. So, there will be plenty of quarry for you all."

Richthofen stared at his pilots again. "I expect great things of you today."

Hans smirked as he noticed Richthofen's glance linger on Althaus, who seemed to cringe.

Then Richthofen's face crinkled into a smile, inspirational in its carefree confidence. "*Kameraden*—good hunting!"

The pilots cheered and dispersed to their airfields. Hans waited for his leader at the bottom of the steps, his wet boots already chilling his feet. He warmed himself by fingering the heavy Iron Cross First Class that hung from his neck.

Richthofen had publicly presented Hans with the medal, together with the usual flowery words about the Kaiser's thanks and Heroes of the Fatherland. But afterwards, the commander had pulled him into the office for a private word.

"You do possess some virtues," Richthofen said. "You have courage, and you may be the best shot I have seen. These are important attributes in a war."

Hans blinked. Praise from Richthofen. *A first. What's the sting in the tail?*

The cold blue eyes moved closer and glowered at him from six inches.

"But you remain the worst pilot in JG1, even though you are now experienced, I want more kills from you. I have talented pilots, young and hungry pilots, begging to join JG1, so if you do not improve your scoring rate, I will replace you."

Alarm flared through Hans. What a fool he'd been to dream! The gods would never stop playing with him as a sport. Twenty kills. The Blue Max. The demise of his family. He should never have let these ambitions take hold.

He found the blue eyes and held their gaze with an effort. "*Nein, Rittmeister! Bitte.* I live only to kill the Kaiser's enemies."

"Then do better. Or else."

Richthofen strode off, leaving Hans sweating but relieved. Yes, it was humiliating for an ace to be treated like a tyro, but what was another little dent in the battered armour of his ego when compared to revenge on his family? For that, Hans would dance bare-foot over glowing coals, never mind put up with a little verbal humiliation. But he needed those kills, and he would bloody well get them even if it involved risks that would make Thor, the god of war, blanch.

Hans reverted to the present as Richthofen strode down the steps, slapping his leather gauntlets against his thighs. His blasted dog, Moritz, bounded up to his master, spraying slobber with such enthusiasm it splattered over Hans. Richthofen laughed and caught the giant paws as Moritz stood on his hind legs to lick his master's face. "Down boy, down!" He cuffed the Great Dane amiably around the huge head and scratched behind the oversized ears. Moritz's tail became a blur and the slobber flew over his master's leather flying coat, but he didn't seem to mind.

Hans turned on his heel and walked towards the airfield before any more dog spittle could fly his way. Richthofen was so absorbed in his stupid dog that he hadn't acknowledged Hans. Not a single word. *Good to know a hero with an Iron Cross First Class comes behind a stinking mutt in the eyes of his leader.*

As Hans climbed into his battered Albatross, Richthofen

finally deigned to walk over and speak with him. "Stick with me whatever happens, Schmettow. Today will be the biggest air fight in history, a giant mess, a *kurvenkampf.* Your job is to protect my back, not go glory hunting, understand?" A hard look reinforced the words and then Richthofen was gone, not even waiting for acknowledgement. Hans wanted to spit but didn't dare do so in front of the fitters.

His mechanics had warmed the engine and the booster magneto started the Mercedes. The airframe shook as the engine bellowed. He throttled it back to a throaty chuckle at 500 rpm, twisted the greaser, and checked the content gauges, magnetos, fuel cocks, and fuel pressure. All good. Hans lowered his goggles and waved the chocks away. He eased the throttle open, and the propeller blurred into a brown haze as the Albatross trundled forward, trembling with eagerness to fly. Hans hardly noticed; he was too busy hating. *You have the wrong man as your wingman, Rittmeister—if you were on fire, I would not even spit on you to put it out.*

22
Polygon Wood

Same day.

100 Wing sailed across the sky as brazen as the Spanish Armada, and Lance reckoned that they had embarked upon an equally futile enterprise. Thirty planes streamed eastwards, stacked from fifteen thousand to twelve thousand feet in neat flights. Arthur led from the front, in an SE5 at the head of A Flight of the wolfpack. Directly behind him, Lance led B Flight so he could keep a watchful eye on Arthur. Arguments or no arguments, no Hun was going to nail Arthur if Lance could help it.

Fifteen hundred feet below and to the left sailed the Brisfits, and below them Thompson's Camels. Smaller formations, friend and foe alike, scattered out of the way of the fleet.

Lance had voiced his objections at the briefing. "Everyone in the sky will see us if we fly in one big gaggle. We'll just get sucked into a giant dogfight with Hun fighters over Polygon Wood while individual reconnaissance planes sneak around us. Better to stretch ourselves in flights of three across the lines like a net to capture any reconnaissance aircraft."

Arthur grimaced. "Direct orders from General Champion. We are to patrol in full force to control the air over Polygon Wood."

"What the heck does that mean? The sky doesn't have a railway line where the German reconnaissance planes must cross at Polygon Wood to fly over Ypres. Don't the fools realise that aircraft can fly across the front lines miles away from Polygon, and then fly north or south to get behind to Ypres?" Lance had grown numb to idiot generals making life more difficult, but this order impacted his father. If the reconnaissance planes spotted the build-up of troops and guns deep behind Ypres, the Germans would add to the machine guns and artillery facing the King's Own Regiment.

Arthur turned and glared. "Didn't you hear me? Orders. When you become a general, then you can give the orders. In the meantime, do me a favour and stop pointing out the bleeding obvious."

That had been the end of the discussion, their first and last since their argument over Megan the previous night.

As they crossed the lines, the familiar barrage of Archie anti-aircraft fire jolted Lance back into focus. The slash of trenches writhing across the muddy morass usually boosted his battle readiness. Today though, a strange lethargy gripped him. His mind wandered, and his feel on the controls lacked precision. He swore, angry at his sloppiness on this of all days. Time for his habitual mental preparation for battle—visualising himself as a leopard stalking prey through the bush. Still his attention strayed. He could not hold the leopard image until it infused his subconscious, and he fretted as the unwieldy wing blundered its way eastwards.

His neck ached. Somehow, he had pulled a muscle and pain stabbed down his right neck every time he turned his head. He tried to work the muscle loose, but only extended the pain down his shoulder blade. He'd woken up this morning listless and short of energy, and nothing had improved since. Tiny things had gone wrong all day, some due to his own distraction, but others were the sort of accidents that suggested his stars were out of kilter today.

Perhaps his visit to Pa this morning had thrown him? The

weather in the morning had washed out all flying and Lance had taken the opportunity for a farewell before the attack. Pa had grown even more gaunt, but his spirits seemed excellent. They had made meaningless small talk at first. Tough to chat to anyone, never mind your pa, when you know it's the last time you'll see them alive. Pa's officers filled some of the conversational gap with their effusive glee over how Lance's escort mission for the gunnery plane had resulted in howitzer shells pulverising the German pillbox.

But when the other officers left the two of them alone, Pa reiterated his intent: he would find a good death in the stumbling charge across the mud into the claws of the barbed wire and the teeth of the machine guns. "If I can get my men past the pillbox, I'll have done my job. The lads will go through the rest of the Hun defences like a dose of salts. Then I can die happy."

Pa seemed sanguine with that idea and nothing Lance said would change it. As they parted Lance made to hug Pa, but ran into a stiff-arm jab.

"Stay alive, Lance. The farm is yours. Go there when peace comes and restore it. Try and find Heidi, or another good woman, and have children. Remember us all. Promise me you'll fight tooth and claw for that life. For me, for Ma, for your brothers."

Tears pricked Lance's eyes. How many twenty-two-year-olds had lost a mother, two brothers, and a fiancée? And now Pa. If Lance wasn't a Jonah, it was still the case that he wasn't exactly blessed. But crying never turned salt into honey. He squared his shoulders and shook hands. "So long, Pa."

The handshake turned into a vice. Bones creaked in Lance's hand. A muscle ticked in Pa's cheek. "Tooth and claw. Promise me!"

Lance looked into Pa's eyes. They always burned with intensity. Now they glowed feverish.

"I promise. I'll fight to stay alive, tooth and claw, kicking and screaming, to the last fingernail."

"Good man! It's ironic, now that I'm dying, that I'm finally learning to live. If you wish me to die happy, let go of your revenge quest and focus on life. After the war I want you and Heidi to raise a glass towards Mt. Kilimanjaro at every sunset and toast Ma and me and the boys. We'll be smiling down on you. Can you do that, for all of us?"

Lance took a deep breath. "I'll try. The Huns have a say too."

Pa smiled. "Stuff the Huns. I have faith in you." He grabbed Lance in a bear hug. "I'm proud of you."

Lance's engine missed a beat, tearing him back to the present. His engine seemed just as out of sorts today as he did. It had refused to start, and Digby went puce in the face from repeatedly swinging the propeller in vain. Just as Lance unfastened his straps to jump from the cockpit, Sergeant Major Smythe shouldered Digby out of the way and bullied the engine into starting with one gigantic heave. Yet Lance worried. The engine sounded rough, and the vibration could loosen fuel, water, or coolant lines and doom him to a dead engine over Hunland.

But under no circumstances would he leave the Wolfpack leaderless as they headed towards the showdown with the Circus. So he clamped down on his worries. Once you had committed to a course of action, doubts served only as shackles.

With Arthur leading the wing from the Wolfpack's A Flight, Lance had dropped himself into B Flight with Jimmy McCudden, Mick Mannock, Rhys-Davids, and Terry. Before take-off, Lance had called them together. Mick Mannock was bouncing off the walls with suppressed energy. "We'll burn the bastards!" he exclaimed every few minutes. Young Rhys-Davids looked pale but determined. Terry's craggy Northern face, dark with his five o'clock shadow, was expressionless except for a rapid-fire tic under his left eye. McCudden was as cool as a man heading for tea with his maiden aunt.

Lance gave them his own briefing. "Listen. This will be a big nasty brawl. Stick together. If you do get embroiled in a massive dogfight and you see two green flares, climb away if you can and reform on me. Better to slash through the dogfight in formation rather than get sucked into a mess where there's collision risk and no time to aim."

Mannock burst into song:

Rule Britannia! Britannia rule the waves
And Britons never, never, never shall be slaves.

Then he laughed, breaking the tension.

Lance smiled at the memory and tested his guns. Their hammering, and the whiff of cordite, gave him a welcome jolt of adrenaline. *Focus, you silly bastard.* He ignored the stabs of pain from his neck and shoulder blade as he searched ceaselessly for ambushers in the heavy clouds.

But no ambush occurred. Above Polygon Wood, a dogfight had already started among the dramatic summer thunderclouds. From a distance the planes resembled a swarm of midges over a lake, a cloud of dark dots zooming and circling. As 100 Wing bored towards the scene, the details took shape. A mixed bag of FE2bs and British SPADs fighting with Albatross, evenly matched with about a dozen aircraft on each side. Planes spiralled in circling combat, some diving away from their pursuers, others jockeying for height. Fireflies betrayed the machine gun fire in the early gloom of summer dusk. Black smoke marked the funeral pyres of the losers, staining the sky with pillars leading to the shadowed earth. From time to time the overall anvil shape of the dogfight billowed into a mushroom, and then morphed magically back into an anvil.

Lance dragged his eyes from the scene in front and searched the surrounding sky. He squinted and frowned. A wave of dots slid towards them on a diagonal course. Lots of dots! He dived under A Flight until he was beside Arthur, triggered a few shots to catch his leader's attention, and stabbed a gloved hand towards the approaching horde. For a while it seemed Arthur could not see them, but as they came closer he nodded and swerved to meet the newcomers.

Lance glanced behind, wincing as the pulled muscle screamed its protest. Rod Andrews and his Bristols were obediently following Arthur. But Thompson had already led his Camels into a headlong dive towards the original dogfight. *Idiot! He can't have seen what's coming or he wouldn't have been so keen to trade away his height.* Now the SE5s and Bristols would be outnumbered.

Lance checked his harness, breathed deeply, rolled his shoulders, and moistened his coppery mouth—the familiar tang of fear. The dots grew into a shoal of shark-shaped Albatross and slender Pfalz. Tremors rippled in his thighs. Together with the planes already fighting, there would be eighty aircraft, an unheard-of concentration. A fifth of all the fighter aircraft in the Ypres sector, from both sides, would be fighting over Polygon Wood.

If the number of planes was breath-taking, so too was the backdrop. Huge as the aerial armadas were, the vast thunder-head clouds, grey castles with thrusting battlements, dwarfed the aircraft. The low sun crowned the tops of the cloud ramparts with ominous orange fire. It was the most magnificent, awe-inspiring, and terrifying arena Lance had seen. Nature's grandeur and man's mechanical might tossed into a late summer's evening cauldron—about to boil to climax. Never had Lance been so aware of the roar of his engine, of the biting cold slipstream tearing at his cheeks, of his shallow mortal breath.

~

JG1, a thundering phalanx of twenty-seven growling engines and fifty-four couched machine guns, hurtled across the sky wingtip to wingtip, nose to tail, flying tight as cavalry on the charge. The kinship between man and machine intoxicated Hans; the throbbing 180 hp Mercedes engine a steed between his knees, the eighteen-foot wings an extension of his arms, the twin machine guns a steel-tipped lance pointed at his enemies. Wind shrieked through the bracing wires as he hummed "Ride of the Valkyries," nodding his head in time as the horns section rose to a crescendo in his fevered mind.

Every plane flaunted different colours, personal heraldry like the shields and warhorses of knights of yore. Hans and his sword brothers, his *Schwertbrüderorden*—the modern Teuton knights—would cut their own bloody legends into the pages of history. Shafts of evening sunshine blazed between towering thunderhead clouds and burnished the planes with a golden glow from the heavens.

Ahead of them, a big dogfight already swirled over the woods. His bloodlust sang. The killing would be good when the full weight of the JG1 charged into that mêlée, and he would break his drought with a kill or two.

The blood-red Albatross ahead of him glistened in the moisture-filled air, rays reflecting off the wings as they waggled urgently and Richthofen's black glove pointed west. Hans's heart thudded with alarm. *Verdammt! Three enemy squadrons.* How could the summer skies of 1917 could be so packed with enemy planes? In April they had fallen like moths before flames, yet now they filled the sky.

The aircraft turned to meet them, swimming from distant dots to distinct shapes: SE5s, Bristols, and Camels. In the hands of skilled pilots, these planes could match or best the Albatross, the plane that a few months ago had dominated the skies. And if this big formation were the chequered, blue-nosed squadrons that dogged JG1, then the pilots were clever and skilled. A chill penetrated Hans's martial spirit. Equal numbers, equally matched planes, no tactical advantages–this would be a slugfest, a test of skill and courage.

Personally? Hans preferred one-sided slaughter.

He heaved a sigh of relief as the Camels dived away to join the original dogfight. Now JG1 had a numerical advantage.

Richthofen led them onwards, pulling five degrees south to help draw the British fighters from the six reconnaissance planes far below them. The Hannovers' dappled brown-black and grey-green camouflage helped them slide imperceptibly across the cratered Flanders mud. Hans spotted them only because of the white British anti-aircraft bursts blossoming below. None of the Tommy fighters plunged downwards. Their eyes must be fixed on the Circus. As Richthofen had planned. He was a cunning bastard, no doubt.

The two aerial armies hurtled towards their joust.

Crimson fingers from the sunset spread from the west, reflected in the swirling clouds that seemed to boil with blood. Below him, the dark earth revolved almost unseen, pinpricks of red flickering in the gloom where shells smashed soil and men into fragments. Then it came to him. *Gotterdammerung! If ever there was a twilight of the Gods, this is it!* The harsh discordant notes of Wagner's finale boomed in his head and meshed the fear and elation with his thumping heartbeat.

Fire flickered from enemy gun muzzles. Spandau chattered in reply. Those were the nervous ones. Richthofen held his fire until fifty metres. Tracer lanced both ways as the charging ranks met, and their formations swirled into chaos.

No room to aim. Just follow Richthofen, who carved violently through the khaki aircraft. Jink for the gaps. Fire short bursts. Every fibre of Hans's focus was on the red Albatross, fighting to follow him in the jostling, bucking airspace.

Hans's engine howled its protest under full power, the Albatross juddering as his guns fired. Valkyrie shrieks thrummed through the wires.

Richthofen hammered a big Bristol fighter from the side. Hans followed, ducking under so the observer could not track him. A huge British roundel filled his vision. He kicked the rudder bar and missed the wing of a diving SE5 by a metre.

A Bristol reefed onto Richthofen's tail. Hans swore in alarm. But before the Bristol could fire, an SE5 reared up in front of it and the two Tommy planes collided, fragmented, and fluttered earthwards.

Black spots danced in Hans' eyes. *Breathe, dammit!* A plane swam into his gun sights. He triggered a short burst. *Idiot, it's a Pfalz!* Twin tracers burned their way over his shoulder. He skidded away. Took a deep breath. *Himmel-donnerwetter!* He was sweating despite the cold. *And we have only just started...*

Above him an Albatross rolled, broke apart, and a flailing body fell. Hans jerked the stick to avoid the body, passing close enough to see the goggled face screaming in terror.

~

A pair of silver and yellow Pfalz raced towards Lance. The bastards were trying to bracket him. *Wait...Wait...Fire!* Missed. Lance ducked as the Pfalz howled over his cockpit. Propwash battered his plane and he caught it with stick and rudder.

A lone Albatross dived diagonally across him. He thumbed the gun paddles. *Missed again! Can't hit a thing today...*

An Albatross hunted an SE5 on his right. Two red streamers flying from the SE5's struts. Arthur! Lance swung to chase. The Hun fired and something whirled off Arthur's plane, but it flew on. Lance triggered a burst at the Albatross and cursed as he missed yet again.

Twin streams of tracers from behind forked into Lance's wings. Lance ignored them and aimed carefully. Both his guns pounded. The Albatross ahead veered sharply off Arthur's tail. Lance stomped on his rudder bar and skidded left as tracers filled the space he'd vacated.

A Camel, blue nose and yellow streamers—Thommo—hurtled towards him. Lance ducked in disbelief as Thommo opened fire. Tracer accelerated like an unfurling whip over Lance's plane. Jerking his head round, Lance saw the bullets lash a striped Pfalz behind him. The German sheered away. Thommo zoomed past to hammer the Pfalz some more. *I owe him.*

Lance reefed into a tight right turn on instinct. Tracers streaked past his left elbow, followed by an Albatross. Rhys-Davids clung to its tail, firing. *Strewth—this is no playground.*

Another Albatross, green with a silver tail, latched onto an SE5 and poured bullets into it. Lance turned to the rescue. Too late. Both starboard wings of the SE5 crumpled. The wreck flipped over and bored earthwards in a corkscrew. Nobody jumped. *Jesus! He's riding that all the way to six feet under.*

Savage anger blasted through Lance. He plunged after the Albatross, dodging through the other aircraft swirling between them. A Camel careered towards him. He flinched but it lifted above him at the last second. The plane bucked through invisible prop wash. *Silver Tail? Still there. Closer.* Crosshairs centred on the pilot. Thumb poised to fire.

Bullets stitched across his left wing. Lance stomped on right rudder. A bracing wire snapped. Tight turn, even tighter. Check behind. Clear. *Where's Silver Tail? Gone. Bastard.*

Ahead, a flaming meteor blazed straight through the massive melee, alight from nose to rudder. *Curved wing tips. Albatross.* A human torch jumped, limbs flailing.

Both sides paused, horror bonding them back into the brotherhood of man. Then the internal warrior resumed, and the pilots again turned into fighting furies, united only in fear and loathing.

Lance searched upwards. Two Albatross climbing for height. Lance too cleared the melee and climbed. He fired two green flares as he pulled above the maelstrom. Soon two SE5s climbed after him as he circled higher. Jimmy McCudden and Mick Mannock. No sign of Rhys Davids or Terry. Lance led his wolves higher, sliding around a thick cloud to hide from the crowd of planes, searching for unwary prey.

~

Hans chased Richthofen through the chaos. Every survival instinct in his body shrieked at him to abandon his leader. He needed two pairs of eyes to follow the twisting Richthofen and avoid collisions. Impossible. His calves grew heavy from stabbing the rudders and his right arm ached on the control stick. He gusted a sigh of relief when the red Albatross led him higher.

Richthofen preferred to hover above dogfights, waiting for prey to leave the arena. Dogfights were a lottery, a cramped space crammed with too much flying lead and too many hurtling planes. Richthofen preferred certainties—his skill against his enemy's. Hans had no complaints about the logic. He followed Richthofen and dragged in lungfuls of air to ease his pounding heart.

Sure enough, an FE2 tried to sneak from the original dogfight, spiralling to the west. Richthofen's hand stabbed down. *A death knell for the British plane.* The two Albatross swooped. Tracers flickered from the FE2b gunner while they were still a long way out. *Waste of bullets. He must be shitting himself. If the Britisher knew it was Richthofen chasing him, he would shit his pants even harder!*

Bullets struck Hans's Albatross like a hammer against an anvil. Splinters flew. Glass exploded. His body clenched rigid, shoulders hunched to his ears, toes curled in his boots.

Seconds passed as hours until the hailstorm of fire ended and the lean killing shape of an SE5 flashed past him.

Before he could take another breath, more bullets ripped into his plane. He glanced upwards to see the square snout of another SE5, its snout alive with flickering muzzle flashes.

He ducked as tracer speared towards him, cutting a bracing wire, which whiplashed into the cockpit and sliced through his thick sleeve. Warm blood ran down his arm. *Tsk! Tsk! Tsk!* His Albatross quivered in agony as more bullets punched through wood and fabric. The diving enemy howled past him with a blur of blue and white chequered nose.

Desperate to escape the maelstrom of lead, Hans jerked his plane into a steep bank and headed at full speed into a thick cloud. Deep breaths of clammy air and cooling mist calmed him. He burst into a patch of open sky and searched frantically. No more attackers. He sucked in deep breaths, pressing his knees together to stop their spastic knocking.

By what miracle was he still alive? His blessed Mercedes engine still purred. The controls worked, but sluggishly. Not surprising. The fabric of his plane was rent and torn as if hacked by an axe, revealing splintered ribs of wood.

He checked the surrounding sky again. Only the ominous grey-red thunderheads kept him company. Where had that humongous dogfight disappeared to? Where was Richthofen? The FE2 had been firing at Richthofen when the SE5s attacked, and Hans had seen no more.

Common sense demanded that he get his damaged plane the hell out of the crowded sky. The current emptiness was a dangerous illusion. But Richthofen might be in trouble and Hans needed him alive or his dream of a Blue Max would be a mirage. Where was Richthofen?

Hans searched the distance. Was that a speck to the north, spiralling lower? He turned to investigate.

Lance's SE5 howled past the two Albatross they had ambushed, too fast to know whether he'd shot them down. For a second, he'd glimpsed the hated red and white Albatross, and perhaps even Richthofen's all red colour scheme. But diving at such speed and with so many planes around, he'd no chance to stay in that fight. Instead, he led the spearhead of his SE5s down into the melee.

They slashed through, scattering Huns. An Albatross shuddered under Lance's bullets and broke apart. He howled in triumph and pulled up in a gut-wrenching zoom to keep height. Gravity rammed him into his seat and blurred his vision. A Pfalz, mottled silver like a barracuda, dived on him. Lance rolled away, skidded, lost control, flicked into a high-speed stall, and spun involuntarily into a large cloud.

As he emerged from the white mist, he kicked right rudder, pulled up, and reefed into a turn in case the Germans had followed him. But the sky had emptied.

It never ceased to amaze Lance how planes disappeared. Minutes before, a collision had seemed imminent every second. Now, not a plane in sight. Only the forbidding clouds glowering over the thin light of dusk.

Not that he was complaining. He'd survived the most tumultuous air battle of the war and even nailed a kill, despite feeling lousy and nursing a dodgy engine and a sore neck.

It had been a while since Lady Luck kissed him. The Lady was as flighty as a butterfly in spring, and her next paramour might be a German pilot with his finger on the trigger and Lance in his sights, but today he would enjoy her blessing while it lasted.

~

Hans eased his plane towards the speck, willing it to be an all-red Albatross. He squinted—friend or foe? *Curved wingtips, an Albatross. A glint of red in the dull light. By God! It is Richthofen!* Hans found himself grinning inanely, but not for long.

His leader fluttered earthward in erratic circles, certain to crash unless something changed. Hans dived towards the wounded plane, his heart thumping.

In the last few months Hans had called down every curse he knew on his commander's head, from *arschloch* to *wichser*. He'd wished death and destruction on the man, but only with the freedom of the knowledge that the maestro was indestructible. In truth, a dead Manfred Richthofen would turn Hans's world inside out. Imagine if he had to fly as Althaus's wingman? If the war stretched for another ten years Hans would never reach twenty kills. Richthofen must live.

He chased the red plane in its ominous descent, willing the slumped pilot to move. Miraculously, the Albatross pulled out of its fluttering dive and levelled out at eight hundred metres, although wavering uncertainly. Hans eased back on the throttle to fly beside the wounded aircraft. Richthofen sat slumped, head on his chest, but somehow he must be piloting the plane. The Albatross itself looked airworthy, almost unmarked. *Most of the bastards must have been firing at me. They didn't realise they had the great Richthofen on toast.*

The red plane lost height steadily as it flew eastwards, and soon a landing became inevitable. Hans saw the head raise a fraction and the engine cut, and the aircraft settled in a slow wobbly glide. Richthofen touched down safely enough, but in line with a telegraph pole and some wires. Hans held his breath as the Albatross ploughed through the wire and trundled to a stop. Hans did a circuit, headed into the wind, and landed as close as he dared. His left wing almost dug in on the uneven soil and his undercarriage creaked and groaned in protest. But his plane bumped to a halt in one piece.

He jumped out and ran to the slumped Richthofen. Hans unbuckled the harness and roughly pulled the unconscious pilot from the cockpit by his armpits. The inert body weighed more than seemed possible. Hans dragged Richthofen onto the lower wing and slid him to the ground. He scooped him up into a fireman's lift and staggered a safe distance from the aircraft. Then he collapsed to his knees and let the body slither from his shoulders to the earth. A smear of blood trailed down Hans's flying coat.

He hardly dared look at his commander. Blood glistened on the face and helmet, some of it congealed by the slipstream into dark red globs. A bullet had slashed a ten-centimetre furrow across the helmet and the skull bone gleamed white through the blood. The pale face and shallow ragged breathing did not bode well.

Hans's chest tightened as it always did in proximity to someone else's imminent death. Every death contained one exact moment when life departed to parts unknown, the body became a corpse, and the soul embraced a new form. It was a privilege to watch that magical moment of transition, to feel you were lifting a corner of the veil between life and whatever lay on the other side. His finger reached out to trace the furrow, to touch the watery blood seeping across the raw bone.

He jerked in shock as someone bellowed in his ear, "You need help?"

A clodhopper infantryman, a brawny Saxon *oberleutnant* with a mop of fair hair, peered down at him. Hans gave the man a glare, angry at being caught in a private moment.

"Get an ambulance. Don't just stand and stare! It's Manfred Richthofen, badly wounded!"

"But Richthofen? Here? Shot down?" asked the big Saxon oaf, unable to grasp the reality of the German *übermensch* laid low in the mud, bleeding like a pig in an abattoir.

"Just get a bloody ambulance. A doctor. Something. Quickly!"

The oaf finally woke up and snapped orders to the men of his company behind him. A *feldwebel* swung into action with a field phone appeared, and a wire layer started repairing and tapping into the wires that Richthofen's Albatross had mown down.

Hans heard the roar of an engine, and an Albatross circled him and came into land. The Saxon peasant gawped as he watched. Whoever was landing, Hans would be glad of the company—happy to share the burden of getting Richthofen to hospital alive. He blew his breath out. When he joined JG1 all this had been furthest from his mind. Glory yes. His own death, maybe. But Richthofen's death? Never.

Hans's hopes of twenty kills, the Blue Max, and his family's grovelling would all be buried with Richthofen's coffin. Even worse, as the wingman who failed to protect Germany's hero, Hans would be infamous, back in the familiar role of villain. Only this time a whole nation would spit on him, not just his family.

~

Lance could not resist an exuberant slow roll when he reached Bailleul. Damn stupid thing to do. If his damaged plane broke apart, they'd give him the tombstone marker he'd threatened his pilots with if they did aerobatics after a fight: "Here lies an idiot."

He did another roll. Just for the hell of it.

Because warriors carry a dirty secret, one they never talk about with outsiders. When you had slaughtered your enemy, directly after battle was the best of times. Never were you so magnificently alive, never were the smallest details so vivid.

The tang of gun smoke reeked fresh. Engine thunder still reverberated in the bones and the ears, and the blood pulsed through the veins fast and free. As the sweat of fear and exertion dried, the memory of the dread faded and the sweet clean feel of rebirth rose. *God, I am so alive!* The shoulders relaxed, breath flowed in an easy rhythm, and the cool air tasted like the finest champagne.

Not just alive, but victors too. Warriors celebrating their vanquished enemies. A gladiator baying at the roaring crowd as he stands over his slain foe. A Maasai warrior chanting his boasts as he cleans his spear of lion's blood.

Theirs was a primeval triumph, the cloak of civilisation stripped to reveal atavistic man—the warrior, victorious.

Lance stretched his next slow roll the length of the airstrip. The sky and earth revolved around him, under his control, interchangeable in his firmament. Before he'd even finished, an angry red flare fired from the airfield. Lance laughed with glee and rolled upright. One advantage of being a commander—no-one would punish him for breaking his own rules. But he cut his engine and glided in to land.

The pilots gathered on the east airfield near the command hut, hands gesticulating as they shouted happily at each other over the engine-induced deafness. Lance joined them.

He winced as Thommo bellowed in his ear. "You owe me, Fitch!"

"Owe you? You shot at me. Your tracers singed my eyebrows. What do I owe you for, missing me?"

Thommo's huge smirk slipped. "You didn't see that black and white Hun lining you up? I nailed the bastard by shooting a yard over you. Helluva shot, even if I say so myself."

"You just want to be top ace. You tried to shoot me down, missed, and hit a Hun through blind luck."

"Balls to you, Lance. You musta been dozing up there. You are kidding?"

Lance slapped him on the shoulder. "Course I'm kidding! Great shooting. You can rescue me like that anytime. Drinks on me."

Thommo beamed. "It *was* good shooting, right? I'll collect that drink from you in the bar tonight."

"It'll be a pleasure."

The Canadian bounded off, leaving Lance only mildly irritated. It wasn't the done thing to rub it in when you saved someone. But what the hell, it's hard to get angry when a man has saved your life. He looked at his still-shaking hands.

"Silly sod," Arthur said from behind him, and Lance dropped his hands to hide the evidence.

"Who, me?" Lance asked, assuming Arthur was going to tick him off for the slow rolls. The few words they'd exchanged since the Megan revelations had not exactly been friendly.

"No, Thompson. He was so busy trying to shoot Huns down he never even checked behind. I twice chased Huns off his tail. McCudden and Rhys Davids did the same, and that is just what I saw in that maelstrom. God knows how he survived. And now he's bragging about saving you."

"I'm not complaining."

Arthur smiled wryly. "I suppose not. You alright?"

"A sore neck but no holes."

"Any day without bullet perforations is a good day. Speaking of which, thanks for shooting that Albatross off my tail."

Lance searched Arthur's honest blue eyes, and on impulse thrust out his hand. Arthur's face fractured into a broad smile and he shook the hand hard. Lance found himself grinning.

"Forgiven?" Arthur asked.

"You? Always."

Lance looked around the airfield at the clusters of pilots exchanging stories, their hands cavorting in the air as they spoke. Then at the blood-wagon as it bumped towards the tent that served as a dressing station for the wounded. His shoulders slumped at the reminder of the SE5 shedding its wings in the dogfight. Who would it be? His eyes met Arthur's and saw the same question.

Arthur wiped his hand across his face, leaving streaks of grimy white beneath the gun-powdered grey cheeks. "I guess we'd better find out today's butcher's bill."

Lance opened his mouth, but the clanging of the fire truck bell forestalled him. He searched the dark sky. An SE5 was approaching the airfield, left wing low as if hunched in pain. A thin stream of black smoke trailed the aircraft and the engine was misfiring. A long strip of fabric flapped from its top wing, but the trailing smoke from the engine worried Lance more. With fire imminent in the engine already, anything other than a good landing invited a firebomb.

When gravity and smoke rode together, the Grim Reaper danced a half-beat behind.

23
Bracing Wires

Same day.
Bailleul Airfield.

The clanging alarm curdled the pilots' joshing and laughter. They watched in silence as the SE5 weaved closer.

"It's Terry," Mannock muttered. "Thought he was a goner...and the way he's flying, he soon will be."

Lance, still bundled in his flying gear, said nothing but watched the plane with anxious eyes. Terry's aircraft skidded and pitched as it turned towards the nearest airstrip, the Camels' Asylum aerodrome. The fire truck headed that way, bell clanging as it charged past the gathered pilots.

The SE5 made a jerky approach. Bullets had chewed away half the tail and shot one landing strut loose. This would be a tough landing for a pilot in good shape, and the erratic flying indicated Terry might be wounded. Lance heard Mannock muttering something that sounded like a prayer.

The nose dropped, and the fighter plunged earthwards. Terry caught it just in time and pulled up, only to over-compensate and pitch almost into a stall. Lance held his breath, but once again the pilot corrected at the last possible second. By now he'd missed his chance on the Asylum airstrip. He lifted gingerly over the pond and hangars and floated towards the pilots on the East Aerodrome. The fire truck turned a circle and raced back.

This time, Terry flared out too early and the nose pitched up. To prevent stalling, he jammed the throttle open. The engine bellowed in protest. A loud bang. A puff of black smoke. A red lick of flame from the engine. "Christ, no!" said a strangled voice. It might have been Lance's.

Now the aircraft was flying too fast for a landing but Terry, presumably desperate to avoid the flames, rammed it down anyway.

The undercarriage snapped. Propeller blades splintered on the hard ground, fragments hurtling through the air as the plane ploughed forwards, throwing shattered parts like a Catherine wheel and trailing a grim banner of pungent smoke. Until one wingtip dug in and a savage ground loop snapped the careering SE5 to a halt 150 yards away.

"Go!" Lance shouted. The collective trance broke, and the pilots ran towards the havoc. Ground crew joined in the race from the hangars on the other side. The fire-wagon, pursuing from behind, hit wreckage and threw a tyre. The truck faltered but ground onwards, metal rims slipping on grass damp with evening dew.

Lance pounded towards the wreck. His flying coat flapped against his driving legs and his wool-lined boots made every stride as heavy as wading through mud. It seemed he had never run so hard; it seemed he had never run so slow.

The ground crew, unencumbered by flying gear, reached the wreck first. One man chopped with an axe at the collapsed top wing that trapped Terry in the cockpit. He threw the axe down and tore free a segment of wing. A second man reached through the gap and fumbled at Terry's harness.

From twenty yards away, Lance heard the deadly *whoof* as the fumes from the nearly empty petrol tank ignited. Flames engulfed the cockpit. The man trying to undo Terry's harness reeled back, clutching his eyes. The axeman leapt away, beating at the sparks in his hair. Red licked over the dark shadow that was Terry. Other ground crew attempted a rescue, but the searing heat sent them cowering.

Still Lance ran, his lungs screaming for air, his pulse thundering in his ears. He reached the crowd and barged through them.

A human torch crawled from the flames on its knees, howling its agony in high notes that pierced even the roar of the fire. It stretched out a beseeching arm. The face came from Lance's nightmares. A leather helmet merged with melted skin. Metal goggles framing smoke-blackened glass fused to the exposed white cheekbones.

Déjà vu triggered the worst memory of Lance's life—Hamisi's wide eyes, lidless in the flames, flesh bubbling. Waves of white surf battered at his sanity with the relentless ferocity of storm rollers grinding at a ragged shore. It sucked him under, roiled him, took his breath, stole his will. *So hard to fight...*

He let go. The savage undertow soothed into calmer waters, where he floated surrounded by a mist that muffled his senses. A dense silence coiled around him, an empty ease of mind. Such sweet surrender.

And yet...from a million miles away, from another life-time...Pa's voice whispered, "Never surrender! Fight tooth and claw, kicking and screaming, to the last fingernail."

With perfect clarity, he saw his futures cleave. One path, where every dawn he would wake, sweat-soaked, guts twisted and mind recoiling from horrors half-recalled, half-dreamed. A life of hard choices with no good answers. A life of bloody thorns. A life fully present in the world.

The other path demanded nothing, just an embrace of merciful oblivion. No grappling nightmares or crippling regrets. A life as all-embracing and undemanding as floating in a cloud. A sort of death. So tempting, so easeful, a sultry siren's song to float above the bitter world, unheeding.

And yet...

"Tooth and claw," he whispered, dredging for the saving rage. Rage, the lover who never left him no matter how low the banked fires burned, his mistress who never surrendered him whatever his faithlessness. He bit his cheek hard and summoned her with the copper bitterness of blood flooding his mouth, with the nails on his clenched fists scoring his palms. He offered her his blood and his pain.

And she came. An angel of deliverance. Fury flooded his veins, shredding the white veil.

He blinked at the wide arc of grey sky, green grass, and the evil black smoke towering towards the heavens.

He had been absent for an hour, a year, a lifetime...yet only seconds. Terry still crawled, haloed with a circle of yellow flame. The fiery scarecrow raised his supplicating arms in a crucifixion pose and toppled over a few feet from the inferno.

Lance pulled down his goggles. He yanked on his leather helmet and gloves and buttoned his flying coat. A deep breath, and he scuttled low towards the fire. The heat was almost a solid barrier, pushing at him, blistering his cheeks. He covered his face with a leather-clad arm and half-turned his back so his thick coat would protect him. Flames roared, deep-throated like a furnace. He pushed closer, bent low to escape the worst of the blaze. Super-heated air scorched his lungs. The stench of burning flesh made him gag.

Lance fell to his knees as he reached Terry. Keeping his back to the searing conflagration, he rolled the flaming body across the damp grass, away from the inferno. He knee-crawled after it. Excruciating heat seared his back. Smoke hot as fire choked his throat, cheating him of his oxygen.

Got to keep Terry rolling.

But without oxygen, his eyes blurred and each movement came slower, like a swimmer weighed down with chains, drowning.

He heaved Terry over one more time, but the effort over

balanced him and he toppled. His cheek hit the cool damp grass. A vague regret filled him. *It's over. Unlike with Hamisi, at least I tried a rescue this time.* A sense of peace drifted over him. Never again would his fear of flames unman him and turn him coward. He had redeemed himself in his own eyes. Worth dying for, that.

A figure loomed through the smoke. Strong hands grabbed his armpits and dragged him into clean air.

"His coat is on fire. Roll him!" The man dropped him and weaved back into the smoke. Someone beat Lance's back. Then hands turned him over and over against the damp grass until the world spun. When they stopped rolling him, they tore off his flying gloves and coat.

Lance sucked in oxygen with racking coughs. The air reeked of burning oil, smouldering fabric, and kindled wood. Charred flakes drifted into his mouth and filled his throat with ash.

It was the finest air Lance had ever breathed.

A figure staggered from the smoke, towing Terry. As they reached safety, the upright one dropped to his knees, chest heaving, whooping for oxygen. Wisps of smoke curled from his shoulders. A fireman emptied a bucket over the smoking rescuer. Other men pulled Terry further from the heat.

The soaked rescuer peeled off his goggles and helmet. Arthur! His red-rimmed eyes stared at Lance, water dripping from his sodden hair. "You alright?"

Lance opened his mouth to thank Arthur, but his clogged throat would only croak unintelligibly. Instead, he reached out to touch Arthur's arm.

Arthur's smile cracked his smoke-blackened face, teeth white against the gloom. "You always were a lucky bastard!"

A choked chuckle escaped from Lance. Then he wished it hadn't. Damn, that hurt his throat. Lance shut his eyes for a second and breathed out gustily. He'd run towards his worst nightmare and emerged relatively unscathed. A flicker of joy sang, "I'm alive!"

Arthur tried to pull off Terry's burnt goggles but singed himself on the smoking metal. "Christ!" Wringing his hands, he looked up at the handful of horrified pilots gathered around him. "Water. Get more water. Now!"

The pilots looked at each other, clueless, but a fireman grabbed a bucket from the wagon and tenderly poured water on the writhing Terry. He moaned as they poured bucket after bucket on him until the steam stopped rising. Then they cut off the leather straps of the goggles and eased away the metal frame.

Lance gagged again as a line of charred flesh peeled off with the goggles, black outside, weeping pink inside. The firemen cut off Terry's clothes, peeling off more burnt skin as they did so. When they poured more cool water on the raw flesh, Terry's screams shredded the pilots' nerves and many edged further away.

Arthur pinned Terry to the grass and whispered something in Terry's ear in a low soothing voice that the rest of them could not make out. The screaming died to a quiet sobbing. The rescuers rolled Terry gently onto a canvas stretcher.

A memory chiselled into Lance's brain. Terry's first patrol. The Hun two-seater going down in flames. Terry's face etched with revulsion and dread when he landed twenty minutes later. Terry had heaved his breakfast over the grass and told Lance to shoot him if he got caught in flames.

Lance staggered to his feet, reached down to his boot, and drew his revolver. He walked towards Terry, weaving on unsteady legs like a drunken sailor. He passed Mannock leaning against the fire tender, face in the crook of his arm, shoulders shaking.

Arthur stood over Terry, his face smoke blackened and his flying coat scorched. He looked up as Lance approached and frowned as he registered the revolver. "What is that for?"

Lance raised the gun and sighted it on the prone body.

"Terry begged me, after he watched a flamer, to shoot him if I ever saw him on fire."

Arthur reached over and slowly pushed the gun down. "He is being taken to hospital and might survive. Let God decide."

"No!" Lance jerked away. "I promised."

Arthur slapped Lance. Lance hardly felt the blow, but the sound of it rang in his ears. His hand with the revolver rose, and he heard the hiss of indrawn breath from the pilots nearest him. Clayton moved towards him. Lance stiff armed the adjutant away with his free arm, still staring at Arthur. Only Arthur had not moved, standing foursquare in front of Lance with his hands on his hips and the wind ruffling his blond hair.

"Sorry, Lance, but it was for your own good. Terry has a wife and a daughter. He has a chance of living. Not a big one but a chance, nevertheless. What gives you the right to deprive his family of a husband and a father?"

"I keep my promises."

"I doubt you promised to shoot him when he was on the ground. It is in God's hands now. Let him be."

Lance pointed his revolver around the circle of officers, who edged away. "If I was in that agony, I'd want one of you to have the guts to end it for me." One by one, they averted their eyes as he stared at them. He aimed at Terry again. The stretcher-bearers kneeling beside Terry froze, eyes wide.

Weston's meaty hand touched Lance's left arm. Lance did not move but curled his forefinger around the trigger.

"I was there when you promised," Weston said. "And I agree we should leave it to God."

"Bully for you. If you'd had the guts to promise then instead of leaving it to me, you could decide now to break your promise. As it is..." Lance closed one eye to sight down the barrel for a neat head shot.

"Do you want to know what I told Terry that made him stop screaming?" Arthur asked.

"No." Lance cocked the hammer.

"I whispered the name of his new-born girl, Annie. To give him something to live for. A chance to see her. Would you deny him that?"

Lance winced. The gun barrel wavered.

He un-cocked the weapon and hung his head. His hand holding the revolver dropped. The stretcher-bearers shuffled to their feet before Lance could change his mind, and trotted their burden towards the medical clearing tent.

Lance stood, with his revolver arm hanging limp. A breeze ruffled his hair, cool across his cheek. The crowd drifted away. Arthur squeezed Lance's shoulder and left him to his thoughts. Clayton started to say something but thought better of it and departed with Arthur. Lance stood alone.

He stared at the smoking wreck of Terry's aircraft. It seemed so harmless now. Just a melted engine block and a partial skeleton of charred wood from the tail. Those evil devouring flames had vanished. Even the red tendrils of the last of the sunset had disappeared.

Lance sighted down the barrel of the revolver at the centre of the charred wreckage. He fired and the pistol bucked in his hand. The explosion made his ears ring. A murder of black crows exploded from the trees at the edge of the cemetery, cawing in alarm. He fired again, five more slow and deliberate shots until the hammer clicked on an empty chamber.

He stood for a while, the gun smoking. Then he turned his back on the burnt-out pyre and strode towards his tent, ignoring the wide-eyed looks of pilots and ground crew as he passed them.

~

Lance slumped on his cot, alone in his tent, staring sightlessly at the ground. What next?

Some things remained clear. Tomorrow the sun would

rise. So too would the RFC pilots and the German air force. And somewhere the flames would dance anew for someone else. Pray God, not at 100 Wing.

A massive lethargy drained every ounce of energy from his body and mind. His eyelids drooped, weighted with lassitude, but he dared not close his eyes. He knew from bitter experience the pictures that would come behind closed lids would be of flames and burning flesh.

He needed company, to crowd out the images from the forefront of his memory.

Also, he must provide an example to the men in his squadron. The war would go on until the Hun bastards broke. A spark of purpose lit inside him at that thought. Curious, that—responsibility for others used to drain him.

Just the act of standing was a major challenge. He willed each muscle to crank into grudging movement, every motion jerky as though his body were a marionette and he an untrained puppeteer. First a shower. That might revitalise him. He stripped off the clothes reeking of smoke, wrapped a towel around his waist, stuck his feet into his boots, and stumbled from his tent.

The field shower consisted of a bag of water hanging from a pole over some duckboards, canvased off for privacy. The cold water shocked his body. He lathered and scrubbed, but even the harsh whiff of the military carbolic soap could not expunge the stench of flame-crisped flesh that lingered in his nostrils.

His back and hands were lightly blistered, and the soap stung the wounds. Lance welcomed the pain. It provided a reminder. *I acted. This time, at least I acted.* And in conquering his greatest fear to help Terry, he had tamed the demons that had haunted him since Hamisi's death. No longer would he call himself a coward in the face of flames.

Those searing memories—whether awake or in nightmares—would always be a part of him. That he knew. It could not be otherwise. But even if the crashing white surf broke over him again, it would not find a flailing swimmer but an indomitable breakwater, standing foursquare and proud. He had saved himself.

So long as he wasn't so stupid as to let anyone under his guard like he had with Albert Ball.

Friends die on you. Feelings make you weak.

As part of the wolfpack, Terry was a comrade and therefore meant more to Lance than most men. But he'd not been a friend. Soon Terry would be just another memory that Lance buried in an unmarked vault deep in his mind. He grunted with the irony. He'd spent his school years honing his memory. Turns out, forgetfulness was more useful.

Lance tilted his head so the cold water cascaded over him like a baptism, a sacrament into a new state of grace.

He padded back to his tent, welcoming the solidity of the earth under his feet. No sound came from the surrounding tents. Some had their hurricane lamps on and shadows moved inside, but a sombre silence ruled.

By the time he reached his own tent, the cold pricked his flesh with goose bumps and he dried himself vigorously. He pulled on his uniform, wincing as the rough shirt rasped his burnt back. When he brushed back his hair and looked in the mirror, he was astonished to see he still looked like the man he'd seen shaving this morning. Apart from a burn blister, hanging like a translucent leech on one cheekbone. He cocked his head. Months of stress and tiredness wreaked havoc on everybody's face. They carved bold lines, sank the eyes, and stretched the skin taut over cheekbones. But each daily increment showed little.

When he reached the Mess, a funeral mood hung like a pall. Terry had died on the way to the hospital field station, not from burns but from loss of blood. In the furore of the crash and the fire, not even the medics had noticed—until

Terry was dead—the two bullet holes in his abdomen. Probably for the best. None of the pilots said it, but Lance could see it in their eyes.

Thank God for small mercies. Terry was out of agony, and Lance would not suffer the anguish Clayton had gone through after mercy-killing his friend on the North-Western Frontier. Lance had Arthur to thank for that.

The pilots lacked the appetite for their usual cathartic binge before dinner. Today's gruesome death differed from most in the RFC. Men arrived, ate with you, played cards with you, drank with you, and then, one day, their chair in the Mess sat empty. Such a death was a vanishing act, without a horrific corpse in situ. On the odd occasion, a fatal crash on the airfield would deliver a broken body. Though such things were undeniably grisly, they were not as traumatic as today. The full ferocity of flame on flesh had shown its remorseless cruelty, in a manner no-one who saw it would ever forget for as long—or short—as they lived.

Dinner itself was a hushed affair, the tinkle of silverware on plates often the only sound. At least the cook had the sense to make it a fish supper—cooked meat would have made Lance spew. After dinner, the pilots drank to the king's health with port, deep-stained like sacrament wine.

It would take a brave man to deliver the requiem for Terry. Lance's eyebrows climbed when Newby volunteered. The youngster looked the schoolboy he should still be—his earnest face clean and scrubbed, wet hair slicked back. But his manner appeared reflective and calm. He held open a book at a chosen page with two cupped hands as though he were about to preach a sermon. He cleared his throat.

"Paul James Terry was of the wolfpack where the strength of the pack is the wolf, and the strength of the wolf is the pack. His death diminishes all of us and is a tragedy, but not a waste. In the words of Kipling's Mowgli, we here tweak the whiskers of Death every day. We do so with a common purpose, a purpose of profound importance. We fight against Junker conquest. Theirs is an evil culture which has pioneered the use of poison gas, bombing civilians from the air, and drowning them at sea. Let there be no doubt that this is a fight worth sacrifice. Rest in peace, Paul Terry. We will not allow his sacrifice to be in vain.

"I leave you with the words of John McCrae, an officer mourning the death of a friend at Mons.

Take up our quarrel with the foe:
To you from failing hands we throw
The torch; be yours to hold it high.
If ye break faith with us who die
We shall not sleep, though poppies grow
In Flanders fields."

Newby's voice was firm, a man's voice, and at last tears came to Lance. For brief moments he released them, until they threatened to overwhelm him. Then he clamped down with all the force of his experience. He wiped the wetness from his cheeks on his sleeve. *It's just another day at war. Just another dead man, and there'll be more tomorrow. 'And tomorrow and tomorrow...Out, out, brief candle!...It is a tale told by an idiot, full of sound and fury, signifying nothing.'*

The Bard always had the best words for everything.

The haunting opening bars of *Clair de Lune* echoed around the room. Clayton was at the piano, playing with his head down and eyes shut. There would be no orchestra tonight, no wild songs.

Clayton was a wise old owl. He knew the form. He would play moving melodies, slowly moving up the tempo and turning thoughts from absent comrades to love songs. Then each man might hum with their own private image of loving eyes and soft lips wedded to warm curves. Maybe Mick Mannock's violin playing would help carry the burden—his "Danny Boy" would be perfect—but the Irishman's seat had been empty all dinner.

Terry's flight commander must be carrying the melancholic torch. Lance knew that sense of lonely guilt too well. Time to rescue Mick.

~

Lance found the Irishman sitting on his tent cot in the dark, his shoulders hunched forward with his hands trapped between his long legs. Dark hair flopped forward to hide his face in the gloom, and huge sobs racked his body. Lance walked over to the cot and put his hand on Mick's shoulder and squeezed. Then he waited, not taking his hand away, letting Mick feel the body warmth of his support.

Eventually Mick looked up at Lance, tears streaking his face, expressive eyes large like a child's. "Why, Lance? Why him, with a baby girl, and why like that?"

Lance gazed at the walls of the tent. The canvas shivered with the constant boom of heavy artillery. Staccato shell flashes in the distance lit the inside with ripples of lightning. Mick's wet face glistened in the unworldly glow.

Lance shrugged. "He made a mistake, or was unlucky, or it was his time. God knows. But you've got to stop. This isn't doing him or you any good."

The anguish and the flashes of shellfire shadowed the stress lines on Mick's face into deep slashes. Terry had been popular, but Lance knew that Mick's reaction owed more to his own fears. Any pilot who'd spent time at the front had escaped death by inches on countless occasions and locked away the fear of each such event. The vividness of Terry's flamer had fractured Mick's containment, and the accumulated stress had geysered to the surface.

Mick took a gulping breath and looked up at Lance. "If they get me in flames, Lance, promise me you'll put me down like you did with that DFW on Terry's first flight. You're the only one with the guts to do it. I've got no wife, no little girl. Just do it!"

"It won't happen, Mick, not if you stay focused," Lance said.

Mick grabbed Lance's sleeve with desperate urgency. "Swear it!"

Lance prised the taut fingers off his sleeve. He'd grown tired of people demanding that he shoot them. "Personally, I'll jump."

"Into the void? Not sure I could force myself. Have you noticed that the only thing that stops one of those big dog-fights is when someone jumps? Both sides stop fighting for a few seconds to gawp at some poor bastard flapping as they fall. I carry a revolver, but I wonder if I'd have the guts to shoot myself."

"If it happens to me," Lance said, "I won't hesitate. I'm jumping. Between the Scylla of fire and the Charybdis of gravity, it's no contest. I hope the void will be calm and peaceful until the big bounce at the end. Then it's instant lights out."

"Oh God," Mick sighed with a gust. "I was terrified of fire before today, and now I'm ashamed I didn't help him like you did. God knows I tried. I just couldn't." Fat tears rolled down his cheeks, but the rest of his face was a stone mask. He stared at the muddy floorboards, but Lance's experiences told him the Irishman saw only flames. After a few seconds, his body shuddered, then relaxed. He sat upright and stared at Lance.

"The pilots are speaking about what you did today. We all admired you as a hard man, tough enough to take on these Junker savages and win. But I admit we had you pegged as a cold fish who didn't care too much about us as people. But not after you pulled Terry from the fire. That was magnificent. Greater love hath no man, etcetera."

Lance looked away from Mannock's intense gaze. "If I hadn't done it, someone else would have."

"We were all there, Lance, and none of us except Arthur could bring ourselves to do what you did, and you had pulled him away from the worst of the flames by the time Arthur helped. Accept it. You risked a hideous death to save him. Take the compliments that brings. You are a prince among men. The Wolfpack is lucky to have you as our leader."

Lance shook his head, feeling like a fraud. When you became a leader, not only did you develop expectations of yourself, but other people also developed expectations of you. Before you knew it, you were acting to fulfil those twin expectations. Had Lance acted for Terry or for himself, to fulfil his own expectations to do whatever it took to protect his men?

Mick stood and scrubbed his face in the basin beside his bed. A huge flash and a deep thud told of an ammunition dump blowing up, emphasising the silence between the two men. Above the rolling thunder of the artillery came the drone of a German night bomber passing over them, solitary in the darkness.

Lance rubbed his jaw, feeling the bristles. "You know, Mick, you could make a difference in the RFC. You're turning yourself into a first-rate scout pilot and you have a rare way with words and men. If folk who understand tactics, like you and Jimmy McCudden, become mentors and leaders, then we might win the war faster and keep more good men alive. Arthur once asked what I wanted my legacy to be. I'd never thought about it, but that's the direction I'm leaning. A legacy of developing pilots skilful enough to both stay alive and destroy the Huns."

Mick paused from soaping his face. "You think I can do

that? Jimmy McCudden should be your main man. He taught me everything I know."

"As far as the number of kills, I suspect Mac will leave us all in his wake. But he's not got your way with words and men."

Mannock shook his head. "I tell you, Lance, he's younger than me by some way but when we speak, he anchors me. He knows his mind, same as you. I can make folk laugh, or raise their anger, maybe even their courage. But you two make us all *believe.*"

Mick grabbed a towel and waved it at Lance. "Mind you, you are both cold fish. Neither of you let anyone through your guard. God knows how you manage. I'd go mad without the craic of friends."

Lance said nothing. The Irishman straightened, checked himself in the cracked mirror. He wet his hands and ran them through his thick dark hair and laughed as he posed with one hand on his hip. "Mick Mannock the mentor! That'd be a fine thing."

Lance smiled in wonder. *Christ, these Celtic mood swings! When I'm down like he was, I'm down for days.*

Mick pulled on his RFC jacket. "I'm starving. I'm going to the Mess to see if they've any food left. Tomorrow we'll burn some Hun bastards in memory of Terry."

Lance grimaced. He would kill Huns to win this war, but he didn't want to burn anyone. He opened his mouth to remonstrate, but the tent flap ripped open to reveal Newby, who was breathing Pernod fumes so strong that his breath shimmered in the night air. Beside him, Elliot Springs clutched a bottle and swayed like a sapling in a gale. On the other side stood Rod Andrews, feet planted solidly apart, as immovable as an oak tree. Behind them loomed other shadows. Lance noticed the bulk of Weston and the gangling figure of Cecil Lewis.

Newby clutched the tent pole, threw his other arm out wide, and declaimed:

We few, we happy few, we band of brothers;
For he today that drinks with me
Shall be my brother; be he ne'er so vile,
This day shall gentle his condition;
And gentlemen in France—

"Excuse me, that should read 'England.'"

in England now-a-bed
Shall think themselves accurs'd they were not here,
And hold their manhoods cheap while any speaks
That drank with us upon this day—

The youngster hiccupped. "Or night, to be more precise."

"Aw sharrup," Elliot Springs said. "What he means is that we—" the American waved his bottle in the vague direction of the band of pilots gathered behind him— "have decided that it is time to persuade you two pitiless and prodigious pruners of Prussian pilots..." Springs paused to inhale a long breath. "Who are also, totally coincidentally, puritanical pillars of probity, to embrace the bosom of bacchanalia. In short, we—"

"Think it's time you should come and get drunk with your mates," Rod Andrews interrupted, thrusting a glass into Lance's hand.

Lance sniffed at it, his nose flaring at its potent bouquet. "Haig's attack starts tomorrow. We'll have to fly. You should all go to bed."

He bent to set the glass down, but Rod caught his wrist. "Mate, it won't kill yer and it may help. The weather boffins say it is a hundred percent certainty we'll be socked in tomorrow. No flying. Give it a go."

Lance looked around the smiling, foolish, drunk faces. Their warmth was seductive. Their warmth was dangerous, a trap laid by the devious Fates. As one weaved the threads of friendship, another sharpened her shears.

He looked at Mick Mannock, who had joined 100 Wing as a teetotaller but that was changing fast. The Irishman caught his eye and leaned forward to whisper into Lance's ear. "You helped me and now I'll help you. Let them in, not one, not two, but all of them. 'No man is an island entire of itself.'"

Lance shook his head. He couldn't do that. Friends died on you. Feelings made you weak. He'd promised Pa he'd fight tooth and nail to live. He couldn't afford weakness.

The pilots shuffled their feet, uncomfortable with being unwanted. Except Rod, who grabbed Lance by the shoulders and swung him around, speaking with rare urgency. "Bracing wires, they keep your wings on. Right?"

Lance nodded.

"When one wire gets shot, do the wings rip off? How many times have you come home with several bracing wires dangling?"

Lance shrugged. "Too many to count."

"See. The other wires help keep your wings on. 'Cos you have lots of them. That's what mates do. Help keep you alive. The Huns can't kill us all."

"Bracing wires and friends." Springs nodded wisely. "Never can have too many. Unlike bottles of booze."

Lance frowned, teetering on the cusp of what felt an important truth. When you fought beside a man and learned you could trust him with your life, you bonded in a manner incomprehensible to anyone who had not experienced battle. Together they had touched the face of death and lived to celebrate their deliverance. They were intimate with the secret lure of death's shadow—that life was most fragrant when you danced on the knife blade above the abyss.

For *this* group, *this* moment was unique. The odds of these men, all of them, sharing such a moment again were infinitesimal. By this time next week, or even tomorrow, some would be dead. New faces would stare from their places at the Mess table. All the raucous banter, the gay laughter, the fumbling drunkenness, none of it could disguise that uncomfortable reality.

But that unvarnished, undeniable truth created the alchemy that made this moment of camaraderie so precious and so poignant. For better or for worse, this was his world until it detonated into flames or broken wings.

"Out of the mouths of babes and boozers," Lance said and clinked glasses with Rod. "Perhaps now is indeed a good time to get drunk with my mates."

"Blessed are those who endure when they are tested," Cecil Lewis intoned.

Lance knocked back a big swig of whatever was in the glass. It burned down his throat and a warm glow spread through him. The glow kindled and took fire as they drank and linked arms and bayed songs with few meaningful words. Yet the singing ached of precious things shared; of friendships present and departed, of promised dawns and lost opportunities, of today and eternity.

24
The Cost to Be Tallied

Same evening - 30 July 1917.
Field Hospital No. 76, St Nicholas in Courtrai.

The JG1 pilots waited on tenterhooks for news of Richthofen. Doctors had chivvied Hans and the others away from the hospital while they operated. Dinner came and went in morbid fashion. The night dragged on, and still no news. Hans lounged in a chair in the drawing room of the Marckebeeke Chateau, watching others wear holes in the carpet. He took another sip of schnapps and savoured the delicious burn down his throat. Lashing rain drummed on the blank blackness of the windowpanes.

When the phone rang, they sat hushed as Adjutant Bodenschatz took the call. He put the phone down carefully and Hans winced. But then a smile lifted the adjutant's stern face. "The *Rittmeister* is awake and talking!"

Bodenschatz commandeered a huge staff car and drove three of Richthofen's favourite officers, plus Hans, to the hospital. When Bodenschatz told Hans he was invited too, the adjutant did so with the look of a man sucking a lemon. "The *Rittmeister* wishes to thank you in person for pulling him from the crash."

Hans sat in the back, with his left side jammed against the car door by Dostler's broad shoulders. The stocky Bavarian commanded *Jasta* 6 and had many more kills than Hans. He was a tough officer in the air and on the ground, and Hans took care to tiptoe around him. The other two, Doring and Reinhard, not so much. They were regular army officers who knew how to shovel Army bullshit. Those virtues had won them temporary commands due to Richthofen's and Wolff's wounds. Hans' lip curled in the darkness. Five kills between the pair of them. The English would be quaking in their boots.

The journey went slowly, but the mood in the car had been buoyant from the moment Bodenschatz informed them that Richthofen wished to see them. "He told me on the phone he would be back in business soon and wanted to tell you that personally."

They splashed through the rain and puddles into the hospital. Sister Kate, crisp of language and starched white linen, rejected them. "You cannot speak to the patient; he needs rest."

Bodenschatz snapped at her. "We are his men. He will see us."

The nurse's face closed. "Wait here." Her shoes clattered on the bare floor. When she reappeared, she relented without grace. "A minute only."

She ushered them in with the reluctance of a sheep dog inviting wolves into her den. The lights in the room were dim, but the whitewashed walls and starched linens gave it an ethereal glow. Hans tried not to gag at the cloying reek of antiseptic lying heavy in the still air.

Richthofen sat upright in bed, pale and wan, the top of his head swathed in a shroud of white bandages. He forced a smile as his relieved subordinates clucked around him. "It was a lucky long-range shot from an antiquated FE2, and I was silly enough to stick my skull in the way." He looked at Hans, his stare direct and challenging. "Thank you for pulling me from the wreck, *Leutnant.*"

Hans ducked his head in acknowledgement. *So that's how he wants to play it.* No mention that he was bounced by SE5s.

No doubt it was better for the legend to be felled by a fluke long-distance shot than ambushed. Fair enough. Maybe it was even true, and Richthofen was falling before the SE5s opened fire? Either way, if Richthofen ever tried to post Hans out of JG1, this was a nice little lever to have. Hans gave his commander a coded smile that his secret was safe. "It was an honour to be of use, *Rittmeister*."

Richthofen nodded, turned to the others and fluttered a weak hand. "Sorry to stay away right now, in the middle of everything, but I will be back soon, very soon."

Hans resisted a snort. Platitudes. The man could barely speak. Sister Kate ushered them out again. The others tried to see Wolff, who was still in the hospital, but Sister Kate gave them short shrift.

As they left the hospital, a British barrage burst over the front lines, many kilometers away. The pilots paused on the stone steps. Behind the looming spire of St. Nicolas, the night sky flickered with flash and flame and the windows rattled with the rolling thunder of the barrage. Lightning lit the sky, the glare freezing raindrops in mid-air before night closed in again. An ill-omened night from the gods. Freya's flickering lightning storm in the heavens, and Odin's guns pulverising the earth. Doring, the new temporary *Führer* of JG1, stood in front of Hans with shoulders hunched against the elements and the coming storm from the Allies. His peaked cap and his sharp nose sloped at precisely the same angle.

"Worse than the Somme," Doring said, gazing at the gun-flashes on the horizon that outlined the rooftops in stark relief.

"Worse than Verdun too," Bodenschatz agreed.

Hans rolled his eyes in the dark. *Ja, ja. We're fucked, as usual. Tell us something we don't know.* "Where's the car?" he asked.

The trip back to Marckebeeke took longer. Already troop reinforcements and ammunition convoys filled the roads. In the darkness, the car beams lit up the endless sea of field grey uniforms—in grinding trucks, on whinnying horses, and on marching feet. The Flanders mud didn't help. Curses and abuse floated through the night to the bass background of artillery thunder. Continuous lightning flashes from the front illuminated the roadside, showing sullen faces under their coal scuttle helmets as the car forced them onto the muddy verges.

General Ludendorff was supposed to have said that Richthofen was worth a division of troops, and right now another division would be useful. Richthofen was more than a gifted hunter. Inside the stuffy, byzantine corridors of the Prussian-led German war machine, only Richthofen could win JG1 favoured status for scarce war material. When Richthofen demanded more benzine, better quality oil, higher compression engines, the latest aircraft, and medals for his men, they soon came. The crown prince and his generals jumped to do the bidding of a twenty-five-year-old.

It seemed the other men in the car cared less about the ground war and more about their leader. The visit had lifted their morale. Dostler wittered that Richthofen was their talisman, their reassurance that JG1 could not be defeated in the air. Hans sneered in the darkness. *They are children. As if one man could guarantee that.* But Hans had to admit that if one man could, then that man would be Richthofen

The austere Bodenschatz positively drooled with relief. "There will be such a cheer when the rest of the *Geschwader* hears the Rittmeister is only lightly wounded!"

Lightly wounded? Am I the only one who noticed those pinprick pupils?

Hans had seen those shrunken pupils when he was an infantryman, on the victims of shellshock as they were led away from the front, shambling like zombies. Richthofen's wound had been a bone-deep furrow ten centimetres long, flecked with bone chips. Richthofen had made light of it, but the bandages and his iron will hid the truth.

Hans felt a chill go through him. Had the bullet that tore the flesh and gouged the bone seared open the psyche too? Germany's champion might be alive, but at what price to the man himself? That cost was still to be tallied.

25
Compass Course Home

Hell slipped its bonds at 3:50 A.M. The earth's trembles shivered Lance's bed. Artillery thunder prowled in his chest and the horizon to the east bubbled scarlet through the canvas walls. Unlike Messines Ridge there was no single massive explosion when the mine blew, but for artillery gunfire this was the loudest, most literally earth-shattering bombardment that Lance had heard. This war set new records in hellfire every month.

Haig's final preliminary artillery bombardment to shatter the German Army had started. Stage 1, the attack on Pilkem Ridge, would lead to a breakout at Passchendaele.

For once, the weather boffins' prediction proved correct. Low clouds squatted over the area and driving rain lashed the airfield. Flying would be suicidal until the storm cleared, which would not be until the afternoon, if at all today.

At 4:30 A.M. Arthur announced to the damp pilots gathered in the Mess that HQ had cancelled all flying for the morning. The hungover men splashed gratefully back to the blessed sanctuary of their beds.

Except Lance.

At five A.M. Lance sat in the cockpit of his solitary SE5, the airframe trembling to the deep rumble of the engine. Sunrise had taken place, in theory. Theory knew nothing of the bruised sky and weeping clouds at five hundred feet. A dawn as grim and troubled as the brew in a witch's cauldron.

Rain drummed on the fabric of his top wing and rivulets cascaded from the trailing edge onto his lap. Thank God for the thick waxed flying coat that deflected most of the damp. Not that it protected him against the miserable streams that snuck their clammy way down his collar and trickled down his neck to soak his shirt.

To his right, the Mess windows glowed, cheery yellow oblongs fighting the gloom, blurred as the rain misted in the driving wind. The smell of cooked bacon tickled his nose and his stomach grumbled in sympathy.

Ahead of him, the poplar trees at the end of the airstrip loomed high and dark, their tops thrashing in the storm, just visible against the low grey clouds that scudded overhead. An eerie dawn, one that touched deep inside a man and awoke ancient superstitions. A stronger gust rocked the SE5. He shivered as though someone was walking on his grave.

Lance reached into his reservoir of courage to drown his doubts and fears. But on this dawn, his courage flowed like bottom sludge from a muddy river. No doubt something to do with the drinks. He'd consumed only two of Rod Andrews's concoctions last night, over six hours ago, but they still blunted his brain and body. A nerve ticked in his cheek. He lifted his face to the clouds, hoping the rain would slap away his mugginess and indecision.

If the attack went well today, the pencil lines on the generals' maps would advance several inches by the close of day. No doubt those pencil inches would cost buckets of blood on the real ground. And Pa would be in the thick of it, looking for a good death, but hoping to shepherd his men past that damned pillbox first.

Lance could not, would not, allow Pa to die alone.

He thrust open the throttle before he could change his mind. The engine bellowed and the plane rolled forward, reluctant through the weight of the wet grass. A dim figure ran from Arthur's office, arms waving in the signal to cut engine. Yellow light from the windows glistened off the puddles. Lance ignored the running man. Arthur had never specifically banned flying this morning, just assumed that no-one would be mad enough.

The SE5 accelerated. Buildings blurred beyond the fire of his exhausts. His goggles streaked with water. He pulled them up and squinted as shotgun pellets of rain stung his exposed cheeks.

The poplar trees raced towards him, towering taller with every second. The tailskid lifted. A gentle pullback of the stick to lift off. Nothing. The SE5 roared onwards, refusing to unstick as the sodden grass sucked at the tyres. A puff of the cheeks, a deep breath, and a prayer, and he eased back harder on the stick. The wheels unstuck. *Thank you, God!*

Lance held her nose down, gathering speed to clear the trees. His belly sucked in as he gauged pace and distance in the gloom. His nerve cracked and he yanked back on the controls. Branches reached for him, thrusting their black claws against the bruised sky. A gust flung him upwards and the plane rocketed over the trees into the wild squalls.

His heart hammered but the hardest part was still to come. Mist and cloud whipped past in dirty grey streamers, clogging all his senses. He scrunched lower into the seat, feeling his way into a state of flow with the aircraft and the elements. In this weather, low flying was pure instinct—"seat of the pants," they called it. The eyes had no time to focus, the mind no time to process information. Shadows of intuition and finely honed reactions took over as the plane bucked in the turbulence.

Ever since Pa had revealed his death plan, Lance had prepared for this day. He'd mapped the route to the pillbox that was the King's Own Regiment's objective. He'd done a dozen reconnaissance flights until he knew the terrain and the compass bearings like the inside of his cockpit. No doubt this storm raised the stakes whilst doubling the odds against. But Pa knew what he wanted, and by God Lance would give it to him.

Lance found the dark scar that was the road towards Locre and Ypres and hugged the left side to avoid Mont Kemmel. That hill might be only three hundred feet high but today that would be enough to kill him before he even saw it. He banked north away from where he knew the church spires of Ypres loomed, then east again to follow the road from Wietje to St Julian, where the King's Own would have kicked off their attack.

Now the smoke from the artillery barrage stung his nose and thickened the grey haze even more. He hugged the ground closer still, flashing past gaggles of troops before they even registered he was there.

Pinpricks of red flashed below him, bright in the gloom. Staccato flashes. Lots of them. Must be machine guns. He'd reached the battle. He flung his plane towards the red pinpricks. Found the ruined pillbox. Zoomed past. The roof was destroyed but men in grey massed behind the rubble and remnants of thick walls, their rifles pin pricks of fire and their machine gun muzzle flashes flickering bright. He banked hard and swung around for another pass. This time he saw khaki soldiers pinned down in shell holes. A muddy blue panel unfurled between them—the King's Own recognition signal for the RFC.

He pulled up slightly to hide in the mist. With so many guns and him the only target in the sky, he was taking no chances.

Weaving until he was on the east side of the wall he sank back down into the marginally clearer air, aiming to make a shallow dive parallel to the defended wall. He leaned his head out of the cockpit, ignoring the sting of the rain that lashed his face. With friend and foe so close, he could not afford mistakes.

There! Grey uniforms, huddled around machine guns battering into the mist. Lance's thumb pressed the triggers.

Tracer riddled the grey uniforms. His bullets mowed them down like threshed wheat. One pass. Zoom, bank, return. Another pass, ignoring the growing ground fire. Muzzle flashes now aimed at him. Some men knelt and fired defiantly, others grovelled against the stone wall, and some ran, arms flailing in the mud. Lance killed them all, sending them spinning in a hail of bullets until grey carcasses littered the pillbox walls under tendrils of wraith-like mist.

By his third pass he was down to fifty feet. Everything flicked past in the blink of an eye. But no more muzzle flashes came from the prone grey figures. British troops, stumbling through mud, flowed over the pillbox. At their head strode a helmetless officer waving a revolver.

As Lance circled in a tight bank, shredding the patchy ground mist, the officer waved both arms and shook them at the heavens. Lance laughed, half at the sheer exuberance and half in disbelief. Every Hun sniper and machine gunner still alive and within sight would be tightening their trigger fingers.

Pa was going out in flamboyant style, not so much tweaking the whiskers of death as embracing the Grim Reaper in a bear hug he couldn't escape. "Daft bugger," Lance said in admiration. Pa saluted Lance with his revolver and turned to gesture his men forward.

Then smoke and mist and clouds closed in and covered the ground like a writhing shroud. Lance could do no more. He zoomed upwards with the vignette of Pa's defiance burned into his mind. The King's Own had captured the pillbox without being massacred, and Pa would go to Valhalla a fulfilled man. Few men could say that on the day of their death.

Lance recalled the serenity that had flooded him when Pa hugged him back in the dugout. That unforgettable infusion of calm certainty and quiet joy that defied description. "I'll raise a glass to you and Ma every sunset," Lance vowed.

He wrapped himself in that warm memory as the storms

of gods and men raged above and below, buffeting his wings as he swung the plane's nose through the blinding mist. The compass needle oscillated and then settled, pointing the way homewards.

Postscript

The assault on Pilckem Ridge was a relative success. The battle towards Passchendaele that followed became an unmitigated disaster, and the British grand offensive to end the war soon bogged down in the Flanders mud and the Germans' skilled and tenacious defence.

Winston Churchill called the battle "a forlorn expenditure of valour and life without equal in futility." The marshes around Passchendaele, created both by the destruction of the artillery barrages on the drainage system and the unseasonal heavy rains, became uniquely synonymous, in a war full of horror, with appalling conditions and losses for both sides.

Siegfried Sassoon, perhaps the best known of the British soldier-poets of World War 1, wrote pithily in one of his poems, *I died in hell—(They called it Passchendaele).*

Neither side would come close to ending the war in mid-summer 1917, and so Fitch and 100 Wing must continue to fly. So too must JG1 take to the crowded skies, with or without Manfred von Richthofen.

Historical Notes

As in the first book of the series I attach some historical notes, mainly on historical characters who die in this book or play lesser parts in the books that follow, or on historical events that take place during this book. Usually, I restrict such outlines to those characters who die in this book, as I do not wish to give the game away in the following books. But occasionally it is worth breaking my self-imposed rule.

Elliot Springs, whose background is accurate in this book, is one of my favourite real-life pilots. He is such an interesting character that I found him enlarging his role in the series. In doing so, I took liberties and invented events for him. However, I was careful to stay with what I believe was his character, as revealed in his own words in his book, *Warbirds*. This was notionally a diary of a pilot friend of Elliot Springs, called John Grider, who died in the war. Most expert commentators regard it as a thinly disguised cover for the author, who attracted some opprobrium in strait-laced America in the immediate post war years, for his revelations about the role of alcohol and sex in keeping pilots sane. Suffice to say that where I have taken liberties with known reality and Elliot Springs, I have done so in such a manner that I hope he would have approved.

Elliot Springs' brush with Absinthe/Pernod did not to the best of my knowledge happen as described in this book, but the tale of absinthe is an interesting one. It was, as described in the book, the drink of the Belle Epoque and the literati, and it was indeed banned by the French government for being detrimental to the war effort, surely a unique accolade during a war where most alcohol was lauded for its part in helping fighting men cope. "Absinthism" was said to lead to addiction, hallucinations and violent mood swings, even murder. Some say Van Gogh cut off his own ear whilst under the influence of absinthe. Pernod was the largest producer of absinthe and today still makes an anise flavoured drink, but without the mind-altering thujon ingredient which is banned by the European Community.

The Procurement Committee set up by Clayton is based on fact. Food waste and the resulting plague of rats was a real problem for many airfields, who under wartime pressure were hardly paragons of sanitation. Rat hunting with revolvers after flying, often by well-lubricated pilots, was banned in some squadrons, and pigs were indeed often the solution—as Weston describes in my book.

Angelique, advertised by Springs in my book as the best officer's brothel in Amiens existed and was described in those terms by some pilots. I hasten to add that although I have given Elliot Springs the lines that imply some knowledge of the institution, this is a fictitious invention on my part. But *Warbirds* describes events that don't make such an invention outrageous.

The scene in Chapter 5 where Newby sees the severed tongue of his training partner sizzling on an engine block, is not gratuitous gruesome invention by me. Captain Victor Armstrong, a South African widely regarded as one of the RAF's top 'stunters' [pilots who excelled in displays of death-defying aerobatics over the aerodrome], killed himself through a rare misjudgment when he pulled out too late and dived his Camel into the ground, presumably biting his tongue off under impact. The question of how it reached the cylinder block fascinated and repelled observers. The worst of it—Armstrong's needless death came two days after the Armistice.

In this book, the pilot's death was caused by the novice pilot diving into the ground while focused on the target he was machine gunning. Such 'target fixation' has been killing inexperienced military pilots in droves since the dawn of military aviation, and probably will continue to do so for as long as there are guns still used in planes.

As WW1 proceeded, the number of colonials and non-public schoolboy pilots grew, and the squadrons became, as this book shows, a fascinating melting pot of cultures. At a time when travel was not nearly as widespread as today, and social classes were more rigidly defined and harder to escape, the pilots found their close-knit existence in their officers' Mess was often their first exposure to other classes and colonials, and vice versa. It was not always a happy experience. Some English complained that the bad language of the colonials was intolerable. On the other hand, white colonial pilots born in Africa were indeed called "Blackies" by some fellow pilots.

Exhibit A in evidence of the social class snobbishness inherent in some squadrons was the infamous case of 85 Squadron refusing McCudden as their squadron leader in 1918. Ostensibly, their opposition was couched in language that implied they thought McCudden was too concerned about his own score rather than the welfare of his own men.

Bluntly, such a charge does not hold water. Firstly, McCudden's record as a flight commander in 56 Squadron was one of, if not the, finest in the RFC/RAF in terms of kills/losses ratio. Shining lights such as Arthur Rhys-Davids and Cecil Lewis left no doubt of his capabilities as a fighting leader in the air, and in fact left the impression that they considered McCudden overly concerned for his pilots. Secondly, McCudden was slated to take over from the Canadian ace, Billy Bishop, who although generous in the bar, was perhaps the most shameless self-promoter in the air force. There were worse commanders than Bishop, but many better. Some historians believe the real reason for 85 Squadron's rejection was McCudden's background as the son of an Irish non-ranker who had himself come up from the ranks as a mechanic, before becoming one of the British Empire's finest aces.

Whatever the real reason, Peter Hart of the Imperial War Museum, calls that rejection "shameful" in his wonderful book *Aces Falling*. Since 85 Squadron subsequently accepted Mick Mannock as squadron leader, it is safe to assume that Mc-Cudden's crime was not being Irish, but a combination of his social class and his reputation as a disciplinarian dedicated to effective air combat.

Lance's tactics based on white hunting lore bears a striking resemblance to Mac McCudden's stalking tactics, although the latter used arcs of fire, quadrants and probability assessments rather than hunting knowledge to arrive at the same place. As far as I know, there were no white hunter aces in the RAF. There were South African aces such as Beauchamp- Procter who appeared late in the war, but he was not a hunter per se. On the other hand, hunters figured prominently on the German side, with both Manfred Richthofen and Werner Voss, two of the greatest, being obsessive hunters. John Buchan, the great novelist of the 1930's, had one minor character in *Mr. Standfast*, Peter Pienaar, who was a great hunter who became an ace. Although hunters today have a bad name, there is little doubt that the stalking and shooting skills employed in hunting dangerous game, would have been valuable in the air during the dawn of military aviation.

Boelke was the first ace to spend a lot of time thinking of tactics, and Manfred Richthofen took on his mantle. The Allied side was far slower to follow suite, such tactics as there were being developed ad hoc largely by individual flight commanders rather than at squadron level. At least until Mick Mannock began to crystallise British thinking on tactics at both an individual and squadron level. Interestingly, while Richthofen ended up controlling five *Jasta*, roughly fifty aircraft, the Allied side only operated at a squadron level, some twelve aircraft. This did allow Richthofen and JG1 to establish critical mass over chosen parts of the battlefield.

What the RAF learned as an institution about flying tactics in WW1 was quickly forgotten. When WW2 started, W.E. Johns, the creator of the famed Biggles series of books who had himself fought in WW1 as a pilot, revealed that many Spitfire and Hurricane pilots reported falling back on Biggles tactics when their rigid, formation-based official RAF tactics proved wholly unsuitable against the German *Luftwaffe,* who had themselves relearned the lessons of WW1 during the Spanish Civil War. For those who enjoy the evolution of flying tactics from 1914 to the Korean war, the best read would be the seminal *Full Circle* by Johnnie Johnson, Britain's top scoring ace in WW2 who became an Air Vice Marshall.

Morgan Budd's line about "stress being an Albatross on your tail" is borrowed and adapted from a line reputedly used by the great Australian cricketer, Keith Miller. Miller fought in the RAF as a Mosquito pilot in WW2 and was scrupulous in not 'bigging up' his service, so the story is probably untrue. Nevertheless, it is said that when asked about stress in cricket, he replied, "stress is a Messerschmitt on your arse, not cricket." If he never said it, he should have! It is probably fair to say that my fictional character, Rod Andrews, is based on my opinion of what the larger-than-life Keith Miller might have done in similar circumstances. If the result is rather a stereotypical view of Australians, I hope it is one the Australians enjoy, and it is done with fondness and respect for both Australians and Miller. I hasten to add that Rod Andrew's womanising and borderline alcoholism is solely my invention.

Like Morgan Budd, some pilots did keep a hammer to try

and correct machine gun stoppages. Weston is a fictional character, but his story about a friend being killed when the hammer slipped from its storage place to wedge beside the control stick as he landed, is based on a true story.

Morgan Budd deserting Lance and Taggart as they are about to attack a vastly superior force of enemy aircraft, is an idea I borrowed from Stanford Tuck's autobiography, *Fly for your Life*, which in my view is one of the top five biographies of WW2 flying. In that book, Tuck, one of Britain's leading aces during WW2, relates attacking a vastly superior force during the Battle of Britain only to have some of his Hurricanes peel away and leave him and others to make the attack on their own. Tuck describes the physical shock of seeing such behaviour, and how it almost undermined his own courage. When Tuck landed, he too pulled a revolver to shoot the miscreant and was stopped by ground crew. The offender was court martialled, stripped of his wings, and later in the war Tuck saw him sweeping floors in another airbase. Lance would have approved.

It is easy to be judgmental of those who failed to beat their fear, but Cecil Lewis in his wonderful autobiography, *Sagittarius Rising*—perhaps the very best of all WW1 flying books as a mix of lyrical writing and action depiction—gives an idea of the strain; *we had to win victories over ourselves long before we won any over the enemy, for it was not impossible to turn back, to tell a lie—not always easy to verify—of faulty engine, bad visibility, jammed guns, and so stave off the inevitable for one day more.*

Kurt Wolff, the nightcap wearing ace of *Jasta* 11 and Manfred Richthofen's protégé, was wounded and did crash as depicted in my book. Those who saw the crash reckoned him dead as the Albatross skidded upside down along the ground. It is said that only his small size saved him, as the scrape along the top of his scalp showed.

Survival in the air war was often a matter of millimeters. As related in this book, the British ace, Cyril Crowe, had the goggles shot off his face in the same series of fights in which Albert Ball died. It is no surprise that Crowe became a heavy drinker, the only surprise was he remained such an effective fighter pilot and commander. Kurt Wolff, however, was never again as effective in the air, but he continued to try damn hard. I am in awe of such men, especially by comparison to today's world where stress is one of the more over-used words.

The background for Clayton's story of fighting Pathans in the Northwest Fronter of India comes largely from John Master's wonderful book, *Bugles and Tiger*. To the best of my knowledge no such specific action as the one where Clayton won his DSO took place, but it was a fact that British and Gurkha soldiers never left alive men behind. If they could not be rescued, it was kinder to kill them. Masters, one of England's pre-eminent novelists in the 1950/60/70s, served prewar in a Gurkha regiment with such a posting. During WW2 he became one of the youngest Lieutenant Colonels in the British Army while conducting the famed *Chindit* raids in Burma. The second volume of his autobiography, *The Road to Mandalay*, describes his WW2 experiences. The two books together are among the most enjoyable and illuminating biographies I have read, as well as being outstanding reads on prewar India, the growth to manhood and command, and fighting in WW2.

Springs' and Rod Andrew's raid on the chateau housing French generals' mistresses is based on an RFC/RAF rumour that such things existed. I have not managed to verify it, but in an age where generals, certainly some French [Petain] and some Americans [Pershing], were infamous for their mistresses, it was too good a story to pass up.

James 'Mac' McCudden and Mick Mannock never served in the same squadron, but McCudden did train Mick Mannock in

England and the two became friends. Although vastly different characters, they shared a passionate professionalism for war flying. Many of the phrases they use in this book are phrases they used. McCudden left an autobiography which is one of the very best of its genre in its lack of 'side' [in the language of the time, bullshit in modern parlance], and clear-eyed analysis. It is also remarkable in its lack of hate for Germans. Unlike Mick Mannock.

Mannock never wrote a book. But one of Mannock's protégé, Ira Jones, who became a highly successful ace in his own right, wrote a wonderful tribute, *King of Airfighters,* which showcases the warmth and charisma of this conflicted genius, as well as his passionate hatred of the Kaiser's regime in Germany. As Ira Jones reports, Mannock often expressed a wish that the enemy planes burned—*Sizzle, sizzle, wonk, wonk, flamerinoes* was another favourite phrase of his.

On a lighter note, aficionados of Biggles might have spotted that Sergeant Smythe exists in those books as Biggles' flight sergeant. My version is perhaps a more terrifying one, but it is one small tribute to W.E. Johns and his magical books. Many today criticise them for glorifying war and for being lightweight, but the author came from a generation that did not dwell on feelings and stress to the same degree as following generations, and Biggles is entirely consistent in tone with most of the books of the age. Since Johns himself fought in the war and was shot down and spent time in a prisoner of war camp, I doubt he was trying to glorify war. As for being lightweight, they are a pleasant antidote to reading the weighty tome, *Winged Victory,* VM Yeates' novel which is often quoted as being a masterpiece. TE Lawrence of Arabia fame himself hailed it as such. Personally, I find it chock full of turgid misogynistic musings although it is undoubtedly realistic in its depiction of life in the front-line squadrons of WW1. Sufficient to say, Johns made a good living from Biggles and would not have done so if he wrote like Yeates, whose book was a flop in Yeates' lifetime. The best Biggles books on WW1 in my opinion are *Biggles of the Camel Squadron* and *Biggles of 266.*

Many in the modern generation do not find the pilots' 'drunks' or 'thrashes' to be amusing. Others may moralise over their womanising. Arthur Rhys Davids would agree on both counts. He wrote to his mother saying Cyril Crowe was a jolly sound chap but a bit loose in his morals around drink and women. Nevertheless, they were a fact of life for the majority of pilots, a coping mechanism. As Cecil Lewis pointed out; *small wonder if, under this strain, pilots lived a wild life and wined and womanized to excess. Stanhope in Journey's End summarises it perfectly: 'To forget, you bloody little fool, to forget. Do you think there's no limit to what a man can bear?'*

The air battles over Polygon Wood in the summer of 1917 were legendary. They were the largest up to that time, and the massive duels to the death among summer thunderclouds remain vividly in the minds of those who took part, and who survived. Until the contour trails over southern England during the battle of Britain in WW2, they were the defining image of a large-scale dogfight.

Taggart is fictitious, but at least one Scottish pilot flew in his kilt. History does not say how many long johns he needed underneath it to protect the family jewels from frostbite. Taggart's story of the First Battalion Black Watch throwing back the Prussian guard at Ypres, and the enormous cost of doing so, is true. So too is the Glasgow kiss, a forehead butt given while wearing a cap with razor blades sown into the peak.

It was Cecil Lewis, author of *Sagittarius Rising*, who told how Rhys Davids once quoted Gray's *Elegy Written in a Country Churchyard [The curfew tolls the knell of the parting day...]* immediately after a patrol. Rhys Davids' speech to

Lance about *being the devil incarnate bursting with the dazzling thrill of playing the best game God ever created*, is a quote from one of his letters. Fair to say it was written in his early days as a fighter pilot before the inevitable strain caught up with him. Richthofen and many others went through the same arc.

The knees knocking together before or after a patrol was a common affliction among pilots on both sides. Not all confessed to it, but I suspect most suffered at some stage.

In real life, Bill Franks did command the Depot Airfield at St. Omer, and did tell Mac McCudden he would be more valuable as a mechanic than a pilot. Although that was intended as a compliment on McCudden's rare virtues as a mechanic. The story of McCudden's background and rise is accurate.

Mick Mannock's background and violin skills were as described. Yet another piece of self-education undertaken by this remarkable over-achiever who rose from lowly beginnings to become arguably Britain's greatest squadron commander of WW1. And that is Johnnie Johnson's opinion as the leading ace of WW2, not mine. Much of that award is owed to Mannock's ability to inspire his men. McCudden was perhaps the superior fighter pilot, and a fine tactician and tactical leader of his flight, but never had the opportunity to lead a squadron. For reasons that will be revealed in a later book.

Mannock's hot-tempered challenges to anyone who did not recognise Fritz Kreisler as the world's finest violinist is well documented, so too his love of boxing matches with other pilots. Since Weston is fictional, his fight with Mannock did not occur, but Mannocks' phrase, used in my book, of *Clack clack, tickets please, all turn up for the show!* was a signature phrase of his.

The scene where Lance consoles Mick Mannock for the loss of Terry is based on a near breakdown Mannock suffered when one of his Irish pilots died. His promise to shoot himself if his aircraft caught fire, was one he repeated often. Mick Mannock was as afraid of flames as is my Lance Fitch.

Sadly, the tales of in-fighting between generals and politicians were true. So too the very real feeling of disenchantment when the pilots went on leave, and saw what seemed to them a very comfortable civilian population either moaning about their hardships or enriching themselves from the war.

The hot-tempered debate between 100 Wing's squadron commanders on the best way to escort bombers was based more on events in WW2, where such arguments raged in both the *Luftwaffe* and the RAF. Certainly, in all my research on WW1, I never came across such tactical debates about escorting bombers. Adolf Galland, who rose to command the Germans' fighter arm before the end of WW2 before being fired for insubordination by Herman Goering [who appears in Books Three and Four of my series], would have agreed whole heartedly with Lance Fitch about the futility of tying a fighter escort too tightly to the bombers.

Arthur's musing about losses and how many of his pilots would see the year out are based on actual statistics, a loss every third day was only that low because in winter many days were 'scrubbed' [the vernacular for a non-flying day].

Richthofen's head wound did come about from an extreme long range, lucky shot from an FE2b, at least according to his version. A FE2b crew claimed to have fired shots at a red Albatross from 1200 feet, an absurd range. Was Richthofen unlucky, or was there a more prosaic truth that would not have suited the legend? That was the starting point for my version, which is pure supposition. However his landing, virtually blind and badly wounded was as described, although he landed alone and not in company with Hans Schmettow. By Richthofen's account he was unconscious while his plan spun from 12,000 feet to around 2,000, only just regaining consciousness and sight in time to land.

The visit by JG1's *Jasta* commanders and Adjutant Boden-schatz to hospital to see the wounded Richthofen is as described by Bodenschatz, minus my fictitious Hans Schmettow whose musings about the long-term damage to Richthofen are all mine. Safe to say, in his written account Bodenschatz did not admit to any misgivings. Instead, he noted that "everything was going well," and that when the pilots heard their leader was talking of returning soon, their chins lifted, and they resolved to wreak revenge on the enemy. Which they did with some success in the following weeks.

Of course, Lance Fitch and 100 Wing will be there to challenge them.

If you've enjoyed the book, an honest comment on Amazon would be wonderful. If you don't like writing comments or reviews, then taking a second just to give the book the number of stars you think it deserves would be most appreciated. These links will take you there.

USA:
www.amazon.com/review/create-review?&asin=B09V6B1Z6C

UNITED KINGDOM:
https://www.amazon.co.uk/dp/B09T2KP5SL

CANADA:
https://www.amazon.ca/dp/B09V6B1Z6C

AUSTRALIA:
https://www.amazon.com.au/dp/B09V6B1Z6C

Acknowledgements

To my friends; Judy Weber for valiantly motivating me after she gamely waded through a stodgy first draft, and Jan Chojecki, Alex Lorenz, Didier Hirsch, and Maura Kuvin, my most reliable and enthusiastic beta readers.

To Kristina Stanley of Fictionary.co who became midwife to the plot lines through all four books. I cannot imagine a more encouraging or tactful coach who does not shirk from pointing out areas for improvement. The highest praise I can offer is to say that her collaboration made COVID incarceration fly past. Apart from being a story editor, her software is amazing too. Although I researched and wrote the books in *Write it Now* software, I found running them through *Fictionary* as well improved the structure enormously.

To Geoff Smith for his accurate, rapid and patient editing. Imagine my surprise when an editor praised by other authors for his understanding of Mandarin, China, electronics and the Mets also turned out to have formidable knowledge of World War 1 and some German. Not to mention a ridiculous understanding of Chicago Style, although I will never understand why Schutztruppe does not get italicized but *Shutztruppen* does! I did choose to break some rules to make it easier for readers not familiar with the genre, so if there are errors, they are mine and not his.

To *Atmosphere Press* who made the process of publishing almost pain free. Special thanks to Nick Courtright for his flexibility and holding my hand through a process that worried me no end; Ronaldo Alves and Mathew Fielder who grasped my concepts immediately and amazed me with their covers; to Erin Larson who made the interior design flow and never sounded aggravated at my 101 changes; and Hayla Alawi who could not have been more efficient or more helpful when it came to marketing and a myriad of other things.

Last but not least, a shout out for Denis Caron of *weekendpublisher.com* who taught me to navigate 'the riddle, wrapped in a mystery, inside an enigma' that is novel and Facebook marketing, and tripled sales whilst doing so.

About Atmosphere Press

Atmosphere Press is an independent, full-service publisher for excellent books in all genres and for all audiences. Learn more about what we do at atmospherepress.com.

We encourage you to check out some of Atmosphere's latest releases, which are available at Amazon.com and via order from your local bookstore:

Among the Alcoves, a novel by Andrew Mitin

Family Crystals, a novel by Amber Vonda

The Truth About Elves, a novel by Ekta R. Garg

How to be Dead—A Love Story, by Laurel Schmidt

Waiting Impatiently, a novel by Andrew H. Housley

A Journey's Promise: The Helio Series, by Johnny Hall

Taint: A Novel, by Janey Kelley

New Shores, a novel by Ciaran McLarnon

Murder at the Olympiad, a novel by James Gilbert

The World Turned Upside Down, a novel by Steven Mendel

Dolly: The Reno Story, a novel by Fern Hammer

Author Biography

Iain Stewart was born and raised in East Africa. Time spent at Kenton College in Nairobi, Fettes College in Edinburgh, and Christ's College, Cambridge was usually enjoyable and often educational. His feeble qualifications as an author of this tale include a childhood fascination with *The Romance of King Arthur*, and obtaining his pilot's license at seventeen. Armed with these, he ventured forth to fly Tiger Moth biplanes and pretended to be Biggles. Who was basically Lancelot in goggles. However, earning a crust at HSBC for over twenty years delayed this book. Nowadays, he staves off reality by living in Miami.

Printed in Great Britain
by Amazon

84429194R00205